UNLEASHED DESIRE

Her cheeks growing an embarrassed pink, Jonty reached for the blanket that had fallen to her waist. Cord shook his head and stayed her hands. "Don't hide yourself from me, Jonty," he said huskily, "I've already seen all of you, remember?"

The pink in her cheeks turned to red as Jonty did remember. As she stared up helplessly at him, he released her wrists and, leaning over her, cupped her face in his hands. She held her breath as he gazed down at her, his eyes illuminated with desire.

"Ah, Jonty," he spoke thickly, "you're drivin' me out of my mind."

A protest trembled on Jonty's lips as he lowered his head to her. She knew his intent, and she would have no part of it. She would not be used.

But the denial died in her throat when Cord's mouth covered hers . . .

NORAH HESS

DEVIL IN SPURS

LEISURE BOOKS   NEW YORK CITY

A LEISURE BOOK ®

April 1990

Published by

Dorchester Publishing Co., Inc.
276 Fifth Avenue
New York, NY 10001

CHAPTER 1

Wyoming, 1871

IT WAS SPRING. TENDER NEW GROWTH ENVELOPED THE earth, and birds sang everywhere. It was a joyous time, a time when the blood raced in one's being, promising a new lease on life.

But there would be no leases of any sort for the slight figure whose breath came painful and hollow from the bed in a corner of the large room. Time was running out for seventy-year-old Maggie Rand.

Her fingers picking restlessly at the wash-faded quilt tucked snuggly around her, the old woman's gaze went often to a door through which she could see a tall, slender figure moving quietly about the kitchen, making a pot of tea, sweeping a long-handled spoon slowly through the bubbling contents of a large kettle, every few minutes stealing anxious glances at the bed.

"Dear Lord," Maggie whispered, "what is going to happen to my little Jonty after I'm gone?"

Her mind clouded with the fever that racked her thin, wasted body, Maggie's thoughts drifted back over the years, and for a while some of the events came to her as clearly as though they had happened yesterday.

She was once again in a small, rock-strewn, weed-filled cemetery at the edge of a little Midwestern town. Sobs shook her body as her husband of twenty years was lowered into his final resting place of sand and clay. Sam had been a good man and husband, aged beyond his years by hard work and privation. But she had loved him dearly and had never complained at their near poverty.

Maggie's mind touched briefly and reluctantly on the following two years of hardship, of scratching out a living on the tiny homestead for herself and her young daughter, Cleo.

Ah, Cleo, she thought sadly, her reminiscences halting at the vision of Cleo, so lovely and carefree at seventeen, in love for the first time—a love that had brought her nothing but heartache and pain.

For the man she was so enamored of was Jim LaTour, a handsome, reckless "breed," born of a white father and an Indian mother. And as so often happened, LaTour had few of the good qualities of either race. He hung out with a bunch of low characters who, running from a life of crime, had made their way to the Western frontier, where there was little law. It was believed by everyone that some day Jim LaTour would step too far outside the law, that sooner or later a posse's bullet would put an end to him.

Maggie's blood had run cold the first time she found Cleo in LaTour's arms, her young face radiating the love she felt for the blue-eyed man. Dread gripping her, Maggie had ordered Cleo into the house, then turned on the breed. She ordered him to stay away from her daughter, said that she was not for the likes of him.

The old woman sighed, remembering the young girl's teary, sullen face as she was told she must never see Jim LaTour again, that he would ruin her life, that he had no honorable intentions regarding her.

Her eyes flashing, Cleo had announced that LaTour loved her, wanted to marry her.

Mental pain entered Maggie's eyes as she recalled the heated arguments between her and her young daughter. Among other dire warnings, she had pointed out that the man could never provide a woman with a normal life, that married to him, her companions would be outlaws and whores, that she would always be running from the law.

A weak sigh heaved the dying woman's chest. Cleo had not heeded her warning and advice, but had continued to slip out nights, meeting the handsome breed. Two months later she was expecting his child. And he was on the run. He and his disreputable companions had robbed a bank, and the sheriff and his posse were hot on their trail.

And while Cleo cried broken-heartedly, Maggie prayed that the breed would be caught and sent to prison for a long time. At least long enough for Cleo to get over him.

There was still the fact, however, that eight months from now her daughter would give birth to a bastard. And in this small Illinois village the people would be scandalized, her daughter ostracized by decent society.

It had taken a month to sell the small farm, accepting half its worth. It was imperative to leave the area before Cleo's condition began to show. She had then packed their meager wardrobe and caught the stage to Abilene, Kansas. She had to put enough distance between them and the people back home that her friends need never know of her daughter's disgrace.

Maggie had also chosen Abilene in the belief that employment would be more plentiful in a larger town, and that she could find respectable quarters for the two of them.

On arriving in the hot, dusty town, Maggie's first disillusionment had been the boarding houses. Anything halfway decent was way out of reach of her slim funds. Finally, shortly before dark, both she and Cleo bone weary from tramping the streets all day, she reconciled herself to inspecting rooms offered for rent, situated between a saloon and a brothel.

The good-sized room she chose was reasonably clean, and the price not too dear. It would suffice until she was working and could rent a house.

Maggie's second disillusionment brought her spirits even lower when she set out the next morning to find employment. It seemed that nowhere in this raw, bustling place was there a job for Maggie Rand. She was politely turned down by grocers and rudely sneered at by the fashionably dressed owners of dress shops and millineries, their eyes scathing over her, saying that such a dowdy-looking person would drive business away rather than bring it in.

She had tried boarding houses next, but was again unsuccessful. One proprietor of such an establishment had kindly explained to her that she was too frail-looking to do the heavy work involved in cleaning up after a bunch of slovenly men.

For three more days Maggie tramped the streets unsuccessfully. What in the world was she to do? she wondered, almost in panic as she trudged wearily back to the bleak room where Cleo waited. After she bought their supper tonight, her shrinking supply of money would be gone.

She was fitting the key in the lock of her lodgings when a gravelly female voice hailed her from the porch next door. She looked up and recognized the heavy-set, red-headed woman as the owner of the brothel, whose rowdy, raucous customers kept her and Cleo awake nights.

"I would like to speak to you a minute, ma'am," the flamboyantly dressed woman said, covering the short distance to stand before Maggie.

Fifteen minutes later, although dispiritedly reluctant, Maggie had found herself a position—cook and housekeeper for fat, frizzy-haired Madam Nellie.

Another fifteen minutes later, she and Cleo had

repacked their bags and walked the few steps to the pleasure house. Nellie gave them a hearty meal of roast beef and fresh vegetables, then settled them into a large room off the kitchen. The next morning, early, Maggie took up her duties, cooking for the madam and her eight girls and overseeing the two maids who did the cleaning and laundry.

Life fell into a routine and the months slipped by. Nellie's girls had big appetites, no doubt due to their strenuous night work, Maggie thought wryly, and she seldom got out of the kitchen before nine o'clock in the evening.

But the fun-loving, good-natured whores were kind to Cleo, asking her no questions, presenting her with tiny gowns and blankets as they counted down the days until the baby's arrival.

Still Maggie dreamed of the day she could take her daughter away from such an environment.

At last there came a bright spring morning when, after a long and difficult labor, a baby girl was born. To Maggie's acute disappointment, the infant, from the time it came from its mother's womb, looked like its father with the same coal-black curls and deep blue eyes.

Cleo had smiled lovingly, tiredly at the tiny, wrinkled baby and murmured, "Her name is Joan, Ma," then closed her eyes. By nightfall, despite everything Maggie could think of doing, her lovely young daughter had hemorrhaged to death.

Almost beside herself with grief, Maggie moved around as though in a mental fog. Nellie helped her with funeral arrangements and a burial plot, while the young prostitutes tended the baby.

It was several days after her adored daughter was laid to rest before Maggie could begin to think clearly. Her first thought was that a brothel was no proper place to raise a little girl. Although her quarters were separate from the part of the house where Nellie conducted her business, one couldn't be sure that some drunken male might not stumble into their private room by mistake. Or even that Joan might wander across the hall into the big room where the customers awaited their turn upstairs.

"Don't go, Maggie!" The young prostitutes begged in unison when Maggie told them that she would be leaving at the end of the week, explaining why she thought it necessary.

"Surely we can think of something," Nellie urged, being very fond of her housekeeper. She knew, too, that she would never find another so competent.

"Well, I don't know what it could be." Maggie finished giving the baby her bottle, then patted the little back to enable her to burp. "I've racked my brain and can't come up with anything else."

"Too bad the kid ain't a boy," Nellie's youngest "girl," said carelessly, tired of talking about the welfare of the child, anxious to get upstairs and prepare for her first customer. Lucy loved her work and very little else interested her.

"Well she's not, Lucy." Nellie threw the uncaring girl a hard glare. Then a thoughtful look came over her heavily painted face.

"You know, Maggie," she said, looking thoughtfully at the woman who had become her friend, "unintentionally Lucy has just given me an idea. You delivered the baby and nobody except us here in the room knows that Joan is a girl. Why not pass her off as your grandson?"

And while Maggie gaped at the madam in confusion, Nellie swept a hard gaze over her "girls," looking each in the eyes, lingering on Lucy's. "It would be our secret, wouldn't it?" Although the question was asked of all the girls, it was Lucy she demanded an answer from.

Lucy shrugged and nodded, then added sullenly, "Of course, a person might forget sometimes."

Nellie's lips tightened and loathing stared out of her eyes as she rasped, "You let this baby's sex be known, bitch, and I'll see to it that your face gets sliced up so horribly there won't be a man alive who'll come near you."

Lucy's face went pasty white at the threat. Nellie had connections, she knew, and could easily make her words come true. It was unthinkable to have men cut out of her life.

"I wasn't thinkin' of myself spillin' the beans, Nellie," she said hurriedly. "I thought maybe one of the others might . . ."

"Don't worry about the others," Nellie snapped. "Their word is as good as gold. You just worry about that vicious tongue of yours."

She turned back to her housekeeper. "What do you think, Maggie? Could we pull it off, do you think?"

Maggie looked down on the sleeping face of her tiny granddaughter. Would it be possible? she wondered. It wouldn't be difficult to deceive the men who came here. They were mostly night visitors and Jonty would be in bed. And she'd have Nellie put bars on the outside of the door that led across the hall to where the men gathered.

"You could save more money," an inner voice whispered. "Try it for four or five years. Put enough aside to enable you to get out of Abilene, maybe buy a small farm."

Maggie looked up at the anxious faces staring down at her. "We can try," she said, and the girls expressed their approval so exuberantly that Maggie didn't have the heart to add that she would be leaving as soon as possible.

So the baby was called Jonty Rand.

The years passed, one sliding into another, and Maggie still kept house for Madam Nellie. The pittance she was able to put away each week grew slowly. But Jonty was happy. The young whores adored her, petted and spoiled her. For now, life was running smoothly, Maggie told herself hopefully. Time would take care of itself.

Then, shortly after Jonty's fifth birthday, Jim LaTour showed up.

Maggie had been baking to fill the never-ending demand for pies when a knock sounded at the kitchen door. Her hands flour-covered from rolling out dough, and Jonty clinging to her skirt, Maggie muttered her annoyance as she stepped briskly across the floor. Some drunk or other had probably stumbled to the wrong door. She jerked the door open, then stared open-mouthed, too stunned to speak for a minute as she gaped at an older, though still handsome, Jim LaTour.

Fighting back a panic that threatened to overwhelm her, and with undisguised hostility staring out of her eyes, she finally croaked, "What are you doing here?"

LaTour smiled thinly. Then, his tone harsh and mocking, he answered, "Why do you think I'm here, Miz Rand—to have a friendly chat with you?" When Maggie made no response, only staring at him stonily, he said coldly, "I've come for Cleo, of course. I've been trackin' you down for over a year."

"Then you've been wasting your time," Maggie said bluntly. "Cleo is dead."

LaTour stepped back as though from a heavy blow. "Cleo is dead?" The blood drained from his face as he echoed Maggie's words. But when Maggie would have closed the door, he snatched it from her hands, his eyes narrowed on her suspiciously.

"I think you're lyin', Miz Rand, hopin' I'll go away. Well, it won't work." He stepped into the kitchen. "You might as well stop stallin' and tell me where she is."

All the hatred Maggie felt for the man who had caused the death of her beloved daughter boiled up inside Maggie. The power to hurt him back, if only in a small measure, was within her hands. Eying him closely, watching to see his reaction, she said in a cold, harsh voice, "You'll find her grave and headstone in the cemetery about a mile out of town."

A bleakness settling in his blue eyes, LaTour fumbled for a chair and sat down. His pain and regret were unmistakable. Maggie stared in amazement at his grief-stricken face. Had this hardened man loved her daughter after all? It was hard to believe that an outlaw was capable of loving. Even so, she knew she had been right in fighting Cleo's attraction for him.

She sat down and folded her hands in her lap, waiting for LaTour to recover, to leave. She gave a startled jump when LaTour said quietly, "Cleo was expectin' our child. I take it this little fellow is my son."

Spots of red appeared on Maggie's cheeks. He had known about the coming baby! Cleo hadn't told her that. Her mind awash with alarm, unable to think straight, she grabbed Jonty up and folded her arms protectively around the small body.

"He is not your son! Your child, a girl, died along with her mother. This little fellow belongs to one of Nellie's girls."

LaTour lifted his eyes from Jonty's small face to look reproachfully at Maggie. "Stop lyin', Miz Rand," he said gently. "Lookin' at the boy is like lookin' at myself in the mirror. You're wastin' your breath tellin' me otherwise."

Maggie's shoulders slumped in defeat. It was true. They were as like as two peas in a pod. "All right." Her chin tilted belligerently. "It's true, but it matters little that you're his father. He will have no part in your life," she finished as Jonty wiggled off her lap and leaned against her knee.

"You think so, Miz Rand?" LaTour said coldly, a dangerous light in his eyes. "I loved his mother, I love him. He should be raised by me, taught manly things. You could only teach him to be a sissy."

"Oh, yes," Maggie snapped sarcastically, "you could teach him manly things all right. How to shoot a gun, rob a bank, rustle cattle. It would be a fine upbringing you'd give him."

If Maggie's stinging words touched him, LaTour showed no sign of it as he rose and squatted down in front of Jonty. Gently brushing a black curl off her forehead, he asked gently, "What's your name, son?"

Blue eyes so like his own peeked up at the breed. "Jonty Rand," came the shy answer.

LaTour looked up at Maggie and pinned her with a hard look. "Had Cleo lived, she'd have called him Jonty LaTour."

Maggie opened her mouth to throw accusations at the man she hated so intensely, to yell that if not for him her daughter would be alive today. But LaTour had turned his back on her and was talking quietly to the child. And to her dismay, Jonty was smiling at her father, playing with the buttons on his shirt.

Oh, dear God, she thought wildly, what if he decides to take Jonty away? There was no way she could stop him. He could be out of the house and gone before she could summon help. Besides, there was no one here but the whores, and they were all asleep.

"There is one slim chance of stopping him," an inward voice nudged her consciousness. "Tell him the child's true sex."

Afraid to hope, but feeling desperate, Maggie spoke to the back of the man who continued to ignore her. "What if I told you Jonty is a girl? That her mother named her Joan."

She received a thin smile. "I would say that you're lyin' again, Miz Rand, that you are graspin' at straws." He ran his hands down Jonty's arms. "Why is he dressed as a boy if he is a girl?"

"That shouldn't be hard for you to figure out. I work in a whorehouse, in case you haven't noticed."

"Oh, I noticed all right, and I'm some surprised. I can't believe that the proper Miz Rand has lowered herself so."

Maggie let the sneering remark pass as she chewed at her bottom lip, her eyes on the clock. It was a little early for Jonty's bath, but this man had to be made aware of his child's femininity. And pray God, he'd have enough decency not to cart a little girl into his camp of outlaws.

"You take a lot of convincing, Jim LaTour," she snapped. Transfering her gaze to Jonty, who now played with the bright kerchief around her father's neck, she rose to her feet and said, "It's time for your bath, Jonty."

LaTour sat back down, calmly watching as Maggie placed a basin of water on the table and dropped a cloth and bar of soap into it. He gazed intently as Jonty was stood on a chair and her grandmother began to disrobe the small body. The little shirt came off, the miniature trousers, then snow-white underdrawers were drawn down over straight, narrow hips.

As Jonty stepped out of them, Maggie looked triumphantly at Jim LaTour. The look of disappointment she'd expected to see wasn't there. The hard features had softened, and in the blue eyes was a great tenderness, a flowing pride of ownership. And while fear gripped Maggie that he would take the child anyway, LaTour rose and walked over to the table. He picked the washcloth out of the basin, squeezed out some of the water, then soaped it liberally.

"So." He smiled and began to bathe the small body. "I have a little daughter. Somehow that pleases me more."

Maggie's eyes darted to the rifle over the mantel, hung out of Jonty's reach. She would shoot the devil before she'd let him take Jonty away.

LaTour followed her gaze, read her intent. "Rest your mind, Miz Rand," he said dryly. "I know my camp is no place for a girl-child."

But while Maggie went weak with relief, he continued, "My plans will have to be redirected for a while. Until she is . . ." He left the sentence unfinished, but Maggie knew what he was thinking. When Jonty was older, he would take her away.

"In the meantime," LaTour went on, "I expect to support her."

"We don't need your money, nor want it," Maggie stated firmly. "Especially dishonestly earned money."

There had been no response to the jibe, but later, after LaTour had played a while with Jonty, then kissed her and left, Maggie found several greenbacks tucked beneath the lamp. Her first instinct was to throw the money in the fire, but her long life of frugality would not allow her to. Instead, she walked to the old trunk sitting beneath the window and, opening it, placed the stack of bills in a small chest.

LaTour had stayed in town a week, visiting his daughter every day, bringing her sweets and once a little toy wooden gun. "To keep up the charade," he had said with a crooked grin. "I couldn't very well bring her a doll."

A warm and affectionate bond existed between LaTour and his child by the time he left Abilene. And Maggie, who had watched the pair together, had to admit, though reluctantly, that the outlaw truly loved his daughter, and that Jonty equally loved her "Uncle" Jim.

For the next thirteen years, a stilted truce existed between father and grandmother as LaTour perodically came to spend some time with Jonty. And for the last five of those years he had nagged Maggie to get Jonty out of the pleasure house.

"I will when I've got enough money put aside," she'd always said to put him off.

He would come back with, "You must have enough. I've given you a small fortune over the years. Enough to buy a small place where Jonty can look and act her sex." At this point he'd say, "You've done your duty by her, Miz Rand. Let me support you both now."

Maggie's answer had always been the same. "I will not spend a dime of your money, nor will I eat a bite of food your money bought."

They'd had their hottest battle of words two weeks ago. As usual, it had been repetitious, the same questions from LaTour, the same answers from

Maggie. There was one difference this time, however. Maggie added to her usual refusal to accept aid from LaTour, "I have made my own plans. We won't be here much longer."

"Well, you had better not be," LaTour warned, "otherwise I'll take matters into my own hands. Jonty can't hide her sex much longer, and I'm not going to take the chance of her being found out by one of Nellie's customers."

"There's no chance of that," Maggie argued back. "Jonty never sets foot in that part of the house. Nellie and the girls watch like a hawk that she doesn't."

"Bah!" LaTour snorted. "What about when the girls are sleepin'?"

"I'm always here. No one would dare touch her."

LaTour looked at Maggie, then searched her face more closely. The usual fire that sparked her eyes was gone. And her face was thinner than ever, almost shrunken. Maggie Rand didn't look at all well.

"Look, Maggie," he said gently, using her name for the first time, "I don't want to argue with you, but I'm giving you two weeks to take Jonty and clear out of here. Otherwise I'll take her away from you."

He had left then, in search of Jonty to tell her good-bye. Weak and trembly from his dire warning, Maggie eased herself into a chair. She sighed raggedly. She had waited too long to take Jonty away. Three years ago, lingering consumption had overtaken her. It had drained her health, robbed her of her strength. It had taken all her will power to hold back her need to cough in front of LaTour. He would have known right away that she didn't have much time left. He would probably have taken Jonty right then and there.

A slight noise brought Maggie back to the present. Her eyes searched for Jonty and found her. The girl moved about the room, half-heartedly running a dust cloth over the furniture. Maggie's fever-bright eyes lingered lovingly on the delicate features, then dropped to the flat chest which she knew was tightly bound. Thankfully, Jonty had matured late and had only recently found it necessary to bind her breasts to keep them secret beneath the loose shirts she wore.

But how much longer, Maggie wondered, could the baggy trousers, cinched in at the narrow waist by a leather belt, hide the gentle curve of her hips, the long, beautifully shaped legs?

Maggie's thin face worked spasmodically. Had she done her granddaughter a disservice, passing her off as a boy all these years? It had seemed the only way at the time. And she had thought to live long enough to see the girl take her rightful place in the world, to fall in love and get married.

The thin chest heaved in a long, regretful sigh. That was not to be, not in her lifetime at least. Maggie continued to watch the slim figure move about. Poor child. She was caught between two worlds, taught to exist in both since she was seven. With her own tutoring of the girl, Jonty had turned into an excellent cook, had learned how to turn a fine seam, and could read and write and do sums. Thanks to her father, she knew how to handle a gun with accuracy, ride a horse remarkably well.

Disapproval flashed in the tired eyes. Jonty was also very adept at playing poker, thanks again to her father. To his admiration, she often cleaned out his pockets in a game of five-card stud.

But Jonty hated pretending to be a boy, Maggie knew. The girl was feminine in every fiber of her being. She longed to shed her male attire, to wear pretty dresses and soft underclothing. But strangely, she seemed to have no desire to attract men. Actually, she seemed to dislike men. At least, the derisive remarks she made about them led a person to think so.

But why shouldn't the child be disgusted with the male species? Maggie asked herself. She mainly only saw those who came to the pleasure house with lust shinning out of their eyes. Of course there was her father . . . and Cord McBain. LaTour never went beyond the kitchen when he visited. She'd give him credit for that. If he whored while in town, he went to another pleasure house.

Cord, however, came with lust to be satisfied. And Jonty had eventually learned that. Foul-mouthed Lucy had seen to that, describing in front of Jonty what went on between her and the wild-horse hunter. Maggie was sorry about that. For up until then, the girl had been almost as fond of Cord as she was of LaTour.

She had tried to explain to Jonty the difference between lust and love. "Listen, child," she'd said, "what goes on upstairs with men the girls entertain is not how it is between a man and a decent woman who are in love. Making love with the man you love, and who loves you in turn, is a beautiful and soul-satisfying experience.

She pointed to the ceiling. "Those people up there, there's no love involved in what they're doing. Not even respect or liking goes into it. Whores are just a convenience to the men who come here, essential to their male drive." She had squeezed Jonty's slender hands gently. "Don't be scared or disgusted by anything you might have heard, all right?"

Jonty's fingers had toyed with the wide gold band on her grandmother's finger, sunk in thought. After a moment, she looked up and said, "I'm not scared, maybe a little disgusted, but I'll tell you one thing." Her blue eyes blazed. "I'd rather scrub floors."

Maggie remembered laughing in relief and of tousling the short black curls. But when she said, "Good girl," then added, "Some day you'll scrub floors for the man you love," Jonty had stiffened and pulled away.

"Maybe," she had muttered, then walked outside, the action saying plainly that she didn't want to talk about it.

That had been when Jonty was fifteen. Was she still wary of men? She called Jonty's name, raising a thin, wasted hand to beckon her to the bed. "We must talk, honey."

Jonty left off staring bleakly through the window and, hiding her anxiety with a bright smile, moved across the room in her natural graceful walk. She sat down on the edge of the bed, and taking Maggie's cold hands into her own warm ones, asked gently, "Talk about what, Granny?"

"About what's to become of you." Maggie paused, gathering strength, then said, "You know that your granny is going to leave you, don't you, love?"

A warm, gentle breeze stirred the thin curtains at the window and a bee buzzed around the bouquet of wild flowers sharing the array of medicine bottles on the narrow bedside table. None of this made an impression on Jonty. Granny had put into words the fear that had haunted her for some time. For the past few months, the cough that often racked the frail body had daily grown worse. She had hoped, had prayed, that with the arrival of spring Granny's health would improve. It had not. Her fingers tightened convulsively on the old ones.

"Don't say that, Granny," she begged, the deep, throaty voice she had practiced for so long coming naturally now. "It's springtime. Everyone gets better then. Besides"—her lips tried to smile—"next week is my eighteenth birthday. Your leaving me to celebrate alone wouldn't be a very nice birthday gift, now would it?"

"I'm sorry, Jonty." Maggie's deeply veined hand reached up to stroke the girl's smooth cheek. "I've hung on as long as I can." After a short pause she said, "Now it's time to talk about your future. Have you given it any thought?"

Jonty blinked back the tears that burned the backs of her eyes. She hadn't been able to think past this old woman's dying and the awful, painful void it would leave in her life. What was to become of her was of little importance at the moment.

She cleared her choked voice and, gently stroking

the gray, wispy hair off the age-narrowed forehead, said quietly, "I suppose I'll stay on here with Nellie, be her housekeeper."

"Oh, no, child!" Maggie tried to sit up in her alarm. "That you must never do," she gasped as Jonty gently lowered her back on the pillows. "You must get away from here. You know what would happen to you if your femininity should be discovered."

Jonty smiled into the eyes that clung anxiously to hers. "Nellie and the girls wouldn't let anything happen to me."

Maggie's lips tightened. "That Lucy would. She'd throw you to the wolves the first chance she got." She shook her small head determinedly. "We must think of something else. Some way to show the world that you are a lovely woman."

"Well, there's always Uncle Jim," Jonty ventured, aware of her grandmother's deep dislike of her friend, but never understanding why. "He's like a relation to me, and he already knows I'm female. He wouldn't let me come to harm."

"Never!" Fire flamed a moment in Maggie's rheumy eyes. "Jim LaTour is a law-breaker, he and his companions a menace to civilization." Maggie struggled again to raise herself up on an elbow. "Promise me, Jonty, that you will never go away with that man."

"But, Granny," Jonty began, then paused and turned her head when a sharp rap sounded on the kitchen door. Before she could ask who was there, the door opened and a tall, broad-shouldered figure stepped inside and closed the door.

"Cord McBain!" Maggie whispered hoarsely and fell back against the pillows again. "Thank you, God," she whispered, "for answering my prayer."

CHAPTER 2

FOR THE GREATER PORTION OF FOUR DAYS AND NIGHTS, THE whip-lean rider had been in the saddle, driving a herd of fifty wild mustangs toward the railyards in Abilene.

Cord McBain, however, was accustomed to long hours in the saddle. He had driven more than one herd on a hundred-mile trip. The hard-faced man was a wild-horse hunter, a wanderer of the wild range in the Wyoming territory.

The Civil war had ended in April of 1865, and a year later Cord was in Wyoming.

He had been a captain, fighting for the North under General Grant. Although he had become sick to death of killing and maiming, he had enjoyed army life itself. The gambling, the carousing, the whoring in between battles had appealed to his wild nature.

His mother had died when he was very young and had left no distinct impression of her on his mind. His father had never remarried, so he had never known the gentle influence of a woman. He and his father had been very close, however, and had even gone to war together. It had torn him apart when the elder McBain was killed in a bloody battle at Shiloh.

At the end of the war, Cord found himself at loose ends. The old farm in Michigan had no appeal for him, if it ever had. A month later, restless, unable or unwilling to pick up the loose ends of his life and put them back together again, he had headed west.

He had wondered if there was something wrong with him, that he didn't hanker for a stable life as he drifted from place to place, gaining only the reputation of a daring gambler, a fast gun, and a bad man to fool around with.

But Cord loved his life of danger, the barroom brawling, facing a quick gun, and an occasional Indian battle. He had lived it so long, it now seemed natural to him.

Then, two years ago he had helped an old man round up a herd of wild horses, and his future was cast. Nothing fired his blood like chasing a wild "broom-tail." After he had corralled fifty head or so, he'd drive them into Abilene. With a pocketful of money, he'd carouse for a few days, drinking and gambling and visiting Nellie's pleasure house as long as he could afford the price of a whore. When he was down to grub money, he'd purchase supplies and head back to the range to start all over again.

The early spring evening had fallen cold, and a keen wind was blowing across the plains when Cord spotted the twinkling lights of Abilene. Ten minutes later, his collar pulled up against the evening chill, he was herding his horses down the main street, hitching his Colt into position with its handle nesting close to his hand. There was no law to speak of in this wild place, and there was some fine horseflesh among the animals that loped ahead of him. It was not unlikely that some shifty-eyed character might make a grab for one.

Cord smiled thinly. After he had delivered them and had received payment for his hard work, the mustangs would be somebody else's responsibility. But until then, he'd take no chances.

An hour later, having had no trouble from anyone, although his herd had been closely watched until note was taken of the gun ready to be plucked from its holster, a deal was struck with a government man. The agent had come west to purchase mounts for the army that was still fighting the Indians, and promised to buy all that Cord could supply him in the future.

Cord's first stop after that was at a Chinaman's bath-house, where he spent close to another hour soaking away the grime and sweat of the trail, changing into clean clothes, then getting a shave. He handed the attendant his roll of soiled clothes before he left.

"Can you have these washed in a couple days?" When he was answered in the affirmative, he ambled outside, swung into the saddle, and turned the stallion down a side street that had more brothels on it than any other kind of business.

"I hope ole Lucy has had a good day's rest," he thought out loud, "'cause she's gonna get a good workout tonight."

A short time later Cord was handing the stallion over to a stableboy, instructing him to give the mount a good rub-down and supply him with a hefty helping of oats. He gave the horse an affectionate swat on the rump, stepped up on the narrow porch, and pushed open the door.

He stood a moment inside the garishly appointed room where a dozen or so eager men waited. Hell, he thought in disgust, I'm not going to wait here like a dog waiting his turn at a bitch in heat. He stepped back outside, leaving behind the jangling music of a heavily drummed piano, the player trying to send his music above the coarse oaths of the men, and the shrill laughter of the whores as they beckoned men up the stairs.

Nellie's pleasure house, constructed of unpainted, rough-sawed boards, had an outside staircase for those who wanted to visit the girls in secret—husbands, businessmen, even one skinny old minister whenever he could get away from his nagging wife. With one foot on the bottom step, Cord paused in indecision. Should he look in on Maggie first—before Lucy got hold of him? He probably wouldn't get away from her until late tomorrow sometime.

A noise mid-way alongside the house caught his attention. He peered around the corner and through the darkness made out two figures. A man, his trousers down around his ankles, had a woman penned against the wall, her dress up around her waist as she straddled his hips. The noise he'd heard was the woman's grunting as her companion thrust furiously inside her. Cord grinned, his mind made up. He had been a long time without a woman and needed what the man in the shadows was getting. He would see his old friend later.

Enthusiastic squeals greeted Cord each time he walked past an open door of a bedroom. He was a favorite here. He was never brutal, and always slipped the girl some extra money, knowing that Nellie took a large share of their earnings. But he refused each invitation with a congenial grin and continued on down the narrow hall, wondering which of the closed doors concealed the girl Joan while she entertained her important client.

He forced the girl from his mind. Nasty Lucy was the whore to visit after a three-month abstinence. She had almost as much stamina as he had himself.

His nose twitched at the rank odor of cheap perfume, unwashed bodies, and the aftermath of spent passion. "That's the one thing I hate about whorehouses," he grumbled to himself. "The damn stink permeates the very walls."

Cord was very fastidious when it came to bedding a woman. The girls here had learned that before he stretched out on their beds he had two rules. Clean linens were a must, and the woman had to bath herself, inside and out. She had better make sure there was no lingering evidence of another man's fluid. He had sometimes wondered what it would be like to bed a virgin, to know that no other man had been there before him.

But virgins were good women, he'd always reminded himself, and he didn't have a chance in hell of ever meeting one.

Cord stopped at the door at the end of the hall. He rapped twice, then pushing open the unlocked door, stepped inside.

Lucy lay sprawled on the bed, sound asleep, her mouth hanging open. Not the most beautiful sight in the world. Cord grimaced, calling impatiently, "Lucy, you lazy wretch, wake up and earn yourself some money. Do you want ole Nellie to toss you out on your dead ass?"

Lucy's eyes popped open, and she squealed his name. The bed springs squeaked a complaint as she bounced up and swung her feet to the floor. When she rushed to meet him with arms outstretched, Cord held her off.

"Hurry and take your bath, woman." His nose twitched. "Then change the sheets. You've got your work cut out for you the next couple hours or so."

Lucy's thick lips pouted. "There ain't no hot water, and I don't relish washin' up in cold. Anyway, I don't know why you have to be so particular. The other men don't care whether I've had a bath or not."

Cord turned to leave. "I'm not arguing with you about it. I'm sure one of the other girls will be more than willin' to step into a tub of cold water for me."

"Oh, Cord, I was only foolin'," Lucy whinned. "You know I'd wash in ice water if you wanted me to."

Her hand snaked down to rub the bulge pushing at his jeans. "And I swear to you the sheets are clean. Why don't you undress and crawl between them while I make myself nice and fresh for you?"

Cord eyed Lucy doubtfully, taking in the soiled and wrinkled dress, the sweat stains under the armpits.

"How come you're not clean and the sheets are? Did your last customer take you on the floor—or did he take his pleasure standing up?"

The insult passed over Lucy's head. She giggled. "Some of the time he was standin' up." She shrugged, and as she pulled the satin dress over her head, she explained, "He was drunk and puked all over the bed. That's why the sheets are clean."

Cord frowned and walked over to the single window and yanked up the sash. Fresh air poured in, and as he pulled off his boots and unbuckled his gun belt, he breathed it deep into his lungs. When he had divested himself of all his clothing, he lay down on the bed and watched Lucy step into a hip-tub whose water had sat all day, having lost its heat many hours ago. He laughed as she eased herself into the water, a squeal whistling through her teeth.

She's going to fat, he thought, watching Lucy's plump rear end disappear into the tub. He shifted his gaze to the large breasts, floating and bobbing in the waves created by her full figure. If she wasn't so good at her trade, he mused, I'd look for someone more firm—one of the younger girls.

"Use a lot of soap and hurry up," Cord called, uncaring for the moment what shape the whore's body was in. "I've got three months of unloadin' to do and I'd like to get started."

Lucy gave him a salacious smile, and a few minutes later when she came shivering to the bed, his arousal was complete, pulsating with need. When she would have stretched out beside him, his restraining hand on her head said otherwise.

"I'll have a little appetizer first." He pushed her head down on his stomach, then nudged it downward. Lucy went quite willingly.

Two hours later, Cord was still "unloadin'" and Lucy was beginning to complain. "Dammit, McBain, I wish you'd give that big thing a rest. I'm exhausted, havin' it rammed into me every half hour."

She ran a disgruntled look over the "big thing" that was tiring her so and snorted peevishly. "You're hung like that damn stallion of yours, do you know that?"

"You think so?" Cord laughed, leaning up on an elbow and looking down at his powerful manhood. His eyes glinted devilishy. "Maybe you're right. Although I have seen a few studs bigger than me."

"Well, go find yourself a mare," Lucy snapped. "I gotta have some rest."

"All right," Cord relented. "You can rest while I have some whiskey to cut a hundred miles of dust from my throat. Have Maggie's grandson bring me up a bottle."

Lucy shoved a pillow under her head and pulled the sheet up around her shoulders. "You don't notice much, do you, Cord? Maggie has never allowed the kid to come into this part of the house." She gave a short, scornful laugh. "I guess she thinks the little sissy will see too much, get ideas."

"Hell, the boy must be all of sixteen by now." Cord frowned. "I'm surprised at Maggie's thinkin'. You girls should have him nicely broken in by now."

Lucy opened her mouth, a malicious gleam in her eyes. She remembered Nellie's threat then, and thought better of the secret she had intended to reveal. She said instead, with a scornful laugh, "I tried to initiate him once and I thought he was gonna slap my face, he got so mad."

"Maybe the kid wants someone young and fresh, someone nearer his own age."

"Yeah, well I doubt if he'll get it. You know Maggie, all prim and straight-laced." Lucy yawned. "Anyway, the old girl's real sick. Nellie thinks she's dyin'."

"The hell you say!" Cord sat up. "I hate to hear that. Maggie saved my life once. Cut a poisoned arrow out of my shoulder, then nursed me back to health."

He lay back down, the whiskey forgotten as he recalled a certain time about five years ago.

He had been heading toward Kansas to check out the town of Abilene. He'd heard that it was an up and coming place, but still raw and wild, and that it boasted more brothels than there were in the whole rest of the state.

He had been riding for a couple of days when he glimpsed the half-naked brave slipping through the trees. But he had ridden on. It wasn't his way to kill an Indian just for sport. When he shot one, it was because the savage deserved it.

An hour later, however, he was sorry he had let his finer feelings overrule his common sense.

He had paused at a small stream to let Rawhide quench his thirst, when the same brave stepped from behind a tree, a long bow drawn back, the cord pulled taut, a projecting arrow ready to let loose. Cord dropped the reins, and with lightning speed the deadly Colt was in his hand. The pointed flint that pierced his shoulder was just a split second ahead of the bullet that found the brave's heart.

His flesh on fire, giddy with the pain that throbbed like a drumbeat, Cord gathered up the reins of the nervous, snorting stallion and pulled himself into the saddle. With a nudge of his heel he rode on, out across the prairie.

His head sunk on his chest, a hand on the protruding shaft in his shoulder, Cord fought off the waves of dizziness washing over him. After what seemed a long lifetime, the big stallion came to a halt in an alley back of a house. He lifted his head, and through pain-filled, fevered eyes he stared at a tall building. Then his weakening grip on the saddlehorn slipped and he fell sidewise out of the saddle.

Cord hit the ground heavily, and in semi-conscious-ness he heard a high, startled squeal. His vision cleared for a second, and he stared up into the bluest eyes he'd ever seen. A strange sensation, almost sensual, ran through his body. Just before he fainted, he raised a hand to brush it over a crop of short, black curls.

Four days later, weak as a kitten and eternally grateful to Maggie Rand for keeping him among the living, he learned that the young lad who had squatted over him on his fall to the ground was Maggie's grandson, Jonty.

"You know, I've always been a little uneasy around that kid of Maggie's." Cord came back to the present, muttering to himself more than to Lucy. "I always get the feelin' he can see into my soul with those tilted eyes of his, read every sin I ever committed, and he finds me wanting."

"He's a strange little baggage." Lucy rose from bed to go use the chamber pot placed behind a screen. "If he's not runnin' wild with the Indian kids, he's got his nose stuck in a book." She got back into bed, adding, "He's a bastard, you know. Nobody dares ask Maggie about the father. It's rumored he has Indian blood in him."

Cord lay back down also. "I'm gonna catch a couple hours sleep, then look in on my old friend. Make sure you wake me up."

Lucy, however, was also in need of sleep, and it was late morning when Cord awakened on his own, the whore snoring at his side. Swearing under his breath, he rose and, filling a basin with water from a pitcher on a small table, scrubbed Lucy's scent off his throat and chest. Then, running a comb through his hair, he hurried down the back stairs.

Cord gazed down at Maggie's worn and wrinkled visage. The tired eyes told him that approaching death was not far away. He glanced at the slender figure holding the old woman's hand, noting the pale, strained face, the blue eyes clouded with pain and dread. What was to become of this strange, sissified lad after Maggie gave up the fight? he wondered.

Jonty sensed Cord's look, and blushing uncomfortably, she released her grandmother's hand and stood up. Cord gave her a curt nod, then took her vacated seat on the edge of the bed. He was keenly aware of the footsteps moving away.

As he took Maggie's cold fingers into his own, he scorned himself for letting a wet-behind-the-ears youngster get under his skin. "What's this I hear that you're not feelin' well, old friend?" he asked warmly.

His fingers were pressed weakly, and he leaned down to hear the low, raspy voice. "I was afraid you wouldn't get here in time, Cord."

"In time for what, Maggie?" Cord asked gently, his insides knotted with deep regret that he was losing a dear, dear friend. "Do you want me to take you to the spring dance that's comin' up?"

As Cord had known she wouldn't, Maggie didn't respond in her usual fashion. Where before she might have quipped, "I've got my dancing shoes all polished up and waiting," this time she pinned him with serious eyes and, licking her dry lips, said, "I'm dying, Cord, and you know it."

"Now, Maggie," Cord started to scold gently, "you don't know . . ."

"Hush now," Maggie interrupted. "We're too good friends to start lying to each other at this late date." The old woman paused, as though gathering strength. Then, "I have something important to say to you, to ask you, and I want you to listen to it."

Maggie's voice had risen on the last part of the sentence, its tone impatient. Cord hastened to soothe her. "Of course I'll listen to you, Maggie. And you can ask anything of me, you know that."

Maggie studied the lean, tanned face anxiously. "I hope you mean that, Cord," she said finally. "For when I'm gone I want you to take Jonty, make a home for him, raise him."

Maggie's request filled the room with a deafening silence.

While Cord stared at the dying woman in wide-eyed disbelief, Jonty, peeling potatoes in the kitchen, grew numb in shock. What in the world was Granny thinking of? Surely not that she would go away with this man—a man who looked at her with dislike, whose lips always sneered when he spoke to her?

She listened intently, a potato in one hand, the knife in the other, both forgotten as she waited for the hard-faced man's answer, praying that he would refuse the unusual request.

She shot a glance over her shoulder, letting her breath out a little. It looked as if he would refuse, for Cord's face wore the same incredible look that she was sure her own did as, half laughing, half begging, he said, "You can't be serious, Maggie. I couldn't give the kid a home. Hell, I don't even have one myself, you know that. I'm on the move all the time."

"It doesn't have to be that way, Cord." Maggie tried to sit up and Cord gently pushed her back. She lay a moment, breathing in short pants, waiting to regain the strength that had been sapped from her by the slight struggle. Then, in the tense silence the old woman began to charter the course she wanted the wild-horse hunter and her beloved granddaughter to follow.

"I have some money put away, Cord. Money I have been saving for thirteen years." Maggie paused, reluctantly remembering that the money had come from the hands of Jim LaTour. She firmed her lips. No time to think of that.

"It's a considerable amount, Cord," she continued, "enough to start you out on your own ranch."

"But, Maggie . . ."

"Hush, Cord." There was determination in the half-whispered words. "It's time you stopped living like an Indian, sleeping on the ground, eating cold rations half the time. It's time you lit in one place and started building yourself a future." Her faded eyes begged Cord. "And take Jonty with you, raise him in a proper manner."

The more Maggie talked, the more panic-stricken Cord became. She was backing him into a tight corner, the tightest he'd ever been in. He couldn't shoot his way out of this one. He could only use reason, and hope that he was successful.

"Look, Maggie," he said softly. "It wouldn't work. I don't know the first thing about raisin' a kid. Besides, I'm not a proper person." He smiled teasingly at her. "Stop and remember how many times you've called me a useless hellion, said that someday I'd hang for my ornerieness."

Maggie waved a weak, dismissive hand. "You know that was all in fun. Inside you're a decent man, Cord McBain. The only person I'd give my Jonty over to. And anyway," she said after a slight pause, "Jonty isn't really a kid anymore. He'll be eighteen next week."

"Really?" Cord shot a surprised look at the rigid figure standing at the dry-sink. Hell, at eighteen Jonty was a man by most standards. He shouldn't need anybody watching over him. And he knew by the stiff stance of the boy that, like Cord, the kid didn't like the idea of stringing along with him one bit.

He turned back to Maggie and said brusquely, "I'm sorry, Maggie, but I don't think . . ."

"You owe me, Cord!" Maggie cried out against the refusal she knew was coming. With panic in her dry voice she continued, "I've never asked you for anything before." Her hand clutched weakly at his arm. "I'm begging you now, Cord. Please do this thing for me."

Jonty saw the weakening in the handsome face, and dropping the knife and potato, she ran out of the kitchen to drop to her knees beside the bed. "Granny, I can go to Uncle Jim. He'll be glad to have me. I'll help him to start a ranch, and he'll provide me a home."

Hope flared in Cord's gray eyes. "There's an uncle the boy can go to, Maggie?"

An impatient sigh whistled through Maggie's fever-cracked lips. "The child is talking about the breed, LaTour. He came through here thirteen years ago, and he and Jonty took a liking to each other. He still stops by occasionally."

"You don't mean Jim LaTour, the outlaw?" Cord looked incredulously at Maggie. When she nodded wearily, he turned scornful eyes on Jonty.

"So, you puny-lookin' runt, you'd pick an outlaw and his gang over me, would you? Is it your ambition to become like him, a parasite livin' off the labor of other men?"

Jonty glared back at the eyes shooting contempt at her. Drawing in an angry breath, she snapped coldly, "No I don't plan on becoming an outlaw. It's just that, unlike you, Uncle Jim would make me welcome."

Cord was suddenly gripped with the unreasonable determination to thwart any alternative suggestions this effeminate boy might come up with.

His mouth twisted in open dislike, he grated out forcefully, "I may not welcome you, young man, but when I leave Abilene, you'll be comin' with me. There ain't no way I'll let Maggie Rand's grandson grow up on the wrong side of the law."

His eyes bored into Jonty's. "And I don't want to ever see him hangin' round you."

And while Jonty's stormy blue eyes glared back into the gray, threatening ones, Maggie gave a happy sigh and closed her eyes. She took Cord's lean hand and brought it to her cheek. "I can go in peace now, Cord," she whispered. She reached for Jonty's hand, and when its narrow length was placed in hers, she said softly, "It will be all right, honey, you'll see."

It won't be all right, Granny, Jonty thought, returning to the kitchen to finish peeling the potatoes. You don't know how he dislikes me. He thinks that because I don't rut with the girls like he does that I'm strange, unnatural.

Jonty added the potatoes to the simmering meat, and idly stirred it as she thought back to the time Cord's careless affection for her had changed to comtemptous disregard.

Nellie's girls took great delight, when Maggie wasn't about, to dress Jonty up in their dresses, paint her face, turn her into the beautiful woman she truly was. Then, giggling and laughing, they'd let customers catch glimpses of her before whisking her away. They had all the men begging to visit the new girl. When the baffled Nellie answered them that she had no new girl, they angrily accused her of keeping the girl for her wealthy customers who sneaked up the back stairs.

One night, after changing back into her male attire, Jonty had slipped out of the room that was directly across from Lucy's. The door was part way open, and when she started to pass it, she froze. Stretched naked on the bed, the blond mat of hair startling against his broad, tanned chest, was her hero. The man she built fantasies around.

Unthinking, she gasped, "Cord!" There was reproach in her voice and in her staring eyes. "What are you doing here?" she asked inanely.

When the startled Cord didn't answer, a mocking voice drawled from behind the privacy screen, "Now what do you think he's doin' here, Jonty? He's here for some of Lucy's special pleasurin'."

The plump whore, also naked, bounced into the room, her heavy breasts jiggling, her large feet slapping against the floor as she crossed the room to the bed. Her large cheeks sticking up in the air as she climbed onto the sagging mattress reminded Jonty of two huge mounds of lumpy dough.

"Lucy knows just how to lower your fever, don't she, big man?" She trailed a hand across Cord's flat stomach, then down across the patch of crisp hair to stroke his long manhood. And while Jonty watched wide-eyed, the whore's fingers curled around the growing member.

A fast glance at Cord completed her disillusionment. He was grinning lazily as he watched Lucy's stubby fingers slowly and knowingly stir his long length into a large arousal. Without conscious thought, Jonty let loose a sound of disgust from between her teeth.

The pair on the bed looked up, and though Lucy

frowned her annoyance, she shamelessly continued to move her cupped hand on Cord. He, however, reddened and hurriedly brushed Lucy's hand away as he fumbled the sheet up over their nakedness.

Flustered, he tried for jocularity. "Get that stunned look off your face, boy, and go get me a bottle of whiskey. I feel like I've got half the dust in Kansas in my throat."

When Jonty made no move to obey his request, the whore sent her a venomous look and swung her feet to the floor. Reaching for her robe, she grunted, "I'll get the whisky." Tying the belt loosely around her thick waist, she turned on Jonty, ordering, "And you, you little bastard, get the hell out of here and take your prudish thoughts with you."

Jonty's gaze moved back to Cord, sure that he would reprimand Lucy for speaking so mean to her. She couldn't believe the change that had come over his face. The smile was gone, an angry dark cloud replacing it. He had regained his composure and was furious for having momentarily lost it. She wheeled and ran for the door, his hurtful words following her:

"Yes, scat, you sissified little pisspot, before I take Lucy right in front of you, show you that thing between your legs isn't only for takin' a leak through."

She had raced down the hall, their ridiculing laughter following her. From that day Cord had barely spoken to her, acting civil only when Granny was present.

Jonty gave a startled jerk, almost dropping the long-handled spoon when Cord spoke from the doorway. "I'd appreciate it if you'd rustle me up a bite to eat. I haven't eaten since yesterday afternoon."

Jonty nodded, and after settling the lid back on the steaming pot, she placed a frying pan on the stove. Fifteen minutes later, a platter of steak and eggs waited on the table. Hurrying back to her grandmother's bedside, she said quietly, "You can go eat now."

She hadn't expected any thanks and she didn't

receive any as Cord rose and stalked into the kitchen. She took his place beside Maggie and picked up the old woman's dry, wasted hand.

The old clock ticked on, the same bee of yesterday continued to buzz around the vase of wildflowers that were beginning to wilt.

Cord returned shortly, and when Jonty would have risen, he motioned her to remain seated and pulled himself up a chair on the other side of the bed. The hours dragged by with no word spoken between them. Twilight came and Jonty rose and lit the kerosine lamp on the bedside table.

How peaceful she looks, Jonty thought as she turned the wick down until only a soft yellow glow shone on Maggie's face. She looks so many years younger with the pain lines smoothed away.

It was several minutes before Jonty realized that her grandmother had slipped away. With a wailing cry of denial, she threw her arms around the frail, still body, sobbing her grief onto the narrow, flat chest.

Cord stood up and moved to the window that looked out on the street, affected by the feminine-sounding sobs. And though he saw the moon rise, saw it bathe the street with a pale light, none of it registered. His thoughts were of Maggie. He would sorely miss the old woman—her warmth, her kindness, even her sharp tongue when she tore into him about the way he was wasting his life. She had meant family and home to him.

His chest heaved in a long sigh. And because of the love he held for this fine woman, he had promised to make a home for her grandson. His lips twisted contemptuously. A damn weakling if ever he'd seen one. He'd certainly have his work cut out. Already he was drawn to the wrong kind of man.

"I'll soon put a stop to that," he muttered to himself, then fell to thinking, and worrying, of the other things entailed in taking over the boy.

His old way of living, for instance. His wild sort of life appealed to him. Could he give it up? Could he settle down in one place? He glanced back at the bed, the still figure on it, and knew he'd have to give it a stab.

Cord's eyes remained on Jonty, impatience growing in them. He knew it was hard to lose the person you loved, one who had raised you and loved you in return, but dammit, the kid was carrying on like a girl.

He walked back to the bed and laid a hand on the narrow, heaving shoulders. "Come on, kid," he said gruffly, "you're grievin' for yourself, not your grandmother. She's at rest now, out of her pain, rid of the hardship she's known most of her life."

Jonty flinched at Cord's stark, unemotional statement of facts, and jerked away from the weight of his hand. Cord McBain was the most insensitive, uncaring man she'd ever known. Her fists clenched angrily in her lap and she parted her lips to speak, but Cord didn't give her the chance to rail out at him, to let him know what she thought of him.

"Dry your tears now," he ordered as he gently pulled the sheet up over Maggie's face. "I'll go send Nellie down to lay Maggie out while I go scout out someone to make a coffin."

Jonty wiped a sleeve across her wet eyes and watched Cord walk out of the room, his flapping chaps keeping time with a clanking of spurs. "Oh, how I hate him," she whispered as he closed the outside door softly behind him. She looked down at the shrouded figure. "You have forced me into an intolerable situation, Granny," she whispered.

Silence and loneliness emanated from the room that Jonty had known as home all her life. She pushed back the tears that welled in her eyes again and, avoiding the bed in the corner, sent her gaze around the large, comfortable room.

There was Granny's rocker, the flower print in the padded seat cover faded and worn; the small table beside it, the kerosine lamp sitting on its smooth surface. She frowned at the glass lamp chimney, which was smoke-clouded. She had forgotten to clean it in her worry for Granny.

Jonty's eyes moved to the low bookcase, every shelf crammed with books, some for pleasurable reading, others from which Granny had taught her to read, write, and cipher. Her gaze then dropped to the square table filled with personal items—a thin volume of poetry from Uncle Jim, the toy wooden gun he'd given her, a grouping of arrowheads and a chipped tommyhawk from her Indian friends.

She paced the floor. "I can't leave it all behind!" Her whisper held her pain, her wretchedness. "I don't care if that arrogant, opinionated devil likes it or not, Granny's things are coming with me—the cow and chickens, too. They'd starve if I left them behind."

On the heels of that muttered defiance came the full realization of what Cord McBain's promise to her grandmother would mean to her. She would have to live with the man, be under his dominance for months, maybe even years. It was such a devastating notion that a dark depression engulfed her. She didn't know if she could bear living with the contempt and undisguised dislike the man displayed every time he looked at her.

She walked over to the window, her shoulders heaving with a deep sigh. With Granny gone now, there wouldn't be a kind word or gesture from him. Her fists knotted on the sill. There had to be another solution, if only she could think of it. Of course, there was always Uncle Jim. She didn't give a whistle on the wind what Cord McBain thought of him, or about his order to stay away from the man who had always been so kind to her. The trouble was, she didn't know how to find this friend. Only he and God knew where he was hidden away.

"I'd rather stay here," she whispered to her reflection in the window pane. "Take the chance of my true sex not being discovered."

A sore tingling in her tightly bound breasts rid Jonty

of that notion. More and more, her body was taking on the soft contours of a woman, and she would be unable to hide her femininity much longer. Granny had been right; she couldn't stay here.

Jonty remembered in alarm at the same time that it also held true that in time Cord would also discover that he was guardian of a female. What would be his reaction? Her lips curled bitterly. He wouldn't like being fooled; it would be another mark against her. He'd probably marry her off to the first man who'd have her.

Sunk in dejection, Jonty continued to stare unseeing out the window. At the moment she had no other recourse but to go with the man who obviously didn't want her and pray that sooner or later Uncle Jim would hear of Granny's death and would come looking for her granddaughter.

She gave a startled gasp when a gentle hand was laid on her shoulder. She turned and gazed into the warm, coarse-featured face of Nellie. "Hello, Nellie," she said softly.

The warm-hearted madam put her plump arms around Jonty's slim, tense shoulders, the odor of her cheap perfume and body sweat almost overpowering Jonty as she said gently, "I'm so sorry about Maggie. She was a grand old lady. I'll miss her dreadfully. She was always so good to me and my girls."

Jonty swallowed back the tears that welled up at the kind words and choked out, "Granny was fond of you and the girls too."

She received a last squeeze before the big woman stepped away from her, explaining, "I've come to lay Maggie out. Where did she keep her best clothes?"

Jonty pointed to a battered trunk sitting on the floor at the foot of the bed. "She kept her church-going clothes in there."

This time the tears would not be checked as in Jonty's mind she saw her grandmother's "best clothes"—a long skirt, black and heavy, and a black blouse, long-sleeved and buttoned to the chin. Jonty swiped at her wet cheeks. Poor sweet Granny had had so little in her life.

Still unable to look at the still figure on the bed, Jonty continued to stare out the window. But as the minutes passed, she became aware of what Nellie was doing. There came to her the sloshing of water in the tin basin as Granny received her last bath, the odor of mothballs stinging her nostrils as the lid of the trunk was laid back.

Her body stiffened and her hands clenched as the outside door opened, and in the mirror-like surface of the window glass she saw Cord and another man carry a roughly constructed pine box into the room. She listened to the scraping of two chairs being dragged across the floor, then the heavy thump of the coffin being set upon them.

Oh, God. Jonty closed her eyes, a sharp pain stabbing her chest when Nellie said, "Wrap her in this knitted throw before you put her in the box, Cord." She could see so plainly Granny's needles flashing with the colorful yarn in the evenings, smiling her pleasure as she read poetry out loud to Jonty. Granny hadn't like Uncle Jim, but she had loved the book of poems he had given her granddaughter.

Nellie's girls came filing into the room, speaking in hushed tones as they paid their last respects to the old woman who had spent countless hours over a hot stove preparing their meals. From the corner of her eye, Jonty noted that, with the exception of Lucy, all the girls dabbed at wet eyes. And that one, she knew, wouldn't cry at her own mother's wake. Jonty was sure the woman wouldn't even be here if Nellie hadn't insisted.

The girls were gathering around her now, saying how sorry they were about Maggie, how much they would miss her. Lucy, of course, wasn't among them. After one careless glance at Maggie's still face, she had left.

The girls finally trailed off, and Jonty was glad to see them go. She couldn't have held back a fresh batch of tears much longer. She had felt Cord's cold eyes upon her, just waiting for her to show such weakness again.

Nellie had remained, and she now sat with Cord at the kitchen table, drinking coffee. Jonty ignored them until she heard her name mentioned. She listened intently then.

"Jonty is a good lad, Cord," Nellie had said, "although as everyone claims, he's different, not like the usual young man his age. As you can see, he's on the delicate side. I think that's why Maggie kinda molly-coddled him, pampered him like."

Jonty let the breath she'd been holding rush out in relief. Nellie hadn't given her secret away. In fact, as Jonty listened, it appeared the madam was trying to smooth the way for her.

"So you must remember that, Cord," Nellie went on, "and take it easy on him until he becomes used to a man's world. He's only mostly been around women all his life."

Whatever Cord's thoughts were about Nellie's advice, he didn't say. "Does anyone know who the kid's father is?" he asked, changing the subject. His chair scraped against the floor as he stood up.

Nellie shook her head. "As far as I know, that knowledge died with Maggie. She never talked about it." Her chair squeaked as she lifted her great weight out of it. "I guess I'd better go round up the girls and take them to supper." A sigh heaved her big bosoms. "I wonder how long it will take me to find another housekeeper. Of course I'll never be able to replace Maggie Rand."

Jonty heard them walking toward the door, then pause. "Maybe the kid is hungry too," Cord said. "I doubt if he's eaten all day."

Hah! Jonty snorted, her eyes narrowing. A lot he'd care if I never ate. He's just saying that for Nellie's benefit.

"Oh, yes, he'll be comin' with us." Nellie's tone said that was a foregone conclusion. "You go tell him that we'll be ready to leave in a half hour or so."

Jonty watched Cord's reflection come toward her. Her back stiffened when he stopped only a few feet away. She could feel his animosity as though it were a live thing beating against her back. Stubbornly she didn't let on she knew he was there, forcing him to speak first.

Cord's forehead furrowed in an angry frown. It would be a constant struggle between them, a fight to best the other. But he didn't have time to wait him out this time.

Cord's frown deepened, and clearing his voice, he said coldly, "Nellie will be down after a while to take you to supper. Be ready."

Resentment flickered inside Jonty at Cord's authoritative tone. She'd let him know right now that he wasn't to boss her around. She shook her head, and her voice cool, she said bluntly, "I'm not hungry."

"Hungry or not, you've got to eat." Cord ran scornful eyes over her slim body. "You look like a damn bean pole as it is."

Jonty's face tightened at his sarcasm. "Look," she spat, "don't pull that fake caring act on me. We both know that you don't give a damn whether I eat or not. In fact, it would please you if I starved to death. You wouldn't be stuck with me then."

Jonty was sure he would leave now that he knew she was wise to him. But she was mistaken. Her elbow was roughly grasped and she was spun away from the window. As she stared in surprise she was given a push that sent her reeling across the room where she finally fell into a chair.

"I know all about you, Jonty Rand." Cord stalked after her. "So don't try any of your tricks on me."

Panic swept through Jonty, and she gripped the seat of the chair, sweat popping out on her forehead. What did he know? That she was female? Who had told him? Lucy?

Cord looked at her curiously. "Why do you look so scared? I'm not gonna beat you for your sissified ways. It's not your fault that Maggie treated you more like a girl than a boy." He narrowed a threatening look on her. "That is, if you change your ways. But if you don't buckle down and start actin' like a young man, I'll take a stick to you."

It was hard for Jonty not to show her relief. Cord didn't know about her sex. Indignation replaced her fear. Take a stick to her, indeed. Her deep blue eyes raked over him contemptuously. "You might as well start beating me now, for I'll act any way I please. And you might as well know also, I'll run away from you the first chance I get."

Cord gazed at Jonty thoughtfully for a minute, then, deciding that the little bastard wouldn't run until after Maggie was laid to rest, he shrugged his shoulders indifferently. He walked toward the door, muttering carelessly, "You weedy-lookin' thing, you can starve to death for all I care."

"Damn fool!" Jonty stared at the door that still shook from the slamming it had sustained. "Couldn't he smell my stew warming on the stove?"

But his tossed-off words stung Jonty, and she was angry with herself that they did. What did she care what that randy tomcat thought of her looks? He was nothing but a low-down whoremonger lusting after that depraved Lucy. If he ever tried to beat her, she'd shoot his rotten heart out.

But it was an empty threat, she knew, as she rose and returned to the window. She could never kill anyone. As she stared out into the darkness, the silence in the room became oppressive. She felt there were spiritual things going on, that at any moment cold hands would be laid upon her. So intense was the sensation that she gave a violent jerk and cried out when a rap sounded on the kitchen door. In her eagerness to have company, even if it were Cord come back to torment her some more, she bumped into the table in her eagerness to answer the summons.

She jerked the door open and gasped. "Hello, honey," Jim LaTour said, his soft voice at odds with his hard, rugged face.

"Oh, Uncle Jim!" Jonty threw herself into his welcoming arms. Then sobbing almost hysterically, she cried, "Granny's dead!"

"I know, Jonty." LaTour held her close, smoothing her tousled curls. "One of my men brought me the news." He held her away from him and searched her small white face. "Are you all right? How come you're alone? Haven't Nellie and the girls been down to see how you're doin'?"

Jonty knuckled her wet eyes. "They've all been down. They've all been very good to me. Nellie laid Granny out. They've gone to supper now."

LaTour glanced through the open door to the pine box suspended on the two chairs. "Who got the coffin for you?"

A sour expression came over Jonty's face. "Cord McBain." She disengaged herself from LaTour and sat down at the table. "The arrogant bastard just took over." She looked up at the tall, handsome man standing over her and cried woefully, "Granny gave me over to his keeping, Uncle Jim, and I can't bear the thought of it."

LaTour sat down tiredly and reached for the tobacco pouch and papers in his breast pocket. "Well, honey," he said, spilling tobacco onto the square of thin paper, "from what I hear, the fellow is decent enough, even if he is as tough as a piece of old leather." He smiled at her encouragingly as he ran his tongue over one edge of the paper, then rolled it into a cylinder. "He'll see to it that you don't go hungry."

Jonty eyed the tanned features suspiciously as they were briefly highlighted by the flame held to the cigarette. It didn't sound encouraging, or like Uncle Jim meant to take her away with him.

"I'd rather go hungry," she wailed. "I don't like the man!"

"Now, Jonty, that's a feeble excuse." LaTour smiled at the obstinate face. "I don't like any of my men, but I put up with them because they're necessary to me."

He drew a fragrant stream of smoke into his lungs,

then looked at Jonty soberly through the exhaled smoke drifting from his nostrils. "We can't always have things the way we want them to be."

"But I feel nervous around him. He makes me feel foolish half the time, always sneering and mocking." Jonty paused, then added confusedly, "He makes me feel strange inside, tingly-like, all fluttery."

Surprise, followed quickly by knowing amusement, flickered in LaTour's eyes. His young daughter didn't know it, but she was feeling the first stirring of physical desire.

He ruffled Jonty's boyish curls affectionately. "If I remember correctly, there was a time when you thought the sun came up just to shine on that horse hunter. I used to be jealous of him."

"Oh, Uncle Jim." Jonty looked at the smiling man sternly. "There's no one who could ever take your place. As for my fondness for that man, that was when I was an ignorant kid. That all changed when I . . ."

She let the sentence dangle and LaTour picked it up. "When he fell off the pedestal you'd put him on. When you discovered that he was like all men, that he, too, needed a woman occasionally."

"But not a dirty old whore like Lucy," Jonty said indignantly. "She's awful. Granny used to say that woman had no morals at all."

LaTour bit his lip to keep from laughing. "Jonty, the Lucies of this world are the kind of woman a man wants when all he's lookin' for is release. she appeals to his baser side. He's got no likin' for such a woman, no respect for her."

LaTour leaned back in his chair, a softness coming into his eyes as he looked backward into the past. "All the goodness in a man comes out when he falls in love with that one special woman," he said softly.

"Hah!" Jonty snorted, then declared positively, "there will never be a special woman in that black-hearted devil's life. Anyway, a decent woman wouldn't have anything to do with him."

Amusement twisted LaTour's lips again. "You're

wrong, honey, on all counts. McBain will find that
special woman someday, and when he does he's gonna
fall for her real hard. It always happens that way with
a hell-raiser." He flipped the butt of his cigarette out
the open window. "Enough of Cord McBain. Let's
take a look at Granny, then you can dish me up some
of that stew that smells so good. I haven't eaten all
day."

Jonty avoided looking at LaTour as she said, "You
go ahead, Uncle Jim. I'll put supper on the table."

LaTour paused in the act of rising and looked
searchingly at Jonty's strained, averted face. Taking
her chin, he forced her to look at him. "You haven't
seen her yet, have you, honey?"

Jonty swallowed the lump that rose in her throat
and mutely shook her head.

"You must, Jonty." LaTour tugged her to her feet.
"You'll feel better." When Jonty shook her head and
refused to budge, he said gently, "Jonty, if you don't
say good-bye, your grief will never know an end." A
bleakness settled over the harsh features. "I know."

And it was true, Jonty realized when finally she
gazed down at the thin, beloved face now at peace.
That hateful McBain had been right. Granny wasn't
suffering any more, and when he had accused her of
crying for herself, he had been right.

Nevertheless, when LaTour led her back into the
kitchen, the tears came again, deep racking sobs that
caused him to draw her into comforting arms. "Cry it
all out, Jonty," he whispered, the words muffled in her
hair.

Neither heard the door open as they stood clasped
in each other's arms, unaware of another presence
until a voice drawled sarcastically, "Now isn't this
somethin'."

LaTour lifted his head and Jonty turned hers.
Leaning against the doorway, his arms folded across
his chest, Cord McBain watched them. Jonty closed
her eyes against the contemptous light in the gray eyes.

"So this is the big attraction between you two."

Cord's voice was tight with withering scorn. "A couple of men lovers." He raked Jonty with condemning eyes and, ignoring her look of confusion, lashed out at her with words that flayed her heart and mind. "No wonder you have no time for women, you little low-life. It's men you hanker for."

He started across the floor toward Jonty, grinding out between clenched teeth, "I'll soon knock such unnatural leanings out of you."

LaTour put Jonty behind him, and his face twisted with rage. But his voice was icy calm when he said, "It's true that I love the boy, but not in the way your low mind is thinkin'. And if you ever lay a hand on him, you'll have me to deal with."

A look of savage glee jumped into Cord's eyes as he reached for Jonty, snarling, "Stop me, breed."

"I'll just do that," LaTour grated back, and with a lunging rush, the two men were at each other. They fought silently, furiously, the only sounds in the room grunts, heavy breathing, and the scraping of feet.

Jonty stood with her fist to her mouth, her eyes wide as twice Cord drove LaTour into a corner, his fists pounding like pistons into LaTour's lean, flat stomach.

The outlaw's eyes were becoming glazed as the hard fists continued to punish him. Then, from his clouded eyes he glimpsed his daughter's frightened face and remembered that this man had threatened to do her harm. At the unbearable thought of rough hands being laid on her tender, helpless flesh, he cleared his vision and renewed his strength. His fist shot out, straight from his waist, all his remaining power behind it. It caught his foe flush below the ear. The blow picked Cord up, then dropped him crashing to the floor, where he lay in a senseless heap.

For a crazy moment Jonty wanted to go to him, to cradle his battered face in her arms. Her mouth tightened then as she remembered all his hurtful words and actions, and her dislike of him was renewed. She turned instead to the fast-breathing

LaTour. She helped him to a chair and sat down next to him.

"I had hoped," she said, "that we could wait until after Granny's funeral to leave. But after this, I guess we should leave as soon as possible—before he comes to." She glanced at Cord's inert body.

LaTour left off examining a bruised knuckle to look at Jonty confusedly. "Leave? You mean, me and you together?" When Jonty nodded eagerly, he touched her cheek lovingly and said gently, "I can't take you with me, honey."

Alarm widened Jonty's eyes. "But Uncle Jim," she cried, "you must take me with you when you leave. I couldn't possibly live with him now, him thinking all those terrible things about us. He'll make life miserable for me."

Hope stirred inside her when it looked as if LaTour was considering her urgent plea. Then a deadness clouded her eyes, for he was saying with obvious regret, "I'm sorry, honey, but right now it's out of the question. Me and my men are leavin' for new territory tomorrow. We'd be gone already if not for your Granny's passin'."

When a small, distressing cry feathered through Jonty's lips, he added hurriedly, "But just as soon as I get settled somewhere, I'll get word to you."

"But Uncle Jim—"Jonty began again. Then Cord stirred and groaned. He felt his jaw, then slowly rose to his feet. He glared first at Jonty, then turned his glacial eyes on LaTour. "Maggie Rand would rise up out of her coffin if she knew what you've turned her grandson into."

"Watch it, McBain." LaTour took a threatening step toward Cord. "You keep it up and I'll beat your filthy thoughts to the back of your head." Before the irate man could retort, he added, "And you might as well know that I'm spendin' the night with Jonty. I'm sure you'll be too busy wallowin' around with your whore to come sit with him yourself."

A guilty red flushed Cord's cheeks. It was his plan to

spend the night with Lucy. It hadn't occurred to him that the kid would be here alone with his grandmother, the whores being busy with their customers. He stood a moment, his fists clenching and unclenching. Then, without a word, he turned on his heel and stalked out of the house. Outside, though, he did not take the stairs to Lucy's room. He went instead to the stables and there hollowed himself out a bed in a pile of hay.

CHAPTER 3

JONTY LAY ON HER SIDE, HER KNEES PULLED UP, HER HANDS tucked under her chin. For the last ten minutes or so she had been staring at the vague shape of the window across from her bed on the floor. The stars had paled in this space of time and the sky turned gray. Dawn was near.

She didn't look forward to this new day. It would be the beginning of so many changes in her life, starting with the placing of her only known relative in the Kansas soil, then leaving the flat prairie and embarking on a new kind of life.

What would it be like, she wondered, the future Cord McBain had mapped out for her? She could see no happiness or contentment in it, living with this wild-horse hunter who made no bones about his reluctance to take her under his care.

Last night came to mind, and Jonty relived the way Cord had stamped out of the room, his lip split, his right eye swelling. She squirmed uneasily. She wished he hadn't found her in Uncle Jim's arms, innocent though it was. For now, on top of everything else, he held against her the belief that she and Uncle Jim were lovers. She could expect that hateful voice to call her man-lover at every turn.

Jonty raised her head, the corners of her lips curving in a smile as she heard LaTour turn over on his pallet and begin to snore in a soft rumble. He had been dead-beat last night when he finally stretched out on the pallet of quilts she had made for him across from her own. They had spent half the night sorting out Granny's belongings, discarding those things she didn't want, packing the items she meant to take along with her—bedding, dishes, pots and pans, the little gee-gaws that colored up the room, making it cozy-looking, a home. Uncle Jim would take apart the bed after the funeral.

Her eyes drifted to the dim shape of the old trunk seen through the door separating the two rooms. She hadn't touched it. Everything in it had been important to Granny and it would go with the others stacked against the wall.

A look of savage satisfaction came into Jonty's eyes. Wouldn't Mister Cord McBain have a raging fit when he discovered she intended taking most of Granny's things with her! He would rant that she was crazy, that he wouldn't allow her to slow them down with such nonsense.

Her lips firmed determindedly. She would be adamant. He could rant and rave and swear until the air around him turned blue. Without the comforting presence of familiar things around her, life with that man would be unbearable.

Her eyes fell on the coffin in the other room and grief wiped out every other emotion from her face.

In the stable back of the pleasure house, Cord shivered and burrowed himself deeper into the hay. Although the days were bright and warm, the early spring nights still had the chill of winter about them.

"I should have brought Lucy out here with me," he grumbled through chattering teeth. A frown darkened his face. "No, by God, I should have gone to her room like I intended before that breed and that big-eyed kid made me feel guilty."

He stared up at the rafters barely visible in the early dawn. His life was going to be radically changed, starting with today, he thought glumly. He would be burdened with the care of a kid whose every word and action stirred anger inside him. A kid who would spit in his eye if he dared.

And as if being strange and ornery wasn't bad enough, it turns out he's queer on top of it.

How did one go about correcting a fault like that in a young man? he wondered. Keep him away from men? Push him into the company of women?

But hell, Jonty had always been in the company of women, he remembered. A thoughtful frown marred Cord's forehead. That could very well be the problem. All his life the kid had associated with whores. God knew that could be enough to turn most men into woman-haters.

However, Cord thought, his brow smoothing out, if the boy was to meet a nice girl, one around his own age, and spent some time with her, by the end of summer he'd know, and like, the softness of the female body in his arms. Jim LaTour would become a repulsive memory to him.

"I'll hire a Mexican family with a teen-age daughter," he thought out loud. Mexican women were beautiful and very loving. Cord warmed to his idea. If anyone could turn a young man around it would be a flashing-eyed *señorita*.

Cord stretched, pleased with himself. Not only had he solved this problem with Jonty, before he fell asleep last night it had come to him where he could make a home for his unwanted ward.

Three years ago he had followed a stallion and his harem of mares across Wyoming's rolling plains, across the North Platte River and into the Rocky

Mountains. There he had lost the small herd in one of the endless gorges. Bone-tired and discouraged, he had sent the stallion upward, into the coolness of the foothills. He hadn't traveled long among the towering Ponderosa pine and Douglas fir when he came upon a deserted set of buildings.

Maybe because he was so beat, so disheartened, the place had appealed to him right off. In the dappled shade of the trees there was a warm and welcoming look to the gray, weather-beaten boards of the scattered out-buildings and the big house with its wide porch. He thought that if he should ever settle down, he would want it to be in a place like this.

But after spending the night in the bare, five-room ranchhouse, he had ridden on in search of another wild herd, never giving the place another thought until last night. He hoped the place was still vacant, and that whoever owned it might want to sell. He wondered how much they might want for the place.

Cord wondered further. How much money had Maggie been speaking of? She seemed to think it was enough to set him up—him and Jonty, of course.

His lips twisted ruefully. Poor old Maggie. To her a couple hundred dollars would seem like a fortune. And it couldn't be much more than that. Look how the kid was dressed. Oh, well. He patted his hip pocket. He still had most of the money he'd got for the mustangs—it was enough to get them started, he hoped.

The buildings will need some work done to them, Cord mused. Some were in bad repair three years ago. Nothing monumental, though. They were all sturdily built, including the corral of spruce poles several yards away from the house. The pen was a big one, too, capable of holding fifty head or so.

In his mind's eye Cord saw the empty house and grimaced. He and the kid would have to sleep on the floor at first, cooking their meals either in the fireplace or outside.

A twinge of excitement stirred inside Cord. Maybe it wouldn't be so bad, this staying in one place for a while. Surely in a couple years he could whip the kid into shape and have him off his hands. Then, if he wanted to, he could resume his old way of life.

His problem solved, or at least thought out, Cord relaxed and turned his attention to the stirring of his manhood. Did the throbbing come from a full bladder, or was it morning desire? Probably both. He grinned, rubbing the now full erection and wishing that Lucy was there.

He stretched, then climbed to his feet. There was much to do today. First a fast trip to ole Lucy, then search the bars and brothels for a crew of rough riders. His face grew sober as he brushed hay out of his hair and off his clothes. And last, to bury his old friend. As he strapped on his gun he remembered he'd have to see about finding a preacher to say the right words over Maggie.

In less than an hour, Cord visited Lucy, ate a hearty breakfast at a diner and was back on the street, starting his search for riders.

He knew the men he wanted, but he didn't know which bar or brothel he'd find them in. He had walked about half a block when one of the men he sought almost walked into him.

"Hey, Jones." He laughed, holding out a hand to a man in his mid-fifties, tall and angular, bow-legged from a life spent in the saddle.

"How are you, Cord?" His hand was gripped and squeezed. "It's good to see you, hoss. Where have you been these past months? We've been thinkin' you'd been kicked in the head by one of your wild horses."

Cord laughed. "I've been out in Wyoming chasin' broom-tails. Brought a herd in yesterday and sold them to the army. What about yourself? What have you been up to?"

Jones shrugged. "Nothin' much, mostly just driftin'. Me and Red worked on a cattle ranch outside of Laramie for a while. Hit town day before yesterday." He thumbed his stetson back off his forehead and leaned lazily against a hitching post. "We ain't latched on to nothin' else yet." He grinned crookedly. "We got to pretty soon though. Our money has just about run out."

Cord jerked his head toward the saloon Jones had just departed. "Let's step inside and have a drink. I gotta lot to tell you, then a favor to ask."

This early in the morning the saloon was practically deserted, with only a couple of red-eyed cowpokes at the bar and a swamper mopping up the floor. Cord called to the bartender to bring a bottle and glasses, then led the way to a table in a far corner.

When the whiskey arrived, Cord splashed some in each glass and began to talk.

Jones shook his head when Cord finished telling him about Maggie, his new charge, the deserted ranch he wanted to buy when he found the owner, and his intention to use it until he did.

"Whew, that'll be a complete change for you, Cord."

That's no lie." Cord agreed. He filled their glasses again. Then, sitting back, he said, "I want you and Red to hire on." When Jones's eyes lit up with acceptance, Cord held up a hand. "I want you to know right off that it will only be bed and board until we drive a herd in."

"Hell, Cord, that won't be the first time that's happened to us. Me and Red will be happy to throw in with you."

"Thanks, Jones, I appreciate it. By the way, where is Red?"

Jones snorted. "Where you might expect. Holed up with a whore in a pleasure house down the street."

Cord grinned. Red's randy nature was well known among his friends. To lie in a woman's arms was food and water to that young man. "Is there anyone else in town we know?" he asked. "I need one more man."

Jones started to shake his head, then paused.

"Paunch is here. He rode in this mornin'. Do you think you'd want him?"

Cord scowled. "Only if I can't find anyone else. He causes trouble everywhere he goes."

"I doubt if you will. The town's pretty empty. Anybody who wants to work is signed up at some ranch."

"You're probably right," Cord said and stood up. He fished some money out of his pocket and laid it on the table. "I'm gonna go talk to Red."

Cord walked a short distance down the street and entered the Belle Pleasure House. He nodded at the stooped man sweeping out the dingy room where the men gathered. His nose twitching at the rank odor of old sweat and sour whiskey, he ascended the squeaking staircase to the rooms above.

The popping and rustling of bedsprings halted him in front of a door midway down the narrow hall. He leaned against the wall until it grew quiet inside, then rapped twice on the door, opened it and stepped inside.

A man in his early twenties, red-headed, slender, and long limbed, rolled from between a pair of white legs. He jerked his head around, frowning angrily. A lazy, genial smile tilted his lips when he recognized the man standing at the foot of the bed.

"Hop in, Cord," he invited. "It'll be like old times, sharin' the same woman."

Cord glanced at the young whore, who hadn't bothered to pull the sheet up over her nakedness, and for a moment he was tempted as he took in the long legs wantonly spread open.

"Thanks, Red." He grinned. "But I've already had a romp this mornin'. I'm here on business of another kind." He quickly recounted the story he'd told Jones.

"Sure thing, Cord." Red agreed readily. "When do we start for this place of yours?"

"Sometime this afternoon—after Maggie's funeral." He started to leave, then swung back. "Do you happen to know where I could find Paunch?"

"That stupid Reb." Red leaned up on an elbow. "He spent an hour or so in the saloon down the street re-fighting the war."

Satisfied humor etched a smile across Red's face. "Finally, some Yank in the place tore into him and beat the livin' hell out of him. When he came to, he headed for Nellie's place. I expect he's pumpin' ole callus-kneed Lucy right now."

Cord nodded his thanks and left. As he descended the stairs and walked outside, he shook his head. Why hadn't he thought of that in the first place? Lucy was a natural for the fat man to look up. They were a perfect pair.

Knowing that Paunch would stay with Lucy until his money ran out, Cord started looking for a preacher. An hour later, he had to give in to the fact that there was only one preacher in all of Abeline, and that one was out of town.

He abandoned the fruitless search, and after making arrangements with an undertaker to have a hearse deliver Maggie's body to the cemetery, he stepped into a store whose sign claimed it sold anything a man or woman could want. Ten minutes later, he left the place with a spade in his hand and directions to the cemetery.

A frown darkened Cord's face when he reached Abilene's burying ground. The breed was already there, the grave half dug. He looked around for Jonty, hoping the kid wasn't around. The little prissy would naturally think that he'd just left Lucy's bed.

Cord's frown suddenly deepened. He'd spotted Jonty's slender frame, off in a meadow picking wild-flowers. He gritted his teeth in frustration. Why wasn't the boy helping to dig his grandmother's grave instead of gathering posies? If the breed weren't there, he'd go over and slap the flowers out of the kid's hands and replace them with a shovel.

He pushed back the desire and, stalking over to the mound of dirt LaTour had already shoveled out, growled, "Take a rest. I'll finish it."

"And good morning to you too." LaTour looked at Cord's black eye with satisfaction. When Cord made no response, he hopped out of the hole and walked away to join Jonty.

Cord watched the straight-backed man hunker down beside Jonty and put his arms across the narrow shoulders. When the curly head dropped onto the breed's chest and stayed there, he swore furiously, attacking the Kansas soil as though it were his enemy.

Two hours later, when the sun was straight overhead, several dozen people had gathered at the cemetery to see the well-liked Maggie Rand tenderly deposited into the gaping hole next to her daughter's grave.

Cord stood staring down at the rough pinewood box. Some word should be said over his old friend. Maggie deserved more than just the prairie soil shoveled over her. He tried to remember a prayer from his youth, but the only thing that came to mind was the blessing his father had sometimes said over an evening meal.

He heard a stirring among the people assembled and looked up. Everyone was gaping at Maggie's effeminate grandson, one they'd had no idea could read. Everyone had in fact always believed he was half-heathen, running with the Indian kids the way he did. But there he stood, a small black book in his hand, reading quietly from it. Cord jerked off his stetson, and with bowed head listened to the softly spoken words that sometimes trembled on the soft lips.

Mesmerized by the husky tone, lulled into a state that bordered on sensual ecstasy, Cord gave a start when the book was closed and only the soft weeping of Nellie's girls broke the silence. He cast a nervous look at Jonty, hoping that he wouldn't start carrying on the way he had the night Maggie passed away. It would embarrass him to see the kid crying like a woman in front of all these people.

But Jonty was dry-eyed. She had cried herself out.

When the first shovelful of dirt was slowly deposited on the pine box, her only indication of the tearing inside her chest was the tightening of her fingers on the Bible and a closer step toward LaTour. When the breed took her arm and held it close to his side, Cord swore under his breath, wheeled and stalked to his stallion a few yards away. When was that bastard going to leave town? Did he have plans to take the kid with him? He hoped not. He'd have to shoot the man and then he'd really have his hands full with the boy.

Cord's three newly acquired hands were close behind him as he pulled up in front of Nellie's place. "When are we movin' out, Cord?" Red asked as they all dismounted.

"As soon as the kid gets back," Cord answered, and passed into Maggie's private quarters.

He stopped short inside the kitchen, a stunned exclamation whistling through his teeth. Besides the several boxes stacked on either side of the door, half the furniture, including a dismantled bed, had been dragged to the middle of the floor.

"What in the hell is that kid up to now?" he muttered, kicking one of the boxes with the pointed toe of his boot. When he would have kicked another, a sharp command behind him ordered sharply, "Don't do that! There's dishes in there."

Cord whirled around and penned Jonty with wintery eyes. "You want to tell me what in the hell all this mess is about?

Jonty grew pale and her pulse raced. Was she up to the battle that faced her, after all? She had never felt so low, so weak in spirit. She slid Cord a glance through her lashes. His dark, scowling face told her that she must. Otherwise this hard-mannered man would roll over her like a herd of buffalo at every turn.

She willed her face not to show her inner turbulence as she said sharply, "This mess, as you call it, are Granny's belongings. I intend taking them with me."

There was a long silence broken only by the ticking

of the clock packed in one of the boxes as the pair glared challengingly at each other. Then Cord was yelling and Jonty was taking a nervous step backward.

"You're plumb exalted in the head, young man, if you think I'm gonna let you haul all this with you."

Stung by Cord's dismissal of her grandmother's possessions, Jonty jumped in front of him, her feet planted in a fighting stance, her small fists thrust against her hips. "And you're crazy if you think I'm leaving Granny's bed to be profaned by a bunch of whores and their consorts," she ground out.

Cord's face grew harder and his eyes glittered dangerously. Jonty's heart plummeted. She was losing the battle. Long, noiseless tears began to shake her shoulders. Big teardrops hung on her lashes, then rolled down her cheeks. "I must take them, Cord," she pleaded, desperation in her voice. "It's all I have left of Granny. I can't leave them behind."

Like the first time Cord had seen Jonty cry, he was affected by her tears. Indecision crept into his eyes and Jonty, seeing the wavering in the gray eyes, shyly put a hand on his arm. "Please, Cord," she said softly. "We might need some of these things when we settle someplace."

Cord brushed her hand away as though it might contaminate him. "You're quite the little homemaker, aren't you?" he sneered.

Jonty's lids swept down to hide her loss of hope. This grim-faced devil was going to say no, was going to enjoy saying it.

She waited, sensing that the three men grouped together also waited for Cord's decision. Not one of them, she was sure, would have stood up to him as she had done. That would be a strike against her too. He'd never back down now, with his men watching him.

Jonty's eyes flew open, happy surprise deepening their blue depths when Cord said, though reluctantly, "You're probably right about using all this." His eyes swept over the jumbled heap of furniture and boxes.

"The place we're goin' doesn't have anything but mice and dirt in it."

He turned to leave, grumbling that now he'd have to scare up a wagon and a couple draft horses. "And a rope for the cow and a crate for the chickens," Jonty called after him, nerves fluttering in her stomach, bracing herself for another explosion of furious denial.

But only a slight slowing of his stride gave any indication that he was nearing the end of his patience. Exasperation in his voice, he muttered, "Why not. Maybe you'd like to pack up the house and take it along too."

Jonty giggled and sighed her relief at the same time. "Thank you, Cord," she said, but the door had already slammed behind him.

"So, Cord McBain." Her lips tilted in a smile. "You can be coaxed a bit, but never, never be pushed."

In the hour it took Cord to purchase a wagon and a pair of sturdy horses, swearing all the way at the extra expense, Jonty walked about the two rooms saying good-bye to an old way of life. She stood a moment at the black, cast-iron range. Poor old Granny had spent more time in front of it than she had anywhere else in their quarters.

With a heavy sigh, Jonty wondered if the day would ever come when she, as a woman, could cook the tasty meals Granny had taught her. She turned when she heard the creaking of wagon wheels.

The amassed contents of the kitchen were quickly transferred into the wagon. It took but a short time to tie the cow to the tailgate. Then came the task of chasing down ten chickens and a scraggly old rooster. Their faces red and sweating, the swearing men spent close to half an hour catching the terrorized, squawking chickens. When the last one, missing its tail feathers by now, was stuffed into the crate Jones had found somewhere, Cord gave Jonty a sour look and demanded gruffly, "Are you ready to get out of here now?"

She nodded, then held out a small chest to him. "I think this is what Granny promised you."

Cord shot a puzzled look at the square, lacquered box shoved into his hands. He had momentarily forgotten Maggie's promise of money. He gave it a shake and heard the rattle of coins. "Look, kid." He pushed the chest back at Jonty. "I don't want your grandmother's money. You keep it, buy yourself some duds. Them things you're wearin' are nothin' but rags."

Jonty's face grew red with shamed embarrassment. The devil didn't have to point that out to her; she knew it well enough. She backed away, shaking her head. "Granny wanted you to have it . . . for my keep. I know it's not nearly enough, but some day I'll square up with you."

Cord shot her a quizzical look. Was there threat as well as promise in those words spoken so calmly? He shrugged finally and said, "Let's go," and motioned her ahead of him.

Jonty stepped outside, then stopped short. The cowboy Red was tying her little mount, Beauty, next to the cow. "Don't tie her there, Red." She walked around behind the wagon. "I'll be riding her."

Red threw Cord an uncertain look as Jonty took the rope from his hands. "I'll just go saddle her," she said and started toward the stables.

She had taken only a few steps when Cord caught her by the elbow. "Not so fast, young man. You're drivin' the wagon."

Jonty could only stare up at Cord, unable to utter a sound. She shot an anxious look at the big, heavy-rumped work horses. She flinched as they stamped their great hooves, tossed their manes impatiently, making the fittings creak and rattle. Her eyes were wide and intensely blue as she looked helplessly at Cord.

"I've never handled a team before."

A cold smile wreathed Cord's lips. "Well then, there's no time like the present to learn, is there?" He kept hold of her arm and marched her back to the vehicle piled high with the last evidence that Maggie Rand had once lived and loved.

"Look, Cord." The red-headed wrangler stepped in front of them. "The kid is kinda puny to control them big brutes. I'll drive them."

Cord stiffened, his eyes narrowing suspiciously on the earnest Red. Was he going to be another LaTour? Was he, too, developing unnatural feelings for the kid? His tone was almost savage when he ground out, "There will be no coddlin' of the kid. He wanted his grandmother's things, so he can haul them."

He swept Jones and Paunch a warning look. "That goes for the rest of you. Don't let his delicate look fool you. He's capable of pulling his own weight, and I'm gonna see that he does." Before he stamped away, he added, "I'll have no interferin' from any of you."

Although Jones frowned and Red grumbled something under his breath, neither challenged Cord. They had seen him in action, and he was a bad one to come up against. Wordlessly, they climbed onto their mounts.

As Jonty looked dubiously at the high spring-seat of the wagon, looking for a step from which to climb onto it, she was grasped around the waist, and before she could take a deep breath she was boosted onto the wagon. She turned her head and glared her dislike at Cord as he tied her mare alongside the cow, then mounted his stallion. He rode to the front of the wagon and motioned her to follow.

Swallowing nervously, Jonty picked up the reins and shook them over the heavy-rumped team. To her relief and amazement, the pair responded and the wagon began to roll.

Abilene was soon left behind as the small group moved westward over the undulating Kansas prairie. The eternal monotony of endless sky and gray, solemn earth brought no relief to Jonty's despair-swamped soul.

By mid-day, Jonty felt that her arms were slowly

being pulled from their sockets. She was sure the team now realized that a very puny strength controlled them, and they took advantage of that fact by wandering along where they willed. She had to constantly fight the pair to keep them going in the direction Cord had set.

The afternoon grew hotter and the air became muggy. Dust kicked up by the riders ahead hung in the air, smarting Jonty's eyes and throat. And topping her misery, her stomach rumbled almost constantly from hunger. She had eaten little the night before, and this morning there had been no thought of food while grief gripped her entire being.

She sat on in a near daze, the sun beating down on her bare head as the miles ran out beneath the wagon wheels. It was near sundown when Cord finally pulled his mount in beneath a large cottonwood and announced that night camp would be made there.

Jonty remained on the wagon seat, letting her shoulders droop, resting them a moment. Cord approached the wagon, and through eyes shadowed with exhaustion, she watched him pull a large piece of canvas from the back and spread it on the ground. Next he pulled forth a burlap bag and emptied its contents onto the white square of heavy material—a coffee pot, pan, skillet, tin plates and cups. Food at last! she thought, hunger a pain inside her. She climbed down stiffly from the wagon and moved toward a large rock, her body crying out for rest.

She was almost at her destination when Cord called out, "Where do you think you're goin'?" When she only stared at him, he ordered, "Go rustle up some wood while the men tend to the animals."

Barely able to stand, her energy spent, Jonty could only look at him in disbelief. What made him push her so hard? Did he dislike her so intently? Was his resentment of being stuck with her that strong?

Her eyes smouldering with resentment, she looked challengingly at Cord and said flatly, "I'm too tired. Someone else will have to do it."

His jaws tightening, Cord stared down at the pale, obstinate face. And as everyone stopped what he was doing and watched the belligerent pair, he grasped the short hair at Jonty's nape and jerked her head back.

"I told *you* to do it," he ground out, "and by God you'll mind me or you'll not eat tonight."

The seconds ticked by as the two glared at each other in a tense battle of wills. But even as Jonty glared her defiance she knew that one way or the other she would be the loser. This devil beating her down with his cold gray eyes made no idle threats. If she didn't gather fuel for the fire, she would go to bed hungry.

The spirit inherited from Maggie Rand came to the front. So be it, Jonty thought. Maybe I'll spend a night of hunger, but this bastard isn't going to have it all his way.

Her eyes blue ice, her tone brittle with fury, she said through her teeth, "Keep your damn grub. I'm not hungry."

Cord stared after the slim figure stamping away, frowning a bit when Jonty stumbled once in her tiredness. Had he been too hard on the boy? The kid wasn't used to hard work. A fast glance at his men showed him that Red and Jones thought he was in the wrong, that he should relent and let him have his supper.

No, by God, he decided stubbornly. The boy has to learn to obey me. He has to toughen up and become a man. If I let him get away with this, I'll have to fight him every time I give an order.

He stamped off under the trees, picking up pieces of dry limbs, stacking them in his arms. Returning shortly to where he had spread the canvas and dropped the gear, he quickly had a fire going. The flames leapt high, throwing into relief Cord's strong features, casting a red glow over them. Jonty, hugging her bent knees some distance away, thought that she never dreamed that the Devil would wear boots and spurs.

While the fire burned down to glowing coals, Red dressed and spitted the seven sage hens he'd shot along the way. He hung them over the fire and soon a mouth-watering aroma lifted above them. The moon was coming up when he announced that supper was ready.

It was a quiet group that sat around the campfire half-heartedly consuming the roasted meat. Everyone looked up when Jones tossed a piece of wood onto the fire and said to no one in particular, "I guess the kid is feelin' the loss of his Granny tonight."

"Yeah," Red agreed, looking over his shoulder at the slim, hunched figure dimly seen in the shadow of a tree. "I remember when I lost my Ma. I was round Jonty's age, about sixteen I guess. It was the awfulest thing that ever happened to me."

Cord drank the last of his coffee and stood up. "The kid will get over it. He's too soft. He's got to learn how to take, and handle, the knocks life is gonna hand him."

Nevertheless, he wondered if maybe he hadn't gone too far in his anger and determination. The boy was too thin as it was. He didn't need to miss any meals. He gave a defeated sigh and an audible sound of relief went up from Jones and Red when he stalked toward the still figure.

Cord smiled grimly. That pair was on the kid's side and it wasn't going to be easy, turning him into a man.

"What does he want now?" Jonty muttered, watching Cord come toward her in his loose, horseman's walk. "To clean up after them?"

She refused to look up when his narrow, booted feet stopped in front of her. She didn't want to see the gloating in his eyes, the triumphant twist of his lips. She was afraid her control would break and God knew what she might say or do. But involuntarily then, her head jerked up and she met gray eyes that had no softening in them. She felt a sick disappointment. She hadn't realized until that moment that she had hoped Cord was coming to make peace between them.

Jonty's own eyes grew hard as she stared back with cool disdain. She had been a fool to think that anything would ever change between them. He had made up his mind about her and that was the end of it.

Cord's momentary softness fled. He had hoped to find the little devil more approachable, that hunger had blunted that stubborn pride of his. It hadn't, so what did he do now? He wasn't about to beg the spoiled brat to eat, to say, "Come on, all is forgiven."

The air had cooled with the coming of evening, and when Jonty suddenly shivered, Cord jumped at the new excuse he could give for having approached her.

Clearing his voice, he said gruffly, "I figured you'd not have gumption enough to bring a coat with you." He shrugged out of his denim jacket and tossed it across her knees. "Put this on. I don't want you comin' down with pneumonia and holdin' us up."

The warmth that had started to grow inside Jonty at what she thought was a kind gesture died away when she realized her welfare didn't enter into it. Cord was only afraid that she might become ill and he might have to delay their journey while he tended her.

And what she had been afraid of happened. Her control snapped. This time he had gone too far with his hateful mouth. She jumped to her feet, and flinging the jacket on the ground began to jump up and down on it. But when she paused to grind a boot into the material, her wrist was caught and held so tightly she thought the bones would break.

Where at the onset there had only been rage in Cord's eyes, now there was violence. "You ornery little devil!" he barked. "Now pick it up."

Jonty glared back, shaking her head and shouting, "Never! Never, never."

His lips clamped together, Cord jerked her wrist behind her and slowly pushed it toward her shoulder blades. "Pick it up or I'll break your arm."

Jonty stopped her protesting. She doubted that Cord would break her arm, but the cold steel in his voice told her that he would welcome more defiance from her, that in his rage he would deliberately hurt her.

After all, he didn't know that she was female.

"All right," she gasped, almost bent double to escape the pressure on her arm. "I'll pick the damn thing up."

"I'll just play it safe and hang onto you until you do," Cord snarled. "You're a tricky little hellion."

Promising herself that she would never forget or forgive this humiliation, Jonty picked up the creased, dirt-grimed article.

"Now hand it to me." Cord released her and held out a hand as she slowly straightened up.

Jonty longed with all her being to fling the jacket in his face. But she had already suffered enough pain and embarrassment at his hands and she wouldn't give him another opportunity if she could help it.

She dared not look at him, however, as she thrust the item of contention toward him. If he should see the hatred and rebellion in her eyes, he might not let her eat in the morning either.

Rubbing her aching arm, she watched Cord stamp away, his body rigid. When he disappeared into the thickness of the trees, she turned her head to the others, who were finishing off their meal with a cup of coffee. How good it smells, she thought, lying down and curling herself into a ball, unappeased hunger knawing at her stomach.

Her grandmother's face swam in front of her, kind and smiling, then Nellie's girls, laughing uproariously at the tricks they played on the men, letting them catch fast glimpses of her rigged out in their dresses. Granny and the girls had formed her character, she guessed. Granny had instilled pride and spirit in her and from the young whores she had learned compassion. With the exception of Lucy, who had chosen her profession, each of the other girls had started out innocent and trusting, and had put their faith in the wrong man.

She sighed and closed her eyes, then leaped up with

a small cry when her shoulder was shaken gently. She looked into Red's sympathetic eyes. "Here, Kid." He shoved a plump breast of sage hen into her hand. "I held it back for you."

"Oh thank you, Red," she whispered, and bit into the meat with unashamed eagerness.

Jonty was licking her fingers, the meat stripped from the bone, when Jones ambled over and tossed a blanket down beside her. "I found I had a spare one in my bedroll," he said off-handedly, trying to hide the softness that made him take pity on the youngster. "Roll up by the fire over there—with your feet to it. Your whole body will keep warm that way."

Tears glimmered in Jonty's eyes, but she blinked them back, knowing they would embarrass the men. They didn't know either that she was female and thus allowed to cry when emotions dictated she should.

"I'm obliged to you both," she managed to say before making her way to the campfire.

In the fringe of the cottonwood grove, Cord stood and watched all that had gone on. On one hand, he was glad the kid had got some food in his gut, as well as the blanket to ward off the cold air, but on the other hand he was not pleased at Red and Jones's interference. How was he to bring this obsinate boy to his knees if those two were always going to be sticking their nose in?

"Dammit, Maggie," he whispered, "you've sure put a load on my shoulders. I hope I'm up to handlin' it."

CHAPTER 4

THE HOUR WAS GRAY, THE AIR STILL CHILL, WHEN CORD came awake. He stretched his lean body and stared up at the dimly seen canopy of trees overhead. If everything went well, three more days should bring them to the old ranch buildings.

He visualized the long valley with its lush grass nourishing the wild horses he and his men would chase down and capture. A tiny frown etched his forehead. It was important to find the owner of the place as soon as possible. He'd hate to put a lot of work and money into fixing up the run-down buildings and then be told the ranch wasn't for sale.

He wondered if the man had moved on to the small town of Cradon, about thirty miles from the ranch. Or maybe he'd gone to a larger city like Abilene.

Cord rolled out of his blanket and climbed to his feet. He'd try Cradon first. If the owner's whereabouts wasn't known there, he'd make inquiries the next time he drove a herd into Abilene.

As he stamped on his boots, then strapped on the

Colt, he hoped they wouldn't have an early winter. He'd like to drive in at least two herds before the first snowfall.

He grinned ruefully. It wasn't a Christian thought, but he hoped the Indians continued the war with the army long enough for him to get the ranch into a profitable state. For once a treaty was made between the Indian and the white man, he'd have to turn his hand to carefully breeding special mares and special stallions, bringing about quality horses—a sleek, high-stepping one for the rich men back east, a sturdy quarter-horse for ranchers and cowboys.

Flushings of pink shaded the eastern sky when Cord moved among the blanket-wrapped figures around the dead fire. He came to Jonty's curled, sleeping form and hunkered down beside it. He hung there a minute, breathing in the smell of clean flesh, gazing at the sleep-flushed cheeks, the long lashes laying shadows on them. His chisled lips softened, and unconsciously he laid a gentle hand on the cap of tousled curls. Why was it, he wondered, that he always had the wish to punish and protect the boy at the same time?

Then the picture of this same boy being held in the breed's arms flashed in front of him, and he jerked his hand out of the silky hair as though repulsed. He shook the narrow shoulders ungently, and his voice was rough-edged as he ordered, "Get up, boy. Get a fire goin' and put on a pot of coffee."

Startled so abruptly from a deep sleep, Jonty could only blink dazedly at the hard-planed face looking down at her. When she continued to stare at him in bemusement, Cord stood up growling, "Come on, get a move on. I want to be on the trail by sun-up." When he accompanied his words with a jab of his toe to her hip, Jonty came fully awake.

Unconcealed fury flashing in her eyes, she jerked upright. "Don't ever kick me again," she warned through clenched teeth. "Animals are kicked, not human beings."

"Is that right?" Cord's hand flashed out and fastened in her hair. She yelped her pain as he tightened his grip and slowly brought her to her feet. "What about hair pulling?" He glared down at her. "Is that allowed?"

Smarting, angry tears gathered in Jonty's eyes and she was about to pull back a foot and let fly a well-aimed kick when her stomach tightened and growled. The piece of meat from the night before had long ago been digested. She dropped her foot back to the ground. The devil wouldn't hesitate to make her go without breakfast if she riled him enough.

She forced herself to stand quietly even though the grip of her hair was pulling the skin tight against her face. And though she didn't know it, her helpless surrender stirred shame in Cord. It was against his nature to hurt someone lacking the strength to fight back. Never before had he used bullying tactics on another human being. Why was it that this green-horn kid made him lose control to such an extent?

He released his hold, and without another word walked quickly away. His self-respect wasn't raised any when he looked down and discovered silky strands of hair clinging to the fingers of his right hand.

And Jonty, chin in the air, rebellion in her eyes and heart, stared after him. "You big bully, you'll pay for this," she whispered. "I'll see you crawl someday."

"He's a bear for gettin' his own way," Red spoke from behind Jonty, making her jump as he set down a pail of water. "The best thing for you to do is not fight him. And keep yourself scarce when he's around."

"I'll try, but it won't be easy." Jonty choked back more angry words as she stooped down and began pulling together small pieces of wood, hoping that she wouldn't have to go out in the near darkness to find more. She had heard the howl of coyotes back there just before she fell asleep last night.

After shooting a glance in the direction Cord had taken and seeing him occupied with saddling his mount, Red squatted down beside Jonty. "Look, kid, I'll make the fire," he said in low tones, taking the

matches from her cold fingers, "and later you can get
the coffee goin'. What the boss don't see won't rile
him." He winked at Jonty. "Now, you watch how I do
this and tomorrow mornin' you won't have any trouble bein' on your own."

Jonty smiled to herself. She had started fires in
Nellie's big kitchen range since she was ten years old,
the exact same way. Of course she'd never tell this nice
young man that. It would be like tramping on his good
intentions.

When the fire blazed high, Red grinned up at her,
then rose to his feet. "Hurry up now," he said out of
the corner of his mouth, "get the coffee goin'."

The morning air was cool and Jonty's teeth chattered as she filled the battered coffee pot with water,
added the coffee grounds and gingerly eased it onto
the flames. An open fire *was* something new to her.
When Cord returned ten minutes later, he found her
alone, hugging her arms, staring into the flames. He
wanted to offer his jacket again, but the freezing look
turned on him aborted the idea. He'd be damned if
he'd give the brat another chance to stomp it into the
ground. Let him freeze.

He studied the regally held head, the proud profile,
and ire and determination swept over him. He'd
break that willful spirit if it was the last thing he ever
did. His hands on his hips, he glared down at Jonty.

"Why are you sittin' there, not doin' anything?
Since Jones has took it on himself to hitch up the
wagon for you, you can go pack the burro."

Red, buckling on his spurs, paused and listened,
while Jones looked at Cord in surprise. And Paunch
watched, hoping to see Cord's suppressed violence
acted out.

Jonty stood up, her eyes glittering. Just how far did
this man plan to push her? She couldn't begin to know
how to pack the little animal. But of course, that was
exactly why he'd ordered her to do it. He hoped she'd
put up a fuss, give him the opportunity to humiliate
her in front of the men. Well, he'd not get the chance.

Somehow she'd get the camp equipment onto the donkey's back.

With an outward calm but fluttering nerves, she shrugged her shoulders and said carelessly, "Why not? Aren't I your obedient servant?"

"You'd better be." Cord scowled at her. Then, informing Jones that he would be cook this morning, he stalked away.

He went but a short distance, however, stopping near enough to keep an eye on Jonty, to see that no one stepped in to help her. And Jonty, her bravado gone, wondered how to go about the task allotted her.

She began by slowly approaching the little gray animal staked out on a patch of grass. Observing the long, laid-back ears, she paused. He was a mean one, she thought uneasily; she'd better watch those hind legs of his. One good kick from one of them and she'd land in Kingdom Come.

She sensed Cord's watchful eyes upon her and, moistening her dry lips, she walked purposefully over to the pile of camp paraphernalia stacked beneath a tree. She picked up as much as she could carry, then gathered her courage and carefully approached the grazing animal again. Keeping up a flow of soothing words, she transferred the first load onto the short, sturdy back. She sighed her relief when the little fellow stood quietly, intent only on cropping the green grass.

Jonty was feeling quite proud of herself when a second armful joined the first without incident. She was struggling the last of the gear onto the seemingly docile burro when Cord's strident voice, rough with impatience, called out, "Pack that load tight, Jonty. I don't want it slippin' and gallin' the animal."

And while Jonty's attention was diverted the mean-eyed little pack animal whipped his head around and took a swipe at her shoulder with broad yellow teeth. She gave a yelp of alarm and jumped back, twisted her foot on a rock, and sat down hard.

Everyone roared with laughter—Cord's the loudest

and most satisfied, Jonty noted. She sat a moment, the breath knocked out of her, grinding her teeth in embarrassment. He had managed to humiliate her after all.

She looked up when a pair of hands came under her arms and lifted her to her feet. "Here, lad," Jones said, a sympathetic smile touching his lips, "let me give you a hand loadin' this mean varmint, give you a few pointers."

Jonty opened her mouth to thank Jones for his thoughtfulness, but Cord was suddenly beside them. His gray eyes like thick smoke, he snarled, "Look, Jones, I thought I made it clear the kid is not to be mollycoddled. He's got to learn how to do the things I set him to."

His angular body bristling with indignation and his face as grim as the man's before him, Jones said with controlled anger, "You're right to a degree, Cord—the boy does have to learn. But dammit to hell, man, you've got eyes in your head! Anyone can see the youngster has never packed a burro before. Do you think he should just naturally know how to go about it? Is it pamperin' him to show him how? When you was a youngin', didn't your Paw or an older friend show you the special knots of packin', the proper way of fittin' things together?"

The older man paused to catch his breath and everyone stared at him. Usually the taciturn Jones didn't say that many words in an entire day.

And when all eyes swerved to Cord, wondering how he'd take these home-truths, the burro went into action. Braying a discordant note, bucking everything off his back, his hind legs lashing out at anything or anyone in his path, he ran through the camp, jumping over the fire, kicking over the coffee pot, and scattering those who sat around it.

After their moment of surprise, the men jumped up and began chasing after the small cyclone, swearing and slapping their hats on muscled thighs.

Surprisingly, it was Jonty who managed to grab a

trailing rope and hang on until help arrived in the form of Cord's powerful arms. Her eyes were sparkling with the humor of five people chasing one ornery small animal, when Cord jerked it to a standstill.

"He sure made a mess of the camp, didn't he?" Her accompaning laugh was warm and genial.

Her observation wasn't returned in kind. Cord's only response was a black scowl and a broad back turned on her.

"Don't let him get to you, lad." Jones noted the hurt look in the blue eyes. "Let's get this brute packed up." He took the rope from Jonty and gave the glistening rump a stinging swat with it. "He'll behave himself now. He's wore himself out."

While Jonty was taught the ins and outs, the special knots of proper packing, Red put on another pot of coffee while Cord tended a frying pan of salt pork. Paunch was ordered to tend the sourdough baking in a covered iron pot.

Paunch got his nickname, the only name he was known by, from the heavy stomach that hung over his belt. Somewhere in his forties, he was not a favorite with the men. He was gossipy and spiteful and trouble-making.

He had, from the first, grated upon Jonty, rousing an instinctive distrust within her. She was aware that his fat-squinted eyes often watched her furtively, and she had made up her mind never to be caught alone with him. Even though he thought her male, that would make little difference to his lustful nature.

When Cord called, "Come and get it," the meal was eaten silently and with hearty appetites. It was all Jonty could do not to wolf hers down. Never had anything tasted so good.

Her salt pork and bread had barely settled in her stomach when Cord stood up and, gathering up the dirty tin plates, ordered, "Jonty, pour us some coffee, then we'll be on our way."

Withholding a sigh, she rose and absent-mindedly smoothed the loose trousers over her hips and dusted

off her rear end. She lifted her eyes to see Cord
watching her, his lips curled in disgust, and realized
belatedly the action was that of a woman. She lowered
her lids in confusion and picked up the coffee pot.

She had filled five cups and was ready to hand them
out when Paunch gave a low, ugly chuckle and
sneered, "If a man got hard up enough, it wouldn't be
half bad, takin' the kid to bed, huh, men?"

A dead silence greeted the words, whose meaning
was crystal clear.

But the fat man, dense to the charged atmosphere
that had sprung up, blundered on. Sliding Jonty a
leering smile, he said, "You wouldn't mind, would
you, kid?"

Jonty flinched at the sly suggestion, aware that Cord
was probably of the same mind. Suddenly all the pain,
humiliation, and resentment that had been building
inside her was released. She was beyond clear thinking
when, with a swiftness that was hard to follow, she
swooped up a cup of the scalding coffee and dashed it
into the leering, fat face.

Everyone but Paunch gasped—and he let out a roar
of pain and staggered to his feet, swiping an arm
across the hot brown liquid that had caught the lower
part of his face and throat.

"You little bastard!" he shouted, and before anyone
could move he caught Jonty across the face with the
back of his hand. She fell flat on her back, the breath
knocked out of her. She cringed as Paunch drew back
a foot to kick her.

But as she lay there, her eyes tightly closed, waiting
for the blow to land, Cord was on his feet, his face
fierce and terrible. Those watching intently saw the
change that came over Paunch's face. He slowly lost
color, his jaw dropped, and his eyes were wide with
naked fear.

"Now look, boss," he said uneasily, backing away.
"The little devil could have blinded me. Anyway, it's
not like he hasn't been rough-handled before. I've
seen you do it."

"You have never seen me strike the kid." Cord glowered at the sweating man. "And if I ever should, I have the right. I'm his guardian."

Paunch laughed a rasping, unpleasant sound. "That covers a lot of ground, don't it?" he sneered.

The words were barely out of the fat man's lips when Cord's rock-hard fist caught him in the fleshy lips. And while his head was still rocking, Cord warned tightly, "Don't ever lay a hand on him again —in any way."

When Paunch stalked away, muttering under his breath, Jonty scrambled to her feet, dreading to meet Cord's eyes. He would be angry with her, tell her that she deserved what she got.

But his eyes got no farther than her mouth. He took in the rapid swelling of her lips, the thin line of blood trickling from one corner. His fists clenched with the desire to hit Paunch again. And while Jonty waited for his abuse to fall on her head, all he said was, "Go take care of your animals." Then he turned and walked away.

With a relieved sigh, Jonty hurried to scatter corn in the chicken coop and take Beauty and the cow to the small stream of water nearby. As she waited for them to drink their fill, Paunch walked past her carrying his saddle. He sent her a malicious look and she knew he would be out for revenge. Another one to beware of. She sighed raggedly.

She glanced back at the now dead campfire. Four of the men were saddling their mounts while Jones hitched up the wagon. She walked a little farther down the stream to relieve a call of nature. She wished desperately that she could wade into the water, lie down in its cool flow, and ease the itching of prickly heat that had formed beneath the bindings of her breasts.

A few minutes later, she led the animals back to the wagon and tied them to the tailgate. She checked to see if the pan in the chicken coop still had water and was relieved to see that it did.

She had just climbed onto the high seat of the wagon when Cord ordered crispy, "Come on, men, let's get goin'. We've got a far piece to go yet."

"A far piece to go," Jonty muttered dryly. That could mean anything, depending on who was judging the distance. Ten miles, a hundred.

She wiped a hand across her sweating forehead. Would this heat ever break? It hadn't rained in weeks and the endless miles stretching out before her showed the results of the arid condition in the limp and shriveled grass, the sparse foliage whitened from the dust.

Her hands loosened on the reins, and as the team plodded on in the haze of heat, Jonty dozed. In her half-sleep, she was unaware of the early dusk coming on, of the dark clouds gathering in the west. It took Cord's loud shout to jolt her fully awake.

"There's a storm comin' up." He rode alongside the wagon. "The small town of Clear Water is just a few miles on. We'll take shelter there."

Before she could make a response, ask where she'd find him once she arrived, he had touched spurs to the stallion and raced away to join the others up ahead. She stared after him as the slower-moving team was left far behind. He was only interested in keeping his own hide dry! She frowned up at the black, angry-looking clouds that rolled and tumbled. It doesn't matter a whit to him that she'd never make it before those clouds opened up.

"But please, Lord," she prayed, popping the whip, urging the tired team to go faster, "don't let it thunder and lightning. . . ."

Jonty's prayer was answered. Fifteen minutes or so later, only a gratefully received rain came. It arrived suddenly, in a heavy deluge. In seconds, Jonty was soaked to the skin, her clothing clinging to her body. Almost total darkness had settled in when she suddenly pulled the team to a stop and clambered to the ground.

"My poor chickens will drown," she moaned, feeling her way through the blinding slash of the rain until she came to the tailgate where the crate had been placed.

As she fumbled for the tarpaulin used to hold the gear and provisions when they camped, the cow lowed hoarsely and the little mare nudged her head against Jonty's shoulder. "I know you're uncomfortable," she sympathized, "but so am I. We'll just have to put up with it."

Finally, by touch alone, Jonty found the piece of folded canvas. Then, guided by the squawking hens, she managed to toss the waterproof material over the wet, bedraggled fowl. "You'll be all right now." She gave the covered crate a reassuring pat before plowing back through the rain and regaining her high seat.

She picked up the reins and, giving them a snap, sent the team on. As the rain beat on her head and ran down into her eyes, she called Cord every name she could think of. He should have stayed to help me, she sneezed. Even if he does think I'm a male, he knows damn well it's hard to handle and guide a team in a downpour. He could have at least thought about the cow and chickens.

A thought that had niggled at the back of her mind, one that she had been reluctant to bring forward and examine, jabbed her now, demanding that she give it serious consideration.

It was plain that Cord McBain disliked her intensely, was resentful of having to be responsible for her. Why, then, hadn't he sent her off with Uncle Jim when he found her being comforted by him? Was it because of the promise he made to Granny, or was it her inheritance that made him hang on to her?

Before handing over the small chest to Cord, she had taken a fast peek inside it. To her surprise, it had been stuffed with greenbacks and gold coins. For all she knew, there might be a small fortune hidden in it.

Jonty shook her head, not knowing what to think as the wagon rolled on, the horses' great hooves splashing mud and water. The chickens had quieted down, but poor Buttercup continued to bellow her discontent.

The cow's unrest added to Jonty's feeling of helplessness. She had no idea if she was going in the right direction, or if they even followed a road. She could only rely on the horses' intelligence to take her to their destination.

It was close to half an hour later that Jonty breathed a deep sigh of relief. Through the beating rain, she glimpsed a string of pale lights which she fervently hoped was Clear Water—or at least a place where she and her animals could find shelter.

Soon the wagon was rolling down a mud-mired street. Her vision blurred as she peered through the slashing rain, and Jonty couldn't believe her good luck when the first building she came to wore a big sign that stated simply, "Livery Stable."

The wide double doors of the place stood open and she wheeled the team through them. "What a sight I must be," she muttered, jumping to the sawdust covered floor and using her hands to wipe the water off her face and hair. And what do I do now? she wondered. Do I just leave the team standing here? Are we spending the night in town? God forbid that devil should ever tell *me* anything.

She jumped when an aged, cracked voice spoke from a dim corner. "Cord said not to unhitch the team, and that you should meet him at the West Wind saloon at the end of the street."

When the owner of the voice didn't put in an appearance, Jonty picked up some burlap bags from a nearby pile and began to rub the horses down. She was becoming attached to them. After all, they were the only company she had, the only ones to listen to her complaints.

After she uncovered the chickens and gave them some corn, she wiped down Beauty and the cow. Then, finally, finding no more reasons to linger in the stable, she reluctantly moved over to the wide doors.

The rain still came down in sheets, beating on the

tin roof like bullets from a gun. The end of the street seemed a long way off. Chilled to the bone, her jaws clamped together to keep her teeth from chattering, her eyes still sparked resentment. I've got to walk it. His lordship says so.

Amazingly, however, Jonty had splashed through the rain but a few feet when it stopped as suddenly as it had begun. The setting sun shone through the remaining thin clouds and bathed everything in a red glow. Her spirits lifting somewhat, she continued on down the wide street that was lined on both sides with stores, saloons, and gambling dens.

Jonty even managed a smile. Now that the skies were clearing, people of every description were spilling out of doors and going about business the rain had interrupted. She was reminded of Abilene a little, and her eyes darted every which way, hoping to see a familiar face.

Satin-clad whores strolled up and down the muddy boardwalk, their hungry, bright eyes roving restlessly, while tall, lean cowboys clanked along with their awkward stride, eyeing every female that passed them. Mexicans, bright blankets draping their shoulders, lounged against buildings, their sloe-black eyes missing little.

Jonty kept her expression blank when she passed two men who were unmistakably gunmen, Colts strapped low on their hips, narrowed eyes ever watchful. Just like Cord McBain, she thought with surprise.

But why should she find that out of the ordinary? She had, on several occasions, heard Cord referred to as a gunslinger. But having known him for so long, she'd never looked on him that way. Maybe she'd better start looking at him more closely. Already, without even trying, she was learning things about him she didn't like—his arrogance, his hard coldness. When he had visited the girls, he had always been jovial, a ready smile on his lips, and he had always been tenderly joking with Granny.

It's me, she thought dispiritedly. She brought out

the meanness in him. She was an itch that he couldn't reach to scratch.

Jonty did an adroit side-step to avoid two bodies that came hurtling out of a saloon. The pair were locked in battle, their fists flaying each other, curses issuing from their mouths. She looked up at the sign hanging over the door and nodded her head. The West Wind stood in front of her.

She stepped around the wrestling bodies, raised her hands to push open the bat-wing doors, then paused. She'd better check her shirt first. The drenching she'd received might have loosened the bindings on her breast. She plucked at the soaked material, thinking that this certainly was no time to have her sex revealed.

When Jonty found that everything was secure, her femininity still concealed, she took a deep breath and stepped through the swinging doors.

The place was crowded, and hazy with acrid blue smoke. Jonty wrinkled her nose. The stench of un-washed bodies was almost overpowering in the muggy heat of the large room. She peered through the milling humanity, searching for Cord and his riders. She spotted them at a table in a far corner. Her stomach rumbled. The four were busily wolfing down huge, thick sandwiches. Would Cord remember that she hadn't eaten since early this morning? She started jostling and elbowing her way through the crowd.

She was only a few feet away from Cord's table when her arm was grabbed. Her body tensed and her hands clenched into fists as she was turned around. She lifted her eyes to the tall man towering over her, and her fear and fight dissolved. "Uncle Jim!" she cried in delighted surprise.

The handsome breed smiled down at her happy face and took the slim hands held out to him. His eyes moved over her and he frowned at her dripping curls, her soaked condition. "Why are you trailin' in almost an hour behind Mister High and Mighty over there? And where is your slicker?"

A sour smile touched Jonty's lips. "I'm running late because I'm driving the team and wagon that's hauling Granny's belongings. As for a slicker, I don't own one."

LaTour ran his hands down Jonty's fragile-boned arms and a dangerous light glimmered in his eyes as he studied the pale, cold, pinched face lifted to his.

"Damn the black-hearted bastard," he ground through his teeth. "It's clear to a blind man that he doesn't want to be bothered with you, yet he drags you along with him. I'm beginning to wonder why."

"That question has entered my mind too, Uncle Jim," Jonty said, "and I've almost concluded that it has something to do with my inheritance. Somehow, over the years, Granny managed to put away a good sum of money—a few hundred dollars, I think."

"Hah!" LaTour snorted. "More like a few thousand."

"How do you know?" Jonty looked at him curiously.

"Oh, I don't know." LaTour shrugged indifferently. "I think she told me once when I offered her some money."

Realizing that for some reason her friend was very upset about the money, Jonty tried to soothe him. "It's probably like he claims. He's putting up with me as a favor to Granny."

"Favor hell," LaTour said. "Maggie Rand would spin in her grave if she knew how shabby he's treatin' you."

Her hands still in LaTour's, Jonty looked wistfully into his blue eyes, urging softly, "Please, Uncle Jim, won't you reconsider and let me come live with you? Cord is so hateful, sometimes I think I can't stand being around him another minute."

Unthinking of how the action might look, Jim LaTour rested his head on Jonty's, his only thought to block out the pleading in his daughter's eyes. But to one man who watched them with blazing eyes, their stance looked very lover-like. And while LaTour tried to explain his reluctance to take Jonty with him, Cord's face was like chiseled stone as he asked himself what the whispered conference was all about.

"Like I told you back in Abilene, honey, it's not a good idea for me to take you with me now," LaTour was saying soberly, unaware of the stormy gray eyes that watched them. "It would be no life for you. I wouldn't want you around my men. They're all failures, lawless, short on morals. I'm not sure you'd be safe from their amorous attention even if they did think you were a boy." He smiled at her and teased, "You're a mighty pretty little feller."

When disappointed tears rolled down Jonty's cheeks, LaTour groaned and begged her not to cry. "You won't always have to live with him, Jonty. Just until I can make a decent home for you. I've been puttin' money aside right along with that in mind. I just don't have enough yet."

He raised his head and looked down into Jonty's tear-streaked face. "In the meantime, I've arranged for a cousin of mine to look after you, to see that you're being treated right. I've told him that if ever things do get beyond your endurance he's to come and tell me. We'll do the best we can if that comes to pass."

The heavy weight in Jonty's heart lessened somewhat at the hope held out to her. Then, shaking her head, she said, "I don't understand. How is your cousin going to be able to look after me? I don't even know where we're going."

LaTour drew a thumb across the last tear slipping down Jonty's cheek. "Don't worry, he'll be with you. Sometime between now and the time you light, McBain will hire him on."

"I don't think so." Jonty frowned doubtfully. "I'm pretty sure that Cord has all the help he needs."

"He'll hire Johnny Lightfoot," LaTour said with conviction. "McBain knows Johnny is the best there is when it comes to trackin' wild horses. He'll be glad to get him."

The outlaw sounded so sure of himself, Jonty had

no doubt it was true. Her face glowed. Smiling shakily, she said, "I'll get through the hellish days somehow
until I can come to you. I'll—" She paused, feeling a
queer chill between her shoulder blades. She turned
her head slowly and met Cord's look of disgust. She
stepped quickly away from LaTour, a guilty flush
staining her cheeks.

Jonty had no sooner taken the step than she was
angry with herself for doing it. What was wrong with
her that she let a mere look from this man make her
act as if she had done something to be ashamed of?
Her chin came up and icy defiance snapped in her eyes
when Cord stalked across the room and stood in front
of her.

"We're having a private conversation, if you don't
mind," she said with undisguised hostility. "I'd appreciate it if you would move on."

Cord's face flushed angrily, and his steel-eyed gaze
raked over her contemptuously. "*You'd* appreciate it,"
he mocked. "Who gives a damn what you'd appreciate, you scrawny little freak of nature." His hand bit
into her shoulder. "Just get your runty ass over there
to my table."

LaTour, his own anger barely controlled, started to
knock Cord's hand away, but then, from the corners of
his eyes, he saw his men push away from the bar, their
hands dropping to their gun butts. A quick glance at
the corner table showed McBain's men now on their
feet, adjusting gun belts. It would be a bloody massa-
cre if both sides let loose with blazing guns—and
Jonty in the middle.

"Look, McBain," he forced himself to speak quietly, "the kid is wet and tired and hungry. You've got to
make allowances." Steel entered his voice. "Couldn't
you have provided him with a slicker? He's soaked to
the skin." He jerked a thumb in the direction of
Cord's table. "Did you even think to get him something to eat?"

Cord stiffened at the scathing words, furious at the
breed and at himself. For everything the man said was

true. He should have noticed that the kid had no rain protection. But dammit, he tried to excuse himself, where that little hellion was concerned he couldn't think straight half the time.

He did feel a little better when he remembered that he had thought about Jonty's hunger. With a heated glower at LaTour, he declared hotly, "I damn well did remember the kid's supper. Jones has him a beef sandwich, wrapped in a piece of oiled paper."

Without further words, Cord jerked Jonty over to stand beside him. Then, stabbing the outlaw with eyes of cold fire, he bit out, "I don't want to ever see you around this boy again. I'm tryin' to get you and your unnatural habits out of his system. I'll have to treat him all the harder every time you come around. So do the kid a favor and stay away from him."

LaTour took a threatening step toward Cord, forgetting the two groups of men who might square off at each other any minute. "In just what way will your treatment of him be harder? Do you intend to beat him?"

"How I treat him has nothing to do with you, breed," Cord answered through his teeth.

His face only inches from Cord's and his eyes flashing blue fire, LaTour warned with dead cool, "If you ever beat this youngster, I'll set the Indians on you. I promise you'll die a slow, painful death."

Cord's eyes shot equal fire, and unaware that his grip had tightened painfully on Jonty's arm, he snarled, "I'm not afraid of your Indian friends, breed. But I want it clearly understood that I don't go around beatin' up on rag-tailed kids—not yet anyway." He ran hard eyes over Jonty's sullen face. "It's hard, though, not to beat this one."

LaTour didn't speak for a moment. Then, lifting a hand, he ruffled Jonty's silky curls. "You're mistaken, McBain," he spoke softly. "To beat this one would be the hardest thing you ever do in your life." His hand moved down to Jonty's narrow shoulder and squeezed it slightly; then he walked toward the door, motioning his men to follow.

"Like hell it would." Cord gave the slender arm a jerk, then dropped it. "It would give me great pleasure to beat the livin' hell out of you right now."

Jonty had to summon all her self-control not to rub her bruised arm. There was no way in the world she'd give this devil the satisfaction of knowing he had hurt her. She flinched when he spoke again, the scorn in his voice shriveling her flesh.

"I'm givin' you fair warnin', Jonty Rand—if I ever again see you hangin' on to LaTour, or any other man for that matter, I will beat you. That's a promise."

Cord's riders arrived at the tail end of his threat. "Why didn't you shoot the bastard?" Paunch demanded.

Cord ignored him, muttering, "Let's get the hell out of here."

Paunch trailed behind the men and Jonty as they left the saloon, his dark thoughts still on Jim LaTour. The breed hadn't used his fists on him that day three years ago. He'd used a riding quirt, the lash of braided rawhide cutting his shirt to ribbons, drawing blood from his back.

It had happened near dawn when he had been with the outlaw group about a month. He was returning to camp after a night of carousing, when he came upon a small group of sleeping renegade Indians. He had stood in the shadow of a tree, his gun drawn, deciding which of the blanket-wrapped figures to shoot first. Then his eyes had fallen on the pretty face of a young girl and he shoved the gun back in its holster.

Stepping slowly and carefully into the camp, he squatted down beside the sleeping girl. His big hand came across her mouth as he swept her out of the blanket. Her back clasped against him, her feet and hands silently beating at him, he slowly eased away from the group. Reaching his mount, he whipped the kerchief from around his neck and tied it across the girl's mouth before she could make a sound. Throwing her onto the saddle, he sprang up behind her and dug his spurs into the horse.

Back at the outlaw camp, he stripped away the girl's clothes and threw himself on top of her. To his surprise, she fought him like a wildcat, clawing his face, finally bringing her knees up into his groin. Enraged and bent over with pain, he grabbed up his short whip and began lashing her with all his strength.

That was when all hell broke loose. The little bitch had snatched the kerchief off her mouth and let out screams that would wake the dead. The next thing he knew, LaTour had jerked the whip out of his hand and was applying it to him.

He had thought it would never stop cutting into his flesh. Finally, beaten to his knees, he had groveled and begged for mercy.

Paunch cringed now. He could still hear the watching men laughing at his humiliation.

"I'll get the bastard." Paunch almost knocked Jonty off her feet as he brushed past her. "I'll get him when he least expects it. How was I to know the damn squaw was his cousin."

Jonty righted herself, throwing Paunch an angry look before turning her attention back to Cord and his men mounting their horses. Would she be offered a ride back to the stables? She gave a startled jerk when Cord suddenly kneed his horse so close up alongside her that she had to step back to avoid being knocked down.

"Well?" he growled, "What are you waitin' for?" He shoved a squashed sandwich into her hand. "Go get the team. We'll be campin' down the road a piece."

Mud and water splashed Jonty's legs as the big black lunged away. "You mean bastard, McBain," she whispered. "You did that on purpose." She blinked back the moisture that sprang to her eyes. With a dejected droop to her shoulders, she walked in the direction of the livery. It was plain that Cord's opinion of her had worsened.

Well, I can't help it, she sighed, and weaving her way among the humanity that thumped along the boardwalk, she unwrapped her supper and bit into it hungrily, wishing with all her being that she could shed her male attire and let the world know that she was a delicate female with a woman's fears and limited strength.

"Someday," she promised herself when a few minutes later she entered the livery, "someday I'll shed these rags and when I do, Cord McBain will pay for every insult, every cruel act he's ever done me."

She climbed onto the wagon and tiredly handling the reins again, turned the team around in the wide aisle and steered them out onto the quagmired street.

The riotous noise of dance halls and saloons died down behind Jonty, finally disappearing altogether. Night descended, dark and silent, with only the creaking of the wagon wheels and her fussily clucking chickens breaking the silence.

She looked up at the full moon moving through the cloudy sky. "Oh, Granny," she whispered, "What have you done to me?"

CHAPTER 5

THE LEADEN GRAYNESS OF THE LOW-HANGING CLOUDS matched Jonty's frame of mind perfectly. Not one day of the four they had traveled, had the sun fully shone. And to add to the gloom that wouldn't leave her, it seemed that with each passing day Cord's face grew harder and grimmer. Oh, he smiled and laughed often enough with his men, she thought dryly, but for me there is only tight lips and harshly barked orders.

If only, Jonty thought, staring through a fine drizzle, she could confide in him, explain that she was not a young boy with unnatural desires, but a young woman who was not up to what he expected of her. Maybe then he would treat her more kindly, not be so angry that responsibility for her had been pushed onto him.

She'd just have to endure whatever he handed out for the present, until sometime in the future her unveiling, so to speak, had to happen. And pray God that time wasn't too far off. Each day the ache of her bound breasts increased. Now, camping out every night, she hadn't dared unbind herself as she had in Abilene at bedtime, hadn't dared give herself those few hours of freedom.

And she longed so much to wear pretty, feminine dresses, to feel sheer muslin petticoats and camisoles next to her skin. And not dresses like those grease-soiled satins that the whores wore, but the rustling taffetas the ladies in Abilene wore, all ruffly and lacy. In her mind she saw those ladies, stepping daintily along, lace mittens on their hands, fancy parasols twirling over their heads.

She sighed and swiped an arm across her wet face, leaving a mud streak on one cheek. That day was far away, if it ever arrived.

The wagon rolled along a rough, winding road, so seldom used that the wheel tracks of previous wagons were dim. A heavy growth of pine obstructed her view for any distance, with only an occasional rift in the timber permitting a glimpse of a distant mountain range. She wondered what part of the country they were moving through as she caught sight of a flat where herds of wild mustangs colored the green grass.

Spotting wild horses was not uncommon, Jonty had discovered. She had seen thousands as the wagon bumped along through brush, across ridges, and around windfalls. And it was on one such sighting that she had learned what Cord had in mind to fulfill Granny's request that he settle down and provide a home for her grandchild.

He had been scouting ahead that day, and when she and the others caught up with him he was sitting his stallion and gazing down into a wild, rocky, and brush-choked canyon. When they had halted around him, he pointed downward and said, "We'll flush many a head of horses out of there once we're settled."

"It won't take long to build up a big horse ranch, boss," Red had said as reins were lifted and horses prodded to move on.

That had rankled Jonty, and it was still a sore spot.

Everybody else knew of Cord's plans, while she was so insignificant that it hadn't been worth his trouble to inform her of anything. Had it even occurred him, he wouldn't have cared that she might be nervous about her future, wondering where he was taking her. In his mind, that he took her at all should be enough.

Her mood desolate and pensive, Jonty followed the fast-disappearing riders up a gentle slope that was indented by gullies choked with brush and stunted pine. A wistfulness filmed her eyes. No one talked much to her anymore. It was Cord's fault, she knew. He had warned the men to stay away from her. She stared unseeing at the team's heavy rumps. Did he have any idea how it felt to be excluded from the bantering exchanges that went on around the campfire at the end of a long tiring day, how it felt to try and join in the conversation only to draw dark threatening looks?

A hint of a smile flickered in Jonty's eyes. Jones and Red forgot sometimes and talked to her—especially if Cord wasn't around. Paunch continued to ogle her when he thought no one was looking.

A fine drizzle had stopped and a pale sun was about to set when Jonty caught up with the others on a level saddle about three miles wide. Camp was being made and she thankfully pulled in the team. She climbed tiredly to the ground and stretched her sore muscles before untying the cow and Beauty.

She was leading her two pets to a creek the spring rains had swollen to a good-sized stream when she checked the animals. From the corner of her eye she had caught a movement in the stand of cottonwoods bordering the watering spot. Irritation firmed her lips when she recognized Paunch lurking beneath them, his thick lips leering, his small eyes watching her like a hawk. Uneasiness fluttered through her when he moved out of the shadows, leading his mount.

"I'll go with you, kid," he said genially. "You never know where some Indian might be layin' in wait. A fine lookin' boy like yourself would be mighty appealin' to some buck." He closed one eye in a salacious wink. "If you know what I mean."

Jonty knew exactly what the bastard meant and she wanted to refuse his company. She didn't trust him as far as she could throw a bear. However, if he was trying to make amends for his previous actions, the least she could do was pretend to go along with him. Besides, they weren't that far away from the others. If necessary, a loud scream should bring somebody to investigate.

But once the creek was reached, she was sorry she hadn't heeded her first instinct. For as she leaned against a rock waiting for the cow and Beauty to quench their thirst, Paunch, no more than three feet away, began to casually undo his trousers as his own mount drank. Before she could turn away, he was relieving himself, his fat-squinted eyes watching her face as his stream splashed against a rock. The other men, including Cord, had often answered nature's call in front of her, but only in the natural way that men did in front of each other. At those times she would shift her gaze or walk away. But she had to force back a gasp of indignation and look away from the fat ugly thing Paunch held in his hands.

Jonty jerked when Paunch asked in his grating whine, "Don't you have to take a leak? You been jostlin' along in the wagon all day, your bladder must be full."

"I went just before we got here," she lied, turning to look at the man. This time she did gasp, her face turning beet-red. Not only had Paunch not returned himself to his trousers, the disgusting man was fondling an arousal.

She shoved away from the rock, repressing a desire to pick up a stick and strike the ugly appendage with all her strength. Wouldn't that make him howl! She almost giggled as she strode over to the animals and pulled their whiffling nostrils out of the water.

As she hurried them back toward camp, Paunch's mocking laughter followed her. Did he know she was female or did he want to use her in the manner some men did with each other? she wondered, then shuddered. She couldn't imagine a woman, or a man, being intimate with that repulsive man.

A damp, blustery wind had risen, cutting like a knife through Jonty's inadequate clothing by the time she finished tending all her animals. She was shivering when she hurried to the brightly burning fire, hoping that Cord wouldn't find another chore for her before she thawed out and rested a bit. She was utterly spent, both physically and mentally. The run-in with Paunch had upset her more than she had realized. She glanced at the fat man, occupied with making bread. She remembered where she had last seen his hands and knew that she would not be eating any biscuits tonight.

Jonty cautiously lowered herself down beside Jones, conscious of Cord's cool gaze upon her. Holding her hands out to the fire, she waited for some cutting word from him. None came. It seemed that tonight Cord's mood was light and relaxed as he laughed and joked with his men. When no order was barked at her, she scooted closer to the fire as the bantering went on around her.

Jonty raised her head with interest when Red asked, "Did you ever give any thought to gettin' married someday, Cord, and raisin' a family?"

Cord threw back his head and laughed. "You gotta be funnin' me, wrangler. A wife and youngins' don't figure in my plans. I'd feel smothered by all that responsibility."

Jonty's lips curled at Cord's disdainful dismissal of marriage and a family. Of course he'd feel that way, she thought. You have to give a part of yourself to a mate and children. And Cord McBain was too damn selfish to do that.

She looked up to find Cord watching her and quickly shifted her gaze back to the fire. That responsibility bit he'd mentioned had been for her benefit. Well, too bad, she thought. He might feel smothered by the obligation he felt duty-bound to take on, but his obligation didn't breathe very easily either.

Jonty pushed Cord out of her mind as her stomach rumbled in anticipation of supper. Paunch had pulled a steaming bean pot off the fire and announced gruffly that supper was ready. They all stood up—then suddenly, every man's hand went to his gun.

Only yards behind them, in the fringe of cotton-woods, the cry of a wolf floated eerily on the air.

"I've never known them to come so close to a fire before," Jones muttered as Jonty took a step closer to him.

"Me neither." Cord stepped to the other side of Jonty, causing a warm feeling of security to flow over her. When his body gave a startled jerk, she looked up, and her own slender body echoed his action.

As though from nowhere, a horse and rider, ghost-like, suddenly stood just outside the circle of firelight. And standing at the feet of the mount was a magnificent-looking wolf-dog. A sharp intake of breath came in unison from several throats when the dog came stiff-legged toward the fire, his nose quivering delicately as though testing the air, sniffing out danger.

Jonty felt Cord stiffen beside her. "Call the animal off, mister," he warned, "or he's a dead dog."

The dimly seen rider spoke quietly to the animal, and the raised ruff immediately smoothed out. While everyone watched tensely, the shadowy figure of the man parted himself from the horse and stepped into the light, his fringed buckskins rustling softly.

With a flash of intuition, Jonty knew that Uncle Jim's relative had arrived. She waited anxiously to see if his plan would work. Someone poked up the fire, and in the new flames created she peered at the stranger, looking for some resemblance to Jim LaTour on his face.

It was there. The man had the same shiny black hair, although unlike Uncle Jim's, it was worn almost to the Indian's broad shoulders. The same hawk-like features were there, but the color of the eyes matched that of his hair. Her gaze dropped to the gun tied low on his leg, the way a hired gunman would wear his.

The same speculation ran through Cord's mind as he scrutinized the still, dark features. The man looked familiar, but he was sure he had never met him before. This was a man you wouldn't forget easily.

The Indian spoke then, in a flat, expressionless voice. "I am called Johnny Lightfoot."

Immediate interest leapt into Cord's eyes. "The hell you say!" he exclaimed. "I hadn't heard that you were in these parts. I heard some time back that you were down in Mexico."

Lightfoot shook his head with a wry smile. "One hears many things, only half of them true. I've been down Texas way for the past three months. Breaking a herd of mustangs for a rancher there."

"Are you headin' anywhere in particular now?"

"No. Just floating around, giving my bones a rest."

"Well." Cord grinned. "If they're rested up enough, I could sure use you. My name is Cord McBain, and I'm startin' up a spread in Wyoming. I can always use someone with your experience. I hope to round up a lot of wild horses."

Jonty ducked her head to hide her glee. For once someone was far ahead of Mister Cord McBain. She yearned to throw that fact in his face, to tell him that he had been set up, that this man's purpose in being here was to watch over her, to keep him in line where she was concerned.

She peeked a look at Uncle Jim's relative. There was a brief twinkle in the black eyes that met hers. However, when he answered Cord his face showed no expression.

"I might as well tie in with you," he said. "I've been at loose ends for a month now."

"Good!" Cord's teeth flashed in a pleased smile. "Meet the rest of the men."

Each man, including churlish Paunch, stepped for-

ward, gave his name and respectfully shook hands
with the well-known tracker and tamer of wild horses.

Jonty, sure in her mind that in Cord's opinion she
wasn't important enough for an introduction, almost
gasped her surprise when Cord waved a careless hand
in her direction and said shortly, "Jonty Rand, my
ward." It wasn't much, she thought, but at least it put
her a cut above the livestock.

But the newly hired hand, much to Cord's frowning
disapproval, wasn't treating the short introduction
lightly. He took the hand she offered, a slow smile
changing the hardness of his features as he carefully
scanned her face as though looking for something.
When she shyly smiled at him, he lifted a hand and
brushed it across her short, black curls. He dropped
his hand then, and gave a peculiar low whistle. The
gray dog stood up and trotted over to him.

"Watch that animal, Lightfoot!" Cord took the two
steps that separated him from Jonty, his hand again
dropping to his Colt.

The Indian lifted a silencing hand, then spoke
quietly to the dog. The huge, muscular animal moved
toward Jonty and her alarmed eyes jumped to Cord
when it suddenly thrust its head against her leg.

"Do not be afraid of Wolf, Jonty." Lightfoot smiled
at her nervousness. "You have a new friend now . . . a
protector. No one will harm you in his presence."

"That's all well and good," Cord said coolly as
Jonty put out a tentative hand to stroke the smooth
pelt between the intelligent eyes, "but I'll give the kid
all the protection he needs."

A lifted eyebrow, followed by a meaningful glance
at Paunch, was the only response Lightfoot made. It
was enough to make Cord frown. He shot a suspicious
look at the fat man, then sent Jonty a searching look.
She dropped her eyes, and he looked again at Paunch.
He knew the brutish man watched the kid, knew what
went through his mind—but surely the man wasn't
foolish enough to try something with his ward?

He'd keep a close eye on him, he decided, then said to Lightfoot, "We were about to eat. Grab a plate and get in line."

The dog, Wolf, walked beside Jonty, and when she sat down with her filled plate he flopped down beside her. With a wary glance at the dog, Cord sat down on the other side of her. When Lightfoot, the last in line, had his share of beans heaped on his plate, the only spot left around the fire was beside his dog. Everyone else stayed clear of the ferocious-looking animal.

The meal was silently and quickly consumed, and it was when they were relaxing with their coffee that the men began plying the Indian with questions.

"How long you been chasin' the broomtails, Lightfoot?" Red asked.

Lightfoot held a flaming twig to the cigarette he'd just rolled. Tossing the burning wood back into the fire, he answered, "Almost since I can remember." He took a deep drag on the smoke and let it drift through his nose. "Taming the wild mustang was always a challenge to me."

"Is it true you can spot their tracks from the back of a galloping horse?" Jones questioned next.

The Indian grinned in amusement. "I've often wondered how some tall tales get started. The truth is, I owe my success with the wild ones to plain stubbornness. Once I get on the trail of a herd I don't let up until I've run them down."

The questions and answers continued, the moonlight grew brighter, the trees cast long shadows. Once the cry of a wolf—wild, lonely and haunting—carried in on the light breeze. The wolf-dog pointed his nose to the sky and answered the call. Lightfoot spoke a calming word to the animal and he settled back down, his huge head between his paws.

Jonty began to squirm uncomfortably, only half listening to the conversation going on around her. Nature was calling and she was afraid to answer it—afraid that Paunch would follow her into the trees.

Finally, she could wait no longer. She eased to her feet and sighed her relief when no one seemed to notice her. They were all engrossed with what Lightfoot had to say.

She had barely left the light of the fire, however, when from the corner of her eye she saw Paunch also rise. He's going to follow me, she cried silently, the pain of a full bladder making it almost impossible to think straight. Then, just when she thought that surely she would wet her trousers, a blur of gray-black fur had sprung in front of the man she detested and feared so thoroughly.

Jonty's gaze swept to Paunch's face and she laughed. He had blanched as he stared fearfully at Wolf's raised hackles, his lips snarled back over long, sharp fangs.

"Call this damn brute off, Indian," he croaked. "I gotta go relieve myself."

Lightfoot turned a face that looked like chiseled stone to the fear-sweating man. "Don't follow Jonty, and he'll not touch you. Like I said before, he's the kid's protection. From now on he'll be his shadow."

Swearing volubly, the obese cowhand wheeled and struck off in the opposite direction, and Jonty hurried into the darkness of the trees.

Cord swore also, silently and angrily, but his anger was directed at himself. Once again he hadn't kept a watchful eye on Jonty. The look he trained on Paunch's retreating back promised that it wouldn't happen again.

When Jonty returned to the campfire, Wolf at her heels, the conversation had lagged as tired men grew drowsy in the comfortable warmth of the fire. In a short time they were seeking their blankets.

To Jonty's surprise, for the first time Cord spread his bedroll only feet away from her. She frowned, not liking the comfortable feeling his close presence gave her. The Wolf came and plopped down beside her and she barely heard the coyotes' piercing notes as she fell asleep.

CHAPTER 6

ON THE FOURTH DAY ON THE TRAIL, WHEN THE SUN WAS dipping westward and losing some of its heat, Cord turned the stallion onto a branch road that led to the Sweetwater River. He and the men followed it until they arrived at a point where the foothills trooped down to the stream. There Cord drew rein and said with satisfaction, "There it is."

Jonty and the team, trailing several yards behind the others, arrived in time to see Cord and the men riding toward a set of buildings. She barely gave her future home a glance. She could only stare in awe at the infinite grandeur nature had created around her. To her right, the tree-lined river wound its way down the valley, shimmering like silver in the sun. She turned her head to the slopes of the mountain range to her left, her eyes moving away into the distance beyond to where the green plains were beginning to disappear into the haze of the horizon.

I could be happy here, she thought, if only Cord were a little kinder. She had worked hard at taking Red's advice, "Stay out of Cord's way as much as possible." But she hadn't had much success in that. It seemed that he was always around, his wintery eyes on her as though waiting for her to put a wrong foot forward.

Jonty was so engrossed with her unhappy thoughts that she didn't hear Cord ride up. She started violently when he spoke, his tone almost friendly. "That's Lost Valley you're lookin' at. It sure is somethin', isn't it?"

Jonty was too surprised at his genial tone to answer him. She nodded silently. "The buildings need quite a bit of work." Cord directed her attention back to the several buildings at the very edge of the foothills, shaded now by tall ponderosa pine and douglas fir. She took her time to study her new home, especially the foremost cabin that sat several yards from the others. Although shabby and neglected, she could see that it was solidly built, erected from the pine that stood thick in the area. Right now, however, the door sagged and the shutters on the windows hung crookedly on their hinges.

"How come you told Granny that you didn't have a place to bring me?" Jonty asked reproachfully. "When all the time you owned this ranch?"

"Look," Cord frowned at the accusation in her voice. "I didn't lie to Maggie, if that's what you're thinkin'. I only remembered this place the night she died."

"Well, who does it belong to then?"

"I don't know, but I'm gonna move in until I can locate the owner, see if he wants to sell, see if I can afford to buy it."

"I don't suppose there was very much money in that chest Granny gave you." Jonty watched Cord closely as she asked the question.

"Probably not," Cord agreed. "I haven't looked yet." His lips twisted wryly. "I don't imagine Maggie was able to put very much aside over the years. Nellie isn't known for her generosity when it comes to money."

Jonty was hard put not to call him a liar. She'd have bet anything that he had looked in the chest, and according to Uncle Jim, there was plenty of money stashed inside it.

"It gets plenty cold up here in the winter," Cord said, breaking her train of thought. "Sometimes it gets twenty, thirty below, what with the wind blowin'. And we get some blizzards up here that are pure hell. A man could soon freeze to death, caught out in one.

"It gets mighty lonesome in the winter time too," he added as an afterthought. "The passes become snow-bound, keepin' out any visitors . . . maybe a few Ute Indians might come by occasionally."

"Oh? Mean ones, like on the war path?" Jonty asked, shivering at the thought.

Cord shrugged. "Not usually. Although they're not the friendliest in the world. They'll rob you blind if you don't watch them. Especially in the winter when they're hungry." He took his hat off, ran his fingers through his hair, then adjusted it back on his head. "You can't blame the poor devils. The white man has practically killed off the buffalo, their prime source of meat."

Jonty nodded in agreement. "I expect hunger can make a man do a lot of things he wouldn't ordinarily do."

It happened so fast, Jonty was stunned. The warmth had left Cord's eyes, leaving them like icy steel. The coldness back on his features, he said harshly, "That's right, hunger does lead men to deeds that are unnatural to them." Before she could make a response, he added, in that hard voice that seemed reserved only for her, "Get on to the cabin. You've got to clean it out before anything can be moved into it." He touched a heel to the stallion and was gone in a cloud of dust.

Jonty watched the stallion until it disappeared, her shoulders slumped dejectedly. Cord's nasty remark about hungers hadn't gone over her head. He was referring to her and Uncle Jim. She picked up the reins and popped them over the team's backs, guiding them onto a dim trail overgrown with grass.

"Someday, someway, I'll prove you wrong, Cord McBain," she muttered. "I'll make you eat every rotten thing you ever said to me."

As she pulled up in front of the house, Red's deep laughter drew her attention to three distant buildings. The wranglers were moving in and out of the largest one, carrying in blankets and gear.

Jonty returned her gaze to the long, low cabin that was to be her new home, thinking that it was very different from what she'd been used to. It wasn't only the house itself, but the solitude surrounding it. In Nellie's big house in Abilene, there was always traffic —men coming and going, laughter and song from the young whores. Would she be terribly lonesome here?

"I think not," her inner voice whispered. "That son of Satan will keep you so busy you won't have the time or the energy to give yourself a thought."

Jonty was silently nodding her head in agreement when Cord spoke gruffly behind her. "Are you gonna set there dreamin' all day?" She turned her head and watched him swing from the saddle, then hop up on the rickety porch. Pushing the door open, he called impatiently, "Come on, bring in that broom you insisted on shovin' in the wagon. I told you the place needs cleanin' out."

Jonty sighed and climbed stiffly to the ground. She stood a moment, stretching sore arm muscles, then walked to the back of the wagon and pushed between the cow and her mare. She swung onto the tailgate and, squeezing past the chicken coop, began rummaging around among the furniture and boxes until she finally routed out the broom. Then she spotted Maggie's old scrub pail, rags, and yellow lye soap still lying on the floorboards.

"I don't remember putting you there," she muttered, dislodging the pail from under a crate of bed linens. Her lips twisted sourly. The pail and soap would get hard usage today, she had no doubt. The pail in one hand and the broom in the other, she mounted the sagging steps, avoided a loose board on the porch, and entered the cabin.

A fast inspection showed five rooms, all rubble-filled and cobwebbed. The large main room, where apparently the previous owners had gathered for an evening, ran the length of the building and was around fourteen feet wide. The huge field stone fireplace centered in the outside wall attested to the severity of the winters in the mountains. Its huge cavern could easily take two-foot-long backlogs that would give a plentiful supply of heat.

The kitchen was at the far end of the house and approximately the same size as the main front room. She visualized bright curtains hanging at the two windows, one looking out over the valley, the other just above a dry-sink and looking toward the out buildings and the mountain. She rubbed a clear spot through the grime on the glass and, peering through it, thought that she would never tire of looking out of either window.

"Evidently, Cord overlooked the kitchen when he said there was no furniture in the house," Jonty mused out loud, scanning a sturdy long table, littered with sand, leaves, and parts of broken bridles and reins. Righting two long benches lying on their sides, she lined them up with the table, thinking that a large family must have lived here before. The table could easily seat ten people.

Dusting off her hands, she turned her attention to a built-in cabinet and several shelves attached to an end wall—a perfect setting for granny's pretty dishes. She smiled, then moved across the floor to examine the small hand pump installed inside the dry-sink. She ran a hand over the bright red pump, not thinking for a moment that it would actually work, produce water. That was too much to hope for.

She moved the handle up and down a few times just

to prove herself right, then yelped in surprise. A gush of cold, pure water poured out of the spout.

"What's all the yelling about?" Johnny Lightfoot stood in the kitchen door, looking at her quizzically.

"I can't believe it!" Jonty's eyes sparkled. "But it works. Watch." She worked the handle up and down again, and again water spurted out.

"There's a spring back of the house," Lightfoot explained. "Whoever lived here before must have piped it into the house."

Jonty eyed the dirt and grime on everything and made a wry face. "How fortunate for me he did. As you might expect, I've been ordered to clean up the place. I really don't care, though," she added, rolling up her sleeves. "I can picture how nice everything will look when I'm finished. I can picture Granny's things placed around, her bright kerosene lamps, her pictures, the pretty dishes and rugs."

Lightfoot frowned and, laying a hand on her shoulder, cautioned, "Don't forget that you're supposed to be a young lad, Jonty, and as such you wouldn't be interested in prettying up a place."

The sparkling excitement in Jonty's eyes died, leaving a dullness in its wake. Jonty's small head drooped on her slender neck. "I'm so tired of pretending, Johnny," she said with a catch in her voice. "I don't know how much longer I can carry on."

Lightfoot studied the slender, graceful body and wondered how anyone looking at it could not see the femininity of its lines. He pressed her delicate shoulder. "I have a feeling it won't be too long before your pretense will be behind you."

He dropped his hand with a smile. "In the meantime, I believe you're marking your eighteenth birthday today."

"Why yes—yes, I am." Jonty's eyes widened in surprise. "How did you know?"

"Your—ah, Jim told me." The Indian reached behind him and picked up a package off the table.

"Happy birthday, little one." He smiled, holding it out to her.

"Oh, Johnny," Jonty's voice trembled with mixed emotions of joy and sadness. Granny had always had something for her on her special day—although sadly, out of necessity, it was always something that would appeal to a young boy, then later something that a young teenager would like. Dolls and pretty dresses had never been for her.

"Unwrap it," Lightfoot urged, anxious to see her smile again, to see the blue eyes twinkle with pleasure.

When the heavy brown paper was laid open, Jonty let out a small cry of pleasure. "Oh, Johnny, I have never seen anything so beautiful." She gazed down at a magnificent looking jacket. She stroked a hand over the soft doeskin, ran her fingers over the colorful beads worked into a design on the sleeves and hem.

"It's lined with rabbit fur." Lightfoot pointed out, laying open the garment. "It will keep you warm in the coldest weather."

"Where did you find such a lovely article? There's hours and hours of work in the beading alone."

"My cousin Naomi made it. She's very clever with a needle."

"She certainly is," Jonty agreed, then stood on her toes to kiss the handsome brave's bronze cheek. "Thank you, Johnny, it's the loveliest gift I've ever received."

The pleased man started to say something, but his body stiffened and his lips remained shut. Jonty saw that his attention had shifted behind her, and turning around, she suppressed a groan. Cord stood in the door, glaring at them from frosty eyes. *Damn*! she thought, *he would have to catch me kissing Johnny*. She blushed and dropped her eyes, all too aware of what he was thinking; she was making overtures to yet another man.

"Why aren't you with the other men, Lightfoot?" Cord almost snarled the question.

The Indian shoved his hands in his pocket and

lounged back against the table. His black eyes challenging, he said quietly, "I just stopped by for a minute to give the kid a birthday gift."

Cord tensed, stared at the man a moment, then swung frowning eyes at Jonty. "Is today your birthday?" When she nodded, he demanded, "How come you didn't mention it to me?"

Jonty shrugged her shoulders. "I didn't think you'd be interested."

Cord's lips tightened. "But you'd tell a stranger. What made you think he'd care?"

"Look, McBain." Lightfoot straightened up, impatience in his voice, "The kid didn't make a point of telling me. He just casually mentioned a couple days back that today would be his eighteenth birthday. With my people that is an important age to reach. I felt he should have something to mark the special occasion." Lightfoot paused and motioned to the buckskin jacket. "And since he doesn't have much in the line of clothes, I thought the jacket an appropriate gift."

Cord picked up the delicately constructed garment, examined it, then tossed it carelessly back on the table. "Looks like it was made for a woman," he sneered. "'Course that would appeal to Jonty." He wheeled abruptly, saying harshly as he walked through the door, "Get on with the cleanin'. I want to get settled in before dark."

"That arrogant bastard." Lightfoot scowled, his lean fingers hovering over the hilt of a wicked-looking knife shoved into his belt. "If it wouldn't make things harder on you, I'd slice him up a bit."

"Don't let him bother you, Johnny. I don't pay any attention to him anymore," Jonty said with an indifference that was contradicted by the trembling of her lower lip and the fast blinking of her eyes.

The Indian pretended not to see the evidence of impending tears, and giving Jonty's arm a pat, he said softly, "That's the right idea, Jonty. Just ignore the swine. Meanwhile"—he turned to leave—"I'll send

Jones over to give you a hand. McBain doesn't seem to mind too much his being around you."

A few minutes later, Jones walked into the kitchen. He looked around and grinned wryly. "I expect the first thing we need is hot water."

Jonty returned the friendly grin. "Gallons and gallons," she agreed. Jones nodded, and while he unearthed a large iron kettle from one of the sheds back of the house, filled it with water, then lit a fire beneath it out in the yard, Jonty got busy with the broom, starting with one of the three bedrooms.

The two worked steadily in companionable silence, no motions wasted. Two hours and many pails of hot water and lye soap later, the sprawling log house held no resemblance to what Jonty and Jones had first attacked.

Gone were the cobwebs and the grime from the windows. The big range in the kitchen now gleamed a soft black, thanks to the wood-ash Jones had vigorously rubbed into it. The long table and benches had been scrubbed until they were almost white, as were the cabinet and shelves. Man and boy looked at each other, well pleased with their hard work.

Jonty tiredly wiped a sleeve across her sweating brow. The shadows on the kitchen floor said that the sun would soon slip over the mountain and darkness would be upon them. She smiled at Jones. "Looks like we're going to make it. Why don't you go get the men to help us unload the wagon."

Jones nodded and left the house, whistling tunelessly through his teeth. A short time later she heard the men coming, laughing, bantering back and forth, Cord's deep laughter rising above the others. A yearning came into Jonty's eyes. If only occasionally he'd share some of that geniality with her.

When Jonty stepped out on the porch to help the men, she noticed immediately that her cow and chickens were gone, as well as her mare, Beauty. She looked around frantically. Where were they? Surely the helpless creatures hadn't just been turned loose to fend for themselves? She grabbed hold of Jones's arm as he was about to hop into the wagon. "My chickens and cow and the mare, do you know what has happened to them?"

"Yeah." Jones looked toward the smallest shed. "Cord put the chickens in there right after you pulled in. Mentioned that we'd have to build them a sturdy pen the first chance we got." He grinned down at her. "I'll get on it tomorrow. And your cow and mare are in the corral with the other mounts."

Jonty's face showed her deep relief. Those pets were the last living things that tied her to Granny. She hoped to keep them for a long, long time.

She was about to drag a box from the wagon when she was tapped on the shoulder. "You go back inside, Jonty, and show us men where you want things put," Lightfoot ordered. "These boxes are too heavy for you to handle."

Jonty didn't argue. Her arms felt like wooden weights, and she couldn't remember ever being so tired. She stepped back up on the porch, then paused, feeling the pull of eyes on her back. She looked over her shoulder and wasn't surprised to see Cord staring at her, his lips clamped in a tight line. She breathed a deep sigh. He must have overheard Johnny expressing his concern for her.

"I don't care if he did," she muttered rebelliously and continued on into the house. "And I'll stay here, for if I take one step outside he'll find some excuse to sweep down on me, like an eagle on a prairie dog."

Amid much good-natured confusion, Maggie Rand's possessions were taken off the wagon and placed where her granddaughter directed. The last article to be carried in was the big four-poster bed. Jonty had directed her own smaller bed to be put in a room for Cord, saving the largest room for herself. He had frowned at her action but had made no remark.

The big bed was put together, the feather tick placed

on it, before the men trooped out. Jonty began to
lovingly smooth clean sheets over the plump mattress
and slide pillowcases over the two fat down pillows.
She had just finished topping the bed off with a
colorful patch-work quilt when she heard the footsteps coming down the hall toward her room. Her
body stiffened as she recognized Cord's quiet steps.

"I'll ignore him," she muttered under her breath,
giving the bright cover a final pat.

She was busying herself at the small bedside table,
unnecessarily rearranging the lamp, moving the book
she had been reading before Maggie took sick, when
Cord, not about to be ignored, drawled sarcastically
from behind her, "So, Jonty, you can turn a fine hand
to housekeeping, I see. You're just full of surprises,
aren't you?"

Refusing to look at her tormentor, Jonty answered
defensively, "I'm just fixing things the way Granny
used to have them."

Surprisingly Cord made no response, and Jonty
remained silent, willing him to go away. The silence
grew strained as Cord continued to lean in the doorway, his arms folded across his chest, no doubt glaring
at her, Jonty thought.

A satisfied grin quirked her lips at the soft sound of
Cord shifting his feet. Good, Mister Cord McBain was
feeling uncomfortable for a change. She started when
Cord cleared his throat, then said gruffly, "I've noticed your saddle has just about had it. I've brought
you over a new one." He hesitated a moment, then
added, "For your birthday. It's out in the hall."

Jonty's heart gave a happy leap. He did care for her,
a little at least. She opened her mouth to thank him,
then Cord spoke again, causing it to snap shut.

"You're gonna be spendin' at least twelve hours a
day astride a horse chasin' wild mustangs. I don't
want you layin' around with a busted leg because a
worn-out saddle snapped and pitched you into a
canyon or a pile of rocks." He left then, saying over his
shoulder, "Get a move on. Supper will be ready soon

and you still have your cow and chickens to take care of."

Jonty gave a defeated sigh as his spurs jangled down the hall, and then outside. The saddle hadn't been a gesture of good will, a liking for her. It had only been a precaution against his losing a spell of hard work from her.

The rich aroma of frying steaks floated into her room, making her stomach rumble with hunger. A wry grimace twisted her face. The desire for a bath and clean clothes was running a close second to her hunger. Sweat had oozed out of her pores all day, and the strips of cloth binding were soaked through. How she longed to scratch the itch of prickly heat between her breasts.

Jonty sighed. A bath would have to wait until after supper, when real darkness had set in. Then she and Wolf would go to the fast-running stream that flowed several yards back of the house. Her lips curved softly. Since the wolf-dog's entrance into her life, she now had privacy and a sense of security. No one came very close to her when he was near.

Darkness was near when Jonty stepped out on the porch, and she took the time to light the lantern someone had hung on a nail beside the door. As she skirted the group sitting around a campfire, she noted that Jones was the cook tonight. The way grease was spattering everywhere, she was thankful he wasn't using the clean kitchen.

Inside the small shed, Jonty ran a gentle hand over the cow's extended stomach as it drank thirstily from the pail of water she'd brought it. "You'll be dropping your calf soon, won't you, girl?" she spoke softly to the animal. "I hope it will be a little girl for future milk. There's enough mouths around here to drink it."

She fed and watered the chickens next, surprised and delighted to find two eggs in a pile of old hay and dried leaves. She carefully picked them up and laid them in a rusty tin can lying on a heap of trash. "I'll save these," she said to a broody hen clucking around

her feet. "When I have a dozen you can sit on them
and hatch some baby chicks. There's a big need of
eggs around here too."

Jonty had just finished visiting with her mare when
Jones called that the grub was ready, adding, "And I
don't want to hear any complaints." When she approached the fire, Wolf trailing close behind her,
Lightfoot scooted over, making a place for her to sit
down between him and Red. She thanked Jones for
the tin plate he handed her, then wondered what in
the world lay inside it. Jones saw her tiny frown and
sourly explained the black, charred pieces of meat.

"It's buffalo steak. And that," he pointed to a large
lump that resembled one of the rocks lying around, "is
sourdough biscuits."

Jonty nodded and tried to smile her understanding,
not wanting to hurt the feelings of the man who had
shown her friendship. Lightfoot nudged her in the
side, and handed her his broad-bladed knife. "I hope
you're hungry," he said in a low voice, "otherwise,
you'll never gag this mess down."

"It will have to be pretty awful for me not to eat it,"
Jonty whispered back. "I'm starved."

"We'll see." Lightfoot watched her poise the knife
over the steak, a flicker of amusement in his eyes.

Jonty sliced into the meat, and immediately her
plate ran red with blood. She stared down at it in
dismay, her appetite gone. She sent a surreptitious
glance at the others, and with the exception of
Paunch, found varying degrees of disgust on their
faces. Her eyes swung back to Paunch when the fat
man spoke to her. "Have you ever et dog stew, kid?"
he asked around a mouthful of meat, sliding a sly look
at Wolf, who eyed her plate hungrily.

Jonty paled at the thought, and while Lightfoot sent
Paunch a stinging look, the obnoxious man asked Red
the same question.

"God, no!" Red gasped. "I ain't never been that
drunk."

"Well, I for one would welcome a bowl of it right

now." Cord growled, tossing his portion of half-raw meat to the dog. "I'm sure it would score high over this mess." He pulled a handkerchief from his hip pocket, wiped his knife, and stuck it back in its sheath. "I've got to hire a cook, there's no two ways about it."

"I'll do the cooking," Jonty burst out impulsively. "I used to help Granny when she . . ."

The rest of the sentence died on her lips as Cord's angry roar jarred against her ears. "No! You're damn well not goin' to do the cookin'. You're gonna pull your weight with the rest of the men."

Jonty was calling herself all manner of fool when Red exclaimed, "Dammit, Cord, at least let him do it until you hire someone. We'll all die if we have to eat Jones's cooking. I say let him have a crack at it. There ain't no shame in a feller knowin' how to cook. All the big ranches have a man cook."

When the others raised their voices in approval, Cord threw up his hands in reluctant surrender. "It's against my better judgment, but I don't see any other alternative at the moment."

He turned frosty eyes on Jonty. "See to it that breakfast is ready by sun-up. So clean up this mess of Jones's and get to bed. It'll be early risin' for you for a spell." He waited for a response from Jonty and when none came, he rose and walked over to his saddlebag lying against a tree. "In the meantime," he said, hunkering down and opening the bag, "We'll have to make do with some beef jerky."

When he finished handing out the strips of dried meat, he ordered, "Come on, men, let's clear out and give the kid room to neaten up around here."

Jonty watched them amble off to the bunkhouse, Lightfoot giving her an anxious look over his shoulder. She heard Jones say, "Maybe I'll give the kid a hand," but Cord shook his head and the older man walked on.

Tears glimmered in Jonty's eyes. "Damn him," she muttered. "He's well aware of the strenuous day I've had. Even if I were the young man he thinks I am, he has to know that I've done the work of two full grown men today."

Wolf shoved his wet nose into her hand and whined in sympathy. Jonty threw her arms around his neck and cried helpless tears into his rough fur. But only for a moment. From an early age, Granny had instilled in her that she mustn't cry unnecessarily, that people would frown on a boy showing such a feminine weakness. "Besides," the old woman had added, "Tears don't solve anything. They only swell your eyes and give you a headache."

Wiping her eyes on the back of her hand, Jonty dragged herself to her feet and got busy. As she chewed the dried beef, her energy was renewed and she soon had everything cleared away, her practiced hands making no unnecessary moves. She hurried inside the house, then, and gathered up the items she'd need, and minutes later she was luxurating in the cool, soothing water of the narrow stream, as Wolf stood guard nearby.

By the time Jonty had finished bathing and rinsing out the pile of clothing she had discarded, coyotes had begun their night barking. She stood outside the cabin for a while, enjoying the solitude, listening to the yelps and the moan of the wind in the spruce trees.

"It smells like rain is on its way." She rubbed Wolf's rough head. A burst of laughter came from the bunkhouse, drawing her attention to the faint light shining through the window. She sighed, wishing she could join the men, but knowing that Cord would send her away. After a moment, she walked into the house, the dog at her heels. She spread her wet clothes on the floor to dry, then disrobed and pulled on her nightshirt and crawled into bed.

She pulled the blanket up around her shoulders, and in the middle of her prayers heavy drops of water thundered on the roof. Their spattering rapidly swelled into a drumming roar of rain.

"I hope the roof doesn't leak," she muttered, and fell instantly into an exhausted sleep.

CHAPTER 7

THE PALE LIGHT OF DAWN WAS CREEPING OVER THE MOUN-
tain when Jonty awakened. She stretched lazily, the
luxury of unfettered breasts making her sigh content-
edly. She had been very careless last night, leaving the
bindings off. Complete exhaustion fuzzing her mind
had been the culprit.

At least she had enough awareness to slip on her
nightshirt. She smiled crookedly. She'd have been in a
fine fix had she overslept and had Cord come in to
awaken her. He would have had a heart attack if he'd
found her naked, the way she liked to sleep.

She plucked the coarse linsey material away from
her body, wishing the mannish garment was made of
fine, sheer muslin with lots of ruffles and lace—and
that when she rose she would slip a full petticoat over
her head, then smooth a lacy camisole over her full,
pert breasts, to be followed by a flowered lawn dress
with a wide velvet ribbon tied around her small waist.

Wolf, hearing Jonty stirring, rose and pushed his
nose against her cheek, bringing her out of her day-

dream. She leaned up on an elbow and scratched the sharp, pointed ears. "Aren't I foolish, Wolf, wasting my time thinking such thoughts?"

The dog wagged his tail as though in agreement, and Jonty slid out of bed. Breakfast by sun-up, her Lord and Master had ordered. She padded across the floor and stood in front of the mirror that had caused her to hold her breath yesterday as Red and Jones worked awkwardly at hanging it. She had expected them to drop Granny's most prized possession any minute and shatter it into a million pieces.

Jonty raised her eyes to her image and gasped. How long her hair had grown! Another inch and she would look like the female she was. She jerked open a drawer, and snatching up the scissors lying there, she attacked the silky mop. In minutes the black curls were cropped close to her head.

"You must never let that happen again," she admonished herself, hurriedly returning the scissors as the clock in the big main room struck four times. "Gosh, I've got to hurry!" She began to rebind her breasts. A moment later she swooped up her hated clothes off the floor, grimacing as she pulled the still slightly damp garments on.

"Damn!" she whispered as she buttoned up, "I forgot to bring in wood last night." She'd have to spend at least an half hour chopping wood for the big black kitchen range.

But when Jonty hurried into the kitchen, the first thing to catch her eye was a large stack of wood neatly piled in a corner.

"Thank you, Johnny." She sighed her relief, knowing it had to be the work of the Indian. Wolf would have raised a racket had anyone else entered the house after she had retired.

She soon had a roaring fire going and a big pot of coffee beginning to brew. She took the time then to wash her face in the basin she had placed in the sink before slicing up a slab of salt pork to be fried later.

When she had finished mixing up a bowl of flapjack batter, she called Wolf and went outside to answer a call of nature.

"Let's stay outside a minute, Wolf," Jonty said, absorbing the elastic breath of the awakening day. The air was still cool with the rain that had fallen during the night, heavy with the scent of the valley and the mountain.

She stared out over the mist-filled valley, reflections of the past days filtering through her mind. Her life had been turned upside down, leaving her with no assurance of a stable future. Cord didn't want *her*; he only wanted her inheritance. Once he owned this property, he wouldn't care what happened to her. And Uncle Jim—only the good Lord knew when he could provide a home for her.

Remembered words of her grandmother came to Jonty. "Life is all God gives us, child. The rest we make for ourselves." With these words ringing in her ears, Jonty straightened her shoulders, telling herself that she would take each day as it came, handling it the best way she could. "Even though Cord McBain treats me as though I'm only a shadow in the dust," she tacked on.

A light went on in the bunkhouse and Jonty hurried inside. The men would soon be coming in for breakfast.

Jonty whipped around in the kitchen, setting the meat to frying, placing Maggie's everyday dishes on the long table. A tall stack of flapjacks were soon keeping warm on the back of the stove, as well as a platter of crisp fried salt pork.

She was standing in the kitchen door sipping a cup of coffee when everyone except Cord left the bunkhouse. She stepped back out of the way as the men came straggling in, yawning and scratching themselves. Good mornings were gruffly spoken, then one by one the men used the basin, splashing water on the floor and the window above the sink.

Jonty frowned at the mud tracked in by high-heeled boots. "You buffaloes can wash up before you come here tomorrow," she snapped under her breath. "I'll have Jones build a bench outside, and I'm sure I'll find another basin around here somewhere."

Her irritation at the wranglers eased somewhat when they dug into the crisp meat and feather-weight flapjacks and heartily praised her cooking skills. Everything was disappearing at an alarming rate, and she was beginning to fear that there would be nothing left for Cord, when suddenly her nemesis entered the kitchen from the hall.

She gaped at him open-mouthed. He hadn't been in his room when she retired last night. How had he gotten in without Wolf raising a ruckus? She unconsciously threw the dog an accusing look as if to say, "You let me down."

She glanced back at Cord. Amusement danced in his gray eyes when he said mockingly, "Good mornin', Jonty, did you sleep well last night?" She tossed her head, gave him a glaring look, then sat down beside Lightfoot.

"Thank you for bringing in the wood last night, Johnny," she said quietly, helping herself to flapjacks. "I was so tired I forgot all about it."

Lightfoot swallowed a mouthful of food before answering, "I can't take credit for that, Jonty. It must have been Cord."

"But Wolf would have barked . . . wouldn't he?" she faltered.

Lightfoot shook his head. "I allowed the dog to know Cord yesterday."

"But why?" Jonty's voice became dangerously high and she lowered her tone to a husky whisper before continuing, "He's the one I need protection from."

Lightfoot shook his head again. "No, Jonty, you're wrong." He sent a knowing look at Paunch, who was intent on wolfing down his breakfast. "There's your danger. Cord's sharp tongue may hurt your feelings, and he drives you too hard, but he'll never harm you despite his threats. For all his rough ways and speech, he's an honorable man."

"Well I'm not going to thank him for the wood," Jonty said crossly, not at all sure that Cord mightn't take a stick to her some day.

"He probably doesn't expect it," the Indian said and resumed eating.

The men were soon tramping outside, Cord trailing along behind them. Jonty waited for a word of praise for the tasty meal she had produced, but his only words as he passed behind her were curt.

"Have supper ready by sundown."

She pulled her eyes away from the broad back disappearing through the door and stared into her coffee. "Fool," she muttered, "did you really expect anything else?" She jumped to her feet and attacked the dirty dishes with an energy driven by anger and frustration. In short order, dishes, pots, and skillets were washed, dried, and put away. She spent close to an hour then, sweeping the floor and scrubbing away the mud stains tracked in.

Wolf whined his hunger, and after feeding him what few scraps were left over, Jonty went to her room and tidied it up. She paused in front of Cord's bedroom, debating whether or not to make up his bed, tempted not to. She remembered then that he had brought in the wood for her last night, and she pushed the door open. Do unto others . . .

It took but a few minutes to put his room to order. Besides the bed, there was only a small table sitting beside it, a lamp, and his shaving material neatly laid out. He's an orderly man, I'll give him that, she thought, looking at his clothes hung carefully on pegs in the wall. Even the soiled clothes he had discarded were folded and placed in a corner. She decided that she'd wash them when she did her own, and swept them into her arms.

She carried them through the house and out onto the back porch, where she stopped and stared. Just outside the door was a small mountain of dirty clothes. Was she expected to do the washing also? She dropped Cord's clothes on top of the others and leaned against a supporting post. She wished she knew more about ranch life—about any kind of life other than what went on in a house of prostitution. She hadn't the faintest idea what a normal life was like, how it was to live as a family.

She hugged her arms. Would she ever know? Would she ever have children? She looked down at her worn, baggy trousers. It looked a long way off.

The rooster crowed and Jonty straightened up. Time to tend her livestock. She kicked the pile of soiled clothes as she walked by. She couldn't wash them today even if she had a mind to. She had only a sliver of soap left and that was for the dishes.

Disappointingly, Jonty found no more eggs in the shed as she scattered cracked corn for the fowl. Admonishing the hens to get busy, she returned to the house and entered her bedroom. She walked to a box sitting in a corner, and squatting down beside it, opened it up. The box contained Granny's little knick-knacks, all the little pieces that had made their one large room so homey. She lifted out a figurine and, stroking it lovingly, wondered if she should put them all out at once, or one at a time. Maybe Cord wouldn't notice if they didn't all show up at once.

She rose and carried the porcelain statue of a shepherd and a lamb into the big main room. She stood a moment, then walked over to the table on which the article had rested since she could remember.

Jonty was debating putting out one more little gew-gaw when she heard hoofbeats coming toward the house. She hurried into the kitchen and frowned when she looked out the window. What was Cord doing home at this hour? She watched him swing to the ground, then tug a haunch of venison from behind the saddle. She pretended to be busy at the sink when he tramped into the house and thumped the piece of meat on the table.

"We'll have stew for supper," he said shortly and turned to leave.

"Wait a minute." Jonty followed him out onto the porch. "Is it expected that I'll wash those?" She motioned toward the pile of dirty laundry.

"It is." Cord frowned at her impatiently, wanting to be on his way.

"Well, I can't do it." Jonty shoved her hands in her pockets and leaned against the wall, not at all sure it was her job to do the wash. "I haven't any soap."

Cord swung onto the stallion's broad back. "Take them down to the river and scrub them with sand the way the Indian women do it." He gave her a satanic smile as he touched spurs to the mount and galloped away.

Jonty indignantly watched Cord until he disappeared into the thick stand of ponderosa pine that grew down from the foothills. "Scrub them with sand," she mocked his taunting tone, then turned back into the kitchen and began cutting the venison into small pieces for the stew.

"I'll roast the rest," she said to the dog who watched her hungrily. "With a big portion for you." She patted Wolf's silky head.

It came to Jonty as wolf whined that he'd probably prefer his share of the meat raw. Most likely he was used to hunting his own food, and that no-doubt pleasurable effort for him had been taken away from him now that he had to stay with her all the time.

A few minutes later, Jonty was carrying a pan filled with chunks of bloody meat out onto the porch, Wolf dancing around her feet, his eyes eager. She watched the dog attack the meat, then went back inside to set the stew to simmering.

As the house filled with the rich aroma of the stew, liberally laced with dried herbs from the jar Jonty had brought from Abilene, she decided to inspect the immediate grounds around the house.

The place had many possibilities, she thought, visualizing grass around the house instead of dirt and weeds, the sagging porch mended and flowers blooming around it. The thought of flowers brought a glimmer of tears to her eyes as she remembered the wild ones she had picked for Granny's grave.

Jonty knuckled her eyes dry. She musn't think back. Somehow she must look forward.

As she wandered around the big log house, she came to a narrow path running through the weeds and she and Wolf followed it. It led them shortly to a shallow cave from which the spring Lightfoot spoke of flowed out, then trickled down the valley.

"What a perfect place to keep perishable food supplies, Wolf," she exclaimed, stepping into the cool, rock-walled enclosure. "All it needs is a stout wooden door to keep the wild varmints out."

She dropped to her knees and started scooping sand and gravel out of the small pool where the water formed before running outside. She lost track of time as she worked at widening the pool and walling it with the smooth, flat rocks that lay around her in plentiful supply.

She looked up, startled, when a tall shadow fell over her. "I've been looking all over for you, Jonty." Lightfoot frowned down at her. "Didn't you hear me calling you?"

"My goodness, what time is it?" Jonty jumped to her feet, wiping her hands down her hips.

"Time you got back to the kitchen, I'm thinking. The men will be here within the hour, hungry as bears."

As they walked back to the house, Jonty explained what she had been doing, and why. "Don't you think it's a good idea, Johnny?"

"Yes it is," Lightfoot answered, then gave a short, dry laugh. "And one that McBain can't find fault with, although it will gripe him."

"Yes, isn't it wonderful." Jonty smiled gleefully, but then her face sobered. "I wonder how long he'll drag his heels before he has the door made?"

"I don't think too long. He mentioned to Jones when we arrived that the house needed some mending, that it should be done before long. Jones is right handy with hammer and saw."

"Good." Jonty nodded and hurried on to the house. Cord would skin her alive if supper wasn't ready on time.

The valley was lost in shadows and Jonty was spooning dumpling mix into the stew when the men rode in. She put the lid back on the pot and went to stand in the doorway. She had put out towels and water, and she meant to see to it that the men used them.

She didn't move out of the way when Red would have pushed past her, Jones on his heels. "There's no soap, men." She stood solidly when Red gave her a nudge. "And you'll have to use the pail until I can unearth another basin. Do the best you can until then."

"Hey." Red chuckled. "I think the kid is tellin' us we got to wash up out here."

"I'd just as soon." Jones stepped back and walked over to the pail. "A feller can splash all he wants to out here."

"Well the runt ain't gonna make me wash out of a pail," Paunch growled and gave Jonty a hard shove that sent her reeling back into the kitchen. But before he could step over the threshold, Lightfoot grabbed him by the arm, jerked him around, and sent him stumbling off the porch. His face tight with anger, the Indian hopped down beside Paunch.

"Come on, fat man," he said threateningly. "Shove me. I'm more your size."

"Now look, Lightfoot." Paunch backed off. "I ain't got no quarrel with you. I just don't think the kid has a right to tell us grown men what to do."

"A kid he might be, but he is the cook, and he is the law in the kitchen. If he don't want it slopped up, it's his right to say so."

"He's right, Paunch." Jones brought his dripping face up from the pail and reached for a towel. "The kid's boss in there."

"And his cookin' is too good to get him riled." Red took Jones's place at the pail. "I ain't ate this good since my Ma used to cook for me."

His face sullen, but knowing he was out-counted, the fat man shrugged his shoulders in acceptance.

Jonty had ladled out the stew and the men had dug in when Cord stepped into the kitchen. She grew nervous, her palms sweaty. What if he started washing up at the sink? Would she have the nerve to stop him?

She sighed her relief when Cord walked past the sink and took his place at the table. Her hands still shook a little as she filled his plate from the pot and moved the bread in front of him. She sat down next to Lightfoot and touched her knee to his in silent thanks.

There was no talking as the men appeased their hunger. Then, as they drank their coffee, Cord spoke. "I don't suppose one of you men would care to make a trip into Abilene for me?"

"What do you need from there?" Red asked, rolling a cigarette. "You needin' yourself a whore?" He looked up and grinned at Cord.

Only Jonty noticed how Paunch brightened up and sat forward.

Cord laughed along with the others at Red's sly question. "Come to think of it, I wouldn't say no to one. However, I need somethin' more important. I forgot to bring along a supply of horseshoes. Rawhide threw a shoe this afternoon."

"What about Cottonwood?" Jones asked. "It's closer, only about fifteen miles."

"I just got back from there. They don't have a blacksmith and the store was out of them."

Everyone looked their surprise when lazy Paunch said that he would go to Abilene. "In fact," he said, "I'll head out right now."

Cord didn't look too pleased at the fat man's offer.

"I want the trip made fast, Paunch," he warned. "No takin' a couple days visitin' the whorehouses."

Paunch raised a beefy hand. "I won't even stay overnight. I swear it."

"All right," Cord agreed finally. "Thanks."

Paunch gulped down his coffee and was gone without another word. The men looked at each other with raised eyebrows when only minutes later there came the sound of hoofbeats pounding down the valley.

"He's in one hell of a hurry to get to ole Lucy," Red said, standing up and stretching. "That's the reason he agreed to go so quickly."

When it looked as if Cord would leave the table also, Jonty spoke quickly before she lost her nerve. "Cord, with just a little work, that spring back of the house could be turned into a perfect place to keep meat. It's really cold in there."

Cord's firm mouth took on a sardonic slant. "Always the little housewife, huh, Jonty?"

"It's a good idea," Jonty claimed defensively, "even if I was the one to think of it."

"The kid has a point there, Cord." Jones set his empty cup down. "I've been back in that cave and it's cold, just like he said. The water that comes out from under a rock chilled my teeth when I took a drink of it." He stood up and reached for his hat lying under the bench. "Meat would keep for a couple weeks in there. We wouldn't have to go huntin' so often."

Cord sent Jonty a look that said, "You've won again." The look was also tinged with the message not to push him too far. He stood up and muttered to Jones, "Make a door for it when you find the time," then left the house.

"Walk quietly around him for a while, Jonty," Lightfoot advised as he too stood up to follow the others outside. "He won't bend to any more requests any time soon."

Jonty knew this was true as she washed the dishes and cleaned the table and stove. She sighed softly.

And there was so much more she wanted done, like a pen for her chickens. It wasn't good for them to be shut up in that dark shed all the time. Maybe she could coax Jones into doing something when he made the door for the cave.

She stepped out on the back porch for a breath of fresh air before retiring. She stared down at the valley, now wrapped in a gray blanket of fog, and wondered if others had stood in the dark gazing down at the lonely-looking place—the rangers, travelers, trappers, soldiers, and missionaries who were the first Americans to come westward in 1779. What brave, tough people her ancestors were.

Jonty turned to walk back inside and almost stumbled over a long, flat package lying on the edge of the porch. Curious, she squatted down and unfolded the brown, heavy paper. She sat back on her heels, gripped with surprise. Before her lay several bars of yellow lye soap, a scrub board, and a long length of rope neatly coiled—everything she needed to wash the clothes and hang them to dry.

What an inconsistent man, this Cord McBain, her guardian, was. First he hatefully told her to use sand, then he turned around and brought her soap. She shook her head in bemusement. She would like to thank him, but knew she daren't. It would only draw some hateful response from him, words that would slash like a whip.

She pulled the package over against the wall, then went inside and on to bed.

CHAPTER 8

THE WEEK FOLLOWING PAUNCH'S DEPARTURE FOR ABILENE was a noisy one at the ranch, as Jones began mending roofs and sagging porches and securing window frames and shutters that hung askew. The big house gradually took on a look of respectable stability.

Making a door for the cave was the next job Jones took on, while Jonty swept the stone floor clean of all debris. Red and Lightfoot carried in large, flat-topped rocks on which crocks and pans could be placed. When the door of sturdy pine posts was fastened to the cavern entrance, Jonty felt like doing a little Indian dance she'd learned from her young friends back in Kansas.

She did do a few little hops, making Lightfoot's somber face twitch with a half-smile, when Jones solved the problem of sunshine for her chickens.

It was a simple operation—he just put half a roof on the shed. He explained that when it rained or snowed and when it came roosting time, the fowl could go into the sheltered side. In the daytime they could sun themselves in the open area.

It was Red's suggestion that turned the long building into an ideal chicken house. "You need to put up some roostin' poles for them ole layers, Jones. They like to be up high like the birds when they sleep."

"That's right," Jonty agreed, remembering how in Abilene Granny's pets had at dusk taken to the big cottonwood in the back yard of Nellie's place.

"And the hens need some layin' boxes," Red pointed out. "With some hay in them so the eggs don't break when the ole cluckers let them drop."

Jones scratched his sweating, balding head. "I ain't never built anything like that before. You'll have to give me a hand, Red."

"Sure, I'll be glad to," the ex-farm boy agreed readily.

So Jonty knew a near contentment that warm noonday as she busied herself ironing the basket of shirts and trousers that had taken her two days to wash.

Her serene feeling wasn't to last long, however. She had just finished pressing one of Cord's shirts when she heard hoofbeats approaching the house. Who could be coming up from the valley? she wondered, bringing an arm across her sweating brow. The men were chasing horses up in the mountain today.

"Oh, no!" she whispered as the mounts came to a halt at the back porch and a gravely female voice called out, "Surprise, Cord! I've come to visit you a spell."

Jonty set the iron back on the stove to keep hot and ran to the window to peek outside. She hadn't known that Cord was around, and she watched his face as he walked toward Lucy and Paunch. The frown on his forehead said that he wasn't pleased at the whore's unexpected arrival.

When he made no move to help the woman dismount, Paunch hurried to do so. When Lucy would have embraced Cord, he put out his hands, warding

her off, his nose twitching distastefully. "So, Paunch."
He eyed the fat man with a cool look. "You've brought
yourself back a bed partner."

"Not just for myself, Cord." Paunch smiled ingrati-
atingly. "I figured we'd all share her—share the
expense."

Jonty giggled at the angry frown that crept over
Lucy's coarse features. Being shared did not appeal to
her. She wanted only Cord. She waited with held
breath for Cord's response to Paunch's suggestion.

"Lucy's comin' here is none of my doin'," Cord
answered shortly. "Maybe the other men will kick in,
but count me out. If I need her services occasionally,
I'll pay for it just like I did when she was whorin' for
Nellie."

"Hell, Cord!" Paunch slammed his hat on the
ground. "You know damn well that Jones and the
Indian won't be interested. That leaves just me and
Red. Nellie wanted a bundle for lettin' Lucy come out
here for a month."

"Knowing you—and Red—you'll both get your
money's worth," Cord said.

"But, Cord." Lucy siddled up to him, her big,
unfettered breasts bouncing with each step. "After I
take a bath, wouldn't you like to rest with me for
awhile?"

Cord looked down into the painted face, sweat-
smeared now, and was surprised that the woman
didn't interest him in the least. Actually, now that he
thought about it, her gross and lewd behavior in bed
hadn't been stimulating to him for some time. Without realizing it, he had been wanting a little tenderness in the sexual act.

He was about to turn down Lucy's offer when from
the corner of his eye he glimpsed Jonty lurking beside
the window. He couldn't resist the temptation to rile
the lad. Smiling down at the whore, he said lazily, "I
wonder how much rest we'd get. I've been a long time
without a woman."

Jonty flinched at Lucy's shrill, pleased laughter. She

hurried back to her ironing when the woman demanded to see the inside of the house and stepped up on the porch, not waiting for Cord's permission.

"Well, Jonty," Lucy sneered as she stepped into the kitchen, "I see Cord has you doin' what you're good at. Wimmen's work."

Jonty didn't bother to look up or answer the slur. But her eyes and ears followed the pair down the hallway to the bedrooms. Her body stiffened when she heard Lucy wheedle, "Can we rest in this bed, Cord? It looks so soft and comfortable."

"Damn them," Jonty swore, "they're in my room and it's my bed the sow wants to lust in." She slammed the iron back on the stove and rushed down the hall.

Cord was on the point of refusing Lucy's request when Jonty burst into the room. But when he saw the fire gathering in Jonty's eyes, devilish amusement kindled in his. And Jonty, seeing this, told herself in desperation that he was going to let the whore have her way. Just for spite he was going to take the hateful woman into her bed!

A black fury came over Jonty, forming her mouth in a tight line. No, by God, he was not going to desecrate Granny's bed! Standing with unconscious dignity, her blue eyes flashing scorn, she spoke through clenched teeth.

"No whore is going to wallow around in my grandmother's bed. I'll burn it first."

"Now just a damn minute." Cord took a step toward Jonty. "You keep a civil tongue in your head, young man, or I'll take a stick to you."

Suddenly it was all too much for Jonty. She was hot and sweaty from standing over a hot iron for four hours, and she was sick to death of Cord's threats. This last insult about to be laid upon her was more than she could bear. Recklessly, she started yelling:

"Take a stick, take a stick, that's all I hear! Well, take a stick and be damned! Better yet, take a stick and sit on its sharp end."

There was a stunned silence for a long moment, Cord gaping at Jonty and she mute with the realization that she had let her anger run away with her tongue. She had ruined all chance of keeping the big bed inviolate.

Cord finally opened his mouth to speak, then Lucy was cutting him off, her shrill voice demanding, "Are you gonna let that little bastard talk to you that way, Cord?" Before Cord could answer, she lunged at Jonty with her riding quirt.

Her lifted arm never delivered its blow. With the lithe speed and grace of an animal, Jonty rushed to meet the bigger, slower woman. The momentum of her charge bore Lucy to the floor where she landed with a loud grunt. She let out an ear-splitting screech when slim, strong fingers fastened in her hair and bounced her head up and down on the floor.

Cord watched the pair, laughter tugging at his lips as Jonty continued to thump the whore's frowsy head and she continued to screech out swear words that most men wouldn't use. But when Jonty drew back a small fist and aimed it at the enraged face beneath her, Cord barked out, "That's enough, Jonty." Grabbing her by the belt, he lifted her off the struggling woman.

"Come on, Lucy." He helped the whore to her feet, then steered her toward the door. "Let him have the bed if he feels that strongly about it. You'll like the bunkhouse better."

"But there's two other bedrooms." Lucy held back, throwing Jonty a murderous look. "I see no reason . . ."

"There'll be livelier company for you out there with the men," Cord cut in, pushing her ahead of him. "I for one am tired of the present company. Besides," he joked, "you wouldn't want all that holiness of his to rub off on you, would you?"

Jonty stood in the middle of the room, breathing heavily, listening to the giggles and low laughter disappear down the hall. "Oh how I hate his wicked laughter," she sobbed, throwing herself on the bed, her hot tears soaking the bright quilt.

Jonty lay on the bed until dusk began to fill the room, listening to the low hum of conversation and an occasional laugh from the bunkhouse. I'd better get supper started, she thought. The hungry buffaloes will be tramping in soon.

She was knuckling her eyes, preparing to rise, when Cord's voice, rough with impatience, washed over her. "For God's sake, are you blubberin'?"

Giving thanks for the semi-darkness so that this harsh man couldn't see her red, swollen eyes, she snapped, "No, I'm not *blubberin'*. I fell asleep for a while."

Cord gave a short disgusted snort. "Naps are for the weaker sex," he said derisively. "Don't get in the habit of it. Maggie might have allowed it, but there's be no time for laziness on a horse ranch."

Finally his verbal abuse ceased. But Jonty knew from past experience that he waited for her to make a rebuttal so that he could lay into her again. So, she reasoned, if she remained silent and gave him no opening, he'd go away. She lay quietly, hardly breathing, praying that she could wait him out. The fussing of her hens as they prepared to roost drifted through the open window.

A cold nervous sweat had gathered in Jonty's palms when finally Cord grated, "I expect supper to be on the table within an hour." When she made no response, his boot heels beat an angry sound on the floor as he stamped to the door, then slammed it shut behind him.

Jonty grinned widely. That's one for me!

The venison roast, mashed potatoes, and beans were eaten rapidly, especially by Paunch and Red, who were eager to get Lucy back to the bunkhouse. As Paunch had complained that they wouldn't, Jones and Lightfoot weren't interested in sharing the whore. Consequently, he and Red would have to bear the cost of her favors—unless, of course, Cord chipped in once in a while.

"What about it, Cord?" Paunch pushed away from the table. "You gonna be down at the bunkhouse tonight?"

Cord looked through his lashes at Jonty's scowling face. After a moment he said carelessly, "Hell, why not. It's been a long, tiring day for me, too. Might as well make a day of it." He slid Jonty another glance from the corners of his eyes as he followed the men outside, Lucy clinging to his arm.

But once outside in the darkness, away from the reach of the kerosene light shining through the window, he pulled away from Lucy. "Go along with the men," he said. "I want to check on my stallion."

"Don't be too long." Lucy stroked a hand down his arm. "We'll have us a high old time."

Cord watched her hurry away toward the lighted bunkhouse, stumbling over rocks in her high-heeled slippers and haste. He shook his head, feeling sorry for Jones and Lightfoot. The pair wouldn't get much sleep tonight with the rutting Paunch and Red would be involved in.

He walked to the stables, and ten minutes later he had Rawhide saddled and was riding down the valley at an easy lope. He sighed his relief. The stallion moved easily, his new shoe fitting him perfectly.

The moon hadn't risen yet, but a billion stars shone brightly, casting a soft glow over the grassy lowland and turning the flowing Sweetwater to a silver sheen. "Damn the kid," Cord muttered in the night quietness, "already he's interfering in the way I live. Hell, I can't even ride a whore without feeling guilty about it."

As the stallion loped on, he didn't remind himself that he had no desire for Lucy, that he'd had to walk up-wind of her to avoid the stench wafting off her body.

* * *

Jonty was up at her usual time the next morning, her heart strangely light. Cord hadn't spent any time with Lucy last night. She had seen him ride out, and had sat in the darkness of her bedroom waiting for his return, a question drumming in her mind. Would he come straight to bed, or would he go to the bunk-house?

She had sat on the edge of the bed for close to an hour when she heard Rawhide's heavy hooves returning. She ran down the hall and into the kitchen where she could see the corral through the window. Her heart gave a leap of gladness when, shortly, she saw Cord coming to the house. She came near to knocking over a chair in her hurry to get back to her bedroom.

She was curled under her blanket when he entered the kitchen and walked quietly down the hall and entered the room next to hers.

Jones and Lightfoot were bleary-eyed from broken rest all night when they entered the kitchen next morning, but Red and Paunch were red-eyed. It was plain the pair hadn't slept at all. Cord shot them a disgusted look as they took their places at the table.

"Made regular hogs of yourselves, huh?" he said shortly.

A leer lifted Paunch's thick lips, but Red blushed in embarrassment.

"Might say we did, huh, Red?" The fat man poked the young wrangler in the ribs with his elbow. "Ole Lucy was in fine shape."

"Well, you two aren't." Cord looked at them stonily. "And if the two of you show up here another morning dragged out like you are now, I'll send your bed partner back to Abilene so fast your back teeth will fall out. I'll have no slackenin' off of work.

"And another thing." Cord helped himself to fried potatoes. "I don't want her stink carried into the house. You'll scrub yourselves up in the river from now on before sittin' down to breakfast."

While Paunch glowered and Red stared into his

plate, Jones raised a complaint. "Me and Lightfoot don't appreciate bein' kept awake all night with their thumpin' and poundin' and Lucy's squealin'."

Cord sighed and ran agitated fingers through his sun-streaked hair. "There's an empty bedroom if you men don't mind sleepin' in your bedrolls. At least it will be quiet." Jones and Lightfoot said that they'd move in as soon as they finished eating.

A few minutes later, they were all filing out of the kitchen. Jonty stood up and began stacking the dirty dishes. "Should I save anything for Lucy?" she wondered out loud. Then Wolf nudged her hand. "To hell with her—huh, boy?" She patted the shaggy head, then scraped all the leftovers into the dog's pan. Let the slut make her own breakfast.

Jonty quickly washed up, then with a soft song on her lips, she made up her bed and entered Cord's room.

It was when she was picking up his discarded clothing that she broke off her song. Her brow pulled into a frown as she asked herself why she should be so happy that Cord hadn't slept with Lucy last night. It was nothing to her if he slept with a dozen whores.

By the time she had the room in order, Jonty had convinced herself that her high spirits came from knowing that Lucy would have her nose out of joint because Cord had abandoned her.

Jonty continued to sing as she fed her chickens and collected two more eggs to add to her batch in the tin can; she had six now. Soon she'd have enough to let the broody hen sit on them. Finally, as she led Buttercup out of the barn and staked her in a patch of grass, she ordered herself to stop being so pleased with herself. Lucy wouldn't be all that cross with Cord. After all, she had Paunch and Red to keep her company.

But Lucy *was* mad. She was furious, Jonty discovered when she walked into the kitchen a little while later. The woman's eyes, almost glazed with hate, glared at her from her seat at the table. "You little bastard," she started right in, "you're real pleased with yourself, ain't you? Goin' round smilin' and singin'."

When Jonty ignored the heated outburst, concerning herself only with setting a large pot of beans to soak, Lucy's anger grew until her face was beet-red. She glared at Jonty, and the desire to leap at the slender figure and beat it into the floor was as plain as though it had been written on her forehead.

Stirring sugar into her coffee, Lucy muttered, as though to herself, "I wouldn't have thought in a million years that Cord McBain would ever want to bed a man."

Jonty hid a pleased smile. Her silence was a better weapon than any words she could say. She felt the whore's small eyes boring into her back as she silently assembled the ingredients for a dried-apple pie and gave a slight start when Lucy demanded suspiciously, "He does still think you're male, don't he?"

"Oh, yes." Jonty broke her silence. "Do you want me to tell him?" she questioned shrewdly, knowing that was the last thing the jealous woman wanted.

She wasn't surprised when Lucy ignored her question, but her eyes did widen when Lucy said slyly, "I've heard it hinted that you and LaTour are lovers. How does he feel about you bein' here with Cord, his maybe findin' out you're a girl?"

Did Nellie and the girls think that? Jonty wondered as she rolled out a circle of pie dough. Or was it only in Lucy's dirty mind? She didn't bother to respond, only shrugged her shoulders indifferently.

"He'll come after Cord, you know, if that happens." Lucy stirred her coffee faster and faster. "And that breed is deadly with that knife of his. He's sliced up a lot of men with it." She paused, her eyes calculating. "If you care anything for Cord, you'll send him to the bunkhouse tonight."

A mixture of mirth and anger warred inside Jonty. The dumb bitch, trying to appeal to her conscience. She hid her mischievous smile and, feigning indifference, said, "Uncle Jim wouldn't come after Cord. He likes him. He'd be happy to share with Cord if it should come to that."

She turned her head to look at the stunned woman. Her blue eyes showing a sham seriousness then, she added, "You see, Uncle Jim is gone so much of the time, he understands that I might . . . you know . . . need comfort once in a while."

Lucy's hatred reached across the table, hitting Jonty like a slap in the face. "You little bastard," she ground out, "I'll fix you, see if I don't." She jumped to her feet and stamped out of the kitchen, slamming the door so hard the window rattled.

All levity left Jonty. What had she done? Why had she let her foolish tongue run on like that? Lucy could take those carelessly spoken words and twist them anyway she wanted to. What kind of story might she tell Cord? A whimper of dread escaped her lips.

CHAPTER 9

AS JONTY WASHED THE SUPPER DISHES AND MOPPED THE kitchen floor, she hummed a bawdy song, learned at Nellie's pleasure house. Two days had passed since her run-in with Lucy, and Cord hadn't asked her about it yet. Evidently the whore was waiting for the right time. In the meantime, she was playing up to Red, hoping to make Cord jealous.

Jonty put the mop pail away and walked out onto the front porch to join the others sitting there. Lightfoot's dark face stirred in a welcoming smile as he patted the space beside him. When she lowered her tired body next to his lean one, Wolf trotted over and crowded in between her and Jones.

"Don't that damn dog ever let you out of his sight?" Paunch eyed the dog with distaste. "He even follows you when you go to take a leak."

"He's my friend." Jonty stroked the big head planted in her lap. "My protector." Her eyes challenged the fat man.

"Well, he's damned dangerous." Paunch's eyes narrowed angrily at Jonty's clear warning. "I don't know why you let him hang around, Cord."

"Don't let the animal bother you," Cord said lazily, leaning back against a supporting post. "Just watch your step around the kid and he'll not bother you."

The second subtle warning in as many seconds was not lost on Paunch. He dropped the subject and transfered his attention to Lucy and Red, who sat apart from the others at the other end of the porch. He peered a moment into the near darkness, then sat forward, his fat-squinted eyes glittering.

Jonty looked to see what had captured his interest, then hurriedly looked away, her cheeks blushing scarlet. Lucy had the young man's trousers undone and was openly fondling him. Her fast glance had showed that Red was caught in a dilemma. He didn't like this public display, but if he should push Lucy's hand away, he chanced making her angry and thus losing her to Paunch for the rest of the night.

A sudden silence told Jonty that the others had noted what was going on but, unlike herself, they were amused at Red's awkward situation. She peeked at Cord and saw that he was grinning as widely as the others.

Curiosity drew her eyes back to the couple when Lucy released a loud, lewd laugh. Despite Red's unease and embarrassment, he had been unable to control the arousal that now filled the whore's hand. At her gasp, Lightfoot spoke, putting finish to whatever the whore intended.

"Red," he warned tightly, "I think it's time you took that heated bitch into the woods and cooled her off. If you don't, I'll dump her into the river."

Blushing furiously, Red stood up, and while the others looked at the Indian in surprise, he jerked Lucy up beside him. As he led her in the direction of the bunkhouse, she giggling and shooting inviting looks at Cord, Lightfoot called after them, "And keep her there until she can't move."

As the pair disappeared into the darkness, Paunch

heaved his great bulk off the floor. "The kid will never wear that one out," he snickered. "I'll just go along with them, give him a hand, take turns at the bitch."

Four pair of eyes watched the fat man walk away, his fingers unbuttoning his fly. Without thinking, Jonty remarked, "Uncle Jim said he wouldn't bed Lucy in a fit."

She immediately wanted to clamp her hand to her mouth, push the words back down her throat. In the uneasy silence that gathered, she peeked at Cord, then dropped her lids against his scowling face. She had unintentionally insulted him. She opened her mouth to apologize, to explain that she hadn't meant any insult, but Cord was on his feet, his gray eyes like storm clouds. Glaring down at her, he said through clenched teeth, "I'm sure *Uncle* Jim wouldn't be interested in beddin' a whore. Or any other woman for that matter, as long as he has you." At Jones's startled indrawn breath, he stalked away.

Jonty stared after him, pain clouding her eyes. When Jones laid a comforting hand on her shoulder and said, "Don't pay any attention to him, kid," Lightfoot sprang to his feet.

"Damn your soul, McBain," he yelled, "you're way wide of the mark. Jonty is just as normal as you are. You'll find that out some day."

Cord kept on walking, disappearing up the mountain trail. The Indian stood a minute, hands on hips, watching him out of sight before sitting back down. "As sure as the sun comes up in the east, I'm going to take my knife and whittle some on that man someday."

Jones shook his head in bemusement. "Cord has sure changed since I saw him a year ago. I don't understand him half the time." He looked at Jonty. "Whether you meant to or not, that was a pretty hard jab you gave him about Lucy. Kinda put him down like, suggestin' LaTour is the better man."

Jonty looked dispiritedly into the darkness. "I

didn't mean to. I just remembered that Uncle Jim had said that once and it just tumbled out of my mouth."

An owl's hoot echoed through the trees, its mournful sound intensifying Jonty's despondency. Her heart and body felt leaden as she stood up, said a quiet good-night, and walked into the house.

The morning was cool, the air keen and sweet, but the sky gave promise of another hot day as Jonty gazed out the kitchen window. In her direct vision was the corral full of neighing, stomping horses, their heads uplifted, regarding the wranglers who approached them with wild, distrusting eyes. Each time a man got too close they'd wheel and move out of range.

Jonty smiled. Every morning was the same. Eventually each rider would catch a mount, throw a saddle on him, and carefully climb onto his back. After a plunge or two, to test the rider, the mustang would then settle down, and after that be easy to control.

When the men rode off, saddles creaking, bits jangling, and puffs of dirt rising from shod hooves, Jonty turned from the window with a heavy sigh. How cool and aloof Cord's eyes had been this morning whenever their gazes happened to meet. He was still smarting from her unfortunate remark last night. Earlier, before the others had come in for breakfast, Lightfoot had tried to lessen her depression by saying that in his opinion, Cord was embarrassed that he had ever lain with Lucy and his anger was actually directed more toward himself than at her.

But be that as it might, Jonty thought unhappily, Cord still thought of her as being unnatural, a degenerate. He probably had more respect for the depraved Lucy than he had for her.

As Jonty set about mixing a bowl of sourdough to rise in a warm place, her mind turned to Jim LaTour. Where was he and how long would she have to wait before she could go to him? Not too much longer, she hoped, for a tension was building inside her that was bound to break free any day. She could not repress much longer the young woman who clamored to be free.

As her brain went around and around with the same questions, she finally told herself to stop fretting about things she couldn't change at the moment and concentrate on those that she could. She would work in the yard, pull the weeds that grew almost to the porch. She was sure snakes and lizards lurked in the tall growth, maybe even coyotes at night.

"I'll need to put on a hat," she muttered. "A person could get sunstroke out there." She moved down the hall toward her room and barely kept from bumping into Lucy backing out it. While Wolf growled threateningly, she asked sharply, "Why are you snooping around in my room? You won't find Cord in there."

"I didn't think I would." Lucy brushed past Jonty and, sticking her chin in the air, swayed her broad hips in the direction of the kitchen.

Jonty turned and followed her enemy, amusement twitching her lips. She had caught the disconcerted flicker in the small pale eyes. Maybe the whore hadn't expected to find Cord there, but she had been looking for some tell-tale evidence that he was in the habit of spending the night in the big four-poster.

"So why were you in my room?" Jonty persisted, going to the small pump and filling a basin with water. "Did you think you'd find something worth stealing? I have no jewelry or face paint."

Lucy plunked her big rear down on a bench. "I was lookin' for a comb." She poured herself a cup of coffee from the pot that had grown cold hours ago. "I lost mine." She grimaced after sipping the stale brew.

Jonty slid a contemptuous look over Lucy's brassy, matted hair. "You leave my comb alone. I don't want head lice in *my* hair."

"Why you little—" Lucy lunged to her feet, then just as quickly sat down.

"Are you two at it again?" Cord's cool question sliced through the tense air.

"Pretty boy won't lend me his comb, Cord." Lucy's thick lips drooped in a pout. "Tell him to let me use it."

Cord raked his eyes from Lucy's tangled, greasy hair to Jonty's healthy, shiny curls. Pumping himself a glass of water, he said before lifting it to his lips, "I wouldn't let you put *mine* through that mess you call hair."

While Lucy spluttered, red-faced, Jonty's shoulders shook with silent laughter. Cord's answer wasn't the one the fat sow had expected. Nor had she, actually. Generally he enjoyed siding against Jonty Rand.

Although there was no friendliness in his voice, Jonty was further surprised when he ordered, "Go saddle your mare, Jonty. You can ride with me while I check out a dry-wash a few miles from here. I saw horse tracks leading into it yesterday."

"Oh, Cord, can I come too?" Lucy leaned forward eagerly. "I get tired of always bein' in the bunkhouse."

Cord looked at her and said dryly, "No one told you to stay inside all the time. There's plenty of work around here that would keep you outside. You could help Jonty with his chores," he drawled mockingly.

"I'm not here to do chores," Lucy flared. When Cord shrugged indifferently, she calmed down and coaxed, "Let me come along, Cord. I'd be much better company than sissified Jonty."

"I'm not lookin' to be entertained, Lucy," Cord said coolly. "I'm takin' Jonty so that he can start learnin' the area for when he starts workin' with the men. But if you want to come with us that badly, you're welcome."

Lucy's eyes brightened and her lips smiled. "How is your herd comin' along?" She fawned, getting up and coming around the table to sit next to Cord. "You've been puttin' in so many long hours."

Cord ignored her question as he slid her a look, his nose wrinkling. "You'd better take a dip in the river pretty soon, woman. You're beginnin' to smell like Paunch."

Jonty couldn't suppress a giggle at the woman's angry start. She quickly choked it back, however, when Lucy sent her a malignant look, warning her that retribution wasn't long off. For a moment, she had forgotten the tale the whore could tell the man sitting next to her.

Cord spoke, breaking into her uncomfortable thoughts. "Saddle a mount for Lucy, too, Jonty, then let's get goin'. I got no time to waste."

Jonty looked anything but happy as she went to the barn to carry out Cord's bidding. She had foolishly thought that her job as cook was secure, that Cord was pleased enough with what she put on the table twice a day to keep her in that position. But his earlier remark proved her wrong. Sooner or later, she would be out chasing the wild ones.

She had Beauty saddled and had just struggled a saddle onto the larger horse Lucy had arrived on, when the pair joined her. She stood waiting, holding each horse by the bit, breathing a little hard from exertion, a film of sweat on her forehead. Without looking at her, Cord jerked a thumb over his shoulder and ordered:

"Lock the dog up in the house. If the herd is still in the canyon, I don't want him spookin' them, scarin' them out of the area."

Wolf whined piteously as Jonty dragged him into the house, and as she closed the door she had the distinct sensation that it was a big mistake leaving the dog behind, that before the day was over she'd have desperate need of his protection. When Cord called impatiently for her to get a move on, she told herself that she was just being fanciful and hurried to swing into the saddle. After all, what could happen to her with Cord along?

For close to an hour Cord led the women straight up the mountain. The air was soft and still and Jonty breathed deep of the thick, hot pine scent. Gradually, as they climbed, the forest thickened, the trees grew larger and the shade darker. Jonty's gaze roamed continuously. She loved this land, the silent places, the solemn mountain, even the animals of this wild and lonely land. She would miss it when she left.

Finally the three arrived at a level spot, a place dotted with wide benches of pine and spruce. Cord led on, traversing the level ground until once again the trail led downward. Another few minutes and he was pulling in the stallion and saying excitedly in a low voice, "There, take a look down in that canyon."

Jonty leaned forward in the saddle and stared down at a stallion and his harem of shaggy-coated mares browsing peacefully in a wide area of "bunch grass." The sun struck fire off the stallion's red coat, and she exclaimed in awe, "What a handsome animal."

"He's handsome all right," Cord agreed. "I'll keep him for stud. He'll sire some fancy ridin' stock. The rich gents back east would pay plenty to own somethin' like him."

They watched the magnificent animal a few moments longer, then Cord said, "I'm goin' down for a closer look. You two stay here and don't make a sound. And be alert that your mounts don't whistle a signal."

He lifted the reins and started Rawhide down the hard-packed trail. Soon he was lost from view among the trees. Jonty shifted her gaze to where he should reappear any moment. Beauty's ears twitched and she leaned forward to clamp her hand against the little mare's nostrils.

It was then that she heard the whistle of the whip as Lucy brought it snapping across Beauty's tender rump. The mare let out an agonized scream, and Jonty, caught off guard, could only grasp the reins and hang on as the little animal bolted and ran madly down the slope, heading straight for the herd of wild horses.

Her hat flew off and her curls tossed wildly, and tears stung her cheeks in the wind created by Beauty's racing hooves. She dimly saw the herd scatter as the mare thundered among them. She heard Cord's angry shout but could do nothing about it. Beauty was running out of control.

Jonty felt her grip on the reins slipping, and knew that soon she would lose her seat. And when she did, she would probably be trampled to death beneath the churning hooves. Then from behind her came the sound of other galloping hooves, and she breathed a thankful sigh when lean brown fingers clutched the bridle and fought the little mare to a winded halt.

She slumped in the saddle, her whole being trembling from the exhaustion of trying to hold the mount in. She looked at Cord to thank him, then cringed at the fury in his face.

"What in the hell do you think you're doin'?" He swung from the saddle, reached up and grabbed her arm, and with one hard jerk she was on the ground. She staggered, reached for Beauty to steady herself, then cried, "Oh, no!"

From rump to mid-flank, there was a long strip of opened flesh on her little pet. Her shocked eyes followed the rivulet of blood running down the delicate, graceful leg. "Oh, Beauty," she whispered, "what has that dreadful woman done to you?"

She spun around at the sound of an approaching mount. Rage burned in her like fire as Lucy scrambled to the ground and hurried to Cord. "I'll kill her!" she ground between her teeth and rushed toward the whore with fingers curved, ready to claw the fleshy face.

Jonty was brought up short of her victim by Cord's lean body barring her way. Lucy, her eyes innocently wide, was crying, "I couldn't stop him, Cord. We were just sitting there when suddenly he said, real mean-like, 'I think I'll rile the bastard a little.' Before I knew it, he brought his whip down across that poor animal's rump and raced away."

At first Jonty was too stunned to respond to the blatant lie, then rage thickened her tongue so, she couldn't utter a denial, couldn't point out that she never used a whip on Beauty, that she didn't even own one.

When finally her tongue was loosened and she opened her mouth to prove Lucy a liar, Cord's arm lashed out, the back of his hand connecting hard against her lips. She reeled, tried to balance herself, but finally hit the ground. She sat there, blood trickling out of the corner of her mouth, pain and bitterness battling each other as she stared up at the unrelenting hardness on Cord's face. In his eyes, and mistaken belief, she had done the unforgivable. She had unnecessarily struck a helpless animal.

"You can't believe that I did this to Beauty!" Her fast swelling lips trembled. "I love her. Besides, I don't even have a—"

Cord took a threatening step toward her, the cold fire shooting out of his eyes stopping her in mid-sentence. "Don't say a word." He glared down at her. "You're lucky I don't lather hell out of you, you revengeful little devil. The only reason I don't is, I might kill you if I got started."

He turned from Jonty then, as though he couldn't bear the sight of her. Picking up the stallion's reins, along with Beauty's, he said, "Come on, Lucy, let's get this mare over to that small stream and see if we can stop this bleedin'."

"Yes, the poor thing." Lucy was all sympathy and caring as she fell in behind Cord. But the jeering smile she turned on Jonty was triumphant. She had waited for the perfect opportunity to get her revenge. She had seen her foe struck to the ground, saw her lip split and bleeding. Her fat body bounced with the satisfaction that filled her.

The water-hole was only a few yards away, and Jonty watched Cord lead Beauty out into the middle of it and then slosh water on the wound with his cupped hand. The little mount flinched and snorted as the water hit her open flesh, but Cord's calm voice soothed her and she stood still.

After about ten minutes of gently bathing the deep, ugly gash, Cord led the mare out of the water, and still holding her reins, he swung onto the stallion's back. When Lucy had struggled onto her mount, Cord nudged Rawhide and they started off, heading up the mountain.

Jonty stared after them. Surely Cord wasn't going to ride off, leaving her sitting here. "What about me?" she called, scrambling to her feet.

"What about you, you miserable little sneak?" Cord wheeled the stallion and raced back toward her, reining in only when it seemed his mount would trample her. "Do you dare to think for one minute that you're gonna ride that poor little mare?"

"No, of course not." Jonty swiped at the blood still seeping from her cut lip. "But I could double up with you."

"Hah! Not likely," Cord spat. "I wouldn't let a vicious thing like you get on Rawhide's back. You can hoof it back to the ranch."

Jonty looked down at her high-heeled boots, then back up at Cord. "But that must be at least six miles."

"Every bit of it," Cord agreed coldly. "And I want you to think of your poor mount with every step you take." He touched his stallion with a heel and galloped back to where Lucy waited with Beauty.

Jonty stared after the retreating figures, sure in her mind that Cord wouldn't go off and leave her alone, afoot, unarmed and with no water. He only meant to scare her a bit, and then he'd return.

But when twenty minutes or more had passed and there was still no sign of Cord returning, Jonty had to admit that he hadn't been bluffing. With hatred for the man and woman a live thing in her breast, she looked up the mountain. Judging by the long shadow it was throwing across the canyon, the sun was well westward. She had wasted precious time, sitting and waiting. It would take some fast stepping to make it back to the ranch before nightfall.

With a sigh of resignation Jonty started out, stepping along briskly. The sun seemed to grow hotter as it beat down on her bare head, and before long her pace slowed considerably. Within the hour, every muscle revolted as she plodded along. Blisters were forming on the bottoms of her feet, and her arches in the high-heeled boots felt as if they were broken. With each painful step she took, her hatred for Cord McBain grew. Her mind dwelled on ways of getting back at him, making him suffer as she was suffering.

She was staggering in a fatigue that was close to exhaustion when she finally reached the spot where the trail again led downward. She paused to rest a minute and to bring some saliva into her dry and scratchy throat. "Another two miles at least to go," she muttered, forcing back the image of the spring that bubbled back of the cabin, the icy cold water that flowed from it.

She heaved herself up, wondering if she could make it to the ranch. Surely Cord would send someone after her if she wasn't back at the house by dark. "Oh, God, he must," she cried, spotting a set of wolf tracks. Her apprehension grew when a little farther on she saw many more tracks in dusty patches.

Did they attack in the daytime? She bit her swollen lips a moment later to stifle an outcry of alarm when, not too far away, a gaunt timber wolf raised his head and sent a wild howl echoing through the mountain.

Her heart racing, Jonty hurried on, ignoring her burning feet as her eyes unceasingly flicked around the area.

She had covered another quarter mile when a soft scuffing noise behind her brought her swinging around. Only yards away, his ruff raised, his fangs bared, a wolf was advancing on her with the silence of a shadow. Gripped with paralysis, she couldn't move, couldn't even open her mouth. It took the animal to move close enough for her to see its gleaming red eyes to release her vocal cords. Her lips parted and a piercing scream tore from her sore throat.

"Oh, God!" her mind screamed. "I am going to die

here on this mountain, all alone." She would never know the joy of wearing pretty dresses and fancy slippers. There wouldn't even be enough left of her to show that she was female.

In terrified fascination Jonty watched the animal bunch its muscles, preparing to spring at her throat. She was praying out loud, "Please help me, God," when seemingly out of nowhere a long shaggy form darted from behind a large boulder and launched itself straight at the snarling beast.

"Wolf!" she cried, and in her great relief promptly crumbled to the ground in a dead faint.

Of the four men sitting on the porch, only Paunch kept his seat when Cord and Lucy rode in, the mare trailing behind them, favoring a hind leg.

"Where's the kid?" Lightfoot frowned. "Why is the mare limping?"

Cord swung to the ground. "Take a look at her rump and flank." His eyes glittered. "See the work of your fine little friend, Jonty Rand."

Lightfoot examined Beauty's nasty cut, then turned to Cord, his jaw taut. "So you took the whip to *him* then."

"No by God, I didn't." Cord's lips clamped in a hard line. "I should have, though, the bloody mess he made of this animal's rump. I left him to walk in instead."

"That's a far piece for a man to walk in boots, if you went to the place you planned on." The Indian ran a gentle finger around the mare's whip lash, then sent a scorching look at the smirking Lucy. "Jonty didn't do this." He looked back at Cord. "It's not his nature to be cruel to animals, especially this pet."

Cord ran slim fingers through his hair. "Look, Lightfoot," he said wearily, "he done it. I was stalkin' a small herd of mustangs and he saw the opportunity to annoy me, so he struck the mare and deliberately raced her among the horses. They're probably still runnin'."

He flung himself down on the porch. "Maybe he didn't mean to hit the animal so hard, but he'll think twice before ever doin' it again."

Lightfoot looked unconvinced, as did Red as he followed Paunch and Lucy to the bunkhouse. The young man knew that if he wanted a turn at the whore, now was no time to anger her with his doubts about Jonty.

Jones offered no opinion either, as Cord and the Indian snarled at each other, but as he led Beauty away to tend to her wound, the black look he sent after Lucy said clearly that he knew where the guilt lay.

The sun continued to move westward as Cord, Jones, and Lightfoot sat on the porch, each man glancing often to the trail that led up the mountain. The dog, Wolf, stood up periodically to pace nervously about, whining anxiously as he, too, watched for a slender figure to appear.

Lightfoot broke the tight silence that had descended. "Can't you go a little easier on the kid, McBain? It's no wonder he gets a little rebellious now and then. You never let up on him."

Cord's face darkened impatiently. "I'll let up on him when he sheds the sissified ways Maggie let him drift into. Until he learns to act and think like a man, he can expect rough treatment from me." He eyed the two men fiercely, daring them to contradict him.

Lightfoot returned the glare, faint amusement in the back of his eyes. You'll have a long wait for that, bucko, he thought. He made no response, however, and silence settled again on the porch. Cord's stoic face concealed the fact that he was just as worried as his companions when the sun neared the mountain rim and there was still no sign of Jonty. He knew that night was a time of danger in the mountain for anyone caught up there. The timber in the high reaches was alive with hungry wolves. His eyes sparked guilt and remorse. The kid was afoot with no gun. He would be helpless against anything that might attack him.

As though his thinking brought it about, the long

yowl of a wolf floated down on the air. When Lightfoot jumped to his feet and stated firmly, "I'm sending
the dog to find the kid," Cord sighed his relief. The
dog would bring Jonty safely home, allowing him to
keep up his pretense of unconcern.

Wolf shot away at a word from the Indian and the
vigil continued. Cord's nerves were so tight from
worry and guilt that he thought they would snap. It
was close to half an hour later, with dusk coming on,
when he decided to hell with pride, he was going after
the kid. He stood up, and at that moment a slender
figure, hanging onto a battle-torn Wolf, hobbled into
the yard area. As three men rushed to meet her, Jonty
gave a little sob and fell into Lightfoot's arms.

"Good Lord, Jonty, you look beat," Lightfoot said
roughly, picking her up and cradling her in his arms.
He carried her to the porch and lowered her onto a
bench. "Let's get these boots off."

"And a drink of water," Jonty croaked, then bit her
lips to hold back a cry as the scuffed footwear was
gently eased off her feet.

"My God, look at this." Lightfoot turned furious
eyes on Cord. "The bottoms of his feet are like pieces
of raw meat."

Jones rushed out of the house with a dipper of
water, and handing it to Jonty swore softly as he, too,
saw her feet.

Cord squatted next to the irate Indian, and grabbing Jonty's slender ankle, he turned the foot over.
His hawklike features revealed nothing at the pitiful
condition of the narrow sole, but there was a huskiness in his voice when he picked Jonty up and
ordered, "Bring a basin of warm salt water to his
room."

Inside the bedroom, he lowered Jonty to the edge of
her bed and silently began rolling up her trouser legs.
His hands paused once, startled at the shapely calf he
uncovered. He shot Jonty a perplexed look, but Lightfoot entered the room just then and placed a basin of
water on the floor. Dropping a towel beside it, he said

brusquely, "I brought some salve too." He set the small jar on the bedside table, adding, "Make sure you put it on thick." He ignored Cord's sharp look as he walked toward the door, pausing there for one last order. "And let him stay in bed for a few days."

Cord's eyes glinted angrily at the Indian's cool dictum, and when the door snapped shut, Jonty waited for a torrent of abuse to be dumped on her head. But curiously, Cord remained silent, speaking only when he lowered her feet into the salt bath. "This will hurt like hell for a minute."

Hell described it perfectly, Jonty thought, flinching as her tender feet felt the first stinging bite of the saline mixture. She would have automatically jerked them out of the basin, but Cord grasped her ankles and held them firmly in the water.

"Don't act so damn womanish," he snapped. "It'll stop hurtin' soon. The salt will draw the soreness out, help the blisters to heal."

His claim was true, Jonty discovered, for within a few minutes the pain was receding and a drawing warmth was taking over. When she smiled her relief, Cord lifted one foot out of the water and began to pat it dry with the towel. She watched the deft movements of his tanned fingers, amazed at their tenderness. If asked an hour ago, she would have declared vehemently that this man didn't have a speck of tenderness inside him where she was concerned.

She transfered her gaze to the intent face bent over her foot. When he began to dry the other one, she thought, maybe, now that he had cooled off some, he would let her explain that she hadn't struck her mare, that Lucy was the guilty one.

"Cord," she began tentatively, "about my mare. I didn't strike her. It was—"

"Look, Jonty." Cord jumped to his feet. "Don't start that again. Just consider yourself lucky that you got off as easy as you did. If one of my men had treated a horse like that, I'd have taken the whip to him."

Tears of frustration swam in Jonty's eyes as he said

curtly, on his way out of the room, "Rub that salve in thick, and like the Indian said, keep off your feet for a few days. Lucy can take over your chores while you're laid up."

He stopped at the door and swung around as though another thought had struck him. "She'll take care of your needs too," he said in harsh tones. "I don't want any of the men in here. Is that clear?"

The door clicked shut, and Jonty, sick to death of his insults and assumptions, grabbed up one of her boots and heaved it at the door. It fell a foot short of its target and she threw herself back on the bed, wishing for the first time in her life that she was a man—a man with a man's strength so that she could beat that black-hearted devil into a pulp.

As she lay there, the events that led her to the present crept into her mind.

She had been returned to awareness on the mountain by a rough tongue licking her face. "Wolf," she scolded, pushing his head away, thinking for a disoriented moment that the dog wanted to play. Then her eyes lit on the long gray form only feet away and she shuddered at the torn throat, the eyes that had glared at her so fiercely now fixed unseeing at the sky. If not for Wolf, she would be lying there now.

She recalled sitting up and hugging the panting dog while she thanked God. Then, scrambling to her feet, she gasped at the pain her weight brought to them. She stood a moment, waiting for a slight dizziness to pass, before hanging onto Wolf's ruff and limping on.

She was wondering if she'd ever reach the ranch when Wolf gave a small yip and relief surged through her in waves. Three men were hurrying toward her.

Had that been regret she saw in Cord's eyes? she wondered as she drifted off to sleep on top of the covers, still fully clothed.

CHAPTER 10

JONTY WAS AWAKENED IN THE GRAY DAWN BY THE HOWL OF a wolf. She shivered, remembering the one that would have ripped out her throat if not for Wolf's intervention.

She remembered something much more pleasurable suddenly, and sat up, smiling widely. After four days in bed, Cord was finally letting her get up. The bottoms of her feet were completely healed, had been for two days. But when she had timidly said that she was able to go about her duties, Cord had growled that he wasn't taking the chance of her feet getting infected so she'd be lying around again for God knew how long.

Anger had flared inside her. He had a nerve, hinting that it was her fault her feet had been in the condition they were. She hadn't said anything, though, and only lowered her eyes, refusing to give him the satisfaction of heaping more abuse on her head through an argument.

The ranch hands, however, after one day of Lucy's

preparing their food, had been eager for her to be up
and at the stove. The second night, as they all sat at
the table, she had overheard Jones complain, "I can't
eat this slop much longer, Cord. And this bread . . ."

Something hard hit the floor and a loud roar of
laughter followed as Johnny Lightfoot observed,
"Even Wolf can't gnaw it. I'd better take it away from
him before he breaks his teeth." There came the sharp
tattoo of high heels, then the kitchen door slammed.

"Shame on you men." Cord looked at Jones and
Lightfoot, his eyes twinkling. "You've gone and hurt
her feelings." And again everyone roared with laughter.

"Cord, seriously, you've got to do somethin' about
our meals." Jones resumed his complaint. "Ain't the
kid's feet about healed?"

Jonty hadn't caught Cord's mumbled answer, but it
wasn't until two days later that he came to her room to
examine her feet. After scrutinizing her soles carefully, he said gruffly that he guessed she could get back to
the kitchen.

She wondered what shape the kitchen was in as she
swung her feet to the floor and took a shirt and pair of
trousers off a peg driven into the wall. She couldn't
imagine Lucy cleaning up after herself. The woman
was downright lazy, grudging everything she had to
do. She was grateful when Jones sent word that he was
taking care of her animals. Lucy would have let them
starve to death.

And how it irked her, having to wait on Jonty. She
grinned, searching for her boots. And she hadn't made
it easy on the whore either. Especially that first day,
when her feet hurt so badly and Beauty's wound was
so fresh in her mind. She had demanded so much
attention that Lucy's snapping eyes said she would
like to strangle her.

But the whore had taken reasonable care of her—
not out of a sense of guilt or compassion, but rather
because she was afraid of displeasing Cord if she
didn't. Since he no longer sought her favors, the

woman was careful not to give him any excuse to send her packing.

Dressed once again in her hated garb, but minus her boots, which were not in her room, Jonty made her way down the dim hall and entered the kitchen. The rancid smell of burned grease struck her in the face as she fumbled for the box of matches. Her fingers closed over it, and extracting one, she scraped it over the floor, then touched the flame to the kerosine lamp sitting in the center of the table, dreading what she would find.

The lamp chimney was smoked black and didn't give off much light, but it shone enough to expose the condition of the big room. A film of grease lay on everything—the stove, the table, even the window over the sink was grime-splattered. Jonty looked down at the floor and shuddered. In her absence, the men hadn't bothered to wipe their feet before entering the kitchen. Would she ever get the ground-in mud out of it?

"I'll get the coffee started first," Jonty muttered to herself, then stubbed her bare toe against the base of a bench carelessly pulled away from the table. "Then look for my boots," she added with a painful grimace.

While the coffee brewed, Jonty searched every corner of the kitchen for her boots, even looked out on the porch. She couldn't find them. "Well, Wolf." She patted the dog's big head, "they'd just about had it anyway, but they were some protection. I guess it's barefoot days for me again, like when I was a kid."

The coffee gave off that special aroma that said it was done. Jonty filled a cup and burned her tongue as she took a long swallow of the steaming dark liquid. For four days she had hungered for it, having passed up the thin mud Lucy called coffee.

She carried the cup to the window and stood looking out onto the back yard. The dawn was cool and fresh, and she breathed deeply of the sharp odor of sage wafting on the air. She had missed this time of day while confined to bed. She sighed, hating to leave the sight, but there was much work ahead of her, and the men would soon be coming in for breakfast.

The big pot of water she had put on the stove to heat was steaming when Jonty turned away from the window. Protecting her hands with a towel, she transferred it to the sink, added a generous amount of soft soap to the water, then started on Lucy's dirt and grime.

She had the table scrubbed and the top of the stove washed down when Lucy entered the kitchen. What an unappetizing sight she must have presented to the men, Jonty thought, glancing at the slovenly whore, who glared at her from red-rimmed eyes. Bitch, she thought, and ignoring the woman, she began to slice strips of bacon from a long slab. As the knife cut through the meat, she sensed the hostility emanating from the chunky figure and knew that it would soon be voiced.

Jonty had counted to five when Lucy sneered, "It's about time you got off your lazy ass and start earnin' your keep."

Jonty drew a deep breath and turned to face the woman. "Well, as you see, I'm up and doing. You can go back to bed now and start earning *your* keep."

The insult went over Lucy's head. "Don't you wish you could earn your bed and board the same way?" She smirked.

Jonty looked at the whore with steady blue eyes. "Not if it made me smell and look like you." She ran contemptuous eyes over the matted hair, the wrinkled, dirty dress and said, "I don't know how Red can stand to bed you. I wish you'd go back to the bunkhouse. You're stinking up the whole kitchen."

"You little bastard." Lucy took a menacing step toward Jonty's slender figure, then quickly stepped back when, with a warning growl, Wolf jumped in front of her.

"You were about to say something, Lucy?" Jonty raised an enquiring eyebrow.

An angry pulse visibly beat in the whore's temple.

"You're real brave when that brute is around," she sneered, "but I'll catch you alone someday, and when I do you'll regret that sharp tongue of yours."

"Do you mean like last week?" Jonty swung around on her. "When you took your whip to my mare?"

"Exactly," Lucy shot back. "Only next time, I'll take the whip to your face. We'll see how attractive you'll be to Cord and the other men then. You won't have them eatin' out of your hand any more."

Jonty advanced on the angry woman with clenched fists. "If you ever use that whip on me or my mare again, you'll be one sorry old whore. I'll—"

"She won't be usin' her whip on anyone, or anything." The words, like pieces of ice, interrupted Jonty.

Both women wheeled around to stare at Cord McBain standing in the hall door. There was a rigidity about his body that sent Lucy blundering in confusion.

"Why—why, Cord," she stammered, "I thought—thought you was still sleepin'."

"Well, you were wrong, weren't you?" And while Lucy stared sullenly at the floor, Cord's eyes met Jonty's in a long look.

Was there apology in the gray eyes? Jonty wondered —regret that he had taken Lucy's word against hers, that he had punished her unjustly?

Maybe, but she had felt the slice of his insults too many times to be deceived into thinking that Cord would ever change his mind about her. Even though he now had proof that she hadn't struck Beauty, that stubborn mind of his would still cling to the belief that she was unnatural.

She looked away and Cord turned his attention back to Lucy. "Pack your duds and Red will take you back to Abilene right after breakfast."

Lucy's small brown eyes tried to stare down the steel-gray ones. She was unable to do so, and after a hate-filled look at Jonty, she stamped out of the house.

"The whorin' bitch." Cord swore, then turned his

burning gaze on Jonty. "Why didn't you tell me that she was the one who used the whip on the mare?"

"I tried to tell you." Jonty brushed past him, setting the table. "I tried to tell you twice. But you were too busy enjoying tearing into me. You didn't want to hear anything good about me."

There was a short silence, then, "So you think I'm quite the bastard, is that it?"

"It's not important what I think about you." Jonty still hadn't looked at him. "More important, what do *you* think of Cord McBain?"

Cord looked at the slender back for several seconds, then he turned abruptly and walked out onto the back porch. Jonty grinned to herself, her spirits high. Cord hadn't said so, but she sensed his self-dislike. "Serves him right, huh, Wolf?" she said to the dog, listening to Cord washing his face, angrily splashing water all over the porch.

She turned around, still grinning, when Jones and Lightfoot left their room and entered the kitchen. "We was hopin' you'd be in here," Jones said, placing a paper-wrapped package beneath one of the benches. Following Lightfoot outside to take his turn at the wash basin, he said over his shoulder, "Another day of Lucy's slop and I'd have been in serious trouble."

Jonty was flipping flap-jacks when she heard Red and Paunch join the men. "Say, Cord, what's this I hear about Lucy havin' to leave?" Paunch started right in, half belligerently. "Her month ain't up for another two weeks."

"Her month ended today," Cord answered brusquly, "when I learned she was the one who struck the mare."

"By God, I knew it," Jones exclaimed, his voice muffled in a towel. "The kid ain't got a mean bone in his body."

"All right," Paunch conceded reluctantly, "I can see that would rile you, but why have Red take her back? I'm the one what brung her here."

"I'm sendin' Red because he'll make the trip in half

the time you would," Cord answered in a tone that said the conversation was closed, as he walked back into the kitchen, Jones and Lightfoot behind him.

"I'll sure be glad to see the back of Lucy," Jones said, piling flapjacks on his plate. "Me and Lightfoot can move back in the bunkhouse. That floor was gettin' damn hard."

"After it's been aired out and all the bedding changed," Lightfoot agreed, passing Jones the syrup.

"I told you, Cord," Jones said over a mouthful of jacks, "me and Lightfoot both told you that Jonty never hit that mare. Hell," he added, "the kid don't even carry a whip. I doubt if he owns one."

Cord didn't lift his head, only concentrated on cutting up his bacon as he conceded shortly, "So I was hasty."

Jones muttered something under his breath, but the subject was dropped, which didn't surprise Jonty. Mister Cord McBain was not about to explain himself further and Jones knew it.

She poured another cup of coffee around, then picked up her own and started to walk to the window. "Come back a minute, Jonty," Lightfoot said. "Jones has something for you."

"For me?" Jonty looked her surprise, resuming her seat.

Jones grinned at her widely, and reaching down picked up the package he had deposited on the floor earlier. Handing it to Jonty, he said, "me and the boys pitched in . . . well, Paunch didn't, said he was broke, and we bought you these." As Jonty untied the string holding the paper together, he added proudly, "I rode into Cottonwood and picked them out myself."

Jonty folded the wrapping back and stared down at a new pair of boots—slim and soft-leathered. Tears gathered in the back of her eyes. How thoughtful the men were! She would have loved to kiss them, but knew she dared not. Cord would send her off with Lucy if she made such a feminine display.

She slid a foot into one and it fit her perfectly. "How

did you know my size?" She stroked the supple
material.

"We took a measure from your old ones." Jones
beamed, pleased at Jonty's pleasure. "There's some
socks, too. Your feet wouldn't have been so blistered if
you'd been wearin' socks that day." He looked darkly
at Cord. "We figured you didn't have any."

Jonty made no response. She was embarrassed that
she was so poor she couldn't even keep her feet
decently clad. She lifted her eyes to thank the men and
caught Cord's frowning gaze on her. He was displeased at the men's gift to her. Well, to hell with him,
she thought, and turning her gaze to the men, she
warmly thanked them.

"I wondered what had happened to my old ones."
She laughed. "I gave my big toe a good stub looking
for them."

When Jones would have elaborated further on the
boots, Cord interrupted impatiently. "Hadn't you
better get goin', Red? I want you back here as soon as
possible. We're gonna start brandin' that bunch we've
got corraled in the east canyon. I'll need every one of
you. When you return, meet us there. We'll be
campin' out for the next couple of weeks."

Everyone stood up when Red did, Cord trailing
several feet behind the men as they walked to the
corral to saddle their mounts. Like it or not, he'd have
to pay more attention to his ward, he thought. The kid
needed new clothes. He'd been shocked at the run-
down condition of the boots Cord had pulled off his
feet last week, and he felt guilty that his men had
taken it on themselves to see that the kid got a new
pair.

Well, by God, that wouldn't happen again. He'd
take a day off and ride into Cottonwood and buy him
some new duds. One more washing of those pants he
had on today and his ass would be hanging out.

Jonty stood at the window, watching the men
prepare for the day's hard labor as they roped and
saddled a mount.

Her gaze was drawn to Cord and Red. They were laughing companionably as they cornered a little pinto in the corral. Cord's men liked and admired him—well, maybe not Paunch. That one didn't like or admire anyone. But he had respect and awe for the gun that always rode on Cord's hip. Cord was deadly swift with the Colt.

He looked the hard life he'd lived, she thought, studying the man who for the present had complete domination over her. Everything about him was hard —the planes of his deeply tanned face, his devil gray eyes.

I wonder if there's any gentleness in him when he makes love? The thought came unbidden to Jonty. Would those firm lips soften, would his eyes grow slumberous with passion? She stirred restlessly, imagining herself in Cord's arms, his naked length against hers, his lips caressing her bare body.

Her face grew scarlet. Had she taken leave of her senses? Never in her eighteen years had she dreamed such things. And to imagine them to be about that hateful man was unthinkable!

Her attention was drawn to Lucy, who had left the bunkhouse and was walking toward the two saddled and waiting horses. As Red took her bundle of clothes and fastened them on the back of her saddle, the whore's eyes sought out Cord. When he did not return her gaze, she allowed Red to help her mount. Jonty drew a deep breath of relief as the pair rode down the valley and out of sight. The evil woman had caused her a lot of grief.

Jonty brought her gaze back to the men and stirred uneasily as she saw Cord walking toward the house. What did he want? Was he coming to voice his disapproval of the men's gift, blame her for their action?

"Get that pugnacious look off your face." Cord frowned at her as he stepped into the kitchen. "I'm not here to do battle with you."

"Well, that's something new," Jonty retorted, coming away from the window and sitting down. "What are you here for then?" she demanded rudely.

Cord's firm jaw tautened and he took a couple of steps toward her before bringing himself up short. Jonty shrank back, knowing that he would like to put his hands on her. And maybe I deserve it, she thought as she watched him gain control of himself. He had said he didn't want to fight.

"I've come to remind you that you'll be alone here for a couple of weeks," he began in a tight voice, "and to warn you to be careful. Keep the dog with you at all times and keep the doors locked, whether you're inside or out. There are still some renegade Indians roaming about.

"Can you shoot that pistol you keep in your room, hit anything with it?"

Jonty nodded. "I'm more accurate with it than any of your hands are with theirs." She waited a second, then added spitefully, "Uncle Jim taught me how to use it, and he's the best."

There was a tight silence for a minute. "You should know," Cord snapped finally, his eyes bright with anger. "And to make sure you don't take off to join that perfect man I'm takin' your mare with me."

"You can't take Beauty!" Jonty jumped to her feet. "What if I should need her?"

"You won't need her if you do as I say—stick around the house and carry your gun."

Before Jonty could retaliate, Cord was gone. She ran to the door yelling at his broad back, "I hate you, Cord McBain!"

The striding figure didn't look back, not even when he swung into the saddle and rode after his men.

Cord waded out into the sun-dappled stream, joining his men who splashed and horsed around like over-grown boys. When the water reached his waist, he cupped water to his face, again and again, rinsing the sweat from a two weeks' growth of whiskers. He'd be back at the ranch before dark, then he'd shave the itching things off.

He was looking forward to going home. He guessed he was growing soft, but he was tired of sleeping on the ground and eating beans and salt pork. The thought of his soft bed and Jonty's cooking brought a smile to his lips.

The little imp of hell had fared well enough while he and the men were gone. Every night for the past two weeks he had ridden down to the house and checked things out. Wolf had known that he was outside peeking through the window, but only a pricking of his ears had shown he was aware that someone was out there in the darkness. The dog knew he had a right to be there, but had it been anyone else he'd have torn the door down to get to them.

Cord's lips quirked. How angry the kid would have been, had he known he was being spied on. He shook his head; unbelievably, he missed their sparring.

It had been an arduous but profitable two weeks. He and the men had broken close to a hundred head of good, sturdy mustangs. And to add to his streak of good luck, Red had brought him some good news. On his way home from delivering Lucy to the pleasure house in Abilene, he had stopped in Cottonwood for a hot meal and a drink and had learned there was an Army agent there, looking to buy horses. That meant he'd no longer have to make the long drive to Abilene, running some of the fat off them.

Yes, things were looking up. Satisfaction softened Cord's eyes as he waded out of the water and dried off his muscular body with a towel he'd used for fourteen days. Donning his dirt-grimed, sweat-stiff clothes, he climbed onto the waiting Rawhide's back and called to the men, "Hurry it up, fellows, let's get down to the ranch, have a decent bath and one of Jonty's good meals."

Cord beat the men home by some fifteen minutes. When Jonty came walking around the corner of the

house at his arrival, he was surprised at the pleasant
feeling the slender figure gave him. Surely he wasn't
glad to see the little imp.

But if Jonty was glad to see him, it didn't show on
her face. Somehow Cord was disappointed that there
was no welcome on the delicate features. "The men
are gonna be here shortly and we'll need lots of hot
water," he said gruffly, reining in beside her. "Drag
the tub out here on the porch and get some water to
heatin'."

"And good afternoon to you, too, Mister Almighty
McBain," Jonty hissed as Cord rode on to the corral
without another word. "He could have at least asked
me if everything went well while I was alone for two
weeks. For all he knows, I could have been raped, the
cow stolen by Indians, and my chickens killed by wild
varmints."

Jonty stamped into the kitchen, swearing under her
breath as she set two big pans of water on the stove to
heat, then dragged the big wooden tub out of the
storage room and onto the porch.

Cord had just shucked out of his clothes and eased
into the steaming water Jonty had lugged from the
kitchen when the men rode in. "Hurry up, Cord," Red
called, "I'm next. I met a pretty little gal in Cottonwood, and I think I'll ride in and visit her awhile."

Jonty kept heating water, with Lightfoot carrying it
outside, saving her the embarrassment of seeing the
naked men as they waited their turn at the tub.

The pile of dirty clothes grew as each man scrubbed
away two weeks of grime and sweat. I'll be washing
clothes for a week, Jonty thought at the sight of the
heaped-up trousers, shirts, and underwear.

Later, when the men sat down to eat, Jonty thought
they sounded like a pack of hungry dogs as they ate.
She squirmed slightly, trying to once again adjust to
the binding wrapped around her breasts. She had so
enjoyed the freedom of being unfettered for two weeks
and it was difficult, being flattened-out again.

At last bellies were filled and Jonty rose to pour the coffee. Ten minutes later she and Cord sat alone in the kitchen.

"Well, how did things go while we were away?" Cord helped himself to a second cup of coffee from the pot Jonty had left on the table.

"About as usual." Jonty held her cup in both hands, sipping at it occasionally. "Wolf killed a snake out by the chicken house. The old broody hen hatched ten eggs." She didn't add how lonesome it had been, nor how at night she had imagined that unseen things were lurking around, hands trying the door knobs.

"Any strangers come around . . . Indians?"

"No, only a couple of coyotes nosing around. Wolf soon routed them."

Cord toyed with his cup, searching for something else to talk about. Strangely, he liked the kid's company when they weren't going at each other. There was a soothing quality about the boy. Maybe it was his quietness, his throaty voice. He laughed to himself. That voice wasn't always husky. When he was spitting fire at him, which was most of the time, it became downright raspy and mean.

He liked that spirit in him, though, Cord mused. It was the only manly thing about him. He gave a humorless smile when Jonty rose to light the lamp, then began gathering the dirty dishes. He was being told that their conversation was over. He watched the narrow back at the sink and unreasonably wanted to start an argument, to stir some life into the still features.

But that would be plain orneriness on his part, he admitted, and rose and walked out onto the porch. He leaned against a supporting post, thinking that maybe he'd ride into Cottonwood also. He, too, had had a rough two weeks and a few drinks and a couple tumbles with a whore was just what he needed.

CHAPTER 11

EVERY DAY WAS HOT NOW, MORE THAN HOT. IT WAS stifling. As usual, Jonty rose with the first tint of pink in the east. And as usual she gave the men their breakfast, watched them ride out, and started her chores.

A pail swinging from her hand, she went first to Buttercup, where Lightfoot had pegged her out in a patch of lush grass before riding out, a chore he did for her every morning. The cow had finally dropped her calf, and each morning and afternoon she let down a gallon of milk to Jonty's coaxing fingers.

At first the men had looked distrustfully at the glass of milk she placed at each plate. But after she threatened that there would be no coffee until the glasses were emptied, it took but one sip of the spring-cooled liquid to make believers of them. And she couldn't keep up with the butter they slapped on her hot biscuits.

Jonty's next task was feeding the hens and the chicks. Actually, they were no longer chicks, but half-grown. Of the thirteen hatched, five were roosters. Before long she could give the men fried chicken occasionally. Wouldn't their eyes pop at that. Already they enjoyed fried eggs for breakfast about three times a week, a real treat for them.

When she had strained the milk through a white cloth kept for that purpose, carried the crock to the cave, and placed another cloth on top of it, Jonty surveyed the small area around the house on which the spruce and pine hadn't infringed yet. Her eyes moved to the greenery flourishing around the kitchen porch. Most of the plants had blossoms of red, yellow, and blue, a bright spot among the gravel and rocks.

The corners of her lips tilted. She and Cord had engaged in quite a row over the plants she had dug up in the valley and transplanted in their present home. He had finally given in when she pointed out that half of them were herbs that she could use in cooking, and the other half were for medical purposes.

Her lips curved into a full, tickled smile. How Cord hated the fact that in the meantime she might derive pleasure from the plants' beautiful display.

Jonty sighed. Cord's attitude toward her hadn't changed. He had, however, surprised her with two new pairs of pants and a couple of shirts. But he still watched her like a hawk, and was always ready to find fault. She always flinched inwardly when he was railing at her about something, but on the surface she managed to show nothing of the pain inside her.

The day passed, and soon it was time to start supper. Although it was still bright and clear at the top of the mountain, down in the foothills dusk was not far off.

She lingered another minute, dreading to enter the hot house. She was gazing up at the sunset-flushed peaks when a scuffing noise behind her brought her swinging around, apprehension running down her spine. Wolf wasn't with her today. Cord had taken him, explaining that there were spots in the canyons that he could chase the wild horses out of. She peered through the dusk. What had made the noise? An Indian, a bear, a cougar?

She started when the shadowy bulk of a man moved out of the shadows and walked toward her. "Who's there?" she called sharply, ready to fly inside and drop the bar across the door.

"It's only me, Paunch." The fat man stopped a couple of feet from her, his heavy mouth twisted in an ugly grin.

Jonty's insides tightened. "Where are the others? I didn't hear the horses ride in."

"They'll be along later." Paunch moved in closer, and Jonty stepped back. "I thought you and me could have a little time together before they came in. Have a little fun."

Jonty took another step backward, fear a twisting live thing in her now. "Go away." She tried to keep her voice calm, not daring to show this man any weakness. "I don't want to spend any time with you. I have to get supper started."

"To hell with supper!" Paunch made a grab for her, and before she could move his fingers were biting into her arms. "I gotta another hunger that's more pressin' than grub." He leered down at her. "I've waited a long time to catch you without that damned dog, pretty boy, and by God I'm not gonna wait any longer to have you."

"Stop it!" Jonty panted, shuddering in revulsion as she was maneuvered against the house wall. "Get your filthy hands off me."

"Not likely," Paunch grunted, trying to avoid her kicking feet. "It was your doin' that Lucy got sent away, so you can fill in for her now." And as Jonty twisted and turned, breathing in panicked sobs, the aroused man's great weight pinned her against the house.

His fat fingers were fumbling with her belt buckle when three words, like slivers of ice, rang out. "Let him go!"

Paunch stiffened, divining the promise of violence in the tone of the order. He released Jonty and stepped away from her. Cord laughed a mirthless sound as the fat man cringed. "You've bit off more than you can chew this time, mister." He advanced on the sweating man, step by slow step. "I'm gonna beat the livin' hell out of you."

"Now look, Cord." Paunch held up a hand, a furtive, calculating look glittering in his fat, narrowed eyes. "The little bastard—"

"You can stop right there." Cord's voice was acid, his eyes coldly furious. His lean finger dropped to unbuckle his gun belt, and Paunch made his move. He lowered his head, preparing to lunge and butt the younger man in the stomach, knock him to the ground.

But Cord had caught the movement through his lashes. He waited, timed his own movement, and when Paunch rushed him, he brought up a knee with all his strength, catching Paunch full in the face. The fat man lay sprawled on his back, a trembling hand feeling his bloody mouth. Cord stood over him when he tried to crawl away.

"Fight, you buggerin' bastard." He grasped Paunch by the collar and dragged him to his feet. "You're up against a man now, not a half-grown kid."

Paunch squared away and Cord drove a hard fist between his eyes. The enraged man let out a painful roar and swung at Cord. Jonty hid her face against the wall, unable to watch as Cord's fists lashed again and again at the hate-filled, snarling face.

Finally, when his eyes were no more than swollen slits in his face, Paunch dropped his hands, refusing to fight any more. His breath coming in gasps, Cord ordered, "You've got ten minutes to get off my property. If I ever see you around the kid again, I'll put a bullet between your eyes."

With a glowering look at Jonty's pale face, Paunch picked up his hat, slapped the dust off it on his leg, then walked unsteadily toward the bunkhouse. Jonty, trembling, watched him leave, then stepped forward to thank Cord for his timely intervention.

One look at his face and she stepped back in bewilderment. His gray eyes were shooting contempt at her. "I hope you learned a lesson just now." His words were clipped. "It don't pay to tease a man like that one. His type can't be turned off and on."

Jonty stared at Cord, her disbelief mirrored in her eyes. "Are you crazy?" she almost shouted. "I didn't tease that man. I can't stand him!"

"Your hatred is probably what teased him." Cord glowered at her. Then, not giving her time to answer, he continued in the same accusing tone, "Because of your little game, I'm short a man now. And you, young man," He said, jabbing a finger in her chest, "are goin' to take his place."

When Jonty made no response, only stood looking down at the ground, biting her lips not to cry, he asked harshly, "Do you understand what I'm sayin'? You'll be doin' a man's job from now on. There will be no more cookin' and fancyin' up the place like a good little housewife."

Jonty nodded silently, her eyes still on the ground. Cord frowned down at her bent head, willing her to look up. When she didn't, he swung into the saddle, saying, "You'll start your new duties in about a week. I'll be ridin' into Cottonwood tomorrow. There's a Mexican family I know there. The wife is a good cook, and she has a daughter around your age. A tumble or two in bed with her should lure you away from the path you're on now."

Jonty stared after the broad back riding away, hating Cord McBain with an intensity she could almost taste. Pray God, someday she could repay him some of the pain he had caused her.

Her shoulders sagging, Jonty walked into the kitchen. She was an expert rider, thanks to Uncle Jim, but she lacked the strength and experience to lasso wild horses. A more unsettling thought hit her. Would she be expected to help break the animals too?

Jonty left off her fretting when she heard the galloping of horses. The men were riding in. She sighed. She'd better get busy. They'd be in before long, hungry as bears. She put the skillet on the stove and slapped venison steaks into it.

Half an hour later, when the men stamped into the kitchen, there awaited them on the table a platter of steaks, mashed potatoes with milk gravy, biscuits, and a bowl of mixed greens.

"I didn't see the fat man around," Red remarked as everyone settled down at the table.

Helping himself to meat, Cord said shortly, "He drifted this afternoon."

"The hell you say?" Jones looked up, a biscuit halfway to his mouth. "He never mentioned that he was ridin' on."

"I guess he got lonesome for Lucy." Cord passed the steaks to his right.

Red laughed. "I can believe that. He's been plenty randy here lately. Always got his hands down his pants. It's a good thing this is a horse ranch. If we worked a cattle ranch, he'd have been after the heifers by now."

"Or one of you men," Cord observed dryly, sliding Jonty a knowing look.

Jonty kept her eyes on her plate, pretending not to see the veiled insult. She felt Lightfoot's eyes on her, and when she looked at him there was apology in his eyes for his companions' frank talk in front of her. She gave a dismissive lift of her shoulders.

Lightfoot shifted his eyes to Cord. "Paunch was the reason I didn't want to take Wolf away from Jonty today. I've read in his eyes that he'd have gone after the kid, given a chance."

"Well, he's gone and we can forget about him." Cord's tone said to drop the subject. He gave his attention to cutting up his meat, then said casually, "Jonty will be takin' his place."

There was a stunned silence. Lightfoot lay his knife and fork down. "You're not serious, of course. You're just ragging the kid."

"I'm dead serious." Cord frowned at the Indian. "I never meant for Jonty to cook for the rest of his life. You men know that."

"I don't know why he can't." Lightfoot gave Cord a hard look. "At the rate we're gathering horses, and the likelihood of traveling farther and farther away from the ranch soon to herd in more, you're going to need a range cook before long. You're not going to find a woman willing to follow along behind a hundred pounding hooves, kicking up dust."

"That's right," Red agreed with the Indian's long speech. "Can't you wait until then and let the kid take charge of the chuck wagon? It would be a pure waste, takin' him away from cookin'."

"Look!" Cord impatiently pushed his plate away. "I'm tired of arguin' about it. My mind's made up. He's takin' Paunch's place with the rest of you men."

After a long scrunity of Jonty's delicate slenderness, Jones grunted, "Shit, Cord, you must see that the kid ain't up to our kind of work. He'll never be able to handle some of them wild horses. They'll pull his arms out of their sockets."

"He'll get strong enough once hard work builds him some muscles. He's weak from doin' woman's work." Cord stood up. "I've said my last word on it." And though half his supper remained on his plate, he stalked out of the room.

"Who's gonna cook for us, then?" Red called after him. "Surely not one of us—nor you either, Cord. You can't cook worth spit."

Cord paused at the door. "Thanks, Red," he drawled, his features easing a bit. "I'm bringin' in a Mexican family next week, so don't worry about your stomach."

He spoke to Jones then. "Get that larger building shaped up, will you, Jones. The new help can live in there." He passed on through the door, and it wasn't too long before the others followed him, mumbling that they hoped the Mexican woman could cook as well as Jonty.

Lightfoot remained a while longer with Jonty. He studied her face as he rolled a cigarette. "Paunch went after you, didn't he?" He struck a match and held it to the smoke.

Jonty sighed and nodded. "Cord caught him and almost beat him to death." After a while, she added, "Of course, he blamed me for the attack."

Cigarette smoke curled to the ceiling as Lightfoot thoughtfully inhaled, then exhaled. "Are you up to it, Jonty?" He looked searchingly at her.

"I don't know, Johnny." Jonty shrugged weary shoulders. "I can ride well enough. Uncle Jim taught me. But lassoing a wild horse, branding it—I don't think I have the strength, or the stomach, for it."

"About the branding, it don't hurt the animals much." Lightfoot smiled at the sad little face. "It scares them more than anything." He laid a hand on hers. "I'll help you avoid the branding as much as possible, and starting tomorrow we'll practice lassoing. It's not hard once you catch the trick of it. It's all in your wrist and keeping the rope taut."

"I appreciate that, Johnny." Jonty smiled wanly, then stood up and began to stack the dishes. She glanced nervously out the door to where the bunkhouse light shone dimly. "I guess you'd better go join the men before that devil comes looking for you."

Lightfoot grinned and allowed that he should. He paused before stepping out into the darkness. "Things aren't always going to be this way, Jonty. Your Uncle Jim is working hard at making a home for you. You just hang in there a little while longer."

The Indian's words of encouragement helped Jonty to finally fall asleep that night.

CHAPTER 12

"YOU'VE REALLY MADE THE PLACE LOOK NICE, JONES."
Jonty stood in the open doorway of the small, four-
room log cabin, watching the tall man slap whitewash
on the walls. "I hope the Mexican family have their
own furniture."

"They probably do. They've been married a long
time." The perspiring man swiped at the water paint
splattered on his face, then sent Jonty a teasing grin.
"I expect you're lookin' forward to meetin' the daughter."

Jonty shrugged indifferently. "It will be nice having
someone my own age to talk to."

Jone's grin widened. "I think Cord has more than
talkin' to her in mind. I think he's hopin' for a little
romance between the two of you."

Jonty blushed and bent over her boot, pretending
an interest in the heel. "I don't care what he wants,"
she muttered. "It's a decision that I will make."

"Hell, kid." Jones kept on slapping paint. "Don't be

bashful. You're eighteen, long past the age of pleasurin' a woman. Why I was only fourteen the first time I had one. I was always big for my age—down there too, where it counts." He chuckled. "The women were always after me."

He turned his head and grinned at Jonty. "Course, I've slowed down considerably these days. I don't need a woman more than once a month or so. I guess I made too much of a hog of myself in my younger days."

Jonty had stopped listening to Jones's reminiscing some time back as her brain worked at something she had momentarily forgotten. Cord did expect more than friendship to ripen between her and the still unknown Mexican girl. He wanted them in bed together.

She supressed a giggle. Wouldn't the little señorita get a shock when she discovered that her bed companion had the same working parts that she did. It would also blast hell out of her disguise, sending shock waves all over the ranch.

"How's the lasso lessons comin' along?" Jones broke the short silence between them. "I see you practicin' with the Indian every day after work. You seem to be doin' all right."

Jonty breathed a relieved sigh at the subject change. "I guess I am. Johnny seems satisfied. I usually settle the noose around the horse's neck. He's lent me a fine little quarterhorse to work with. That means a lot."

Jonty stayed on while Jones gathered up his paint paraphernalia, then said she guessed it was time she started supper. "The last one I'll make, I expect. Cord will probably be back tomorrow with his new cook. He's been gone for four days."

"I hope she's as good as you are, Jonty." The wrangler smiled at her. "I'm gonna miss your pies and cakes. I don't think Mexicans go in for that kind of sweets very much." He sighed. "It's too damn bad you ain't female, Jonty."

"Yes, it is," Jonty agreed, and stepped outside, smiling to herself.

The next morning, after Jonty had seen to her chores and set some sourdough to rise, just in case she had to make supper again, she saddled Beauty and headed for her favorite place. A secret place, a place hidden among a stand of spruce that no one else knew about. There she shed her tears, and afterwards gathered her courage to return to the house.

In all honesty, though, she hadn't cried in a long time, she reminded herself as she urged the little mare up the mountain. She had learned not to mind Cord's churlish ways with her, to turn a deaf ear when something about her didn't please him. And she loved her routine of cooking, cleaning house, and taking care of her animals. She wondered who would tend her pets now, and if they would get the proper care.

In a short time, Jonty was lounging in warm content on a triangular outcrop of stone overlooking the ranch house below. Nearby, with dangling reins, Beauty nibbled daintily at a patch of grass while she herself watched a ribbon of smoke drifting from the chimney below.

What new twist would her life take now? she wondered. She knew she would fail miserably as a wrangler. She absolutely hadn't the strength for it, and all the practicing in the world would not give it to her.

Unconsciously, Jonty picked the wildflowers that bloomed abundantly around her. She had a handful when her fingers grew still. She had heard the distant clip-clop of hooves and the creaking of wagon wheels. Her shoulders sagged. It was the end of four peaceful days. Cord had arrived with her replacement.

The flowers gripped unnoticed in her hand, Jonty flattened herself out on the rocky shelf and watched the action around the house. Besides Cord and the Mexican family riding inside the wagon, four more riders were drawing rein. Cord slid from the saddle, and the four strangers followed suit. In a matter of seconds, Jones and the others were filing out of the bunkhouse and Cord was introducing them to the new help. She watched them shake hands, then leaned forward when Cord turned to the wagon that was piled high with furniture.

A middle-aged woman clung to his hand as she climbed from the high wagon seat, then a young lady stood up, waiting to be assisted to the ground. Cord lifted his arms, and with a laughing squeal, she jumped toward him.

It was too far away for Jonty to distinguish features, but the sun shone on blue-black hair that hung down the middle of the girl's back. Her whole being was envious of the red blouse and vivid flowered skirt that swirled around slim brown legs as Cord set the girl on her feet. What she wouldn't give to wear such garments, her own black hair hanging to her shoulders!

She shifted her gaze back to Cord, now speaking to Jones. Her lips curled. He was asking about her, she knew. He was probably angry that she wasn't there to greet the new people, especially the girl.

She giggled when Cord made for his mount in long, angry strides. He was coming to look for her. Her lips curved smugly. He wouldn't find her.

A few minutes later, however, nothing seemed funny any longer. For coming through the trees, a grim look on his face, rode Cord. He knew about her hideaway!

She jumped to her feet as he drew the stallion in, almost on top of her, and she braced herself for his rage. It began as soon as he swung to the ground and slapped the flowers out of her hands.

"Don't ever let me catch you doin' any more woman-stuff. Pickin' flowers, of all things. What's wrong with you? What if the girl, Tina, had been with me? What would she have thought of you?"

Not giving her time to answer, he shoved her toward the mare. "Now get on your horse and get yourself down to the house. And for God's sake, try to act like a man in front of the new people."

"I'm not going to make up to the girl, if that's what you're hinting at." Jonty's eyes smouldered her resentment. "You can bed her," she spat. "I'll choose my own bed partners."

"Oh, yeah?" Cord's fingers bit into her arm. "Just who do you have in mind? One of the new men who just rode in with me?" He shook her until her curls bounced. "You listen to me real good, young man, you are to stay away from them. I will not have you embarrassing me."

A stony silence developed while Cord waited for Jonty to make a response. When she only stood quietly, her face pale, refusing to look at him, uncertainty replaced the anger in Cord's eyes. He recalled the Indian accusing him of being too hard on the kid. He nudged the limp pile of flowers with the toe of his boot. They were pretty. A kid raised by Maggie might be tempted to pick flowers. He released Jonty and stepped back. He would say no more about them.

He swung onto the stallion, and as Jonty mounted her mare, he said before leading off, "You'll continue to live and sleep in the house. Don't let me catch you around the bunkhouse."

Tina Perez was very pretty, with red lips and sparkling black eyes. Her short body was curvaceous now, but later, after a couple of babies, those curves would turn to fat if she weren't careful, Jonty thought the first time she saw the girl up close. She had a bubbly nature and rolled her eyes provocatively whenever there was a man around. And though she flirted with all the males on the ranch, she made it clear that her real interest lay in Cord McBain.

She sought him out at every opportunity, hanging over him at meal times and urging him to take more meat, another helping of potatoes. Jonty's eyes twinkled with wicked amusement each time a discomfited Cord caught her watching Tina making up to him. For other than treating Jonty like a younger brother, the girl showed no interest in him, whom she believed to

be a green lad. And while this pleased and relieved
Jonty, it didn't set at all well with Cord. His plans had
gone awry and he couldn't blame his ward this time.

In the first few days after Tina's arrival, Jonty had
tried to talk to her, to build a friendship. She was
hungry for feminine companionship. Cord had been
pleased at her effort, for she had caught him nodding
his head in satisfaction a few times. But Tina had soon
let it be known that she had no time for skinny Jonty
Rand.

Jonty sighed now, as she looked out her bedroom
window. Cord still found fault with her. According to
him, everything she did was wrong. She didn't throw
her rope right, she didn't keep control of the mustangs
she chased out of the brush. He eyed her with suspicion every time one of the new riders spoke to
her—especially the one called Jake, a young man in
his twenties who had a stocky build and laughing eyes.
He took few things seriously, and was fun to be
around.

She shook her head ruefully. Cord saw to it that she
didn't enjoy Jake's levity very often—or anybody
else's, either. Except for Jones and Lightfoot, of
course. Jones was too old, and the Indian paid no
attention to Cord's warnings.

When Jonty could no longer penetrate the wall of
darkness outside her window, she turned away from it
and began preparing for bed. Another grueling day
would be upon her before she knew it.

The rising red ball of the sun shining through the
window warned that it would be another hot day.
Jonty grimaced. If this day was going to be as hot and
rigorous as yesterday, she didn't know how she would
get through it. Yesterday, when Cord had finally called
it quits for the day, she had been almost sick with
fatigue.

She rolled out of bed, stretched, then whipped the
nightshirt over her head and rebound her breasts
before pulling on her shirt and trousers. Lightfoot had

installed a bolt on her door, assuring her of privacy
when she was in her room. How blessed it was to be
relieved of the bindings for a few hours.

Thank goodness for him and Jones, she thought,
stamping on her boots. The pair always kept within
her vicinity, helping her out whenever they could.
This had to be done on the sly, though, away from
Cord's ever-watchful eyes. That one would spare her
nothing, and that was the reason she had determined
from the first day that he would never see her weariness. No matter what it cost her, she always forced a
spring into her step whenever he was around.

Being young and healthy, after a good night's sleep,
Jonty felt refreshed. After a hearty breakfast, she
stood ready for another day's hard work. As everyone
filed out of the kitchen, the first words out of Cord's
mouth brought her spirits drooping.

"I've decided," he said, "that we'll not gather any
more horses until we've branded the ones already
penned in the north canyon. Gather up the brandin'
irons, Red, and let's get started."

Dismay filmed Jonty's eyes. This was just what
she'd been dreading. There was no way she'd ever be
able to bring herself to putting a piece of hot iron to an
animal's skin. He could beat her to death first.

They were all riding out then, and fifteen minutes
later reached the ragged gorge. It was yellow and
crumbled, grass-covered at the bottom, spruce-
trimmed on top. Jonty guided her mount after the
others as they squeezed single file through a narrow
opening.

The wild ones raced away at their approach, but
didn't get far in the box canyon. While Jones built a
fire and stuck the irons in it to heat, Red and the new
men chased after the horses, their lassos flying. Within
a short time, each man returned with a mustang
straining against the rope around his neck. The branding began.

Jonty watched in fascinated horror. "I can't bear
it," she whispered when the third animal, a young

colt, its eyes rolling in terror, was thrown on its side
and a hot iron was pressed against its rump. The
sizzling hair, the odor of scorched hide, was sickening
to her. Without conscious thought, she wheeled her
mount and raced away.

She heard Cord's angry roar as she slowed the
quarter horse's pace to send him through the narrow
opening of the canyon, and ignored his strident call as
she steered the mount on an upward course she had
never been over before. She didn't care where it would
take her, she only knew she had to get away from what
she felt was cruelty to animals.

As Jonty climbed higher and higher, she grew more
calm, and finally surrendered herself to the peaceful-
ness of her surroundings, to the cool, quiet, endless
solitude. Later she would have to return to Cord's
wrath, but only after she had soothed her nerves and
strengthened her will. For when she next confronted
Cord, she was going to tell him flatly that she would
have nothing to do with the branding. He could take
that stick he was always threatening her with, and beat
her, but she wouldn't do it.

She was riding along the rim of a narrow deep
canyon, listening to bird song, when a coiled rattlesnake hissed at the feet of the wiry little mount. He
reared frantically, swerved, and she went sailing over
his head, rolling and tumbling. But before she could
even scream, she found herself standing on solid
ground.

She peered upward. It was a heaven sent miracle.
She had fallen about twenty feet before landing on a
ledge—a very narrow ledge, no more than two feet
wide. She stood a long time, facing the stone wall,
willing her heart to slow its beat, her trembling to
cease. What was she to do? She was afraid to go to her
left, afraid to go to her right. Either way the ledge
might peter out to nothing. But below her was a sheer
drop of at least fifty feet, with jagged teeth of stone at
the bottom, waiting to crush the life from her body.

"But I can't stay here forever," she whimpered. She

said a heart-felt prayer, then pulling her nerves together, she slowly lowered herself to her hands and knees.
She stayed there a minute, then began to slowly crawl
forward. Stones and gravel cut into her palms, rubbed
through the material at her knees. She bit her lips and
moved on, wondering if the ledge would take her
anywhere.

When she came to a bulge in the stone wall, nervous
sweat bathed her body. What would she find on the
other side? Would it go on, or would it drop away to
nothing? Calling on all her will power to find out, she
inched her way around the protuberance, then let
herself go flat, finally letting her tears flow in the relief
that gripped her. A wide outcropping of rock extended
as far as she could see and was easily scalable. In just a
few minutes she would be out of here.

She rose to her feet, and then it started—started
with a low crash, then slowly a rising roar that hurt her
ears, and finally a rattle of sliding earth and rock. A
landslide!

Before Jonty could move, she was swept up in its
path and carried helter-skelter to the rocky bottom
below. As she lay on her back, stunned, a hundred
different cuts and bruises all over her body, she
thought she had never heard a sweeter sound as the
slide finally ceased with a crackling of stone on stone.
She moved her arms, and then her legs. Nothing
broken there. She had no difficulty breathing, so
evidently no ribs were broken.

But her clothing had been reduced to rags, and her
hat was gone. She laughed hysterically. Cord would
raise hell about that too.

She rose, wobbling, to her feet and stood searching
the terrain. Nothing was familiar, not one landmark.
She was totally lost. She looked up at the sky and
found the sun straight overhead. There was no help
there. Then, as she stood in indecision, wondering
what direction to take, high in the mountain a panther
screamed. A shuddering fear rippled through her. It
sounded savage, sinster, yet so human. Now she didn't

know what to do. Should she move on, no matter in what direction, or should she hide among the boulders and wait for someone to come looking for her. She was sure that, if not Cord, Johnny Lightfoot would search for her.

She limped painfully to two tall boulders and eased herself between them and waited.

Jonty had been in her hiding place a scant ten minutes when the cat's cry came again, but not from the same spot. He was moving, seeking a crack or crevice where he could steal swiftly down and pounce on his prey below. And Jonty knew in her bones that she was that quarry. The animal had either seen her or caught her scent.

A swift upward glance stopped her heart. On a ledge about thirty feet up, was a flat-nosed, fang-toothed face whose eyes flamed fiercely green, and whose snarling jaws promised death.

Involuntarily, she let out a piercing scream, followed by, "Help! Help!"

Two voices answered her—one a feline snarl, the other Cord's anxious voice. She snapped her head up in time to see him jerk the Colt from its holster. A red flash leapt from its barrel, and then in a swirl of blue smoke she saw the cat disappear.

Her relief was so great, she gave a little moan and fainted dead away.

"This time I will take a stick to him," Cord swore between clenched teeth as he sent the stallion thundering after the little quarter horse that was disappearing up the mountain trail. "I'll beat the hell out of his worthless hide, then kick him off the ranch."

But as he climbed higher and higher, his eyes on the tracks he followed, he knew he made an empty threat. No matter how badly he might want to be rid of the kid, wily Maggie had made it impossible.

Last night he had finally opened the chest Jonty had handed him. He was still reeling from the amount of money it contained. A small fortune had stared up at him. How had she ever saved so much? There was not only enough money to pay for the ranch, there would be some left over. And in all fairness, the kid should be an equal partner. When he was older, and a little tougher, Cord would make him one.

Cord was in deep thought when he came upon the little quarter horse. It stood riderless, its head drooping, its sides quivering with fear. With a sinking sensation in his stomach, Cord reached down and grabbed up the trailing reins. His whole being full of dread of what he'd find, Cord urged Rawhide on, back-tracking the little mount.

He had ridden close to a mile when he came upon the spot where the quarter horse had spooked, evident by the way the ground was trampled and by the long, slithering trail of a snake seeking cover among the rocks. An accomplished sign reader, Cord knew the snake must have startled the horse and thrown Jonty.

Cord's eyes feverishly searched the area. There was nothing that didn't belong there. Cold sweat broke out on his forehead. That left the canyon. He swung to the ground, moved to the gorge's edge and peered down. Could the kid possibly be alive after a fall like that? His hands clenched helplessly. He didn't think so. It would be a miracle if he was.

A hard knot formed in his chest as he tried to visualize the ranch house without the strange boy in it. How empty the rooms would seem without the kid's occasional trilling laughter, his silky, throaty voice conversing with the men.

As Cord prepared himself to look for Jonty, dreading what he would find, he took one last downward look, then froze. There, crouched between two tall boulders, was a small figure. Relief in tumultuous tides washed over him when he saw it move. Unbelievably, the kid was alive. He hurried along the canyon's edge, looking for a place he could descend without breaking a leg.

It seemed to Cord that he'd walked a mile before he

found a spot that looked hopeful if he navigated it carefully. He gave a start as he stood, charting his course. From down below, there had came a high scream, followed by a panicked, "Help! Help!"

A broad smile lit up his face. It's the kid, he thought, and scared witless. He cupped his hands around his mouth and loudly called Jonty's name, then froze. Jonty's name hadn't even echoed back to him when the scream of a panther chilled his blood. He jerked his head to where the sound still hung on the air, and missed a heartbeat. Belly down, on a ledge several feet below him, was the biggest cat he'd ever seen. Its large paws were gathered together, ready to spring on the figure below.

His reflexes working at excessive speed, he had the Colt out of its holster, his trigger finger squeezing it. The panther flopped on its side, the fierce eyes glazing. Before the smoke cleared away, Cord was slipping and sliding down the canyon wall. He reached the rock-strewn floor and hurried to kneel beside Jonty's still body.

Surely the kid wasn't dead, he prayed, feeling for a pulse in the slender wrist. He sighed his relief when he found it beating strongly. "Shit," he growled, frowning, "I'm damned if he hasn't fainted." His swift hands then felt for broken bones and found none.

Unconsciously gentle, he brushed the sand-covered curls off Jonty's forehead. "I guess you can't help bein' a scaredy-cat." His eyes ranged over the still form. He noted the shirt that hung in shreds from the narrow shoulders. "These duds are sure shot."

He was about to uncap his canteen and sprinkle water on the small, dusty face and revive the limp body, when his attention was caught by the wide strip of white cloth circling the narrow chest. "What's this?" he muttered, undoing the three shirt buttons that were still intact and folding back the edges. "I wonder when he hurt himself, and why didn't the little idiot tell anyone?"

Cord's long fingers unpinned the binding, then, lifting Jonty in order to unwind the cloth, he laid her back down, the material in his hands.

His face drained of color as, with a sharp intake of breath, he sat back on his heels, his mind refusing to believe what his eyes saw. It wasn't possible—but nevertheless, Jonty Rand was a woman!

His heart hammered. To the man used to the sagging breasts of whores, these firm, pink tipped mounds were mesmerizing. In wonderment, he lifted a hand to stroke the flush-tipped flesh, then hurriedly dropped it. It wasn't the thing to do, with the kid out of it.

Kid, hell! He gave a mirthless laugh. This was no kid lying here. His eyes ranged over her features, noting the delicate structure of the face, the straight nose, full lips, and creamy skin. Jonty Rand was all female, and he couldn't believe he hadn't seen it before.

"You didn't for a simple reason," his inner voice pointed out. "Ever since you've known her, you've been conditioned to believe she was a male."

There marched before him all the cruel, hurtful words he'd ever said to Jonty, all the harsh acts he had visited on her. In his mind he saw her blistered, bleeding feet, remembered the times he had laid rough hands on her, heard the insults and accusations he had hurled at her.

An agony of regret swept across Cord's face as he continued to gaze at the perfect loveliness of the upper torso. It would be too much to think that Jonty would ever forgive him. He had seen hatred of him flash too many times in those blue eyes.

But just a damned minute! A welcome thought hit Cord. He had some apologies coming too. She and her grandmother, Maggie, had played one hell of a trick on him, a trick that had made him handle a woman roughly, something he had never done in his life.

When Jonty stirred and opened her eyes, she looked into a face vastly different from what it had been when

Cord first discovered her secret. She stared into the angry eyes, waiting in dull misery for the scornful words that were bound to come. She had fainted from fright, and this hard-faced man knew it. To him, it was an unforgivable act for a male.

Her uneasiness increased as Cord spoke no word, only quizzed her with slate-hard eyes. Please get it over with, she begged silently, then caught her breath. Cord was gesturing to her chest and asking coldly, "When did you plan on tellin' me about these?"

She cast a swift look downward, and with an alarmed gasp, snatched at what remained of her shirt and tried to cover her nakedness. Clutching the edges together, she ventured a glance at his face. She had wondered many times how he would react if he should learn of the deceit perpetrated on him. Now she knew. If she were to go by the dark scowl on his face, he would like to strangle her.

"So, you and Maggie have played a fine trick on me, huh?" The question was shot at her so abruptly, so harshly, that Jonty cringed.

While she tried to gather her thoughts to make some response, he shot another question at her. "Why the pretense all these years? What did Maggie hope to gain, passin' you off as a boy?" When Jonty was too scared to answer and could only stare at him mutely, his mouth tightened and he grated forcefully, "Well, dammit, say somethin'."

Jonty sat up, grabbing at her ruined shirt when Cord's eyes dropped to her partially covered breasts and lingered. She felt her nipples hardening under the heat of his gaze, and, with her rising anger that they should, the mental fog she'd been thrust into began to lift.

She flung a hand toward the arousal pressing against Cord's trousers and cried out bitterly, "She did it to protect me from the men such as you who visited the whorehouse."

His face beet-red, Cord jumped to his feet and jammed his hands in his pockets, silently cursing the desire that had risen in his loins. His voice was gruff when he told his lie. "I'd have no trouble keepin' my hands off a weedy-lookin' thing like you. Maggie could have told me your secret before foisting you off on me. I had a right to know."

Smarting from Cord's description of her, Jonty made no response for a moment. She supposed she was weedy-looking in her tattered clothing. She wrapped her arms around her body to hide the thinness he had scorned and said quietly, "I suppose she was afraid you wouldn't take me if you knew. She was worried sick that she'd die and leave me unprotected in Nellie's pleasure house."

Cord hadn't missed Jonty's shamed covering of herself, and felt a jab of remorse. He shouldn't have spoken to her so. Anger at himself had made him do it, for in truth, he had never seen a lovelier body.

Yet, when he spoke, none of this sounded in his voice. "You supposed right. There's no place in my life for a clingin' woman."

Jonty stiffened, all nervousness fading. "Look, Cord McBain," she burst out furiously, "I never wanted to be pushed off on you. I begged Granny to let me go live with Uncle Jim LaTour, but she wouldn't hear of it. The poor old misguided woman thought you the better man to entrust me to."

"Hah! That's not surprisin'. That half-breed hangs around with the scum of the West. You'd have been safer at Nellie's." He frowned down at her suddenly. "Does LaTour know you're female?"

Jonty looked away from the penetrating gray eyes as she acknowledged faintly, "Yes. He's always known."

Resentment and hurt pride flashed in Cord's eyes. "How come a damned outlaw knows about you and no one else does?"

"I don't know," Jonty answered, having often wondered about that herself. She'd imagined he had probably stumbled onto the fact accidentally at some point. "Nellie and the girls have always known, too," she added. "Maybe one of them told him."

Cord looked stunned. He couldn't believe that so many women could keep such a secret. He thought back to the fondness Nellie and her girls had always shown the *boy*, the time he'd had pneumonia and they had hovered over him as though he were a dear brother. Nellie had had a hard time pulling them away to entertain her customers. He was remembering how Lucy hated Jonty, when Jonty spoke.

"Uncle Jim would never let anything bad happen to me." She looked hopefully at him. "Can I go to him now?"

Cord's eyebrows pulled into thunderclouds. "You can like hell. Maggie gave you over to my keepin', and you'll stay with me until I can figure out a suitable way of gettin' rid of you.

"But I wouldn't be a burden to *him*," Jonty insisted doggedly. "He wants me."

"I just bet he does." Cord snorted sardonically. "He wants you to share his bed." Suddenly he gripped Jonty's shoulder painfully. "Maybe he's already had a taste of you." He pinned Jonty with stormy eyes. "Has he? Has that breed made love to you?"

Little flecks of devilment flickered in Jonty's eyes. "Me? Are you loco? A weedy-looking thing like me? He likes his women to have lots of curves—like you do."

Cord's eyes blazed and his fingers tightened until Jonty flinched with the pain of them. "Answer me, damn you."

"No, he hasn't." Jonty's own eyes shot sparks. "He doesn't feel that way about me. He treats me like a sister, a niece." She tried to free herself from the steely grip. "You've got a dirty mind, Cord McBain."

Cord shoved her away. "And you've got a mind full of cotton if you think he wouldn't take advantage of the situation I just ran into." He looked meaningfully at her barely covered breasts.

"He would not!" Jonty denied hotly, unaware that in her agitation the torn shirt had shifted and one breast was revealed in all its beauty.

Cord tore his eyes away and picked up the strip of binding from the ground. "I'll never know, will I?" He shoved the cloth into her hand. "Wind this back around yourself, then you can put my shirt on." He turned his back to her and began undoing his buttons with fingers that shook slightly.

"I take it I'm to continue my disguise then?" Jonty said when he tossed her the shirt.

"Yes, for the time bein' at least. Even though the men believe that you're a boy, I've caught some of the younger ones sneakin' lustful eyes at you. I'd have my hands full if they discovered you're a girl."

"Oh? I don't see that happening with Miss Perez. They all seem to be able to control themselves around her."

Cord ran a condemning glance over her slender shape as she finished buttoning up his shirt. "Weedy lookin' or not, you're the kind of woman men fight over."

But not the great Cord McBain. Jonty's lips curled as Cord took her arm and they began to climb out of the canyon. It would be beneath *him* to fight over a woman.

They scrambled over the top of the wall, and every muscle and limb protesting, Jonty approached the little quarter horse. A surprised breath caught in her throat when Cord picked her up and sat her astride the horse. Had he still thought her male, he would have let her struggle into the saddle the best way she could.

She picked up the reins and sent her mount after the stallion, wondering what turn her life would take now.

CHAPTER 13

IT WAS LATE SUMMER, AND THE SUN WAS STILL SCORCHING hot. Jonty lifted the pointed ends of the neckerchief tied around her throat and wiped her forehead with it. Was this heat never going to break?

It hadn't rained in weeks. The grass was gone and the foliage was gray with dust, and every sandy wash was bone-dry. Each day they had to ride farther and farther from the ranch to find the wild horses that were on the move, searching for graze.

"Until it rains, we'll break and brand those we've already rounded up," Cord had said the night before as they all sat out on the porch. "It's crazy to drive new ones back here and let them starve to death. There's bound to be an end to this drought soon."

He looked up at the sky and pointed out, "See, there's a ring around the moon. That means it will rain soon."

The wranglers had hooted laughter at his claim, declaring that it was only heat-haze he saw. But

Lightfoot had said that Cord was right, that it would
rain sometime tomorrow, and the men had taken his
word as gospel.

Wry amusement twitched Jonty's lips. The riders'
willingness to believe Lightfoot was simply because he
was an Indian and was supposed to know those things.
She could have told them her Granny had had the
ability to read nature, and she couldn't claim an
acquaintance with any Indian.

From her position far down the canyon, Jonty
picked Cord's tall frame out of the swirling mass of
riders and horses. She sighed unhappily. Nothing
much had changed between her and Cord. Although
he mostly ignored her these days, she still felt ill at
ease around him—more so now that he knew her sex.

She thumbed the sweat-stained hat off her forehead.
It was a relief, though, not to have Cord pushing her at
the flashing-eyed Tina anymore. She had grown to
dislike the girl. There was something about her ready
smile, her soft speech, that didn't ring true. No one
was ever nice and sweet all the time. Human nature
just wasn't that way.

Jonty's lips curled scornfully. A man might not see
it. His big ego made him see what he wanted to see. He
would never look beyond the ripe red lips and provoc-
ative figure. But a woman would be wary of forming a
friendship with the señorita.

Had Tina lured Cord into her bed yet? Jonty
wondered. Lately, in the evenings, he often left the
cabin for long stretches of time. Did the Mexican girl
meet him somewhere? Did they make love, perhaps
alongside the murmuring Sweetwater?

She told herself scornfully that the little pang in her
heart at the thought had nothing to do with jealousy.
Why should she care if he met a dozen women? She
couldn't stand the arrogant, bossy man.

Uneasiness washed over Jonty when she saw that
same man lift the reins and send his mount in her
direction. What had she done now to displease him?

He didn't make her attend the branding anymore. Had he changed his mind? Was he going to send her down there, to smell and hear the animals' distress?

Her teeth worried at her bottom lip, but as she waited for Cord to join her, her face showed none of her apprehension. He pulled the stallion in and frowned down at Jonty's heat-flushed face. He sensed her unrest by her white-knuckled grip on the reins and felt a mingling of irritation and contrition. Was she never going to forget and forgive his previous treatment of her, never trust him?

Jonty eyed him suspiciously for several seconds, then snapped, "All right, out with it. What have I done wrong now?"

Cord's frown deepened and his eyes flashed angrily. "You little hell-cat, why are you always on the defensive with me?"

"I'd think that wouldn't be too hard for you to figure out." She looked at him stonily, then said, "You're not in the habit of seeking me out for friendly conversation."

"Well, you're not the friendliest person I've ever come across," Cord taunted, his gray eyes softening in amusement. When Jonty refused to carry the sparring further, he said, "I rode over to tell you to take the rest of the day off. It's gettin' too hot for a female to be out in. With all the men out here, you can take a dip in the river, cool off a bit."

Jonty stared at him in some confusion, for never had he considered her comfort before. He motioned her toward the ranch, adding, "Take the dog with you."

Still a little disconcerted, Jonty nodded, then wordlessly trotted off, the dog loping along beside the horse.

Cord's gray eyes watched her out of sight. Since that momentous day of discovery, he had found himself thinking more and more of his ward, seeing in his mind too often the beauty of her perfectly shaped breasts. Her face would suddenly come between him and whatever he might be doing, even staring out at him from the flames of a campfire.

He bowed his head in acceptance of the truth. There were no two ways about it. He hungered for the girl who had been left in his care, and he was ashamed of it. A ragged breath escaped his lips. But that didn't seem to make a blind bit of difference. No matter how he fought it and called himself a low-down cur, every time he saw her, or even thought about her, he got an erection. He seemed to go around with a perpetual arousal.

Cord turned the stallion back toward the men, his loins aching. He had to do something about Jonty, but God knew what. He didn't think he had the will power to send her away, so the question was, did he have the strength to keep his hands off her?

Jonty unsaddled the little quarter horse and put him in with the corraled herd of wild ones that pawed the ground and tossed their lean heads at their approach.

It took only minutes for her to gather soap, wash cloth, towel, and a change of clothing, not forgetting the hated binding cloth. Then, with Wolf at her side, she followed the narrow branch of the Sweetwater until a bend in it took her out of sight of the house. In the shade of lacy aspens, she kicked off her boots and stood a moment wiggling her toes in the grass, stretching out the anticipation of the cool water against her heated flesh.

She shed her clothes, then entered the river and waded out into its center until it reached her waist. With a graceful shove of her body, she began to swim. Her tired and aching muscles relaxed with each stroke of her arms.

Jonty had splashed around in the water for about half an hour and had just finished soaping her body and hair when she became aware of the weather change. The air had become sultry, and grim-looking clouds had built up in the west. They were steadily drifting toward the mountain, sending ominous shadows over the ground.

With a cry bordering on terror, she dived fast under the water to rinse away the soap, then she was splashing out of the water. She grabbed up the towel, wrapped it around her shivering body, and sprinted toward the house, giving no thought to her clothes or the soap or the washcloth that was slowly sinking to the river bottom. Wolf scampered at her heels, barking, wanting to play.

By the time she reached the house and shot through the door, the great black clouds had shut off the sun completely. When she glanced out the main room window, the out-buildings and corral were only dim outlines. She swung away from the growing darkness outside and began pacing the floor, her nerves growing tighter and tighter. When the first crash of thunder exploded, making the windows rattle, she screamed.

"I must get hold of myself," she muttered, trying to think rationally as the rain came, lashing against the windows and doors. "I should check if any of the windows are open."

She had taken a faltering step into the hall when a flash of lightning drove everything but the terror from her mind. She flew back into the big room and, like a threatened animal, curled herself into a shivering ball in one corner of the fireplace. She clapped her hands over her ears, trying to shut out the fury of the raging wind that seemed determined to get inside the house.

It took a minute for Jonty's near-crazed mind to recognize a sound outside that wasn't the shrieking wind and pelting rain. She lifted her head from the protection of her arms when she heard the rapping of boot heels on the porch.

"Thank God," she whispered, scrambling to her feet. "Johnny has come to see about me."

The door opened and a tall figure stepped inside. Water ran in small rivulets from a rain-darkened stetson and a long black slicker. A tanned hand removed the soaked hat, and blond hair was raked back by long, slender fingers.

With an inarticulate cry, Jonty flew across the room and, ignoring his drenched condition, threw herself against Cord McBain's chest.

A little less than an hour had passed since Cord sent Jonty home when he became aware of the change in the sky. There were mushrooming clouds, through which the sun burned a fierce, fiery hue. The hard, hot wind that had burned all day was suddenly gone. They were in for one hell of a storm. He thought of Jonty, alone at the house, and turned the stallion homeward. She would be frantic. He recalled the story Maggie had told him once, about Jonty's deathly fear of storms, as he kept the mount at a hard gallop.

When Jonty was ten years old a tornado had swept through Abilene, practically demolishing the entire town. The roof had gone off Nellie's place and several windows had blown in. Jonty had been sitting with one of the young whores in the kitchen when a flying shard of glass struck her companion in the throat, severing her jugular. Blood had spurted from the deep wound, spraying Jonty's face and clothing. She had screamed and gone into shock, her face chalky white, her eyes staring.

From that day, the usually spunky kid turned into a mindless, cringing wreck every time it stormed.

As Cord pulled up in front of the porch, he doubted that the years had changed Jonty's deep-rooted fears. He opened the door and stepped inside and was almost knocked off his feet by her charging body.

"I knew you'd be scared out of your wits," Cord said huskily, his arms going around Jonty's slender, shivering frame. Then, as the soft pliable curves pressed into his hard, muscular frame, he felt a stirring, a leap in his loins. Never had he wanted a woman like he did this one.

But you can't have this one, he told himself, and

tried to put Jonty away from him. Her arms only tightened around his waist, not knowing or caring that the front of her was getting soaked from the wet slicker.

As her cheek pressed under his chin and her body pressed closer and closer, as though to climb inside him, Cord's voice was raspy as he coaxed, "Let me get out this wet slicker, honey. You're gettin' all wet and I'm not doin' the floor much good either."

Jonty reluctantly released him, but stood at his elbow as he shrugged out of the dripping garment and hung it on a peg just inside the door. A blinding flash of lightning sent her springing back into his arms before he fully turned around.

This time Cord felt no stiff, unyielding material between them. As Jonty's body pressed into his, he felt every soft curve as they burned through the towel and into his flesh. A spasm of raw need was visible in his hooded eyes when a bolt of lightning lit up the room as it hit a nearby pine. When Jonty screamed hysterically, he scooped her up in his arms and carried her to the fireplace. Kneeling down, he laid her on a bearskin rug, then stretched out beside her and gathered her close in his arms.

Cord determinedly ignored the firm breasts flattened against his chest, the nipples two spots of heat burning into him. This is Jonty, he reminded himself. She's half out of her mind with fear, and all I should be thinking about is calming her down.

He began a slow stroking of his hand along her back, much in the same manner he would use in soothing a fractious horse. When the worst of her shuddering began to leave her firm, silken flesh he didn't know whether he was glad or sorry. She felt so good in his arms.

He was about to reluctantly leave off the calming movement of his hand when a gust of wind tore loose a shutter with a screeching of released nails. As the slatted wood went skittering across the porch, slamming and banging against the wall, Jonty lifted a face to him, so white, so terrorized that he groaned a curse. Gently grasping her delicate jaw, he lowered his head and placed his mouth over her trembling lips.

And though his lips moved and coaxed on hers, they had no effect on Jonty. Her lips remained as stiff as her body. When the stroking of his tongue against them brought no response, he placed a finger on the lower one and pressed gently until it parted for him. His tongue plunged into the sweet inner recess, at the same time that his fingers released the towel from around her body.

The coarse cloth fell away and Cord cupped a full, firm breast in a callused palm and slowly, sensuously, stroked a thumb across the pink nipple. His eyes glittered with satisfaction when the soft nub hardened into growing passion. Releasing her mouth, he lowered his blond head and drew it between his lips.

Minutes passed as he hungrily suckled one breast and then the other, something he had never done to any other woman, had never had the slightest desire to do.

The gentle tug of drawing lips, the sensual sound their tasting made, all combined inside Jonty and there grew in her a need so strong that she became oblivious to the storm that raged outside. The ache in the core of her being clouding her mind, her body squirming a mutual affinity, she raised a hand and stroked the thick blond hair that lay just beneath her chin.

Cord's body stiffened, and his lips grew still when her fingers tightened in his hair and she moaned, "Please, Cord, help me. I hurt so."

With a ragged sigh and a drugged look in his eyes, Cord sat back on his heels and let his eyes devour every inch of the lovely body stretched out before him. They roamed from the white breasts with the pink nipples his sucking mouth had swollen, down to a small waist that curved delightfully to softly flaring hips, a curly black triangle nestled between them, then down the long length of shapely legs.

"I knew you would look like this," he said hoarsely, placing his palms on her waist, then running them down over her hips, "all satiny soft, sweetly curved."

Jonty gazed up at him, her blue eyes stormy with desire. She slid a slender hand inside his shirt, but when she would have trailed her fingers across his muscled chest, Cord grasped her hand and firmly pulled it away. He didn't dare let her touch him. He was barely holding on to his control as it was.

Before Jonty could hurtfully ask why she couldn't touch and caress, his tongue was once again laving her breasts, nibbling her nipples. She forgot everything but the ache that knotted and pulsed inside her.

Then her twitching body grew motionless. Cord was moving his head down her body, his tongue hot and exploratory as it brushed against her stomach. When he moved lower yet and flicked his lips across the valley of her hips, her control shattered like a fine piece of china. "Please, Cord," she whimpered, "I hurt."

"I know you do, honey," Cord rasped, wondering how he could keep himself from ravishing her. "It's comin' to an end soon."

He lifted his head, and with a lithe movement knelt at her feet. Gently, he parted her legs and slid his hands beneath her narrow buttocks. Jonty gasped weakly when he lowered his head and slowly moved his warm mouth over the smoothness of one inner thigh, pausing occasionally to nip gently at the tender flesh with his white teeth, then lick his tongue across the tiny mark he'd made.

Jonty, almost weeping from the maddening throb between her legs, gave a strangled cry when Cord's slim fingers gently parted the vee of black hair that guarded the moist core of her desperate need. "Oh, Cord!" she gasped in sweet agony when his tongue invaded that special, unexplored territory.

Her fists clenched, she thrashed her head back and forth, sure that she could not bear the waves of ecstasy that grew and pulsated inside her.

But she bore it, sustained the wave that snatched her up, carrying her to a crest that made her slim hips buck wildly before giving a great shudder. She called Cord's name, then slid into soothing warmth.

When the tremors ceased wracking her body, and her breathing settled to a normal rhythm, she smiled lazily into the slate-gray eyes that watched her face intently.

"Oh, Cord," she whispered huskily, "I never knew . . . had no idea that anything could feel so . . . so fine and beautiful."

Cord leaned over her and smoothed the dark hair off her damp forehead. "You liked it, huh?" he murmured, his gray eyes smoldering.

"Oh, yes." She smiled, then blushed prettily. A tiny frown creased her brow. "But what about you? Didn't I strike a fire in you?"

"Oh, you started a fire all right." Cord laughed ruefully, stroking a palm down the huge bulge straining at his fly. "But I'm an old hand at fires. It will burn itself out."

Jonty leaned up on an elbow, unaware of what her bareness was doing to the man still kneeling between her legs. Pinning him with searching eyes, she asked with a ragged edge to her voice, "Will you let it burn out on its own, Cord, or will you take it to Tina to be quenched?"

Cord stroked the delicate arch of her eyebrow. "Would it bother you if I did?"

"You know it would," Jonty answered, her eyes telling him everything she felt. "I want to take care of what I started, Cord. I don't want the passion I aroused taken to another woman."

"The thing is, Jonty, you didn't start anything." Cord rose to his feet. "I started it, so I can finish it when and where I please."

Jonty lay stunned, her fingers clutching at the bearskin, the clean, woodsy smell of Cord's body clinging to her own. She couldn't have been more hurt if he slapped her across the face. It was clear he didn't please to find relief from her.

She sat up, and gazing at him gravely, asked bluntly, "Just why did you start it, Cord? Was it a new way you thought up to hurt, to embarrass me, to make me dependent on you for even that?"

Cord stiffened and looked at Jonty, too stunned by her accusation to readily answer her. Naturally she would think those things about him. He had led her into other traps before, when he thought her a boy and had been determined to bend him to his will. *Damnit!* he thought, I never do anything right where she's concerned.

After a long, tense silence, he said curtly, "I had no trick in mind. You were petrified of the storm and that was the only way I could think of to get you through it—build one inside you more wild than the one that raged outside. Which, by the way," he added casually, glancing out the window, "is also over."

Cord's unemotional explanation hit Jonty with the force of a kick in the stomach. For a moment she could only stare at him in disbelief. How could anyone be so cold, so unfeeling?

Jumping to her feet, she grated out as her naked body stamped past him, "Thanks awfully, but do me a favor and send one of the new men to calm me the next time it storms."

Cord watched the graceful figure disappear down the hall and flinched when the bedroom door slammed. He leaned over and picked up the discarded towel, muttering, "Like hell I will," as he held it to his face. He breathed in the clean, rose scent of the delightful body that had responded so wildly to his love-play. A love-play that in the end made her hate him more than ever. He dropped the towel and left the cabin.

There was a somber austerity about a forest after a rain, Cord thought, steering the stallion through the trees. He had been riding the mountain aimlessly for the past few hours, trying to erase from his mind the girl he'd left back at the house, bewildered and on the point of tears.

But dammit, he was bewildered too. Never before had he paid such homage to a woman's body, never had he even thought to do so. But with Jonty, it had seemed natural and right. He sighed. It was going to take everything within him to keep his hands off her. And she would be no help. She had responded all too readily, and would again despite how angry she might be at him now.

He reined the stallion in at a break in the forest and sat looking glumly at the valley below. He could have had Jonty back there, done what his body was screaming for him to do—bury his throbbing arousal deep inside her, receive the relief only she could give him.

Two things had stopped him. First, his liking and respect for the dead Maggie and his promise to look after her grandchild, and second, the thought of giving up the freedom of being a bachelor. For making love to Jonty would never be a one-time occurrence. One taste of her and he'd want her for the rest of his life.

His lips gave a bitter twist. Even if Jonty should by some miracle agree to marry him, it would never work. He was too old for her and in time her eyes would begin to wander to younger men, men who hadn't lived as hard as he had, experienced as much.

No. He shook his head decisively. There was only one thing to do. He must continue his coldness toward her. He would also make up to the girl, Tina, whenever Jonty was around, make her think that his interest lay with the Mexican girl.

Jonty listened to the outside door close quietly, heard Cord walk across the porch. A tear rolled down her cheek as she heard the stallion gallop away. He was on his way to Tina's arms.

She listlessly took clean underwear from the dresser, then lifted a shirt and pair of trousers from a peg fastened to the back of the door. As she did up her buttons, she thought of the clothes she'd left on the river bank. She could imagine what shape they must be in, beaten into the mud.

Jonty's stomach growled, telling her that she was hungry. And what was she to do about supper? She wasn't ready yet to meet Cord's mocking looks. There was no doubt in her mind that he had derived a devilish satisfaction out of refusing her offer of love.

Love? She closed her eyes in defeat. She knew suddenly, unwanted and unwelcomed, that she did love Cord McBain, and it was a bitter discovery. Nothing would ever come of it. The man didn't even like her, much less love her.

She threw herself across the bed, hopeless tears running from the corners of her eyes. There was nothing she could do about it but hug the knowledge to herself in silent misery. If Cord should find out, he'd laugh himself silly.

CHAPTER 14

AUTUMN CAME, DULL AND GRAY, WITH THREATENING clouds hovering over the mountain. Before long winter would be upon them again, with its snow, ice, and piercing winds.

Cord shivered, remembering past winters of sitting around a campfire in freezing weather, the long nights hunched up in his bedroll, never quite warm. Suddenly, surprisingly, he realized that his old life no longer appealed to him. Why? he wondered. What was dulling the wild side of him?

"I don't like these changes in me," he said aloud. His lips tightened when a pair of blue eyes flashed in front of him. "Jonty. She's the cause of it."

What was he going to do about her? He asked the often repeated question. She was looking more feminine every day. It was just a matter of time when, just as he had, one of the men would accidentally discover the delightful shape beneath the loose-fitting shirt and baggy pants. He'd have to do something then, or keep a constant eye on her.

The house came in sight and Cord's mind switched to another and different aggravation. Tina Perez. The charade he had started with her for Jonty's benefit had backfired on him. Everywhere he turned, she was there. Her cloying, clinging sweetness was wearing to a man's nerves—at least to his, when all he wanted to do was grab Jonty up and carry her off to bed. He went through hell every night, knowing that she was sleeping only a few feet away. He pictured her lying on her back, one arm flung over her head, the man's night-shirt riding up around her waist.

He knew the way she slept. He had slipped into her room many nights and stood beside the bed, watching her sleep, battling with himself not to slide in beside her.

He shook his head ruefully. Not only had his pretense with Tina gone awry, but every time he went riding with the girl, Jonty spent the evening in the bunkhouse with the riders. Playing poker with them of all things. And usually the big winner. He had been secretly pleased at her ability with cards—until he learned that Jim LaTour had taught her the game.

LaTour, Cord thought with a grimace. He still wasn't completely satisfied in his mind just what the relationship between Jonty and the breed was. She called him Uncle, and claimed that was how she felt about the older man. But the breed was known as a womanizer and if he was aware of Jonty's sex, he wouldn't be feeling like a relative toward her. If nothing had happened between them yet, the man was just biding his time.

Cord's eyes narrowed at the thought. Maybe Jonty had lied to him. Maybe the outlaw had already known the joy of her body. Maybe for some time. According to Lucy, LaTour had visited Maggie and Jonty several times a year, but had never taken any of Nellie's girls to the room upstairs. Was that because he had a bed and a partner downstairs?

No. Cord shook his head. He was wrong, wrong about everything. First, Maggie would never have allowed it, because she had hated LaTour, and second, Jonty was too innocent, too unaware of her body's needs.

Or she had been, he reminded himself. She knew all about them now, thanks to his own craziness. He had started fires she might want fanned again. Maybe her visits to the bunkhouse meant she had an interest in one of the new men, one she had chosen to be her fire-tender.

Jealousy, a new emotion for Cord, gnawed at his insides. His eyes darkened with defeat. If it was true, there wasn't a damn thing he could do about it, and Jonty knew it. In his mind's eye he saw the triumphant smiles she always sent him as she ambled toward the bunkhouse, the riders walking close beside her, laughing and joking, touching, secretly watching her, at the same time looking sheepish for being attracted to what they thought was a young boy.

He sighed raggedly and rode on, his broad shoulders drooping a bit.

The sun had passed over the mountain rim and dusk was settling in, soft and pine scented. As birds, preparing to roost, swooped among the trees, Jonty stepped out onto the porch. She stood a moment, a smile on her face, listening to the birds calling to one another. She relaxed on a bench then, sinking into thought.

Johnny Lightfoot should be returning any day now. A week ago, he had gone looking for Uncle Jim. He hadn't wanted to, pointing out that he was sure his cousin was still holed up on a distant mountain about fifty miles away. "It's no place for you, Jonty." He had finished his argument.

But she had been adamant, declaring tearfully that she was at the end of her tether. She told him forcefully that she couldn't take much more of Cord McBain's dictatorial, high-handed ways and that, if necessary, she would return to Nellie. Johnny had agreed then to search out his cousin.

Jonty smiled in dry amusement. As far as Almighty Cord McBain knew, Johnny had gone to visit his people for a short time. Which was true in a way. Uncle Jim was a part of his people.

She stared down at her clasped hands lying in her lap. She had lied to Johnny when she claimed it was Cord's hateful ways she couldn't stand. It tore her apart seeing Cord and Tina together, watching them disappear into the darkness each night, a darkness that would screen them as they made love.

She stared into the near twilight, tears glittering in her eyes. Cord knew now that she was a woman, so why did he still treat her in the same cold way? She could understand his doing it in front of the others, who were still ignorant of her sex, but even when they were occasionally alone together, his eyes were always veiled, unreadable, his restlessness saying he was impatient to get away from her.

Jonty sighed softly. There was one little piece of consolation she clung to. For although Cord had flung her offer of love-making back in her face, treating very casually what had happened between them, there had been nothing casual in the way he had kissed her. There had been passion and intensity in the lips claiming hers, and she hadn't imagined the tremors that had shuddered through his body. Maybe *he* didn't like her, but his body did.

She gave herself an impatient shake. "Give it up, Jonty," she whispered bitterly. "You're beating a dead horse. Outside of your inheritance, the man has no use for you, so you'd better get away before you start begging him to make love to you." And wouldn't that please him, she thought, blinking back a tear. What pleasure it would give him to laugh in her face.

Jonty gathered her feet together to rise, then sat back down. The man who claimed so much of her thoughts had just ridden up to the porch and slipped off his horse.

Cord didn't see Jonty at first, sitting at the far end of the porch, and when she spoke his body went still.

After a moment he said stiffly, "I didn't see you hidden over there."

"I wasn't hiding." Jonty laughed nervously. "I was just enjoying the twilight. It's my favorite time of day."

"I'm beat." Cord started for the door, flexing sore muscles.

Jonty stood up and ventured shyly, "I'm good at rubbing away soreness. I often massaged Granny's poor old back when it ached."

Cord's mocking eyes held her gaze a moment, then he said cruelly, "No doubt you brought relief to Maggie, but it takes a little gal like Tina to relieve my soreness. She knows just where to rub."

Cord passed on into the house, hating himself for the shattered look he left behind.

Jonty watched the distant black dot come closer, quickly growing into a horse and rider. A smile lit up her face as she recognized the thick-chested roan. "It's about time you got back, Johnny Lightfoot." Her voice was eager.

Two weeks had passed since her friend had ridden off on his errand, and for the past week she had watched every day for his return. She lifted the reins, thumped Beauty with a heel and raced across the valley to meet the Indian.

The two mounts came to a plunging halt, only inches apart. Jonty and Lightfoot grinned affectionately at each other. "You've been gone a long time, Johnny," Jonty said accusingly. "I was beginning to think that something had happened to you."

He looked away from her eager young face, his own reddening a bit. "You know how it is, a person gets held up sometimes."

"Yeah," Jonty teased, noting the dark flush on the bronze cheeks, "especially if it's a pretty little Indian girl doing the holding up."

The Indian grinned, but made no response.

"Well, tell me," Jonty said impatiently, "Did you

see Uncle Jim?" Lightfoot nodded. "Did you tell him how desperately I want to get away from here?"

"Let's move on and I'll tell you while we ride." Lightfoot nudged his mount in motion. "Cord may be watching us and become suspicious. You know how he is where you're concerned."

"First, there's something I should tell you." Jonty rode along beside Johnny. "Cord knows I'm female."

The stunned look on the usually stoic face made Jonty want to giggle. Instead, she reminded him of the day she was thrown and fell down the canyon, then briefly explained how Cord had discovered her femininity.

Suspicion grew in the black eyes watching her face. "What did he say? Better yet, what did he do?"

"He didn't *do* anything, but he was really angry when he got over his shock. He said Granny had played a dirty trick on him, saddling him with a girl."

"I hope he continues to feel that way about it. I don't want him getting other feelings about you, if you know what I mean."

Jonty grinned. "I know what you mean, friend. I was born and raised in a whorehouse, remember? Anyway, you don't have to worry, he still can't stand me."

When Johnny said nothing, Jonty twisted around in the saddle and looked at the Indian, suddenly wary. He was slow in bringing up Uncle Jim. "You didn't find him, did you?" she asked, a tremor in her voice.

Lightfoot gave her a resentful glare. But as he drawled, "Have you lost faith in my tracking ability, Jonty?" she saw the gleam of amusement in his black eyes.

"Of course you found him!" Jonty laughed happily. "It was foolish of me to ask such a question."

"Yes it was," Johnny chided, reaching out and giving her curls a tug. "It took me awhile, though. My cousin don't spend all his time in his usual haunt anymore. He's mostly living in Cottonwood these days."

"But Johnny." Jonty started to pull her mount up, her eyes wide. Lightfoot caught Beauty's bit and urged her on. "Doesn't Uncle Jim realize he's taking a big chance, showing himself so openly in such a small town?" Jonty finished.

"I doubt if he's in any real danger. Cottonwood is a wide-open cattle town, if you remember. It's still raw and violent, with not much law and order. Jim will fit right in."

"What's he going to do there? I hope he's not going to . . ."

"Rob banks?" Lightfoot laughingly cut across her sentence. "No, believe it or not, for your sake, my cousin is going to try going straight. He's dickering to buy a saloon. He expects to take it over any day now."

"Then—" Jonty paused, afraid to ask. "Does that mean I can go to him?"

The Indian chuckled as the hope and dread of his answer chased across her face. "You can go to him any time you want to."

Jonty let out a whoop that startled both horses. When the animals had been calmed down, she said, half jesting, half serious, "I'm ready to turn Beauty around right now and leave this mountain—and Cord McBain—forever."

The corners of the Indian's eyes crinkled in sympathy. "I understand your feelings, girl. You've had a rough few months with McBain. But we have to make a few plans, not go off half cocked. Cord would never let you just up and go, you know that. We'll have to leave on the sneak."

"I expect that would be best," Jonty agreed. "But he would only object in an obligatory way—his promise to Granny, you know." And the money she gave him, she thought to herself.

Lightfoot made no response, but the look he slid Jonty said he doubted that would be the only reason McBain would refuse to let her go. He'd bet that under the rough clothes Jonty hid herself in, there was a lovely body. And womanizing McBain had seen a part of it. He'd be wanting to see the rest of it as soon as possible.

"Today is Thursday," he said. "We'll leave this coming Saturday. At night, when everyone is asleep."

The house stood in front of them and nothing more was said on the subject.

"I'm going over to the bunkhouse and grab a couple hours' sleep before supper," Lightfoot said. "I'm beat. I've been in the saddle since daybreak this morning."

Jonty nodded. "You go ahead. I'm going to take a ride, let this good news sink in."

Without conscious thought, Jonty followed the now deeply cut trail to the canyon Cord had discovered. Mixed emotions battled inside her. She swayed between the relief of getting away from Cord, and wondering at the same time what life would be like with him not in it.

"You idiot," she finally reproached herself. "Your life would be pure hell with that man in it. He'll never change. He'd continue to trample on your feelings, shove his women under your nose. Be thankful you can get away from him."

Jonty forcefully pushed thoughts of Cord from her mind as she came to the gate that blocked the only entrance to the valley of wild horses. She slid from the saddle and swung open the barrier; then, leading Beauty through, she dragged it closed behind her. Back on the mare again she gazed down at the huge expanse of green, waving grass.

I will miss this, she thought sadly, swinging her gaze over the part of the valley she could see. It had to be the most beautiful spot in the world. Her attention was caught then by black dots and clouds of dust away in the distance—tell-tale signs of running horses. The wranglers were cutting out special mustangs to be branded, then broken to saddle.

With a light touch of her heels, Jonty urged the mare down the gentle slope for a closer look, probably for the last time. Her sympathy with the horses, she watched the graceful animals dodge and elude the whistling nooses whipping over their heads. According to Johnny, a wild stallion was the most cunning of all wild animals, his speed and endurance above all others.

"Of course Cord would argue that the wolf beats them all hollow," he'd added, then said with a laugh, "there's some who say he's akin to the wolf."

The shrill piercing whistle of a stallion brought Jonty twisting around in the saddle. Off to her right she spotted Cord, astride Rawhide, moving in on a beautiful white stallion. "Cord, you fool!" she exclaimed, "riding a stallion among those wild ones."

She held her breath as she watched the white horse stamp and snort defiance as Cord cautiously kneed Rawhide closer, a looped rope in his hand. His ears laid back, the handsome white gave another shrill clarion call and Rawhide neighed a blast in return, stopping to pound the earth with his own iron-shod hooves.

"Oh, my God!" Jonty's heart seemed to stop. "They're going to fight!" Her eyes flew to Cord. He was trying to hold Rawhide in, the strain of it on his face even from this distance. And while she watched, terror stricken, the stallions raced at each other. They met and stood on their hind legs, their forelegs striking out at each other.

Round and round the two great stallions circled, long bared teeth nipping at vital points, hind legs kicking at each other in furious rage. "Oh, be careful, Cord," Jonty whispered, as a lethal hoof came dangerously close to him.

Then, in a blink of an eye, it seemed, Cord did catch a blow from a flashing hoof. On his right temple. As in slow motion, his body slumped, then tumbled to the ground.

"That devil will stomp him to death!" Jonty cried, then held her breath as Rawhide, his nostrils distended, his eyes blazing, stood protectively over his fallen master.

"Oh, you brave, brave animal," Jonty sobbed, automatically unsheathing her rifle. "But there's danger for Cord from your own hoofs."

Breathing a grateful thanks to Jim LaTour for having taught her the use of the weapon, she swept it to her shoulder, caught the white stallion's broad chest in the rifle's sight, then slowly squeezed the trigger. The beautiful horse went down, shot through the heart. As Jonty raced Beauty to the fallen Cord, Rawhide sped away, becoming lost among the scores of other horses.

The mare barely coming to a plunging halt, Jonty was off her back and kneeling beside Cord's inert body. The lean face, usually so vital, was still and pale. She stared at the imprint of a hoof that left a half circular mark on his forehead before disappearing into his hair line. Blood poured freely from the wound, trickling down over a blond eyebrow and onto a cheek that had lost its tan.

She frantically felt for a pulse in his wrist and thanked God when she felt it, faint but regular. She looked up as some of the riders came thundering toward her. Jones, the first out of the saddle, ran and knelt down beside her. "Is he all right?"

Her own face as ashy pale as Cord's, Jonty said shakily, "He's alive, but he's had an awful blow to the head from that stallion." She jerked her head in the direction of the dead horse.

"I saw you bring him down." Admiration was in Jones's voice. "It was the best shot I ever saw a man make."

It was doubtful if Jonty heard the words of praise as she whipped a clean handkerchief from her back pocket and pressed it to the wound. "We've got to get him to the house as soon as possible," she cried as the cloth immediately turned red from Cord's blood.

She jumped to her feet, and catching up the mare's reins, vaulted into the saddle. "Get him up here in front of me."

"Can you handle him?" Jones cast a doubtful look at the slender, impatiently waiting figure. "Cord weighs close to a hundred and ninety pounds."

"Come on, Jones." Jonty glared down at the concerned face. "We're wasting time. I'm stronger than I look."

Shaking his head, still doubtful, the older wrangler motioned to one of the men, and together they carefully picked their boss up and placed his limp body in the saddle. Jonty pulled Cord back to lean against her slight frame, and with his head resting against her narrow shoulder, she nudged Beauty with a heel, one hand on the reins, the other keeping the cloth pressed to Cord's forehead.

Although it took less than half an hour to cover the distance to the ranch house, it seemed like hours to Jonty as Cord's blood continued to seep through the make-shift bandage and trickle through her fingers.

When she pulled up in front of the house, the Perez family burst through the door, Tina leading the way. "Jonty, what has happened to Cord?" Maria pressed forward to stand beside the little mare whose head hung and sides heaved.

"He was kicked by a stallion," Jonty answered as Jones and the young rider lifted Cord down and carried him up the steps and onto the porch. She gawked at the two men a moment. She hadn't even been aware that they had followed her.

She hurried then to hold the door open, saying briskly to wide-eyed Tina, "I'm going to need your help. Hurry and bring me a basin of cold water and some clean white rags." When Tina didn't move, only stood wringing her hands, she demanded angrily, "Why are you standing there like a statue? I need that water before Cord bleeds to death."

"Oh, Jonty, I can't." Tina backed away from the blazing light in Jonty's eyes. "I can't stand the sight of blood . . . of sick people."

A picture of this flashing-eyed beauty fawning over

Cord, taking long rides with him, probably making love with him, flashed before Jonty. She was gripped with an anger that made it hard for her not to slap the soft, silly face.

Her lips tightened. "It seems that this great passion you have for Cord disappears when he's hurt and helpless." She gave the cringing girl a push that sent her staggering against the wall, then turned to Maria.

The shame-faced mother said hastily, "Go to Cord, Jonty, I'll bring the water and cloths."

Inside Cord's sparsely furnished bedroom, Jonty stared down at him, thinking that his face wasn't much brighter than the pillow his sun-streaked head lay on. Someone had removed the handkerchief and she felt weak with relief to see the bleeding had lessened somewhat, with only a slight oozing in a few places.

Jones spoke from across the bed. "It's not as bad as we thought, Jonty. It looks like he only caught a glancing blow. If he'd have got the full impact of that hoof, it would have crushed his skull."

Jonty shuddered at the dreadful thought of a world without Cord McBain in it. To her he seemed invincible, proof against any obstacle life might put in his path. And though she wanted no part of his life, she wanted him to have one.

As she stared down at the handsome face, so much younger-looking in its vulnerability, she found she liked him this way, rendered weak and dependent on his fellow man. It made him like the rest of them, with the same frailties, the same need to lean on another once in a while.

But there's concussion to worry about, a small voice whispered inside Jonty. She looked at Jones. "I'll be back in a minute," she said and rushed out of the room.

Inside her bedroom Jonty hurried to the big trunk placed against a wall. She threw the lid back, and with anxious fingers, she rummaged around in its contents.

"Aha!" she grunted after a moment, dragging forth Maggie's old medical ledger. She flipped through its frayed pages, looking for information on concussion.

She found the page, then sighed, a mingling of disappointment and relief griping her. There wasn't much written under the heading "Concussion of the Brain." In her neat, spidery hand Granny had only penned, "A condition of unconsciousness and shock resulting from a severe blow on the head."

That first sentence was her disappointment, the second one her relief. It read, "Concussion is rarely fatal."

Jonty's relief grew when she returned to Cord's room and found that Maria had cleaned Cord's wound and washed his face. Her eyes mirrored her hope when she looked at Jones and half-whispered, "I believe he's regained a little color, don't you?"

"Yeah, I believe he has, lad," Jones answered in a normal tone, "and you don't have to whisper. Cord wouldn't hear the crack of doom right now." He looked at Jonty and grinned. "Now's your chance to say all them things you've been wantin' to say these past weeks. So go on, tear into him, unload yourself."

Jonty returned the grin but shook her head. "Oh, no. That one's subconscious would take in everything I'd say and then in a week or so he'd remember them. You know what my skin would be worth then."

"Go on, are you tellin' me that you're scared of Cord?" Jones teased.

"Scared to death, half of the time." Her eyes twinkled.

But while Jonty and Jones laughed softly together, Maria interjected a serious note. "I think Cord might need a couple stitches in that one spot, Jonty. It looks a little deep." She looked up from her seat beside the bed. "Can you do it? I'm not sure I know how."

Jonty recalled the many times she had watched, then later helped Granny to sew up busted heads, gunshot wounds, and knife stabs. She had become quite proficient at it over the years. "I'll do it," she said, and as she left the room Maria advised the men to undress Cord.

Maggie's small case, holding several thin needles and a good supply of cat-gut thread, lay on top of the trunk's contents. Jonty grabbed it up, hurried back to the sick room, then stopped in her tracks. She wasn't sure she could do it. It was altogether different, sticking a sharp needle through the flesh of someone you knew. Cord wasn't a stranger she would probably never see again. He was the man she loved.

And since she loved him, she willed herself to approach the bed. She placed the slim case on the small table beside the bed, next to the kerosine lamp and shaving paraphernalia. "Can you find me some whiskey, Jones?" she asked.

The tall man nodded and left the room. Heaving a deep sigh, willing her pulse to slow down, Jonty chose a slender needle from several other sizes. Next she picked up a length of suture material and threaded it through the narrow eye.

"Here you are, Jonty." Jones stood beside her, a bottle and glass in his hand, panting slightly from his hurried errand.

Jonty took the bottle from him, uncorked it and poured a good amount of the liquor into the glass. Jones's eyes widened when she dropped the needle and thread into it. "Pour some over my hands now," she instructed, holding her hands over the basin.

Jones looked at her searchingly and she explained, "It will kill any germs that might be on my fingers."

The wrangler did as directed, but his expression was woeful as the last of his whiskey splashed over Jonty's hands and into the pan of bloody water. Maria smiled and patted his bony shoulder. "You can get another bottle." Jones nodded, then watched Jonty lean over Cord's face, the dripping needle poised.

Jonty was once again gripped with doubt that she could unemotionally slide the needle through Cord's flesh. But three people stood watching her expectantly, so, catching her lower lip between her teeth, she began, flinching each time he did at the sharp prick of the needle.

It was done finally, and Jonty straightened up, drawing an arm across her sweaty brow. "That should do it." Her voice quivered slightly, her eyes on the three neat stitches.

"You did a fine job, Jonty." Admiration was in Jones's voice and eyes. "A doc couldn't have done better. Thanks to you, Cord won't hardly have a scar to mar his handsome good looks."

Jonty thought of all the women who had marched through Cord's life, the ones still to come, and knew a moment's regret that she had been instrumental in enabling him to continue attracting every female within his range.

Jealousy of all those women jabbed at her heart. "I hope that some day a woman will touch your heart, Cord McBain, and when she does, I hope she won't have anything to do with you."

Enough of this wishful thinking, Jonty silently scolded herself and snapped the needle case closed. "I expect you want to get on with making supper, Maria." She smiled at the housekeeper as she stood up. "Let me have five minutes to catch some fresh air, then I'll sit with him."

"Of course, Jonty," Maria hastened to agree. "Take all the time you need. Tina can mind the pots."

Jones and the young wrangler followed Jonty outside, but as though sensing her need to be alone, they moved on to the bunkhouse. Jonty sighed her relief at their thoughtfulness and shivered slightly as she leaned against a supporting post. The air had cooled to chilliness with the deepening twilight. Fall is coming, she thought idly, twitching her shoulders to relieve the nervous tension that knotted her muscles.

She was massaging the back of her neck when she heard the soft sound of scuffing, moccasined feet. "How is he?" Lightfoot stepped upon the porch and stood beside her.

"He'll be all right." Jonty smiled tiredly. "It would take more than a kick in the head to kill that one."

"His head is as hard as his heart, huh, Jonty?" The Indian teased gently.

"Almost," Jonty agreed, her blue eyes shadowing with pain.

"Does this change our plans for Saturday? Will we still be going?"

"I don't know." Jonty ran slim fingers through her curls. "I feel obligated to tend him until he's on his feet. Maria has enough work to do without having to care for him too."

Lightfoot stepped off the porch and stood looking up at her. "We'll put a hold on our plans for the time being. See how McBain comes along."

Jonty nodded. "I don't think he'll be bed-fast very long." Satisfaction entered her voice. "He's going to have a large headache for a while, though."

The corners of Lightfoot's eyes crinkled, then lifting his hand in farewell, he disappeared into the gathering darkness. With a deep sigh, Jonty turned and walked back into the house. She had so looked forward to Saturday—to turning her back on Cord and the heartache he seemed to always cause her.

CHAPTER 15

THE SUN WAS DROPPING OVER THE MOUNTAIN, SENDING long shadows over the valley. Jonty sat hunched upon a small boulder, her arms folded over her bent knees. She was in no hurry to go back to the house, to start fetching and carrying for that arrogant, demanding man.

For five days she had been at his beck and call, tending to foolish requests, biting back the words that would give him the satisfaction of knowing he was getting under her skin. Why, she wondered, was he so hateful to her, so down right ornery? What did he see when he looked at her with those gray stormy eyes? He was a very knowing man. Could he see that she was in love with him? Did the fact repulse him?

She gave a dry grunt. That first night spent in delirium, she hadn't been repulsive to him . . . at least her body hadn't.

In those first few hours she had swung between wretchedness and joyful surprise. For though Cord had sworn at, yelled at, and even threatened Jonty

Rand in his high fever, it had been only her hand on his brow, her low, throaty voice that could calm him. Once, to her intense pleasure, he had turned his face into her hand and, murmuring her name, kissed her palm. She had been thankful that they were alone at the time. What gossip that act would have started had one of the hands been there to see it.

Jonty laid her head on her bent arms, remembering how she had been more thankful for their privacy when, in the early dawn hours, Cord had done something that had completely unnerved her.

His fever had reached its zenith, and she, in her nightshirt, was leaning over the bed about to lift his head and press a glass of water to his mouth when suddenly his hands fastened around her waist. As he jerked her down on top of him, she loosened her grip on the glass and it fell to the floor, rolling across the room. While she gaped at him in surprise, he pulled her head down and fastened his lips on hers. She struggled but a moment, then willingly accepted the thrust of his tongue and the tightening of his arms around her.

A big mistake, Jonty thought morosely, lifting her head and staring unseeing out over the valley. But there had been a sweet savagery in his kiss, and instead of listening to the warning flashing through her brain, she had arched herself into him and returned the kiss with equal fire. She thrilled to his callused palm sliding up her thighs, over her small buttocks, squeezing them gently before continuing to the small of her back.

When, as in a dream, Cord asked with ragged urgency, "Can't you take this damn thing off?" she had, without hesitation, sat up and whipped the nightshirt over her head. In the path of the moonlight striking across the bed, Cord's eyes grew stormy as he gazed at her breasts. His hands came up slowly to gently stroke their fullness, watching the nipples grow and become pebble-hard.

"Beautiful," he rasped, and taking her by the shoul-

ders pulled her down until a pink-tipped point
brushed against his lips. He held her there, his mouth
opened and his tongue moved hotly against her nipple. She could feel her heart beating with slow, thick
strokes, and with a moan of intense pleasure on her
lips, she breathed his name.

Jonty slid off her stone perch and stared up at the
sky, bitterly remembering how disappointingly that
beautiful beginning had ended.

It had ended as abruptly as it had started. At the
sound of his name on her lips, Cord had given a start,
sighed a ragged breath, then seemingly dropped off
into a deep sleep. For an astounded moment, she hung
over him, telling herself that it wasn't possible, roused
as he was, to fall asleep.

When she dragged herself off the bed, weak and
trembling from unfulfilled need, she doubted that
Cord slept at all. She suspected that hearing his name
spoken had pulled him back to reality, and he had
been appalled to find that it was weedy-looking Jonty
Rand he was making such fierce love to.

Her mental anguish had eased a bit, however, when
an hour later she laid her hand on his brow and found
it damp and cool. His fever had broken, and his chest
now rose and fell in the rhythm of deep, natural sleep.
Maybe, she thought, nature had stepped in at that
precise moment of love-making and had sent him off
into a healing sleep.

Would Cord remember any of it if that were the
case? she wondered later, lying on a pallet of blankets
laid out next to his bed. When she finally dropped off
to sleep, she still hadn't decided whether she wanted
him to remember or not.

"And I still don't know," Jonty burst out, causing
Beauty to lift her head to look at her. Most of the time
she thought that Cord hadn't been aware of dragging
her to him, taking her lips in raw hunger. He still
treated her in the same cool manner, barking orders at
her, never satisfied with anything she did. It seemed
that every time she opened her mouth, her words

angered him for some reason or other. No matter how calmly a conversation might begin, it always ended with Cord becoming angry.

On the second day of his recovery, she had brought him a bowl of stew. He had smiled and said that he was starving. Encouraged by his show of friendliness, she had sat down on the edge of the bed and watched him spoon the meat and vegetables into his mouth. A warmness grew inside her as, with a rush of desire, she remembered how his lips had moved on her breasts.

Then, halfway through his meal, he had looked up at her and said, "I'm told that you saved my life, that the stallion would have trampled me to death if you hadn't shot him."

Flushed with pleasure at his admiring tone, she had unthinkingly answered, "Thanks to Uncle Jim, I'm an expert shot."

Without warning, Cord's face was darkly furious. He pushed the bowl of half-eaten stew away from him with such force that the gravy splashed on her arm. She jumped to her feet, staring down at him in bewilderment.

"Everything comes down to *Uncle Jim* with you, doesn't it. Uncle Jim says, Uncle Jim does, Uncle Jim doesn't! I'm sick and tired of hearing that breed's name."

She had wheeled and run to the door, almost colliding with Tina as she went through it.

Bitterness darkened Jonty's eyes. Now that Cord was almost recovered, Tina was firmly back in his life, lying on the bed with him, practically crawling beneath the covers. Almost every time she entered his room, the pair were clenched together, unaware of anything around them as they kissed, long and hard. And if by chance they weren't locked together when she arrived, it would be but moments before Cord was pulling Tina into his arms.

"But it's still me who fetches and carries," Jonty muttered disgruntedly. "He never so much as asks Tina for a glass of water."

Determination glittered in Jonty's eyes. All that catering to him was coming to an end. The great man was on his feet most of the time now, well on the way to recovery. She had no reason to stay on and she would speak to Johnny after supper. Maybe they could get away tonight.

Her decision made, Jonty felt more at peace with herself. An owl hooted and a wolf mourned as she gathered up Beauty's reins, swung into the saddle, and headed down the hard-packed trail to the ranch.

"Where in the hell have you been?" Cord demanded brusquely from his leaning stance on a porch support as Jonty reached the house and slid from the mare.

She glanced at him curiously, caught by an odd tone in his voice. It was as if, beneath the anger, there was excitement. "I went for a ride," she answered shortly. "I was tired of being cooped up in the house." She resisted adding, "And damned tired of waiting on you."

Cord's lips parted as though to find fault, then snapped his mouth shut. Jonty would have pushed past him and gone into the house, when he spoke again.

"A stranger came by while you were gone."

"So?" Jonty asked when he didn't add to his statement. "It's not unusual for someone to stop by for a meal."

"I'm well aware of that, you little weed, but this man happens to know who owns this place. And more important, the owner wants to sell it."

"That should make you happy. It's what you've been wanting."

"Yeah. The only trouble is that this old man, Barker, lives in Abilene. That's a long trip, as you know, and I'm sure I'll have to do some dickerin' with him over the price. I could be gone two or three weeks."

Jonty lifted an indifferent eyebrow. "So? What does that have to do with me?"

"Dammit!" Cord snapped impatiently. "You'll own half of the place. While I'm gone, I want you to keep an eye on things."

Jonty sent him a startled look. "Own half of it? Me?"

Cord moved down a porch step. "Yes, you'll own half of it. It's mostly Maggie's money that will be payin' for it, and as you very well know, I promised to look after you."

Look after me! Jonty thought of the way he'd looked after her so far and wanted to laugh at the ridiculousness of it. She could do without his brand of looking after. Her full-throated laugh carried a faint mockery.

"You can have it all," she dismissed carelessly. "I want no part of the damned place. It gives me no satisfaction," she lied. "It's done nothing but draw the strength out of me ever since I set foot on it."

There was contrition in Cord's expression for a minute. In those days when he thought her a male, he had driven her hard, intending to toughen her up. He hadn't done it out of meanness. And dammit, it hadn't been that way since he learned she wasn't a frail young boy. He had spared her all he could, considering the ranch hands still thought her male.

His face hardened. She was an ungrateful little wretch who didn't appreciate anything. She should know how hard it was for him to do the honorable thing by her—keep his hands off her, pretend a romance with Tina.

"That's pretty big talk," he ground out. "I suppose you have other plans, like goin' to that breed."

Blue eyes challenged gray ones. Then, starting for the door, Jonty answered flippantly, "You don't have to concern yourself about me. I am nothing to you, and you are nothing to me."

A small cry of pain escaped her as her arm was gripped and she was swung around. Cord stared down at her with furious eyes. "You've made that clear right along, you insolent little baggage. But I'm going to keep my promise to Maggie, whether you like it or not. Once and for all, put that breed out of your mind."

Jonty stared into the glittering, stormy eyes and suddenly realized with shock that more than anger stared out at her. Cord was jealous. He wanted her. He didn't like her, but against his will he desired her. It had been there in the heat of his eyes every time he looked at her, and she hadn't recognized it until now.

She had a sinking feeling in the pit of her stomach. It was an intolerable situation. She loved him too much to let him use her, and he'd attempt that before too long. She remembered the night it had almost happened. She had been helpless against his lovemaking then, and it would be the same the next time. Tonight wouldn't be too soon to leave the mountain.

Jonty opened her mouth to say something, anything that would disguise what she was thinking, but the words never came out. They froze on her lips as from the kitchen issued the sound of a pot clattering to the floor, followed by a piercing cry of agony from the housekeeper.

Jonty dashed ahead of Cord, pulling up short in the kitchen doorway. Maria sat on the floor, cradling a foot in her hand. Painful tears ran down her cheeks as Tina looked helplessly on. Nearby a pot lay on its side, hot, thick lard still running from it, spreading across the floor. It told a clear story. Maria's bare foot had been in the way as it spilled its contents.

Stirring into action, Jonty rushed to kneel beside the suffering woman, Cord right behind her. He picked up the foot that was already turning red and stared at the white bubbly blisters that were rapidly forming. He looked at Jonty and asked over Maria's sobbing, "How are you goin' to fix it?"

Jonty blinked. Cord had automatically assumed that she would be the one to take care of Maria's injury, that she had the skill to do so. Exultation swept over her. Wasn't that proof that he looked on her as a responsible adult after all? That, as such, he wouldn't try to take advantage of her?

She took over. "First we must get Maria to her own quarters and to bed." She turned to the hand-wringing Tina. "Go get your father to come help Cord carry her."

Cord was helping Maria to her feet when Carlos hurried in, concern in his dark eyes. He took a moment to speak soothingly in their native tongue to his wife, then together, he and his boss lifted the heavy-set woman.

Jonty followed them out the door, calling over her shoulder, "Tina, bring me a basin of cold water, some clean white rags, and a box of baking soda."

In a short time Maria lay stretched out on her bed, and Tina, having for once moved swiftly, arrived breathlessly as the men were stepping away from the bed. Jonty grabbed the box of soda and emptied half its contents into the basin. She took up one of the rags and swirled it through the water. When the liquid was milky-looking, she began to gently bathe the red, swollen foot.

"The soda will draw the sting out," she explained to Cord and Carlos who hung over her. "Does it feel a little better, Maria?" She smiled at the woman, who had grown quiet.

"Oh, yes, Jonty, ever so much better." Maria returned the smile. "You have such a gentle touch. Healing hands, my madre would say." She looked up at her boss. "Would you not say so, Cord?"

Cord looked uncomfortable, and avoiding Jonty's eyes, finally said that he reckoned a person could say that.

Jonty drew in an angry breath at his reluctant acknowledgment of her skill. In truth, though, she hadn't expected that much from him. She stood up, muttering that she would be right back with some salve for the burns. Maria caught her hand, holding her back.

"Thank you for your kindness, Jonty. You are a fine young man, and I can rest easy knowing that you can take over the cooking while I recover."

Jonty struggled not to show her alarm. It hadn't occurred to her that she would be expected to take over the housekeeper's duties.

She withheld a disappointed sigh. She could forget about leaving tonight. Although it was dangerous to her fragile emotions where Cord was concerned, she couldn't in good conscience go off and leave him without someone to cook for the hard-working wranglers. Tina was as worthless as spit in the kitchen.

Her bound breasts rose with a sigh she could no longer hold. She'd be stuck here at least another two weeks. She slid a glance at Cord and found him watching her suspiciously. Did he suspect anything? Sometimes she thought he could read her mind. She hurriedly gave Maria a short nod and left the small house.

A week of raw chill, leaden skies, and numbing wind visited the mountain. October was grinding to a bleak end. November was drawing near.

As Jonty guided the mare up the often-traveled trail, the western sky was drapped in dark clouds and the autumn smells were dank and woodsy. Any day now the drenching fall rains would come, and she must get away before that happened. She shivered. Otherwise she'd be bound to the house, unable to escape the sight of Cord and Tina touching, kissing, and Tina tittering while Cord laughed his low, husky sound.

There was something else bothering Jonty this gloomy day. Cord had fully recovered from his run-in with the wild stallion, yet he showed no signs of wanting to make the trip to Abilene. Not only that, he hung around the house almost constantly, transferring more and more of his responsibilities to Jones. It seemed that every time she turned around, he was underfoot, watching whatever chore she was about. She hadn't drawn an easy breath in the past week and a half.

Her soft lips tightened. To add to her vexation,

three days ago Cord had taken over the third bedroom, turning it into his office. Jones had knocked together a long table and a small bench, rough and full of splinters. Cord had then informed her that considering Maggie had taught her to read and write and do figures, he was putting her in charge of the books—to keep track of the horses sold, the ledgers balanced.

And that, Jonty expelled a long breath, put her all the more in his company. For he rarely left her alone in this room. He stood over her as she worked, leaning so close sometimes that his cheek brushed her curls.

She closed her eyes, remembering. What torment she went through during those times—feeling the heat of his body washing over her, his breath on her face, his clean smell of pine, horses, and sage. She'd catch herself breathing in his scent, then become angry with herself.

Finally, yesterday, she could bear it no longer. "Do you have to hang over me?" She'd jerked away from him. "It's hot, I can't breathe." That naturally raised Cord's ire and he had cut back at her with some hateful remark and stamped out of the room, calling for Tina.

A thoughtful frown furrowed Jonty's forehead as the mare clomped on. The evening walks and rides Cord and Tina had used to take had ceased. She wondered why. The daylight hours only provided them with kisses and embraces, never any romps in Cord's bedroom. Had Tina's father put a stop to the nightly rides? Mexican fathers were very protective of their daughters.

Jonty was jerked back to the present by the increasing velocity of the wind. It blew cold against her face, tossing her curls all over her head. A fast glance at the sky showed the sun well westward, time she returned to the cabin and saw about supper.

She turned Beauty around and started back down the mountain, aggravated with herself for spending the whole time with thoughts of Cord McBain. What a waste of brain power.

CHAPTER 16

JONTY SNIFFED APPRECIATIVELY OF THE BEEF ROAST SLOWLY cooking in the oven as she deftly set plates and eating utensils on the scrubbed pine table. Cord had traded a horse for a steer from a distant rancher and it would be a welcome change from the wild game she was getting so tired of. She tied a fustian towel around her waist. She had only to add potatoes to the roast and make a couple of pans of biscuits.

As she stood at the sink peeling a large pan full of potatoes, Jonty swung between her usual dread and anticipation of sitting at the table with Cord. What would be his mood tonight, his attitude toward her? Would he be genial, or cold? Or would those gray eyes, when he looked at her, glimmer with a light she hadn't been able to put a name to?

She felt a jolt to the heart when from behind her came an attention-getting cough. She didn't have to turn around to know that Cord had entered the kitchen.

But she did turn, and she couldn't keep her eyes

from moving over his splendid body. Against her will, they ranged from where his shirt strained over his broad chest, to the sleeves rolled up just below his elbows, then on past the leather belt where tight, low-riding trousers molded the shape of his manhood.

Realizing what Cord must be thinking about her perusal of his person, she blushed and forced herself to look at his face. Their eyes met and clung in the tense atmosphere, oblivious to everything around them. Cord took a step toward her, then Tina's high piping voice shattered the intimate moment.

"Cord." Tina pouted, wrapping her short fingers around his arm. "I waited for you down at the stables."

A swift shadow of annoyance swept across Cord's face. His voice was cold as he said evenly, "I don't remember tellin' you that I'd be there."

"You didn't have to tell me." Tina chose not to see the irritated drawn brows. "You're most always there at this time."

Cord made no response to the coyly spoken words, only turned on his heel and left the room, his spurs jangling musically. Tina ran after him and Jonty turned back to the potatoes, a dejected curve on her lips. Why hadn't she thought of the stables? It was a perfect spot for a man and woman to meet . . . plenty of hay to lie on.

The wind sighed outside and rustled softly through the cabin. Jonty hitched her chair closer to the fire, thinking that Jones hadn't done too good a job rechinking the cracks between the logs in the walls. She stared moodily into the fire, watching the blue-edged flames lick along the burning logs. Cord hadn't shown up for supper tonight. They'd had another row today, one of their worst in a long time.

She sighed. And it had been so nice at the beginning when they sat down to lunch. Cord had been in a jovial mood, chatting with Tina, even tossing a few words her way occasionally.

He had finished the meal with a couple of cups of coffee, then left, headed toward the corrals. She had then set the displeased Tina to clearing the table while she gathered up the left-over scraps to give to Wolf, carrying them out to the porch.

She was rubbing the big dog's head when Red rode up and pulled his mount in. They exchanged a few pleasantries, then the young rider lifted the reins and rode on. She gave the dog a final pat and started to rise.

She had barely straightened up when her arm was caught by hard, biting fingers. She swung around, bewilderment in her eyes, wondering what had set Cord off this time.

She soon found out as Cord said contemptuously, "So, Red is the one who draws you to the bunkhouse to play poker. I thought it was one of the new men you had chosen to quench the fire I started in you."

Jonty gasped at the injustice of his accusation. Good Lord, couldn't she even pass the time of day with a friend without him charging her with licentious intent?

Well, she'd had enough. And since it was useless to try to convince him that he was wrong, she'd just feed his dirty suspicions a little.

Smiling coolly, she said, "Why not? You're too busy with Tina to take care of my fire, and you must admit that Red is very good looking, very virile. And he's trustworthy too. He'd never give away my secret."

While Cord glared at her, his mouth formidably tight, she looked at him unblinking and drawled, "Naturally, he wouldn't want the others to know . . . give him competition."

As Cord stared at her, his jaw working, she jerked her arm free and left him there as she wheeled and walked back into the kitchen, muttering to herself, "Chew on that, Mister McBain."

Jonty jumped to her feet and paced the floor. There were no two ways about it, she had to get away from here. Maria's feet were almost healed, and Miss Tina could muddle through somehow for a few days.

The clock struck nine. "I should be getting to bed." she sighed the words. "But I'll be forever falling asleep, with so much running through my mind. Maybe I'll read for a while."

The wolf-dog, stretched out in front of the fire, thumped his tail as if in agreement.

Five minutes later, Jonty had changed into her worn nightshirt and chosen a thin volume of poetry from her small supply of reading material. As she settled herself in bed and bunched the two pillows under her head, she hoped that Uncle Jim had found her some new books. She knew her old ones by heart, she had read them so often.

The poems gripped Jonty's interest and the pages fell away, along with the moving hands of the clock. Then Robert Burns began to lose his pull and, only half aware, her lids were drooping and she was scooting deeper into the covers. Shortly, her breasts rose and fell gently in sleep.

She did not hear the outside door open quietly, nor the indrawn breath of the tall man who paused in her doorway. She did not hear the cat-quick steps move across the floor, then stop as the man hunkered down beside the bed. She did not feel the slim fingers that lifted a black curl and let its silkiness slide caressingly across his palm.

The sun had set hours ago, and the coyotes had started their yelping, sharp and impudent. Cord continued to sit the stallion, unaware of the moon edging over the mountain top. His mind was racing with the question that demanded an answer.

What was he to do about Jonty? Things could not go on as they were. It was driving him crazy—being around her, desiring her all the time, lying awake half the night, knowing that she slept only the slight width of a wall away from him. He knew he'd lose control some day and be false to the promise he'd made Maggie Rand.

As Cord sat on in his solitude, his all-consuming love for Jonty eating away at him, he came to the only conclusion that would heal his heart, rest his soul. He must marry Jonty, regardless of the age difference.

But Jonty hated him, and with good reason. Cord's throat convulsed. He remembered the ass he'd made of himself a few hours back. Deep in his heart, he had known that it had only been a friendly talk between her and Red. Red had never shown her anything but a careless fondness for what he thought was a green kid.

"You jumped all over her because you're raging jealous of any man who comes near her," his inner voice pointed out.

"Yes," Cord whispered. "but how do I go about makin' amends?"

"You can start by treating her better—like a woman should be treated, even court her a little. And for God's sake, stop making up to the little señorita in front of her. Trying to make her jealous is no way to smooth her feathers. She probably thinks of you as a rutting buffalo, straddling any cow that comes along."

Cord could only nod in agreement as he lifted the reins and started back down the mountain. He had his work cut out, he thought, wrapped in a gloom he had never experienced before. There were so many harsh words and actions that he must erase from Jonty's memory.

His dejection remained with him until he spotted a glimmer of light in the ranch house. Maybe Jonty didn't hate him that much after all. She *had* left a light burning for him.

His spirits raised, Cord unsaddled the stallion, turned him into the corral, then walked slowly to the house. He pushed open the kitchen door and his spirits dropped. The light came from Jonty's bedroom. She hadn't left a light burning for him.

He shook off his disappointment. At least she was awake. Maybe he could say a few words to her, start his campaign of winning her trust, her affection. He'd had that once.

Jonty's door stood open, and the hand Cord had raised to knock, dropped back to his side as his eyes kindled. The delicately boned face was relaxed in sleep, an open book lying on her flat stomach. Without conscious thought, he crossed to the bed and squatted down beside it. He gazed at her for a long moment, then reached a hand toward the tumbled, soft curls.

Jonty came awake to gentle fingers stroking her throat. She blinked her eyes sleepily, focusing in the man who hunkered beside her bed. "Cord?" she whispered, puzzled.

"In the flesh." He smiled down at her, his long fingers still on her throat.

"You weren't here for supper. Are you hungry?"

"I'm starving," he whispered back, his voice thick and raw.

Jonty came up on her elbows. "I'll get you something," she began, then stopped in confusion. Cord's eyes were fastened on her breasts, clearly outlined beneath the thin material of her nightwear. As his hot perusal continued, seeming to burn into her flesh, she felt her nipples harden. When his darkened eyes leapt knowingly back to her face, she knew he was aware of their aroused condition.

Her cheeks growing an embarrassed pink, she reached for the blanket that had fallen to her waist. Cord shook his head and stayed her hands. "Don't hide yourself from me, Jonty," he said huskily. "I've already seen all of you, remember?"

The pink in her cheeks turned to red as Jonty did remember. As she stared up helplessly at him, he released her wrists and, leaning over her, cupped her face in his hands. She held her breath as he gazed down at her, his eyes illuminated with desire.

"Ah, Jonty," he said thickly, "you're drivin' me out of my mind."

A protest trembled on Jonty's lips as he lowered his head to her. She knew his intent, and she would have no part of it. She would not be used.

But the denial died in her throat when Cord's mouth covered hers and his lips moved gently, persuasively. Her firm resolution died swiftly when he lay down beside her and gathered her in his arms. His heart slamming wildly against her breasts, his lips forced hers apart. Every nerve inside her awakened as his tongue teased her own. Her arms came up around his shoulders and clung. She made no demur when he slid a hand inside her nightshirt and gently stroked a breast. When he moved his lips to settle them over its rosy peak, she moaned and pressed his head closer to her soft flesh.

Cord pulled the pebble-hard nipple into his mouth, and when he felt Jonty's answering need rippling through her in sharp spasms, he smiled his satisfaction and settled down to suckle her. Slowly and gently he dragged and pulled at the swollen breast, thinking that in her mind Jonty might hate him, but certainly her body didn't. If necessary, he would win her through her passion. He would make her so dependent on his love-making that she would be happy to marry him.

As he lifted her nightshirt up to her throat, Cord refused to listen to the little voice that whispered inside him, "Passion is not enough. You must gain her love, or your marriage will be a hollow thing."

Jonty readily helped Cord pull the shirt over her head, then waited impatiently when he stood up to rid himself of his own clothes. He stood before her then, splendidly naked, his eyes inviting her to look at him, to know him.

Her eyes slid slowly over his broad chest and wide shoulders, taking in the blond hair that swirled around his chest, then slanted to a vee at his waist. With a little shiver of eagerness, yet shyness, her eyes dipped down to the triangle of hair where his long manhood was swollen with desire for her.

Cord stepped closer to the bed, stopping when his knees came up against the mattress. "Touch it, Jonty," he whispered huskily. "Hold it."

Jonty's fingers trembled as she timidly reached and stroked the throbbing length, then curled her hand around its thick fullness.

Mesmerized, Cord watched her slender fingers move on him. Never had anything aroused him so. With a low groan, he folded his fingers over hers, and keeping them on his hardness, he lay back down beside her.

Smoothing the curls off her forehead, he said shakily, "I want you so desperately, Jonty, but seein' you lie here, so slender and delicate, I'm afraid I'll hurt you."

Jonty reached a hand to lovingly touch his cheek. "You won't hurt me." She smiled at him trustingly, and pulled him on top of her.

There was still doubt in Cord's eyes as he tenderly parted her legs and positioned himself between them. And for all the exquisite care he took when penetrating the thin barrier that protected the gift he'd longed for so long, Jonty's cry of pain would have rung through the house if he hadn't caught it in his mouth.

"Should I stop, honey?" he whispered, holding his body perfectly still.

Jonty shook her head and tightened her arms around him, urging him on. This time he would not go to Tina for release.

And hating himself for the pain he was causing the woman he loved, but unable to stop, Cord continued his slow entry, stretching and filling her warmth. Jonty bit her lips, holding back her cries as the instrument of torture moved deeper and deeper inside her.

She was telling herself that she was willing to suffer any pain in order to bring pleasure to this man she loved with her entire being, when suddenly the pain was gone. She was left with a sense of sensual delight.

Slowly, at first, she began to move, to respond. And Cord, feeling her hips reach to meet his, relaxed his caution a bit and began a slow, rhythmic thrusting. The spiraling passion that built in Jonty then was almost as painful in its way as had been the breaking of the thin membrane.

Lost in the blissful rapture of Cord's working body, Jonty was unprepared for the explosion that sent her straining into Cord's large, shuddering frame. He moaned her name and she felt the flow of his spent desire, warm and soothing to her stretched and torn femininity.

She smiled in wonder as she lay exhausted, Cord's sweat-dampened head lying in the curve of her throat and shoulder, his breathing harsh in her ear. She had never dreamed making love could be so mind shatteringly wonderful! Would it be like this with any man? she wondered, or could only Cord bring her this mindless losing of herself? She smiled. She had no desire to test the question.

She gently stroked Cord's shoulder when he said softly, "I've wanted to make love to you for so long."

When she made no response, only continued to run her palm over him, he leaned up on an elbow and looked searchingly into her eyes. "Didn't you ever want the same thing? At least think about it?"

Jonty wanted to say that what had mostly been on her mind was the hope that some day he would return her love. But since he hadn't mentioned that important word, she wouldn't either. Instead, she teased, "It's entered my head once or twice."

"Once or twice, huh?" Cord growled, bucking his hips at her, making her feel the manhood that still merged their bodies together.

Jonty joined his playful manner by bucking back and pulling his head down to her breasts. Lifting one, and inserting the nipple between his lips, she murmured, "Maybe if you work at it, you can make me think about it a third time."

Cord gave a throaty laugh, and as he sucked noisily on one breast and then the other, Jonty felt him growing inside her. When he slid his hands under her small rear end and lifted it several inches off the bed, she leaned up on both elbows and watched his long length stroke her.

Cord's eyes grew stormy as he saw what she was doing and decided that he would like to watch their coupling too. So, bending his head to look at the space between their bodies, he slowed his movement, withdrawing almost completely before thrusting back inside Jonty.

Watching the slick slide of his slowly working manhood, Cord thought to himself that he could watch his mating with Jonty forever. Then she was throwing herself back on the bed, grasping his shoulders, pulling him against her, whimpering for release. He grasped her hips, held them steady for the mad thrusting they were about to receive.

A pinkish gray showed outside the window when Cord and Jonty had at last satiated their need of each other. Jonty wiggled her derriere into the nest of Cord's body. She smiled as she fell asleep. Cord loved her. Oh he hadn't said so, but his every action tonight had said it.

Cord wrapped his arms around the sleeping Jonty, savoring the feel of her soft, curled body. Not since he was a child and loved his parents had he cared so deeply for another human being. And now, having all that love centered on this girl—no, woman, he had made her a woman tonight—was almost frightening. It would kill him if he ever lost her.

He stroked the black curls, his eyes caressing the sleeping face. "Ah, my lovely," he whispered, "I'm too damn old for you, I have lived life too hard, seen too much, but I love you and I'm going to keep you.

"And I swear to you, Maggie Rand, your granddaughter will never have cause to regret marryin' me."

Cord eased himself away from Jonty when, from the back of the house, her big leghorn rooster crowed. As he sat up, he remembered with amusement the fight she had put up to bring her chickens along. What a

little scrapper she was. He grinned, swinging his feet
to the floor and standing up.

He gathered up his clothes, lying in a crumpled
heap where they had been tossed last night, and
hurried into them. Everyone would be up and about
soon, and he didn't want to be found in Jonty's bed.
He wanted no sly looks or remarks made to, or about
her. Shoving his feet into his boots, he left the house to
answer a call of nature.

Cord was on his way back from the stand of trees
several yards behind the house and was about to step
up on the porch when Tina stepped into his path.
Before he could put out a hand to stop her, the girl
threw herself against him, her arms coming up around
his neck.

"Tina!" He spoke sharply, grabbing her arms, trying to break her hold without hurting her. It wasn't
her fault that he had falsely led her on, and now he
must find the words that would let her down gently,
explain that there would be no more kisses, that he
loved another.

"Look, Tina," he began, still struggling with her
arms. "There's something—"Then the girl's mouth
was on his, cutting off his words.

He was trying to free his head from the grip Tina
had on it when he heard the anguished cry behind
him. Wrenching his mouth free, uncaring now whether or not he hurt the clinging girl, and turning around,
he gazed helplessly at Jonty. His heart ached at the
disillusionment in her blue eyes.

Jonty was semi-aware when Cord left her side. She
smiled dreamily and rolled over on her back, then
supressed a groan. Her nipples were still tender from
Cord's drawing lips, and her hip bones ached from the
repeated thrusting of his against them.

She sighed happily, but regretfully. The kitchen
awaited her, the making of breakfast. Sliding out of
bed, she walked stiffly to the big dresser and took out
clean clothing. As she wrapped the wide binding

around her sore breasts, she giggled. She wouldn't be wearing the hateful thing much longer. Cord couldn't very well pretend he was marrying a man. He hadn't said so, but she knew they would become husband and wife.

Dressed, Jonty walked down the short hall to the kitchen, then paused in the doorway. Her own call of nature had nudged her. Before she did anything else, she must visit the little outhouse that had been erected for Tina and Maria's use.

She stepped out onto the back porch, then froze, her heart twisting painfully. Cord and Tina stood locked in each other's arms, lips fastened, bodies straining against each other.

With sickening clarity, she realized that she had allowed Cord to use her after all. Her pain was so great that she couldn't withhold an anguished cry. Through tear-blurred eyes, she saw Cord push Tina away, then come toward her, a hand outstretched, guilt on his face. Humiliation and fury blinded her. Was there no end to what this man would do to hurt her?

Her face working convulsively, she sprang at Cord with tiger-like ferocity, crying, "I hate you, Cord McBain, I hate you!" Her fierce attack sent him stumbling backwards. Before he could raise his arm to protect his face, her curved fingers raked down his cheeks.

With Tina whimpering at his elbow, Cord stood a moment, too stunned to move as blood oozed from the long gouges on his face. And though there was a stinging pain from his wounds, he didn't feel it. His only concern was the contempt that glittered in the pain-filled eyes.

"Jonty." He held out a hand to her again. "It's not the way it looks."

Jonty stepped back, gritting through her teeth, "You, Cord McBain, are lower than a snake." She wheeled and dashed back into the house, through the kitchen and into her bedroom. She slammed the door, and through the tears flooding her eyes, shot home the bolt with finality. As she threw herself on the bed, she heard Cord's rapid footsteps coming down the hall.

The door knob rattled and his frustrated voice cajoled, "Open the door, Jonty, I can explain everything."

"Like hell you can," Jonty muttered and pulled a pillow over her head to shut out his words. Never again would he sweet-talk her into anything. She knew what she had seen. The randy tomcat hadn't been satisfied with an entire night of releasing his lust on her, there had still been enough left over for his true love, Tina.

She was beginning to feel smothered beneath the feather pillow when finally Cord's muted words ceased. But she had no sooner uncovered her head than he spoke again.

"Look, honey, I'm leavin' for Abilene as soon as I have a bite to eat and a cup of coffee. I'm goin' to see the man about buyin' the ranch. We've got to talk when I get back."

In the silence that followed, Jonty knew that Cord waited for some response from her. A minute later, when she made none, she heard him walk heavily away, then brusquely order Tina to start breakfast.

"Good," Jonty grunted when Tina whined a complaint and Cord's only answer was the slamming of the kitchen door. Little Miss Perez was getting a taste of what she had endured all these past weeks.

Flinging the pillow that held Cord's scent to the floor, Jonty stared dry-eyed at the ceiling. She had cried her last tear over Cord McBain. He wasn't worth one more tear, one thought. His leaving for Abilene today couldn't have come at a better time. She would stay in her room until he was gone, then she and Johnny would leave. There would be no one to stop them. And if he dared to try to follow her later, he would have Uncle Jim to contend with.

She slid off the bed a minute later and began gathering up her clothes. They didn't make a very large bundle as she rolled them together and tied them with a strip of rawhide. Placing the roll beside the door, she looked around the room in which she had spent so many miserable nights. A grimace of regret furrowed her brow. There were things she hated leaving behind—her books, the little knick-knacks Granny had treasured, the big four-poster. No doubt Cord would move Tina into it.

She sighed and sat down to wait. Wait for the time she could ride away forever.

An hour passed before the men came tramping in for breakfast. Jonty heard the familiar scraping of the benches as the hands took their places, then grinned when they began grumbling about the food.

"Where's Jonty?" Jones demanded. "Why isn't he out here doin' the cookin'?"

When Tina's high-pitched voice started to tell what had happened, Cord cut her off with a sharp, "Jonty's not feelin' well this mornin'."

There was a short pause, then Lightfoot asked suspiciously, "What's wrong with him? Did the two of you have words?"

"No, we didn't have words," Cord grated, and Jonty knew without being there that Tina had received a warning look from him.

Nothing more was said, and shortly the men were filing out of the kitchen, some of them still grumbling about their breakfast and expressing the hope that Jonty would recover by supper time.

Jonty smiled grimly. "You'll eat no more meals cooked by me, boys. I am no longer Cord McBain's slave."

Several minutes passed before the wranglers had saddled up and ridden off, leaving it quiet outside. Jonty rose and walked to the window, stepping to one side of it. Cord would soon ride by, on his way to Abilene. Concealed in the shadows, she waited for him to appear.

She hadn't long to wait before the beautiful black stallion came pacing along, Cord sitting easy in the saddle. She noted that his double saddle bags were well filled, and that two canteens of water swung from the saddlehorn. Her eyes drifted to the bedroll tied snuggly behind him, and she was reminded of when she had made the trip here to the ranch. How miserable those four days had been for her.

The big mount clomped past the house, heading for the trail that would lead into the valley, and on to Abilene. Horse and rider were about to ride out of sight when Cord reined in and sat grazing back at the house, straight at her window.

Her lips curled in a sneer. "I hope he doesn't think I'll be standing here to wave good-bye to him."

Still, despite her rage and burning hate, when Cord lifted the reins and rode on, Jonty's heart felt empty.

CHAPTER 17

SHE HAD SUSPECTED THAT THE INDIAN WOULD HANG around, that he hadn't been satisfied with Cord's explanation of her absence. He would remember that never before had she been allowed to stay in bed simply because she didn't feel well. Also, there were the scratches she'd put on Cord's face. Johnny was bound to be curious about those.

Having unbolted the door after Cord rode away, she called, "Come in, Johnny," and the door swung open.

Lightfoot stepped inside, then his body stiffened. He studied the tear-stained face and swore softly at the shattered look in the blue eyes. As he had worried the past days, the bastard had seduced the girl. Wordlessly, he opened his arms, and Jonty flew into them.

Several minutes passed as she sobbed out her story, ending with the gut-wrenching pain of finding Tina in Cord's arms. "I've got to get away from here, Johnny." Her fingers clutched the buckskin material of his shirt. "Today! Right now!"

"Yes," Lightfoot soothed, stroking her curls, calming her. "We'll go whenever you like." He held her away. "Are you sure you're up to leaving today? There's no great hurry. Cord has taken off for Abilene and probably won't be back for a couple of weeks. Maybe you should rest today. We can leave tomorrow."

"No!" Jonty pulled away from him, scrubbing a knuckle across her wet eyes. "I'm fine, Johnny, and there's no way I'll spend another day in this house." As she urged him toward the door, she didn't add that she couldn't bear to be around Tina.

"Get the mounts ready," she said, following Lightfoot out of the room and adding, "I'll be ready in about fifteen minutes."

Tears stung her eyes as she picked up her clothes and jacket. She ran a loving hand over the bright quilt Granny had patched together, rumpled and tossed now by two bodies that had strained against each other through the night.

Remembering those hours when she had so freely given of herself, thinking that her love was being returned, she removed her hand as though she had touched something unclean.

With an angry jerk of her head, telling herself to put the past behind, she firmed her lips. A new chapter was opening in her life, the old one finished and best forgotten. She picked up the bundle of clothes, draped the jacket over her arm, and with downcast eyes, unable to look at the familiar furniture as she walked through the big main room, she walked out onto the porch.

Tina and Lightfoot approached at the same time. Tina coming from the "necessary" and the Indian from the stables. He rode his quarter horse and led Jonty's little mare. Curiosity smoothed the pout from the Mexican girl's face as she took in the rolled-up bundle under Jonty's arm. Her eyes shifted to Lightfoot and the two mounts.

"Where are you going, Jonty?" Alarm flared in her dark eyes, showing plainly that she was thinking of the large supper to be prepared, that if Jonty was going away, that duty would be hers.

Jonty brushed past the girl who had shared in the cause of her humiliation and grief, and as she tied her clothes to the back of the saddle, she tossed over her shoulder, "Nowhere in particular, Tina. Just away."

"But, Jonty," Tina wailed, taking a step toward her. "What about all the work to be done around here? You can't leave me to do it all."

Jonty swung into the saddle, and as she controlled the impatient mare, wicked amusement shone in her eyes. Looking down at the spoiled, lazy Tina, she said, "I did it, and more. Surely you can do as much for the man you're so in love with."

Tina's black look scowled after the pair who touched a heel to their mounts and trotted away without a backward look.

The foothills were still shrouded in gray shadows when Jonty and her companion reached the valley floor. White frost covered the ground, crackling underfoot. Jonty shivered and considered donning her jacket.

But as the sun rose higher, shining on the aspen thickets, bare and leafless now, stark against the gray sage, the air became warm and pleasant. An hour passed with no words spoken between them before Lightfoot grunted and pointed.

"Take a look at that, Jonty."

Jonty's gaze followed the pointing finger and a smile curved her lips. A hundred yards or so to their left a small herd of wild horses grazed, along with several head of elk and one hump-backed shaggy buffalo. "Wouldn't it be wonderful if only people got along so well," she mused out loud.

"That has not been so since the beginning of time," the Indian grunted, and they rode on without further words. When Jonty's thoughts strayed to Cord, she repulsed them, ordering herself to think of her future instead.

But as she had no inkling of what she'd find at the end of her journey, she decided it was fruitless to lay any plans. She smiled widely, thankful that soon she would see Uncle Jim and finally let the world know that Jonty Rand was a woman.

The lack of sleep last night caught up with Jonty, and her head nodding, she drowsed off and on in the rocking motion of her mount's easy gait. When, some hours later, the sudden halt of the little mare snapped her eyes open, they widened in astonishment. It was raining.

The rain fell monotonously for the rest of the day, a cold rain swept slantwise by the wind, biting into the marrow of Jonty's bones. An early twilight came on and it was night when Lightfoot grunted and pointed. Through the slashing rain Jonty glimpsed the lights of Cottonwood. They were faint and blurred, but to her tired body they beckoned a welcome.

Her heart beat stepped up. Soon now she would be with Uncle Jim, be folded into warm arms of love and protection.

Lightfoot led the way down the wide, single street, through ankle-deep mud. Stores, saloons, and gambling dens lined the wooden sidewalk. Each building had a wide overhang that now sheltered a populace of gamblers in black coats and wide-brimmed hats, satin-clad women, cowboys, and one or two buckskin-clad mountaineers.

It was a rough town, Jonty thought as Lightfoot pulled in his mount before a saloon that was larger and fancier than the others. "This is it, the Trail's End." He grinned at Jonty and slid to the ground.

Jonty gazed up at the impressive false front of the saloon, its name printed boldly in red paint. Through the bat-wing doors came the shuffle of boots, murmuring voices, loud laughter, the clink of glasses, and the whirr of roulette wheels.

Nervous, and a little afraid, Jonty was dismounting when bursts of gunfire errupted down the street. At her start and small cry, Lightfoot lay a calming hand on her shoulder.

"Get used to that sound, Jonty," he advised. "There's no law to speak of in this town, and gunplay is pretty common."

Jonty smiled wanly at her tall friend and followed him through the swinging doors.

Despite its grand appearance, the Trail's End had the same odor as all the saloons in the West—sweat, smoke, spirits, leather, and sage. As Lightfoot jostled his way to the long bar, Jonty was hard on his heels. She had never seen harder-looking people.

"He's upstairs in his office," the surly-looking bartender answered to Lightfoot's query. "First door on your left."

Climbing the wide, worn stairs, Lightfoot said dryly from the corners of his mouth, "You can see these steps have had a lot of use."

Jonty missed the innuendo in Johnny's words. Her mind was on something else, fretting about her welcome from Uncle Jim. She had faith in his wanting her—still, maybe he'd have liked a little warning that she was coming.

LaTour's door stood open and everything but the joy of seeing the big man sitting behind a desk left Jonty's mind. When she happily called his name, the glad light that came over the handsome features was all she needed.

"Jonty!" LaTour stood swiftly and came toward her. "Jonty," he repeated softly as he gently folded her into his arms.

Jonty sighed and snuggled her head under his chin. He smelled of whiskey, soap, and cigarettes. She breathed deeply of the familiar scent, feeling secure for the first time since Granny had passed away.

After a moment LaTour put Jonty away from him and they studied each other. Jonty saw a man that was still hard as nails, still slim and handsome. And

LaTour, as he gazed at the delicate face, saw that more and more it looked like the young girl he had loved so totally.

He drew her back into his arms, pain in his blue eyes as he laid his head on her wet curls. "It's good to have you with me at last, little one," he said huskily.

Jonty drew back to look searchingly into LaTour's eyes. "I can stay with you always, never have to go back to Cord McBain?"

LaTour stroked her smooth cheek. "I promise, you'll never have to go back to him . . . unless someday you might want to."

"Hah!" Jonty snorted. "That will never happen. But there's the slight possibility he might come looking for me. Because of his promise to Granny. He's strong on keeping promises."

"Then I'll just have to handle him, won't I?"

Jonty's face paled a shade. "I wouldn't want you to kill him, Uncle Jim."

"That one wouldn't be easy to kill." LaTour gave a short laugh. "He's got the reputation of bein' a bad one to draw on. It's said that he's the fastest gun in these parts."

Alarm grew in Jonty's eyes. "You stay away from him then. I don't want you dead either."

"Don't worry about it, honey." LaTour hugged her, then releasing her, added, "I doubt that gunplay between us will ever come to pass." A satanic smile twisted his lips. "Just a plain old knock-down, drag-out probably. It would give me a lot of satisfaction to mess up that handsome face of his a little."

Jonty made no response, but the black-haired man saw the small frown that gathered between her brows. Was she as he half suspected, and despite her show of hostility toward the wild-horse hunter, in love with the man?

LaTour's face showed none of his thoughts when he said, "I expect you and Johnny are tired and hungry." He took Jonty's arm. "I've got your quarters fixed up

downstairs, honey. I had a big room added on back of
the kitchen."

Jonty held back when Jim would have escorted her
downstairs. A room back of the kitchen . . . She had
lived in such quarters all her life, except for the short
time spent at the ranch. She had grown used to, and
loved, the freedom of moving about, going where she
pleased.

"Why can't I live up here?" she began, then grew
quiet as a scantily clad whore walked past the door,
her arm around the waist of a drunken cowboy. Her
face reddened and she said faintly, "Oh, I see."

LaTour heard the disappointment, the disapproval
in the three words. He ran distracted fingers through
his hair and looked sympathetically at Jonty. "I'm
sorry, Jonty, to be sticking you back in the same
situation you suffered at Nellie's. "But," he sighed,
"out here saloons and whores go together. The men
won't come to your place if you don't have women
they can take upstairs."

"I know." Jonty patted the hand he laid on her arm.
"I don't feel bad," she lied. "And now, since you
mentioned it, I am tired and hungry and would like to
get into some dry clothing. So, if you'll show me to my
quarters . . ."

A few curious glances followed the wet, slicker-clad
boy and stony-faced Indian who followed along behind the owner of the saloon. Nothing was said,
however, when the three disappeared into the kitchen.
Nobody ever questioned Jim LaTour.

Jonty's nose twitched at the rancid smell of old
grease and older dust as they passed through the
kitchen and into a dark room. She waited patiently
while Jim fumbled his way to a kerosine lamp, her
appetite fast disappearing. She doubted she could eat
anything that had been prepared in that filthy room
behind her.

There came the rasp of a match and the big room
came softly alive. Jonty sniffed deeply as she looked

around. The room was large, smelling of new wood and the earthy odor of clay chinking between the log walls. She looked down at the floor. It was laid with rough pine boards, but a plentiful supply of bright Indian woven rugs were scattered about—One each in two comfortable padded rocking chairs, a long running one alongside the bed in a corner, and a huge one beneath a table placed under the window that looked out on a small plot of weed-filled ground, except for a cleared spot where an axe was resting on a tree stump next to a pile of chopped wood.

Not much to rest your eyes on there, she thought wryly, but turning to LaTour, who watched her anxiously, she smiled her delight at the room's coziness. "I love it, Uncle Jim." Her eyes roamed over the colorful quilt spread over the bed, the bright blue window covering. Her smile widened when she discovered a small wood-burning brazier off in one corner. She could heat water for the hip-bath sitting beside it, brew a pot of coffee on it, in a pinch cook on it.

She flew to Jim and hugged him around the waist. "I'll be so happy here."

"I'm glad, honey." Jim hugged her back. "I've been workin' on it for the past month."

"Well, you've certainly done yourself proud. The only thing left to make my world complete is pretty dresses, fancy slippers, and letting my hair grow. And getting rid of these terrible bindings." Her slender fingers plucked at the white material that flattened her so painfully.

LaTour's smile faded and his eyes became serious. "About that, Jonty," he began softly, "I think we'd better wait awhile for your unveiling, so to speak. As you've seen, I've got practically the same set-up here as Nellie had in Abilene. Maybe even worse, considering some of the characters that come in and out of town."

"But, Uncle Jim," Jonty wailed, seeing all her dreams melting away. "Am I never to be a woman?"

"Don't cry, honey." LaTour tilted her chin and swore silently at the disappointment in the blue eyes so like his own. "Your time will come, I promise. I plan on someday havin' a ranch. You can have all the dresses you want then."

He turned to Lightfoot, who had been silent through the whole exchange. "Come on, Johnny, I'm goin' to order some supper and hot water brought to Jonty." When his cousin opened the door and stepped into the kitchen, LaTour told Jonty to bar the door behind them.

When the big dog shoved his nose in her hand, Jonty called out, "Bring Wolf something to eat also." She heard the pair laugh and knew she had been heard. She dropped the bar in place across the door and began a closer perusal of her new abode.

Her eyes grew wistful as she moved around the large room. How pretty Granny's little treasures would look in here. She sighed. The loss of them was the price she'd had to pay to escape Cord.

What was she to do with her days? Jonty wondered glumly, sitting down in one of the rockers and putting it to motion with a shove of her feet. She was used to being busy from early dawn to late at night. Time would certainly hang heavy.

A knock on the door interrupted her morose thoughts.

"Who's there?" She stood up as Wolf growled warningly, his ruff raised.

"I got your supper here, kid," a gravely voice answered. "The boss ordered it."

Jonty drew the bar, and was almost knocked over by the large, bearded man who stamped into the room, bearing a large tray. He plopped it on the table and turned to give her a scathing look. "From now on, young man, you eat in the kitchen. I ain't got time to fetch and carry for no snot-nosed kid, even if you are Jim's nephew." He spun on his heel and stamped out of the room, jostling a gangly youth just entering the room, a pail of steaming water in each hand.

"Watch it, you fat tub of lard," the teenager snarled as hot water splashed on his legs. The rotund cook cuffed him on the head and slammed the door behind him.

Wordlessly, the sullen-faced boy emptied the pails into the enameled tub, then left, also slamming the door. "Well," Jonty sniffed, "Uncle Jim doesn't have the friendliest help in the world."

Although Jonty had been sure she couldn't eat anything prepared in the dirty kitchen, her hunger said otherwise. And surprisingly, the steak was juicy and tender, the baked potato flaky, and the stewed squash was spicy with herbs. She would be hard put not to eat Wolf's share.

The coffee was fresh and fragrant as later she sank into her bath, sipping it as she soaked the tiredness out of her body. Half an hour later, she sank into the feather bed with a long, relaxed sigh. Outside, the rain still hissed against the window. She barely heard it as she sank into a deep, dreamless sleep.

The stallion was tired and limping a bit when, in the distance, the foothills came in view. Cord was weary too. Weary of the saddle, the hard ground for a bed. He was also hungry. He'd ran out of grub that morning.

But he was possessed by a spirit of elation and eagerness. After long hours of dickering with the crusty old rancher, he now owned a thousand acres of land—half in timber, the other half in grassland that included the secret valley where his thousands of wild horses grazed and bred.

His blood sang for another reason also. In another half hour he would be with Jonty again. And this time he would make her listen as he explained about Tina Perez.

He grinned crookedly. He couldn't believe that he'd been in Abilene for two days and nights and hadn't visited any of the pleasure houses. He hadn't even been tempted to do so. The best whore in the whole city couldn't compare with the way Jonty made love. He could hardly wait to feel her smooth body beneath him again, rising to meet his eager thrusts.

He reached behind him and patted the bundle tied to the saddle. Wouldn't her blue eyes sparkle when she saw the three dresses, the pretty underclothes and dainty slippers he'd purchased in Abilene, not to mention the bars of scented soap.

Cord laughed out loud, startling Rawhide. Wouldn't there be some surprised faces when Jonty stepped out of the house, a breath-takingly beautiful woman in one of those new dresses.

He visualized how the material would hug her proudly jutting breasts and immediately felt himself grow hard. He shook his head in dry amusement. He had only to think of her and his loins went crazy. There was no use trying to deny it. Jonty had become an obsession with him.

He reached the foothills and soon the stallion came to a halt in front of the house. His face darkly shadowed by a week's growth of beard, Cord grinned down at Jones and Tina sitting on the porch.

"Where's Jonty?" he asked, doing away with greetings as he swung stiffly to the ground.

Jones stood up, cleared his voice gruffly and, his thin face solemn, answered, "Lightfoot and the kid have sloped. They left here less than an hour after you left for Abilene."

For long seconds Cord stared at his friend in disbelief, his shock and pain unmistakable in the widening of his eyes. His hands clenched. She was gone!

He leaned against Rawhide, as if for support, and it came to him as though something whispered it in his ear, that the Indian and the breed were related. He swore savagely under his breath. He had been duped. The Indian had been sent to his camp that night with the sole purpose of watching over Jonty—to take her away if she so desired.

His shoulders sagged and he shot a cold look at the

Mexican girl. Catching him with that little bitch had given Jonty a reason to leave him.

He forced the dejection from his mind and stiffened his spine. All he had to do was find LaTour and he would find Jonty. And he must be fast about it. Before Uncle Jim coaxed her into his bed.

There was a slumbering threat of violence when he spoke to Jones. "Do you have any idea where Jim LaTour is holed up these days?"

Jones scratched his balding head. "I don't know if it means anything, but one day I overheard the Indian and the kid discussin' Bolten Pass, and I heard LaTour's name mentioned."

Cord nodded, staring at the ground. Bolton Pass was just such a place as the breed would hide out in. He had been there once himself, hunting wild horses. It was the ruggedest, wildest country he'd ever visited.

He lifted his head to look at Jones. "I'm gonna grab a bite to eat now. In the meantime saddle me a horse. Have him ready in about fifteen minutes."

"Man, you're loco. You look beat." Jones stepped to the edge of the porch. "Get a few hours' rest under you. One more day won't make a blind bit of difference."

The raw pain in Cord's eyes stopped any further argument that hovered on the older man's lips. And though confused that Cord would be so concerned about a kid for whom he had always held such contempt, he merely said, "Okay, Cord." He stepped off the porch and headed for the corrals, leading Rawhide behind him.

"Fix me something to eat, then pack me a week's supply of grub," Cord ordered over his shoulder to Tina as he ran after Jones to retrieve the package from the saddle. As he returned to the house and stepped inside, the up-until-now-silent Tina ran after him.

"Cord," she coaxed, "you need rest. Like Jones said, what difference does a few hours make?" She scowled when Cord made no response. "I don't know why you make such a fuss over a scrawny little bastard kid anyway. He's—"

Cord's lean body went rigid. When he ground out savagely, "Don't ever call Jonty a bastard again," the Mexican girl stepped back in alarm, then wheeled and ran for the kitchen.

Cord stalked into his room, noting with gloomy eyes Jonty's closed door as he walked past it. He shoved the package of women's clothes under the bed, away from prying eyes, then locked the property deed papers in a tin box. This document was very important. Jonty's name, as well as his own, was on it. If something should happen to him that he didn't return, like getting shot to death, he would have at least provided a home for her.

Five minutes later he had changed into fresh clothing and was grimly strapping a cartridge belt around his lean waist. He didn't doubt for a minute that he would have to use the Colt he automatically swung low on his right hip. LaTour wouldn't easily give Jonty up. He carefully tied the bottom of the holster to his leg, a precaution against the accidental snagging of a weapon when a rapid draw was essential.

Tina watched silently as Cord wolfed down the salt pork and eggs she'd prepared, a pout on her pretty face. The expression turned to anger a few minutes later as, without a word to her, he picked up the grub sack she had filled and strode out of the house. Her thoughts of Jonty Rand weren't very nice as she stormed around the kitchen, banging pots and pans.

A fresh mount stood ready for Cord when he walked outside—a big roan, chomping his bit, eager to run. "You've got about another hour of daylight left," Jones said, hanging a canteen of water on the pommel, then handing Cord the reins. "Good luck, and be careful."

With a lift of his hand, Cord turned the mount around and headed him down the valley. A short time later he struck a cross trail, one that would take him southward to the rough country. He kept the mount at a slow lope as he searched the ground for a sign.

Jones's promised hour's daylight came to an end and Cord sighed as the sky darkened. He had picked up no sign of anything, not even the print of a deer hoof. His eyes ached and burned from studying the ground so intently, and when he came to a low-sweeping pine he steered the roan beneath it. He gathered a supply of dead wood lying about, then strapped a feed bag over the mount's nose.

"I'm sorry, old fellow," he said, slapping a heavy rump, "but there'll be no water for you tonight."

While the horse munched his supper of oats, Cord brewed two cups of coffee. One for tonight, and one for the next morning. He had to be careful of his water supply—he had no idea when he would come across a water hole. He poured the alloted coffee into a tin cup, and while it cooled, he dug into the grub sack and pulled out a beef sandwich.

The moon rose as Cord's strong, white teeth bit into the meat and bread, his thoughts on Jonty. Where was she tonight? By now she must be with LaTour. He shook his head vehemently. He would not dwell on what she might be doing at this hour of the night.

Cord finished his coffee and, standing up, piled more wood on the fire. A cold and cutting wind had come up. The fire flared up, and in its new light he unrolled his blankets and unbuckled his gun belt. Placing the Colt handy to his reach, in case he had to use it sometime during the night, he pulled off his boots and rolled himself in the blankets. Exhausted in both mind and body, in minutes he was falling asleep to the faint mourn of a hunting wolf.

Each morning at sunrise found Cord in the saddle, pushing farther into the wild country. He had been riding steadily upward for the past three days. The spruce had grown smaller as he climbed, at length becoming dwarfed and stunted. Today they had failed altogether. Now there was nothing but rocks, boulders, and gullies. He had, however, come upon a couple of watering holes, where the roan had quenched his thirst and he had filled his near-empty canteens.

His sweat-stained shirt clung to his heated body. Indian summer had arrived, its sun as hot as a day in August, and his lean, whiskered face showed his exhaustion. But inside, his blood thrilled.

Yesterday, just as darkness was coming on, he'd come across a lightly marked trail, called a trace by hunters and trappers. The recent passing of two horses was clearly marked in the faint path. It was the first sign he'd seen of human habitation since starting out. The Indian knew every trick and guise in covering his tracks. Evidently, he had felt at this point that he was far enough away that it was no longer necessary to hide his trail.

A brisk wind had sprung up in the late morning, blowing sand across the open spaces, stinging Cord's face and bringing tears to his eyes. Coyotes stole along in the brush, and lizards ran swiftly across the trail. He saw none of this as he urged the tired mount on, his rifle now lying across the saddle pommel. It was cocked and ready, for each boulder he approached a man could be crouched behind, a rifle at his shoulder.

Cord had been following the slant of a ridge for the past hour when he came to a break in the bluff. His heartbeat quickened with an instinctive sense that the end of his search was drawing near. He guided the roan through an opening that was so narrow, the horse rubbed against the sides as it passed through. And even when they had squeezed through the passage, the way was nearly impassable. The trail threaded around large boulders, huge rocks, and thickets of brush.

Cord came upon the roughly erected shack without any warning. Suddenly it was standing there in front of him, a scant ten yards away. He steered the mount behind a tall, thick bush and quietly searched the area

with his eyes. He saw no mounts, but a straight
column of blue wood-smoke rising from the chimney
gave evidence that someone was there.

He had just decided to dismount and slip up on the
building when gravel was kicked up around the
mount's feet, a sharp crack of a rifle sounding on its
heels. He sat statue-still. The shot had been a warning
one, telling him to keep back, to ride on. He lifted the
reins and, seemingly, rode away. At this close range
whoever handled the firearm could easily pick him off.

When Cord felt he had put a safe distance between
him and the small clearing around the shack, he
circled around until he came up behind it. He slid to
the ground, and with the reins looped over his arm, he
advanced slowly, slipping from boulder to boulder.
When he was three feet from his object, he let go the
horse and dropped to the ground. He waited a moment, then, running in a crouch, he came to the back
wall of the slab-board shack.

He stood there a minute, catching his breath before
standing up and adjusting the Colt. Then he moved
slowly to the clay-and-stick chimney. He leaned in its
corner and listened to the raised voices inside.

He could distinguish three different tones. If Jonty
and LaTour were in there, they weren't saying anything. He pressed his ear closer to the wall, trying to
make out the words being spoken in anger. He was
sure that once that he heard the breed's name mentioned, but he couldn't catch why it had been spoken.

Could he take all three, he wondered, if in fact there
were only three? For all he knew, there could be half a
dozen. And there was no way he could find out
without exposing himself to those inside. The building contained one window, and that one was in front,
right next to the only door in the place. There was no
way he could sneak up on them.

Cord remained in his corner for what he thought
was at least fifteen minutes, listening intently for
voices other than the original three. He heard none,
and was relatively sure there were no others.

Now, what was his best course of action? Should he try to take them by surprise, burst in with blazing guns, or should he wait for one to come out alone? He could capture him and make him tell where Jonty had been taken, for he was satisfied she wasn't inside.

The decision was suddenly taken away from him. There came the sound of chairs being scraped back, as though from a table, and someone was saying distinctly, "Come on, let's get the hell out of here."

It's now or never, Cord told himself, and in three running strides he was around the building and standing in the open door, his gun drawn.

"Stay right where you are," he ordered the three men who gaped at him in surprise.

"Who in the hell are you, mister?" A short, sharp-faced man finally recovered sufficiently to ask.

"It's of no importance to you who I am," Cord answered. "All you have to do is give me some answers. I'm lookin' for three men. The breed LaTour, an Indian, and the boy who is travelin' with them."

There was a flicker of knowledge and confusion in the eyes of the three men as Cord's gaze ranged over them. LaTour was obviously no stranger to them, but he wasn't sure they knew anything about Jonty.

The ferret-faced one spoke sullenly. "You're barkin' up the wrong tree, stranger. We don't know no breed or kid."

Cord started to say that the man was a liar, when he saw the man at the edge of his vision suddenly drop his right shoulder. "Get the bastard!" the small man yelled as a gun appeared in the man's hand.

With lightning-like speed, Cord's Colt leapt in his hand. There was a red flash, a thundering report, a hoarse cry of agony. The gun that had been pulled on him dropped to the floor from nerveless fingers. The man fell, face down on the floor.

In the same second, Cord spun around to find another muzzle pointing at him. His bullet caught the little man in the chest. The outlaw staggered, clutched at his wound, then sank slowly to the floor.

Cord swung around, swearing bitterly at the sound of hoofbeats fading into the distance. The third man had escaped, taking with him his last chance of discovering Jonty's whereabouts.

The odor of smoke and gunpowder began to lift, to float out the door and up the chimney as Cord sheathed his gun. He walked outside, his shoulders sagging in defeat. He had no idea where to look now. The Indian could have taken Jonty to a dozen different places.

"But I'll find her," he muttered, catching the roan's reins and swinging onto its back. "I'll never stop lookin', and someday I'll run into LaTour or the Indian, and by all that's holy, they'll tell me where she is."

Twilight of the seventh day found Cord once again approaching the foothills, the house less than a mile away. He's aged, Jones thought when, a few minutes later, Cord slid wearily from the saddle. He shook his head sadly as Cord walked into the house without a word.

CHAPTER 18

IT WAS LATE OCTOBER AND THE MORNING AIR HELD A NIP-
ping edge of frost. November would soon arrive.

Jonty rode bareback, hunched low over the mare,
her knees high on the mount's back. Her motion one
with the animal, she urged Beauty on to a greater
speed. She had a sense of exaltation as the wind blew
across her face, caught her curls, and tossed them
about her head.

It felt so good to be away from the saloon, the
squalor of Cottonwood, if only for a short time. Uncle
Jim didn't know she was out here, riding like a wild
Indian. She grinned. He would skin her alive if he
knew.

She recalled all his arguments about her riding
alone, the rebuttals she had given him.

"There are too many undesirables out there,
Jonty," he'd declare. And when she pointed out that
anyone she might run into would think her a boy and
would not bother her, he'd been ready with another
danger to warn her of.

"Dammit, Jonty, there's panthers on top of every bluff, and wildcats roamin' the mountains that are as big as Johnny's dog, Wolf. Anyway," he finished, frowning at her, "I don't know why you want to ride alone. What difference does it make if Johnny or one of the other men rides with you?"

She had only shrugged her shoulders at his question. She couldn't tell him that she wanted to be alone to think about Cord. That though she hated herself for it, she missed him, and every day she longed for the ranch, the tall spruce and pine, the freedom, the wilderness.

And that was why, when she rode out of town this afternoon, only Tillie had seen her leave. And Tillie wouldn't tell. Tillie was devoted to her. For Jonty had rescued the ex-whore from the street. Too worn out to work her trade any longer, the woman had been scratching out a living by collecting the bottles drunks had thrown on the ground. The saloon owners paid her for their return.

Jonty slowed the mare to a long, easy lope, remembering with a smile how Uncle Jim had blustered and carried on the morning he'd found her giving Tillie a hot breakfast.

"Jonty," he'd started quietly, trying to be calm, "you can't take in every destitute you see on the street. This town is overrun with them. And this old hag"— he'd jerked a thumb at the woman whose face was practically in her plate—"is probably full of disease."

That last had brought Tillie's head up sharply, and angry light shone in her eyes. "I ain't got no disease in me, LaTour. If I did, I wouldn't come within a mile of this sweet boy."

Uncle Jim had run contemptuous eyes over the dirty old body and muttered, "Probably not. No germ could ever penetrate all that filth."

"Then I can keep her?" Jonty had rushed to grab his arm and look pleadingly into his face.

A gentle smile curved Jonty's lips. As usual, Uncle

Jim had not been able to deny her. He had only said gruffly, "She's not a stray dog, Jonty. You can give her a corner to sleep in, food for her stomach, but you can't *keep* her. You can only befriend her."

Embarrassed blood flushing her cheeks, she had answered, "I know that, Uncle Jim. I just used the wrong words."

"I know, honey." He had kissed the top of her head, then left the kitchen.

While Tillie had continued to eat—and eat—she had put two big pans of water on the stove to heat. When they began to steam she took from the wall the big wooden tub used for laundering the clothes. By the time Tillie had finally pushed away from the table, warm bath water awaited her.

Jonty smiled at her, handing over a towel, wash cloth, and a bar of soap she had brought from her room. "Have a good soak while I go rustle up a shirt and pair of pants until we can get you some dresses."

And today, Tillie looked ten years younger. Three meals a day had fleshed out her bones, and the previous lank, greasy hair was now softly white and shiny with health. Strength that the woman had thought gone forever returned, and she now helped in the kitchen from early morning until late afternoon. She spent the time before retiring to her cot in a blanketed-off corner of the kitchen sipping at a glass of whiskey and smoking a cigarette.

Jonty shook her head ruefully. It hadn't taken long before Jonty was in charge of the kitchen, taking over the role of cook. The fat, gruff man who had made her the steak her first night at the Trail's End had gotten drunk once too often. Uncle Jim had sent him packing when the customers started demanding food and the cook was passed out in the kitchen.

But actually, she was glad the way things had turned out. She liked to cook, and she was going loco penned up in one room all day and night. She would have gladly taken over Tillie's old job of picking up bottles.

Uncle Jim had been against her taking charge of the

meals, but in her usual fashion she had ignored him and dug in.

But dig wasn't the right word. Scrape and shovel was more like it, she remembered with a grimace. It had taken her and Tillie two days to rid the big room of its grease and grime. Gradually, then, she had started increasing the fare offered by the saloon.

She had begun by adding pies, along with beef sandwiches. Then, one day, as an experiment, she put up a sign in the barroom announcing that stew would be available to whoever might want it. From then on, nightly meals were served. Sometimes stew, another night beef or venison roast or sometimes steak. It was not unusual for her and Tillie to bake twenty-five loaves of bread a day, and as many pies.

As the extra money from her labors poured in, Jonty was thrilled. She felt less and less like she was sponging off Uncle Jim.

The mare slowed to a walk of her own volition and Jonty pulled her in. As Beauty chomped at some tufts of grass, she gazed down into a wild rock- and brush-choked canyon. It was so like one of those back at the ranch that she experienced a wrenching pain in her chest. She visualized Cord and the others chasing wild mustangs, yelling and swearing as they raced after the wild ones, trying to throw a loop around a graceful, slender neck. A sadness, a regret, grew in her eyes. Cord *had* gone looking for her, but at the wrong place. She and Uncle Jim had been having lunch the day the man rode into Cottonwood, interrupting their meal, swearing vengeance on Cord McBain. "The bastard claimed he was lookin' for some kid who was travelin' with you and the Indian. I told him we didn't know nothin' about a kid, and when Snake and Jimbeau drew on him, he shot them both."

The man had paused for breath, then said, "As soon as I saw that fast-draw I knew who he was and I got out of there. Are you goin' after him, boss?"

LaTour shook his head. "No, McBain will come to see me soon enough."

And that, Jonty suspected, was the real reason Uncle Jim didn't want her riding alone. And, truthfully, wasn't that why she wanted the solitary rides, hoping she would run into Cord?

"God, I hope not," she scolded herself. "How could I still love a man who only wanted to use my body—and even then didn't find it sufficient to his needs?

"For Heaven's sake, forget Cord McBain," she ordered herself, kneeing the mare and reining her around.

Jonty tugged at the bindings around her chest. Each day her breasts became more tender and sore. And added to that was the way her body was filling out. The trousers Cord had bought her were becoming a little too tight, and she could no longer tuck in her shirt, but had to let it hang free to hide the new curve of her hips.

"Someday." She sighed and lifted the reins, pressing Beauty into a lope. "Right now it's time I got back and started on the pies for supper."

Jonty arrived back in town shortly and was unsaddling the mare in the shed back of the saloon when the sound of coarse laughter sent a chill down her spine.

Paunch! She'd heard that snorting sound he made too many times not to recognize it. What was he doing in Cottonwood? She moved to peer through a crack between the loosely fitted boards. And who was that poor creature with him? she wondered as her eyes fastened on the thin frame of an Indian woman following abjectly behind the fat man as he skirted the side of the saloon, making for the front door.

"I hope he's just passing through." Jonty said a small prayer, hurrying to the back and sliding into the kitchen. Tillie looked at her curiously as she paused to shoot the bolt on the door, something they never done in the daytime.

"Are you runnin' from someone, youngin'?"

Jonty gave a embarrassed little laugh, then unlocked the door and swung it open. "Just a habit, Tillie."

Tillie's wise old eyes studied her a minute, taking in

the pale face, the remnants of fear still lingering in the blue eyes. "You're with Jim LaTour now, honey," she said softly. "You don't have to fear no man."

Jonty smiled wanly. "You're right, Tillie. I forget that sometimes." She began to assemble the makings for a dried apple pie on the table, trying to shut out the sound of Paunch's voice in the barroom, his coarse oaths as he mistreated the Indian woman.

After a moment, Tillie jerked a thumb toward the closed door separating the kitchen and the bar. "The fat one is broke." Her lips curled. "He's in there tryin' to sell the squaw's favors."

"You know him?" Jonty swung around, her hands full of dough.

Tillie nodded. "He's a mean one. Kicked me one time because I didn't get out of his way fast enough to suit him." The cackling laugh that followed was full of devilish glee. "I fixed him, though. When he went into the saloon, I put a burr under his saddle. An hour later when he came staggerin' out and climbed on the mount, that animal bucked him flat on his lard-ass. You should have heard how everybody laughed."

Tillie grinned in remembrance a moment before adding, "Nobody likes the big bullyin' braggart."

Jonty turned back to the pan of dough. "He lives around here, then?" there was a tone of disquiet in her voice.

"Yeah, worse luck. He works in one of the saloons down the street, doin' odd jobs and such. A flunky," Tillie answered, contempt in the cracked voice.

Jonty put a ball of dough on the scrubbed table and picked up the rolling pin. Was there a chance that Paunch might run into Cord here? If so, he was bound to mention that she was living in Cottonwood, for she was sure to cross paths with the fat man sooner or later. She recalled the circumstances under which Paunch had left the ranch and doubted that he would even speak to Cord if he saw him.

She was filling a pie plate with the sugary apple

mixture when Tillie asked softly, "Have you ever been mistreated by a man, Jonty?"

"Mistreated, Tillie?" Her head jerked sharply around. "In what way do you mean? Are you asking if I've been beaten?"

"No." Tillie looked away from her uncomfortably. "You know . . . forced to make love."

It was Jonty's turn to look uncomfortable as she remembered Paunch's attack on her at the ranch. She tried to laugh, but it came out a tiny squeak. "I'm a male, Tillie. How could I be forced to make love?"

There was a long silence while neither woman looked at the other. When Tillie finally spoke, there was a firm certainty, as well as a gentleness in her voice. "I know you ain't no boy, Jonty."

The quietly spoken words so stunned Jonty, she couldn't speak for several moments. She looked blindly at the pie waiting to be put into the oven and asked finally, "How did you find out, Tillie? I thought I had my femininity well concealed."

"You do, child." Tillie came to stand beside her. "LaTour is the one who got me to thinkin'. I know that he totally loves women, wouldn't even consider doin' anythin' with a man. So, when his every action toward you is gentle and lovin', father-like, I knew you had to be a female. I started lookin' for womanish things about you, and I found them—the way you walk, the proud tilt to your head, the dainty way you use your hands."

Jonty sighed and looked at her friend anxiously. "I hope you won't say anything to anyone about your discovery, Tillie."

Tillie gave her a wounded look. "It hurts me that you even think you need to ask me that question. I'd let my tongue be cut out first."

Jonty threw herself into the boney arms held out to her. "Oh, Tillie," she cried, "you're almost like having Granny back with me." When tears flooded down the ex-whore's wrinkled cheeks, Jonty wiped them away with a corner of her apron, telling her not to cry.

It was nearing sundown, and Jonty and Tillie were filling plates from the pots keeping hot on the big black range. "How many go upstairs tonight?" Tillie asked, licking the thumb that she had accidently jabbed into a mound of mashed potatoes heaped beside a juicy steak.

"Six, so far," Jonty answered absent-mindedly. Her attention was on a question she had been muddling about in her mind for the last couple of hours. Should she break the rule Uncle Jim had laid down, that she was never to enter the barroom?

She finished filling another plate and placed it with the long line of plates already sitting on the table. She reached for the next one and forked a steak onto it, ignoring her companion's idle chatter. Paunch was still in the saloon and she wanted to face him, get it over with. And she wanted to do it in the presence of Uncle Jim, so that the man would know beyond a doubt that she had a protector and that he had better let her alone.

By the time Tillie had stacked a large tray with steak dinners and left to carry them upstairs, Jonty's mind was made up. She was going to do it and chance Uncle Jim's anger. A minute later, carrying a large tray herself, she entered the barroom.

The bartender, Jake, looked at her in surprise when she set the tray on the bar. "What are you doin' in here, kid? You know it's off-limits for you."

Jonty smiled easily. "Tillie's real busy upstairs tonight, so I thought I'd give her a hand."

"Well, you'd better scoot back to the kitchen before Jim gets back."

Jonty lifted startled eyes to the big man. "Isn't Uncle Jim here?" She suddenly didn't feel so safe.

Jake frowned at the wariness in her eyes. "He had some business to take care of. He said he'd be back around dark." He paused to look where Jonty was suddenly staring.

"That lousy bastard," he grunted, taking in the sight that had brought an appalled look to Jonty's face. "This is the first time he's ever brought his squaw in here. He usually takes her to the lower dives down the street."

Pity and anger grew in Jonty when she looked at the Indian woman who stood with bowed head, passively accepting the inevitable as Paunch bargained with a few interested men gathered around. She lost all reasoning when a dirty buffalo hunter roughly took the Indian woman's arm and jerked her toward the door so he could use her in the alley. She sprinted across the floor, Jake's startled cry following her.

She caught up with the pair at the door, her hands fastening in the man's waistband. "Take your hands off her," she ordered, and gave a hard jerk that brought the man stumbling backwards, finally sitting down hard. While she glared down at him amidst the loud laughter, the woman whimpered and shrank back. Her enraged owner was stalking menacingly toward the slight figure who had stepped in on her behalf.

When Paunch's heavy hand grabbed Jonty's shoulder and spun her around, his dark scowl turned to one of stunned surprise.

"Well, well, well. Look who we got here." He grinned maliciously. "Cord McBain's little whoreboy. What happened, pretty boy? Did he tire of you and kick you out? Whose little plaything are you now?"

Jonty knocked away the fat hand still holding her. "I'm nobody's plaything, nor have I ever been, you big tub of buffalo dung. Did Lucy get tired of your smell and kick you out? Are you reduced to abusing helpless Indian women now?"

Paunch's face tightened at her sarcasm and the tittering laughter that ran through the room. "No woman throws me out!" he roared. "Lucy's dead." He gave a short ugly laugh. "She died the way she would have wanted to. Pumpin' her ass beneath some man."

"You, no doubt," Jonty sneered.

"No, not me." Paunch shook his head. "He was a big mountain of a man, and he was drunk. The doctor said it looked like he'd passed out right in the middle of his humpin' and Lucy couldn't move him off her. He squashed the air out of her lungs."

Jonty blanched. She had never liked the woman, but what an awful way to die. She jerked and stepped back when Paunch would have grabbed her again. "Would you like to trade places with the squaw, pretty boy?" His gaze roamed around the room where the men watched intently, "or have you already chosen McBain's replacement?" Without warning, he grabbed Jonty again.

"You piece of filth, let go of my arm!" Jonty tried to twist free of the steely fingers biting into her flesh.

"A piece of filth, am I?" Paunch snarled as he twisted her arm behind her back. "We'll just take us a little walk in the alley and change your mind about me."

The angry muttering that started from some of the patrons was silenced as Tillie slammed open the kitchen door. Wolf came charging across the floor, coming to a bracing halt in front of the struggling Jonty. His lips were pulled back in a low snarl, and the hair on his neck bristled.

Paunch's face turned white. "You've still got that damned dog, I see." He grunted. "Well, once and for all I'm gonna put an end to that mangy beast."

Jonty felt him reaching for his gun and screamed. "Run, Wolf! Run to the kitchen!"

The burly bartender stirred into action. He came from behind the bar, a heavy club in his hand, as at the same time a broad-shouldered figure pushed through the swinging doors.

A hush fell over the room as Jim LaTour said

quietly, the words reaching each corner of the room, "I'll take care of this, Jake."

Silence filled the blue-hazed room, giving off a quiet threat as the breed advanced on the fat man. When his hand closed firmly over the hilt of the broad-bladed knife stuck in his belt, Paunch released Jonty's arm, his face devoid of all color.

"Look, LaTour." He held up a hand. "I didn't know the kid was—"

The slap LaTour delivered to the fat face cracked like a pistol. "Don't say it, scum. Don't even think it." He motioned Jonty to his side and when she hurried to huddle against him, he put an arm around her shoulders protectively.

"The kid started it." Paunch looked at them sullenly. "He came runnin' over here, interferin' with that man takin' the squaw outside."

"So, you're still mistreatin' Indian women, huh?" LaTour's eyes bored into the fat-slitted ones. "I thought I'd taught you a lesson about that." When Paunch made no response, LaTour raked him with contemptuous eyes. "I'll give you five minutes to get on your horse and ride out of town. If I ever see you around here again, you're a dead man."

Paunch looked up and tried to glare down grim blue eyes. Those watching interestedly saw the defeat when it clouded his face. He turned to the shrinking squaw and muttered, "Come on, bitch."

When the woman wearily moved after him, Jonty grabbed Jim's hand. "Don't let him take her," she implored. "He not only sells her to men, he abuses her terribly."

"Dammit, Jonty." LaTour looked down into her pleading eyes. "Are you askin' me to let you *keep* another pet?"

Jonty nodded. "Please, Uncle Jim."

After a moment, he grinned and ruffled her hair. "All right." His eyes stabbed the glowering fat man. "Leave the squaw, Paunch."

"What the hell!" The irate man took a belligerent
step toward LaTour. Then the hand that dropped to
the knife again, a thinly veiled threat, stopped him
cold. With a muttered curse, and a malicious look at
Jonty, Paunch turned and lumbered out of the saloon.

Conversations were resumed, drinks turned back
to. LaTour draped an arm across Jonty's shoulders
and led her toward the kitchen. When they were
inside, he sat her down at the table and ordered, "All
right, young man, talk. What were you doin' in the
bar?"

Jonty looked across at Tillie, who was trying to look
serious. She looked back at Jim and made a decision.
"Tillie knows my sex, Uncle Jim."

"Where'd you get that information, old woman?"
LaTour growled.

"She figured it out for herself," Jonty answered
before Tillie could speak. She rose and filled a plate
for LaTour and placed it before him. Then, taking a
chair across from him, Jonty gave him a big smile.
"Now tell me where you've been. Do you have a
lady-love?"

"Don't try to change the subject, young lady."
LaTour gave her curls a tug. "If I ever catch you in
there again serving food I'll blister your little rear end.

"And you, Tillie." He pretended a sour look. "Have
you been teachin' this youngin' to be disrespectable to
her elders?"

"I think she mostly gets her pertness from the man
sittin' at the table with her," Tillie retorted.

"You think she's a chip off the old block?" The
handsome man eyed the cook suspiciously. "Are you
tryin' to figure somethin' else out, old woman?"

Tillie hurriedly dropped her eyes and stammered,
"No—no, Jim."

LaTour picked up his cup and drank the last of his
coffee. "What about the squaw you took away from
Paunch?"

"I forgot about her," Jonty exclaimed. A frown

marred her forehead. "Do you suppose she speaks English?"

"She does," Tillie said grimly. "I've heard her beg the fat one not to beat her."

There was silence as each one pondered the cruelty of some men.

Jonty yawned suddenly. "I'm going to bed, Tillie, I can't hold my eyes open. Would you mind bringing the Indian woman in and giving her something to eat?"

As Jonty disrobed and climbed into bed, outside the Trail's End Paunch lurked in the shadows. His face was twisted with hate. Once again he had been humiliated by the breed. Again men had laughed at him.

"It's the last time, you bastard," he muttered. He slunk away in the darkness, his mind working on ways he would kill his enemies. First LaTour, then Cord McBain. Or whichever one he came across first . . . alone, out on the range someplace . . .

CHAPTER 19

JONTY STOOD AT THE KITCHEN WINDOW, WATCHING THE daylight fade as twilight came, blotting the distant mountains from view. All day it had been damp and overcast, and the gloomy weather was having its usual effect on her spirits.

She gave herself a shake, as though to throw off the gloom that had followed her all day. It wasn't her nature to fall into these fits of depression. She should be happy, contented. Wasn't she with Uncle Jim now? Hadn't she escaped Cord, his arrogance, his falseness?

She withheld a sigh and turned away from the window as unrestrained ribaldry began to issue from the barroom. The merry-makers and drunks would want to eat before long.

Word of the good food to be had at the Trail's End had spread, and each day brought new customers to the saloon. Tillie had become a fine cook and was a great help. Also, she was a pleasant companion, with a good sense of salty humor.

She thought of Nemia. Would that one ever laugh and joke? The Indian woman had been a pitiful looking sight the night Tillie had gone into the saloon and found her huddled in a corner, looking half dead. Tillie had finally coaxed her into the kitchen, but when she had placed a hand on a thin shoulder to press her into a chair, the woman had cried out in pain. Afraid that the shoulder was broken, Tillie had awakened Jonty.

Tears had swum in their eyes when Jonty eased the doeskin shift over Nemia's head. She was so thin, each rib could easily be counted, and there was very little flesh on the wasted body that wasn't bruised. That the woman was still alive was a miracle to Jonty.

She found that a broken collar bone had caused Nemia's cry of pain. But that could wait for the moment. If she kept her arm down she wouldn't be too uncomfortable. First she needed warm food in her stomach.

She said as much to Tillie, then, bringing down every curse she could think of on Paunch's head, she went to her room to fetch a blanket for Nemia. When she had wrapped it around the frail body, Tillie placed a bowl of soup and half a loaf of bread in front of their companion.

Two more bowls of soup later, Tillie gave Nemia a sponge bath, then slipped one of Jonty's nightshirts over her head. Jonty fashioned a sling to hold her arm, to take the pressure off the broken bone. A cot was set up in Jonty's room, and Nemia was helped to bed.

"That Paunch!" Tillie flared out. "I wish Jim had killed the no-good. He hasn't seen the last of that man. That one is very vindictive. One of the madams here in town refused to let him in her place, he was so brutal to her girls, and a week later she was found in an alley with her throat cut. Everyone suspects he did it, but there's no proof. He left town for a few weeks, then turned up with Nemia."

"How old do you think she is?" Jonty whispered.

"Probably younger than we think," Tillie answered in the same low tone. "Even a week with that man would age a woman."

Jonty's musing was interrupted when Tillie entered the kitchen from the back door and LaTour stuck his head in the room from the saloon. "This bunch out here is beginnin' to beller for food," he said. "Is that roast about ready, Jonty?"

"Give me fifteen minutes. I have to mash the potatoes and make the gravy."

Both women bustled around the kitchen. It would be this way for the next couple of hours.

"Whew! My feet are killin' me," Tillie groaned, bolting the kitchen door. "I was beginnin' to think that bunch upstairs would never get their guts filled." She plopped into a chair.

"The same thing at the bar. I must have made up fifty plates. I'm going to take my bath and go straight to bed."

"Here, let me help you carry that." Tillie jumped up and took hold of one side of the big pan of water that had been slowly heating on the back of the stove.

As they carried it through to Jonty's bedroom and poured the contents into the hip-tub, Jonty said as she stripped off her clothes, "I think a man should take the trays upstairs. They're too heavy, and you have to make too many trips."

"Don't worry about me, honey," Tillie said as Jonty stepped into the tub. "I'll let Jim know if it gets too hard."

Jonty stood rubbing her breasts a moment before easing down into the comforting bath. She threw a disgusted look at the strips of cloth lying on the floor. "My breasts are so sore I can barely stand to touch them. They even seem swollen."

Tillie's eyes narrowed on the young body as it disappeared into the water. "You seem to be gainin' weight too," she said thoughtfully.

Jonty laughed wryly. "I am. My britches are really

filled out these days. You'd think I'd lose weight, the way I have to hustle around here."

Jonty washed and rinsed her hair before Tillie spoke again.

"Have you been feelin' all right, Jonty—maybe a little pecky in the mornins'?"

Jonty chuckled as she slid the bar of soap over her shoulders and breasts. "Who can afford to feel pecky around here? As it happens, though, I have felt a little nauseated a few times. Probably from having to bolt down my food most of the time."

A somberness grew in Tillie's eyes. When Jonty stood up and reached for a towel she asked softly, "Have you ever been with a man, Jonty?"

"Tillie!" Jonty exclaimed reproachfully. "What a question to ask."

Tillie nodded. "Yes, I agree that I'm bein' very personal. I'll put it another way. Did you have your period this month?"

Jonty frowned as she finished drying herself and slipped on her nightshirt. She was getting a little perturbed at Tillie's prying. But something told her to think back, to count. When she realized that she hadn't had her woman's time for close to two months, a pallor spread over her face. Bitter tears springing to her eyes and clinging to her lashes, she looked at Tillie, silently begging her to say it wasn't so.

But no such words came as her friend wrapped her arms around her shivering body. As she cried on the bony shoulder, Tillie said gently, "I know nothin' happened to you here. Did someone rape you at the ranch?"

Jonty wanted to cry out, "Not rape in the sense that you mean, Tillie, but rape nevertheless. My brain was assaulted by honeyed words, my body tricked by caressing hands and warm lips. It was a rape of the senses."

Before she could get started telling Tillie it hadn't been rape, that she had been a willing partner, a knock sounded on the door between the kitchen and the saloon, and LaTour called, "It's me, Jonty, open the door."

"Tillie! Don't open the door." Jonty clutched at a bony arm.

"I've got to, child. He knows we're not asleep." The knock sounded again, only louder, and Tillie hastened into the kitchen.

Jonty tried to compose herself, to stop shaking. But her mind was too frantic with the discovery she'd just made. There was a new life growing beneath her heart, a life put there by a man's careless seed. And equally strong was the dread of what Uncle Jim would think of her. Would contempt leap out of his eyes when he learned that she was no longer an innocent?

She was knuckling her tear-wet eyes when LaTour entered her room, Tillie close behind him. His gaze immediately took in her red eyes and swollen lips. "Jonty." He frowned, hurrying to her. "What's wrong? Why have you been cryin'?"

"It's nothing, Uncle Jim." Jonty tried to smile brightly. "I'm just tired. I served a lot of meals tonight."

"I'm sorry, honey." LaTour was contrite. "I haven't realized how hard you've been workin'. I'll get someone in to help you and Tillie."

An impatient frown darkened Tillie's face. What was wrong with the foolish girl? Didn't she realize that a woman could hide a big belly only so long? Why avoid the inevitable? She took a deep breath.

"Jonty is gonna have a baby, Jim."

LaTour's face went pale, as though he had taken a blow to the stomach. After a jagged indrawn breath, he slumped down on the edge of the bed. "It didn't take that whore-chasin', rake-hellion long to discover that you are female, did it?" He spoke as though thinking out loud. While Jonty supressed more tears, and Tillie wondered who the rake-hellion was, Jim jumped back on his feet.

"I'll kill the bastard," he raged, pacing the floor.

"I'll ride out to his ranch and put my knife in his heart."

With a small cry of protest, Jonty reached out and grabbed his arm. "No, Uncle Jim, please! You mustn't kill him! He is, after all, the father of this child I'm carrying." She couldn't add that despite everything, she still loved her child's father.

LaTour gazed down at the delicate face so like her mother's and wanted to weep himself. His hands clenched as he swore to himself that, unlike the woman he had bred his daughter on, he would be here to see Jonty through it all.

He drew Jonty into his arms. "I won't kill him." He nuzzled her head with his chin. "But if he should come here lookin' for you, he'll wish that I had before I'm finished with him."

Jonty's lips tilted in a weak grin. "I wouldn't mind that. I'd do it myself if I had the strength."

LaTour and Tillie smiled at each other, Tillie's eyes saying, "An apple doesn't fall far from the tree."

Jim picked Jonty's old flannel robe off the bed and handed it to her. "Put this on, honey, then come into the kitchen. We've got things to discuss."

As Jonty and LaTour sat down at the table, Tillie took the warm coffee pot off the stove and gave it a slight shake. When there came a sloshing sound, she reached for three cups, and when the coffee was poured, she took a seat next to Jonty.

LaTour wasted no time. "Tillie," he began, "you take over Jonty's duties tomorrow. And you, Jonty, start gettin' your things together. Do you know how to sew?" At Jonty's nod, he continued. "Tomorrow mornin', go over to the General Store and buy all that frippery women need, and some flannel to make baby clothes out of." He stood up. "I want you and Johnny to be out of here by early afternoon. I didn't tell you, but when I was gone the other day, I bought a small ranch. I want you and Johnny to run it."

He was gone then, leaving Jonty and Tillie looking

at each other. What a turn the evening had taken! Mixed emotions shadowed Jonty's eyes. All her dreams were coming true, but in less than eight months she would be a mother.

"Well, this has been a surprisin' night, huh, honey?" Tillie rose and gathered up the empty cups.

"It surely has." Jonty smiled weakly. "My head is still spinning and my heart is still trying to jump out of my chest." She stood up also. "I might as well start getting my things together."

Tillie took up her shawl and swung it around her shoulders. "While I look up Lightfoot, you make a list of the things you'll need to take along to your new home."

Jonty nodded. "When you return, you can help me think of what to purchase in the line of clothes." She smiled wanly. "I don't know too much about women's . . . *frippery.*"

It was past midnight by the time Jonty and Tillie got to bed. It had taken Tillie quite a while to find Lightfoot. She had stuck her head into half a dozen saloons before remembering that Indians weren't served liquor.

She found him finally at the livery stable, quietly conversing with some other Indians. She stood quietly in the doorway, waiting for him to speak first. Women did not interrupt Indian men. She had great respect for Jonty's friend and would not shame him in front of his companions.

When Lightfoot came to her, she related why she sought him. As they returned to the saloon, she was careful to walk behind him. Only Jonty was privileged to walk beside the tall, proud Indian. As for that, even in front of him if she so desired.

It hadn't taken Jonty long to gather what she would take with her tomorrow. At first she had packed shirts and trousers for her and Nemia, who she had decided would go with her, then with an impatient sound, she gathered everything up and shoved it all into her little stove, muttering, "I'm not thinking straight. I won't be wearing these rags anymore."

The closing of the stove door awakened Nemia, and Jonty sat down on the edge of the cot and explained that they would be leaving Trail's End tomorrow. "You'll like it at the ranch Uncle Jim purchased, Nemia. You'll grow strong and healthy again."

Fear flickered in the frail woman's eyes. "Will there be just me and you there?"

Jonty ran a soothing hand over the long black hair. "Don't be afraid, Nemia. Johnny is going with us. You needn't worry about Paunch anymore."

The thin face relaxed in relief. "I'm glad Johnny will be with us. He is a brave and good man."

"He is indeed," Jonty agreed softly, and tucking the covers around Nemia's shoulders, she climbed into her own bed. As she pulled the blanket over her, she heard Tillie enter the kitchen and quietly bolt the door.

Jonty's sleep was restless and filled with nightmares. In one, she and Cord tugged at a baby between them, and one of its arms came off in Cord's hand. Then, she was at the ranch house Jim had sent her to and it had no roof or windows. And while she was telling Lightfoot that he would have to do something about it, he suddenly turned into her enemy, Paunch. When he stalked toward her, calling her Pretty Boy, she sat straight up in bed, her body drenched in sweat. Dawn was streaking the sky, so she rose and got dressed. She'd had enough bad dreams.

Jonty was half-way to the General Store the next morning when Lightfoot caught up with her. "I've got the wagon packed." He shortened his stride to match hers. "There's not much room left in it, so don't buy too much. Jim must have bought out that furniture store at the end of town."

The furniture store was only a long shed which a German carpenter had taken over recently, fashioning most anything a woman would want in her home. Jonty knew from the pieces in her room that the man did fine work.

"Did you get everything on my list?" she asked.

"Yes, plus a couple things you forgot."

"Such as?" Jonty frowned, trying to remember what she could have forgotten.

"Tobacco and whiskey." The Indian grinned down at her.

"Oh, yes!" Jonty smacked her forehead. "How could I have forgotten two such important items." Her lips twisted in a teasing smile. "Especially that last one."

"You're real sharp this morning, huh, curly-top?" Lightfoot gave her hair a tug, then left her, walking in the opposite direction.

Jonty spent close to two hours in the store, choosing the items she'd longed for for so long. The petticoats, chemise, and camisoles weren't of the finest material; the place catered mostly to farm and ranch women, but compared to men's rough underwear, they were fancy enough in Jonty's eyes.

However, the pleasure she had anticipated in purchasing the articles was missing. The worry and frustration of learning she was going to have a baby had predominance in her mind.

Her spirits rose somewhat when she spotted a rack of ready-made dresses. She wouldn't have to waste time sewing. She could wear a dress as soon as she arrived at the ranch.

Finally, six dresses lay over her arm. They weren't the fanciest she'd ever seen, calico and chambray, but she had chosen the brightest colors available. To her, they were grand and beautiful.

Jonty carried the gowns to the counter and placed them on top of the undergarments. She smiled at the clerk who watched her curiously from the corners of his eyes as he waited on another customer, then walked over to the stacks of yard goods. For later, when she grew large with child, she would have to make some clothing that would accommodate her new growth. Her eyes fell on a bolt of white flannel. She'd need several yards of that for baby clothes.

Jonty waited patiently while Mr. Jenkins finished with his customer, a young cowboy purchasing a shirt. When the bell attached to the door jangled behind the buyer, the owner of the establishment moved down the counter to her.

"Good morning, Jonty. You're up and about early this morning."

"I have a busy day ahead of me." Jonty smiled at the middle-aged man, then indicated with a wave of her hand the three bolts of yard goods she'd carried to him. "I'll have two dress lengths from each, and six yards of the white flannel."

The material was measured, cut, and wrapped in brown paper. When Jenkins began to neatly fold the dresses, he said in a slightly sneering voice, "Jim's girls will turn their noses up at these dresses, Jonty. They ain't fancy enough for them. They send back to Abilene for their things."

"They're for Tillie." She gave the man a cold look, not liking his remark about "Jim's girls."

Jonty's displeasure passed over Jenkins' head. "Now, they might like some of them," he said as she lingered over a display of scented soap and toilet water.

She picked up one of the bottles, coated with a film of dust, and wondered how long it had been on display. The hard working women of the area, toiling under the hot sun to make ends meet, wouldn't be likely to waste their money on such "fripperies." As for the prostitutes—she uncapped the bottle and sniffed the delicate fragrance—it wasn't nearly strong enough for them.

When Jonty added two bottles of the scent and six bars of soap to the dresses, the proprietor lowered his lids to hide his relief. He had been stuck with them for over a year. After he toted up her purchases, she paid and left the store hugging her treasures to her chest.

The next two hours passed swiftly as Jonty wrote down recipes for Tillie, got Nemia out of bed, and readied her for the trip.

It was around one o'clock and threatening rain when Lightfoot pulled the wagon up behind the kitchen. Jonty handed her packages up to him, then helped Nemia to climb up on the tall seat. She smiled shyly at Lightfoot, who waited patiently for Jonty to say her good-byes.

Tears shimmering in her eyes, Jonty gave Tillie a hug and kiss, reminding her to come visit soon. She turned to LaTour. He pulled her jacket collar up against the cold wind that had risen, then hugging her fiercely, said, "You take care of yourself. I'll be out one day next week to check up on how you're doin'."

Jonty hugged the big man back, ordering, "You take care of yourself too. Stay out of those barroom brawls. I couldn't bear it if I lost you too."

She stepped out of LaTour's arms, slapped the wide-brimmed hat on her head, and climbed up beside Nemia. As Lightfoot lifted a hand to his cousin, then snapped the reins over the team's back, Wolf leapt into the back of the wagon.

The dark clouds that had hung overhead all day spilled their first drops of rain as the wagon began to roll. By the time it reached the end of town, the rain was coming down in earnest. As the two mounts and the cow tied to the tailgate snorted their displeasure, Lightfoot ordered, "Get the slickers out, Jonty. This is not going to let up for awhile."

Worried about Nemia in her weakened condition, Jonty helped her first to shrug into the long, rubber garment, buttoning it all the way up to the woman's chin. She handed Lightfoot the second one, then donned the third. All three laughed when Wolf jumped to the ground and ran along beneath the wagon to escape the downpour.

About a half mile had been covered and Jonty was checking the waterproof canvas thrown over her packages when she heard the thunder of many hooves. She peered through the slashing rain and made out a large herd coming toward them.

"Mustangs!" Her heart beat harder. "Could they possibly be Cord's?

Even as Jonty asked herself the question, she spotted Cord's black-slickered figure astride the big stallion, Rawhide. She hunched down in her own cover and pulled the sodden, floppy hat further down on her head, thankful for its wet condition that made it fall around her ears and face. She noted that Lightfoot had drawn his collar up beyond his chin and tugged his hat farther down on his forehead. He, too, knew who was leading the wild horses. If only he doesn't see Wolf, she thought, clasping her hands in silent prayer.

Although Jonty kept her eyes straight ahead, she knew exactly the moment Cord rode past her. Her hands gripped each other. God help her, she could walk straight to him in a black dark room filled with a dozen men.

Tears ran down her cheeks, mingling with the rain as riders and horses splashed out of sight. Her heart ached to tell Cord that he was going to become a father. She sighed raggedly. That was out of the question, of course. For if she should bear a son, it wasn't unlikely that Cord would try to take him away from her. It would appeal to him—having an heir without the bother of a wife. She doubted seriously that, no matter how much he cared for Tina, he would ever marry the girl.

The flames in the fireplace threw long shadows into the corners of the room. Silence held the house, broken only by the sough of the wind-beaten pines outside the window as Cord sat quietly staring into the flames. This was not an unusual occupation of his. Sometimes he'd sit thus by the hour. A month had passed since Jonty left him, and she continued to haunt him. Her face danced in front of him in everything he did.

The feeling of helplessness that suddenly gripped him forced him to his feet. He paced over to the window and stared out into the darkness. If only he had the barest hint of where to look for her. One long-fingered hand clenched into a fist. It was as if she had disappeared into the air—she, the dog, Lightfoot, even LaTour. He hadn't been able to find a trace of any of them.

The soft opening of the door interrupted his gloomy thoughts. He turned around, a slight frown marring his forehead. "Did you want somethin', Tina?" His voice held impatience. It was hard to be civil to the girl anymore.

The Mexican girl advanced into the room, her eyes holding a boldness, and yet an underlining of uncertainty. Then, as though remembering when he had pursued her in the past, she walked up to Cord and laid a caressing hand on his arm.

"Yes, I want something." Her eyes told him plainly what it was. There was no coyness in her manner when she asked, "Why have you changed toward me? What have I done that you no longer ask to walk with me, to ride with me?"

Cord squirmed inwardly at the blunt questioning. The girl had every right to be curious, hurt. He had led her to believe that she appealed to him. She had no way of knowing that even if he hadn't been tied up in knots over Jonty, he still wouldn't have taken her to bed. He had too much respect for her parents. Tina was a ripe little piece who wouldn't waste any time in making up to the new wranglers he had hired. Still, he had to handle this carefully, try not to hurt her feelings.

He laid a hand over the small one clutching his sleeve. Squeezing it gently, he said, "Tina, you have every right to be bewildered, even angry at my recent behavior. You're a lovely girl and I was strongly attracted to you, but a month back I fell in love with another young woman and I plan to marry her."

At Tina's little cry of dismay, Cord added hurriedly, "I'm too old for you anyway. You should be interested in one of the young wranglers. They would show you a good time, take you to dances."

He smiled coaxingly into Tina's sullen face. "If you think about it, you'll find I'm right." He took her shoulders and turned her toward the door. "Go help your mother with the dishes now. And tomorrow morning, when the men come in for breakfast, look them all over, choose one, flash your pretty eyes at him, and he'll make you forget all about me."

He didn't see the angry glint in the young girl's eyes, the black snap that said she had no intention of giving him up. He was a big *ranchero* and she would do whatever it took to land him.

But Jones, who barely had time to step out of Tina's way as she flashed past him, saw the look of fury on her face. He gave a low whistle as he stepped into Cord's room.

"What's got into Miss Pepper Pot? She's really roiled up." He grinned at Cord. "The fire comin' out of her eyes singed my whiskers."

Cord shrugged. "She didn't like the way our conversation went."

"Aha." Jones laughed, helping himself to a glass of whiskey from the bottle that always stood on the mantle. "You threw cold water on her high expectations, huh?"

"Somethin' like that." Cord took the chair next to the man he'd made foreman a few weeks before.

"I hope you don't think this is the end of it," Jones said after tossing the amber liquid down his throat. "It was foolish of you to take up with her in the first place."

Cord leaned his head back on the chair with a ragged sigh. "It was more foolish than you know, friend. It's probably the most foolish thing I've ever done in my life." He closed his eyes, remembering how his action had lost Jonty to him. "There's no use

rehashing that," he told himself and, pulling himself
back to the present, asked Jones, "Did you go to
Cottonwood and talk to that government man?"

"Yeah, I just got back from there. The man wants a
hundred horses for the army. I told him we'd deliver
in a couple weeks."

Jones stood up and stretched. "I'm beat. I'm gonna
get a bite to eat, then crawl into my bunk."

Cord nodded and was ready to slip back into his
gloomy reflections when the announcement Jones
made from the door brought him sitting up straight.

"I almost forgot, Cord. While I was in Cottonwood
I saw the Indian's big dog, Wolf. He was layin' in front
of a saloon."

"Are you sure, man?" Cord's hands gripped the
chair arms. "It could have been one that looked like
him."

"Naw, it was that same mean bastard that always
tagged along after Jonty. I spoke to him—from a
distance you can bet—and I saw recognition in his
yeller eyes."

"Well?" Cord was on the edge of his seat now. "Did
you see Jonty or Lightfoot?"

"Nope. And I went inside and looked. There was no
sign of either one of them." Jones paused for a
moment, as though debating the wisdom of voicing
his next words. Finally he said, "I saw Jim LaTour,
though. Turns out he owns the place."

Cord caught his breath sharply. The slashed grooves
alongside his mouth deepening, he demanded,
"What's the name of this place?"

"It's called Trail's End. It's a pretty fancy place for
that hell-hole town. It's got gamblin' equipment,
pretty whores . . ." Jones's words trailed off as Cord
jumped to his feet.

"Go ahead and get your rest, Jones." Cord looked at
him, his eyes filled with a light that hadn't been there
for a long time. "We've got a lot of hard work ahead of
us tomorrow. I plan on setting out the next day."

Jones eyes widened. "You gonna go along?"

"That's right. That dog is gonna lead me to Jonty. Either he will, or I'll beat the information out of LaTour."

"I don't know, Cord." The recently appointed ranch foreman frowned. "LaTour has some tough-lookin' characters hangin' round. You'd better be careful."

Cord smiled thinly. "There'll be no one around when I face him. It will just be me and him. I've waited a long time for just such a moment."

The gray of dawn stole over the eastern range and the blackness of night retreated. Half an hour later, horses whinnied and ropes whistled. His trousers clinging to his lean, muscular hips, his shirt straining across his broad chest, Cord pulled his collar up against the thin, cool air as he glanced up at the sky. Those gray, lowering clouds promised rain before the day was over.

The chill of November was upon them, the cold of winter not far away. "It's probably snowin' back on the mountain," Cord mused out loud, swinging onto Rawhide's back.

The rains came, as Cord had prophesied, coming down steadily as he glimpsed Cottonwood through its slashing force. His heartbeat picked up. At last, only half a mile distant, he would either see Jonty or learn of her whereabouts.

He steered Rawhide against the lead mustang, directing them away from a wagon coming their way. His mind was so taken up with Jonty that Cord barely glanced at the occupants, nor as he rode by did he see the large dog trotting beneath the wagon. As for the two mounts and cow running along behind, there was nothing unusual about that. It was a common sight.

When riders and horses entered the town, Cord rode up alongside Jones. "Lead them to the holding pens, Jones. I'm gonna go take care of the business I came here to do."

CHAPTER 20

JONES DIDN'T GIVE HIS USUAL, "RIGHT AWAY, CORD" BUT sat on, his angular face drawn into a worried frown. "Cord, why don't you wait and go along with us into that den? Like I told you before, it's a mean bunch that hangs around there."

"And like I told you before, It'll just be me and him."

"All right." Jones gave in, lifting the reins and nudging his mount with a heel. "I just wish you had eyes in the back of your head. And remember, that breed ain't no ordinary man. You look out for that knife he carries."

Cord watched his friend splash away. "I hope the bastard draws his blade," he muttered, his eyes going hard and cold. "I'd like nothing better than an excuse to put a bullet between his eyes."

He tightened his grip on the reins, sending Rawhide into a walk that took them down the middle of the single street. It was deep in mud, strewn with empty bottles and rubbish of every kind imaginable. The buildings were all low structures, made of rough, unpainted boards. A few sported fancy false fronts, the fanciest being the Trail's End.

Cord drew rein in front of Jim LaTour's place and sat for a moment, scanning it carefully. A raucous din surged from behind the bat-wing door—laughter, shouts, the shrieks of women, a rattle of dice, the clicking whirr of roulette wheels.

"This is a fine place you've run to, Jonty." He scowled darkly, swinging from the saddle and looping the reins over a hitching post. He stepped up on the narrow porch, paused to adjust his holster, then pushed open the swing doors. He stepped to one side and paused again, scanning the large room.

Trail's End was indeed a hard-looking place, full of hard-faced men and painted whores. His gaze moved to the far end of the room where at least a dozen games of chance were being played—and bringing in a lucrative business judging by the people crowded around them.

The man he sought wasn't among the players. Cord's eyes moved to the bar and narrowed. He had found his man. LaTour stood with elbows on the shiny mahogany bar, idly talking to a male companion. Cord stared at the handsome face in profile, and bitterness and hatred boiled inside him. If not for LaTour, Jonty would still be with him, all misunderstandings cleared up.

His face a cool, impassive mask, Cord moved forward, ignoring the women who looked at him boldly as he made his way to the bar. When he stood directly behind LaTour, he slid the Colt from its holster and jabbed it into the man's ribs.

"Don't turn around, LaTour," he said quietly, for his ears alone. "Just lead me to a place where we can talk privately."

Blue eyes met gray ones in the mirror behind the bar. "I've been expecting you, McBain." LaTour's lips twisted wryly. "Upstairs in my office, all right?"

No one paid any attention to the two men mounting

the stairs. LaTour was always going up there with someone. "I have to take the keys out of my pocket." LaTour stopped in front of a door at the head of the carpeted steps.

"Make sure it's just your keys you're goin' after, breed, or you're a dead man."

"You've got the upper hand at the moment, McBain," LaTour muttered as he unlocked the door.

"Now, relock it and hand me the key," Cord ordered as they stepped inside the small room.

"You're a trusting bastard, aren't you?" The words were growled as the order was obeyed.

Cord let the remark pass as, flushed, they glared at each other, in the eyes of each a challenge. "Where is she?" Cord wasted no time, his voice raspy.

LaTour didn't pretend to misunderstand the question. "She's where you'll never find her."

"Oh, I'll find her. If I have to tear this town apart, I'll find her."

"Tear ahead." LaTour smiled mirthlessly, leaning lazily against his desk. "But before you do, I wish you'd satisfy my curiosity. I'd like to know just why you're so all-fired up to drag her back to your ranch. What are your plans for her, now that you know her sex? Somehow I can't believe that they're honorable."

Cord's only response to the charge was an angry narrowing of his eyes. Instead, he asked of the fiercely glaring man, "I'd like to hear from you why *you* want Jonty. What are *your* plans for her?"

"It's very simple," LaTour answered after a slight pause. "I love the girl, always have. As for my future plans for her, that is none of your business."

Cord stiffened, a muscle working in his jaw. "Does marryin' her figure in your future plans for her?"

Laughter exploded from LaTour's throat. "No." He finally managed to say, "I'll never marry Jonty." His mouth relaxed in a lazy smile. "I don't love the girl that way."

With a sudden plunging rush, Cord went for the man who stood in the way of his marrying the woman he loved so desperately. "You bastard," he gritted through clenched teeth, "you'd make her your whore!"

LaTour, quick as a cat, accustomed to rough-and-tumble barroom fights, met Cord's rush, low and hard. They grappled each other to the floor, fighting as though for life, silently, perspiration streaming from their faces.

But right was on the breed's side. He was fighting for his daughter's honor, for all the wrongs done to her by this man. "You've bucked the wrong tiger this time, McBain," he panted, and settled down to placing his fists where they would do the most damage.

Soon Cord's left eye was swollen shut and his nose a bloody smear. When he finally managed to pull himself up, LaTour landed a fist to his chin that sent him back to the floor, where he lay in a senseless heap.

Cord drifted back to the living when his stallion snuffled at his face. He had immediate recall. LaTour had beaten hell out of him, then thrown him into the street. Through swollen eyes, he peered at the rain that had become a drizzly sleet that could turn into snow any minute. He felt his sore jaw and longed to put a bullet through the breed's heart.

Where was Jones? he was wondering when a sly cackle brought him painfully to one elbow. He focused his gaze on an old woman standing in the doorway of a shack, puffing on a clay pipe.

"The breed worked you over pretty good, didn't he?" The old crone watched him through rheumy eyes. "I'm surprised he only gave you a beatin'. Usually he just puts his knife in them who are foolish enough to tangle with him. He must have a soft spot for you."

"Hah!" Cord felt his face again. "I didn't notice it if he does." He gave the woman a calculating look. "Do you happen to know what happened to the young lad who worked for LaTour?"

"You must mean Jonty. A fine young lad. Cooked

for LaTour's customers. Used to give me a plate of food every night for supper." The faded eyes grew gloomy. "I'm gonna miss him . . . and his food."

Cord's shoulders slumped as he helplessly cursed his bad luck. "I don't suppose you know where he went?" He looked at the old woman. "Or when he's comin' back?"

"No, I don't. I only know that he left with the breed's cousin and a squaw . . . and a big, mean-lookin' dog."

Cord sat up, fighting the pain that rocked his head. He flinched when Jones stood over him, loudly exclaiming, "Good Lord, man, what happened to you?"

"The damn breed beat the livin' hell out of me, that's what happened," Cord growled.

Jones reached a hand down to him. "We've got to get you dried off before you catch pneumonia."

"I'll build a fire as soon as I get out of this hell hole." Cord grunted, coming to his feet. "Where are the rest of the men?"

"In a saloon down the street. I'll go get them." He paused. "They're not gonna like it, though. They're tired and want to live it up a little before we start back."

"I can understand that." Cord picked his hat off the muddy street and slapped it on his head. "You and the men stay over night and rest up. But stay out of Trail's End," he added. "And that's an order, Jones."

"I'll not be stayin' myself." Jones climbed back on his mount. "But I'll make sure the men understand your orders."

Cord gazed after his friend for a moment, then turned back to the old woman. He shoved a hand into his pocket as he walked over to her. "Here," he said, pressing some money into her gnarled fingers. "My name is Cord McBain, and I have a ranch at the foot of Devil's Mountain. If you should get a line on where Jonty is, and get word to me, you'll get more."

He received a peering, suspicious look, then, "Do

you mean to harm the lad? Me and LaTour wouldn't like it if somethin' bad happened to him."

"Jonty will come to no harm from me, Granny," Cord said quietly, convincingly.

After another close scrutiny, the white-haired woman nodded. "I'll be keepin' my ears and eyes on the alert. And my name is Janie."

Cord nodded, said, "Glad to know you, Janie," and swung onto Rawhide's back. Twenty minutes later and a couple miles out of town, he sat before a fire he'd kindled beneath a large pine. Steam rose from his wet clothing as the snow began to stick to the ground, forming a thin white blanket over everything.

Cord's angry thoughts dwelled on Jim LaTour. He'd like to put a bullet through the man's heart, but something told him that if he did, he'd never win Jonty. And win her he would. He'd set men to watching the Trail's End and sooner or later they'd either see her, or LaTour would lead them to wherever he had hidden her.

An hour ago the rain had turned to sleet and the sleet into snow. The whole world seemed smothered in a dense white shroud. Jonty couldn't see a yard ahead, could barely make out the rumps of the horses only a few feet in front of her. She felt lost in a soft, soundless obscurity.

She scooted closer to Lightfoot, to share his warmth. Nemia had long since deserted them for the shelter of the tarp that covered the furniture and supplies. Jonty's lips moved in amusement. Wolf had soon joined the Indian woman.

"Johnny, are we almost there?" she asked through chattering teeth. "I'm about frozen."

As though her voice had triggered an unseen God who looked down and took mercy on them, the snow stopped and a pale westerly sun strove to shine.

Lightfoot looked at Jonty and smiled. "We'll be there in just another few minutes. The ranch buildings are at the end of this valley."

"Thank goodness." Jonty hunched lower into the heavy jacket Lightfoot had given her on her eighteenth birthday. Her friend now snapped the reins over the horses's broad backs, urging them to a faster gait. Jonty let her gaze travel over the area.

The valley was approximately half a mile wide, she judged, and its length she couldn't tell. It ran beyond the sight of her eyes. It was bordered on one side by tall spruce and a clear stream flowing along on the other side. She smiled dreamingly, visualizing cattle grazing on the rich, grassy level come spring.

Lightfoot guided the team nearer and nearer toward the river, and soon, just a short distance away from it, beyond a tall stand of pine, he drew the horses in. Jonty had her first view of her new home.

She stood up, her hands clasped together, her gaze eagerly taking it all in. Except for the sturdy log cabin, the other few buildings were pretty much run-down and would need extensive work done to them. She thought of Jones and his ability with saw and hammer, and wished that he was there. But the surrounding mountains were beautiful, and pride of ownership burned in her breast.

"What do you think, Nemia?" She turned and smiled at the Indian woman as she stuck her head up and gazed around. "Do you think you can be happy here?"

"Oh, yes," Nemia answered on a long, happy sigh. "Nemia has dreamed of such a place for a long time."

"Poor Wolf." Jonty laughed when the big dog jumped out of the wagon and ran to lift his leg against a tree. "I wonder how long he's been wanting to do that?"

Nemia laughed softly. "No longer than I have, I expect."

"Me too." Jonty chuckled and looked around. "I wonder where we can go to relieve that condition."

Lightfoot whipped up the horses, explaining, "There's a privy back of the cabin. Jim had it built special for you ladies," he said a minute later as he helped Jonty out of the wagon. He turned to help Nemia then, adding, "While you two visit it, I'll go inside and build a fire."

By the time Jonty and Nemia left the narrow little building and hurried toward the cabin, smoke curled up from the chimney. They left running foot prints in the snow as they dashed for the cabin. Jonty jerked the door open, and Wolf almost knocked both women down as he, too, made for the fire that crackled inside a huge, fieldstone fireplace.

The savory odor of brewing coffee was just beginning to waft through the single room as Jonty and Nemia held their hands out to the fire's warmth. Jonty glanced over her shoulder at the single piece of furniture in the room—a big black cooking range, in which a fire also roared. Lightfoot was just pulling a brand new coffee pot to the back of the stove where it would simmer slowly on the lesser heat.

The familiar scent of new wood brought Jonty's gaze sweeping the room, settling first on new window sills, a new door, and several shelves attached to the wall, close to the range.

"We'd better get settled in, Jonty," Lightfoot said interrupting her inspection. "It will be dark in another hour."

Darkness had arrived by the time Jonty and Lightfoot had emptied the wagon, the Indian carrying the heavier pieces on his back. All that was left to do now was make up the bed and put away the supplies.

Nemia had not been idle either. She had buried four potatoes in the hot ashes in the fireplace, then went through the hamper of food Tillie had packed for them. She withdrew a good-sized beef roast and slipped it into the oven to warm, then rummaged through the boxes holding cooking utensils until she found a pot. Carrying it to the stove, she emptied a crock of squash stew into it. Half an hour earlier, she had lit the kerosine lamp and placed it in the center of the table, the first article of furniture to be carried inside.

Jonty stood in the middle of the floor, smiling her content. The big room was warm and cozy, brightly lit by lamp and leaping flames in the fireplace. She turned to express her delight to Lightfoot, but he had picked up the axe, placed earlier beside the door, and walked outside.

She was setting her new table with new dishes when the Indian returned, the wind swirling in behind him, causing smoke to spiral from the fire. His arms full of spruce boughs, he kicked the door shut with his foot.

"For Nemia's bed," he explained at Jonty's questioning look. He dropped the greenery in a corner, then dusted off his hands. "Jim hadn't planned on her being here when he ordered the furniture a month ago."

"I had planned that Nemia and I would share the bed," Jonty began, but Lightfoot shook his head.

"Best you sleep alone, in your condition."

His thinking made no sense to Jonty, but she made no response. She and Nemia watched him carefully stack the branches together, weaving their ends so that no sharp points would poke the sleeper. Expertly then, he covered the make-shift bed with a soft buffalo hide. He looked up at Nemia. "You can put sheets and blankets on it if you want to, otherwise I have another hide you can cover up with."

A pleased smile stirred his stoic features when Nemia said shyly, "I would like to use your hide, Johnny. Like I did in my people's village."

"Where will you sleep?" Jonty looked at the tall Indian suspiciously. Nemia was under her care now, and the woman wouldn't be forced to sleep with any man again, not even Johnny.

Lightfoot's lips twisted slightly as he slid Jonty an innocent look. "Why, in my bedroll, of course. Where did you think I'd sleep, Jonty? Out in the stables?"

Jonty blushed an embarrassed pink. "Of course not!

I only wondered if you were going to make another pallet," she lied.

The Indian ducked his head to hide another smile. The sly little fox had read his mind. He had thought to share Nemia's bed. Now that she had regained her health and put on some weight, Nemia was quite a handsome woman. But now, what with Jonty having subtly challenged him, he'd have to work on Nemia to obtain her favor before spending the long winter nights in her buffalo robes. Jonty wouldn't object if Nemia was willing.

And while he unrolled his blankets close to the fire, promising himself he'd soon be in the bed of pine boughs, Nemia fished the potatoes out of the ashes and announced that supper was ready.

Hungry appetites made short work of the meal. Jonty had started on her second cup of coffee when she remarked with concern, "I forgot about Buttercup. I'd better hurry up and milk her. Her udders are probably near to bursting."

Lightfoot looked at Nemia. "I don't suppose you ever milked a cow?" At the helpless shake of her head, he rose and took the lantern off its peg in the wall beside the door. "Dress warm, Jonty," he said, raising the chimney and applying a lighted match to its wick. "The wind has come up again." He snapped the glass globe back in place.

Bundled to her eyes, a milk pail in her hand, Jonty followed the Indian outside. When a fierce wind buffeted her back, lashing at her face, he took her arm and held on to it as the lantern shone the way to the barn. He held the door open with some difficulty while Jonty slipped inside. She was greeted by a pain-filled low, and she hurried toward the tortured sound.

Jim LaTour had scoured Cottonwood a week before to find a cow that had recently dropped a calf and would supply Jonty with the daily milk he felt important to nourish her and the baby growing inside her. Lightfoot, knowing the importance his cousin put on this belief, had stabled the cow, named Buttercup in memory of the one left at the ranch, in a corner stall, well away from the blast of cold weather.

It grew quiet in the barn with only the slash of milk hitting the pail. When Jonty had stripped the last drop of creamy fluid through her fingers she stood up, gave the cow's rump an affectionate pat, and murmured, "Thank you, Buttercup," before following Lightfoot outside.

Snow was falling again as they made their way toward the lamp shimmering in the kitchen window. The wind had died down and it was eerily quiet with only the howl of a wolf off on a distant mountain to break the silence. The lonely yowl made Jonty think of another ranch, far away in the foothills of a mountain. Was it snowing there also? Was Cord sitting in front of the huge fireplace, Tina wrapped in his arms? She slipped on a piece of ice and almost fell as tears blurred her vision.

The cabin was warm and cozy when Jonty and Lightfoot stepped inside. It would be that way all night, the flames lazily eating into the huge backlog Johnny had placed deep inside the fireplace. Jonty wondered about their wood supply as she placed the pail of milk on the table, then took off her jacket and hung it over the back of a chair.

She was pleased to see that Nemia had washed the dishes in her absence and had unpacked most of the boxes, placing everything on the new shelves. With a small smile on her face, she took down a big brown crock, a white folded square of cloth resting on its bottom.

"Where will I keep this?" she asked as she tilted the pail over the crock, letting the milk spill slowly over the white square. "If I set it outside it will freeze or some animal will drink it. I'm afraid it will sour here in the heat of the house."

Lightfoot jerked a thumb toward a door which Jonty had believed led outside. "There's a storage shed through there." He walked across the floor and swung the door open. "In the cold months we can keep our perishables in there, and in the hot months we can use the cave just a step or two behind the cabin."

Jonty placed a clean towel over the bowl of milk and walked into the slant-roofed room. "I'll straighten it up for you tomorrow." Johnny Lightfoot frowned at the litter on the dirt floor, chopped pieces of wood thrown haphazardly into one corner. He righted a good-sized chunk of wood and patted its level top. "For the time being put the crock here."

When they stepped back into the big main room, they looked at each other and grinned. Gentle snoring was coming from Nemia's pallet. "She still tires easily," Jonty whispered. "Poor woman, she lived in hell with that no-good Paunch." She shook her head in wonderment. "Why is it, Johnny, that some men are so cruel?"

"I don't know, Jonty. I think Paunch was just born mean. I think some men are. Women, too, as for that. I've seen some mean examples of the weaker sex. Remember Lucy? That one didn't have a tender feeling in her whole body."

Lightfoot stretched and said at the end of a long yawn, "I think I'll turn in too. I want to get an early start tomorrow to hunt us some fresh meat. It'll be easy tracking in the snow."

When he had removed his moccasins and slid under the buffalo hide, Jonty entered her room, lit the lamp on the small table next to the bed, then returned to the main room to extinguish the lamp there. She smiled wryly. Already Lightfoot's snores were joining Nemia's.

Back in her room again, Jonty moved to the large wardrobe where her new clothes hung. She swung open the double doors and gazed inside. It was hard to believe that the dresses were hers. Finally she was going to wear the kind of clothing meant for her.

After stroking a hand over each dress, debating which one to wear tomorrow, she took down a long flannel nightgown and laid it on the bed. It was soft blue, its collar and cuffs trimmed in white lace. After ridding her body of the despised trousers and shirt, and the wide binding strip, she drew the gown over her head. She sighed. How soft it felt against her skin.

Jonty blew out the light and climbed onto the thick feather mattress. She was asleep almost before she pulled the quilt up around her shoulders.

The next morning when she awakened, snow was drifted on her bed. She had left the window open a crack. She lay a moment listening to the Nemia move about in the kitchen, preparing breakfast.

"Get up, lazy bones," she chided herself. "Buttercup needs to be milked." She sat up, swung her feet to the floor, moving them about, feeling for the fleece-lined moccasins, the only article she would keep from her old wardrobe. Finding them and shoving her feet into their warmth, she rose and padded across the cold floor to the wardrobe. Today would mark a milestone in her life. From now on, everybody would know that Jonty Rand was a female.

She patted her still-flat stomach and grinned. As if that secret could have been kept much longer.

Shivering in the brisk coolness of the room, Jonty lost no time choosing a dress, but took the first one her hand fell on. She was equally quick to jerk open a dresser drawer and pull out a petticoat and stockings. She draped everything across her arm and hurried to the warmth of the fireplace.

She smiled a greeting at Nemia as she dropped the clothes over the back of a chair, then crossed to the window to look outside. It took her several seconds to scrape away enough frost to enable her to see through the glass.

Jonty gasped in wonderment. There had to be at least two feet of snow where it had drifted in spots. Thank God the snow had finally stopped falling. As it was, she was afraid that uncle Jim wouldn't be able to get through to visit her. Her gaze lifted to the remote jagged peaks of the mountain rising impassively to the sky, glistening from the sun glancing off the snow. She sighed raggedly. Cord was up there somewhere. Cord and Tina.

The outside door banged open and Lightfoot hurried inside, loose snow swirling in behind him. He slammed the door shut, and as he wiped his feet on the heavy woven rug Jonty had placed there for that purpose, he panted, "I just finished shoveling a path to the necessary, and to the barn. You women dress warm before you stick your necks out. In fact, Jonty, don't be in a hurry to throw away your britches."

"Oh no!" Jonty shook her head vehemently. "Nothing is going to keep me from wearing a dress today. Other women manage in the cold weather."

"Well, then, put the damn dress over the pants if it means that much to you. Otherwise you're gonna freeze that runty ass of yours."

"All right!" Jonty conceded, used to the derogatory remarks made about her rear end. "But only when I go to the barn to do the milking. Now turn your head while I get dressed."

Ten minutes later, she told Lightfoot he could look at her now. When the Indian turned around and only stared at her, she faltered nervously as she smoothed the full skirt over her hips, "Do I look . . . silly?"

The dress was her brightest one, a deep red background with tiny white flowers woven in it. It was cut low on the breasts whose beauty was allowed to show for the first time. The bodice was tight, hugging her narrow rib-cage to her tiny waist.

"Go ahead and say it, Johnny." She looked ready to cry. "I look ridiculous in a dress. I look like a man got-up in women's clothing."

Lightfoot finally realized that he was gaping and closed his mouth. Never again would Jonty be accused of being runty.

A chill of foreboding gripped him. Cord McBain knew of Jonty's beauty, and having held her in his arms, made love to her, he would never let her go. The big rancher would search the ends of the earth to find her if he had to.

Lightfoot sighed inwardly, dreading the day McBain and his cousin clashed over the girl. He hoped fervently that neither man would die. It would kill Jonty to permanently lose either of them, despite what the rancher had done to her.

He spoke finally. "You're as pretty as a mountain flower, Jonty," he said softly, walking over to her and running a gentle hand over her curls. "Jim will be so proud when he sees you."

"I hope so." Jonty flushed with pleasure. She returned Nemia's admiring smile then, and was thankful to have the attention taken from her when the Indian woman announced that breakfast was ready.

An hour later, as Jonty battled the wind to the barn, her old trousers felt good to her legs. Also, she discovered, dresses had their drawbacks. The long skirt flapped and whipped about her legs, impeding each step she took. It was something she would have to get used to, she told herself, lifting the heavy bar that kept the domestic animals safe from the wild ones that roamed the range.

Beauty whickered softly when Jonty stepped inside the barn, and Buttercup stuck her head over the stall. Jonty rubbed the spot between her soft brown eyes, then entered the enclosure. Bunching the full skirt around her, she squatted beside the cow, washed off the teats from a pan of water she'd brought for that purpose, and began persuading the milk from Buttercup.

The chore was done quickly, and soon Jonty was hurrying back to the cabin, the warm milk steaming in the cold air. As she reached the door, Lightfoot opened it and stepped outside. She looked at the rifle on his shoulder. "Are you off to hunt now?" she asked.

The Indian nodded. "And while I'm gone, make sure you keep the door locked, and don't let anyone in unless you know them real well," he warned. "There are a lot of rough characters around these days. Our fat friend Paunch might put in an appearance. That one carries a grudge for a long time. Not only will he be mad about losing Nemia, he'd do anything to hurt Jim, and he knows that he could do that through harming you."

Jonty's face blanched a little, remembering the run-in she'd had before with the fat man. "Rest your mind about me being careful, Johnny." Her lips firmed in a tight line. "Both door and windows will be kept locked," she assured him.

Lightfoot nodded his satisfaction. "I'll be back before dark," he said, and struck off through the snow, his webbed snowshoes moving easily over the ice-crusted snow. The big dog watched him a moment, then turned and followed Jonty into the cabin.

"You're getting spoiled, Wolf," Jonty scolded as the dog flopped himself in front of the fire, "but I'm glad you stayed behind." She recalled the times he had come to her defense and felt safer with him so close by. There weren't many men who would stand up to Wolf when he came at them, his hackles high and his lips pulled back in a vicious snarl.

CHAPTER 21

THE DAYS PASSED, TURNING INTO WEEKS, AND THE WIND continued to come from the north. Sometimes it rattled the windows as it howled around the cabin in icy waves.

Jonty had settled into her new home and was almost content. But often in the evenings, as she and Nemia sewed on tiny baby clothes, Lightfoot would glance up and catch a sadness in her eyes. He felt confident that she was thinking of Cord McBain. He had brought the rancher's name up once, giving her the opportunity to talk about him if she wished, but she had quickly turned the conversation to something else.

Lightfoot rose and placed another small log on the fire. He sat back down and, looking at Nemia, said, "Do you remember how as youngsters we would entertain ourselves when the winter nights were so cold we didn't dare stick our heads outside?"

Some time back, in the evenings, he and Nemia had started reminiscing about the days before the white man overran their prairies and mountains. Tonight, as he came to the end of a story, Jonty smiled at him apologetically.

"You and Nemia must miss those days, as well as your people," she said softly.

Lightfoot stared into the fire as though seeing those happy days in the flames. He turned his head and smiled at Nemia. "Perhaps someday Nemia and I will go back to my village and remain there. White society, for the main part, hasn't been kind to her, and most of their ways are not mine."

Jonty looked at Lightfoot and said earnestly, "I wish you both could have known better white men. The majority are good and decent people, interested only in making honest livings."

"I know." Lightfoot fondly brushed his hand over the black curls that had grown to Jonty's shoulders now. "And believe it or not, Cord McBain is one of those men. It's true he can sometimes be meaner than a rattlesnake, but I've never seen him do any man dirt, be it red man or white."

When Jonty made no response, only continued to sew on the tiny garment, he let the subject of the wild-horse hunter drop, and puffed quietly on his clay pipe.

The small stitches Jonty was taking in the baby gown blurred as bitter tears gathered in her eyes. To a man's way of thinking, maybe Cord was a decent man, but in her mind he wasn't. Not when it came to his treatment of women, at least. He might not cheat a man, but he didn't hesitate when it came to the weaker sex. Look what he had done to her and Tina. He loved the Mexican girl, yet had thought nothing of cheating on her, hadn't cared less that in the cheating he had taken a young girl's virginity, made her wrongly think that he loved *her* as he carelessly planted his seed in her womb.

No, Cord McBain was not honorable. Jonty blinked back her tears. But fool that she was, she loved him none the less.

Jonty started and came back to the present when

the clock on the mantel started a mellow striking. She silently counted the muted bongs. Ten. Time to retire, a routine that had been set by Johnny, when and how she couldn't remember. She looked up in time to catch the look that passed between Nemia and the Indian and, smiling to herself, thought that maybe she knew after all.

It had started around this time of night shortly after the three of them had moved into the cabin. Like tonight, it had been bitterly cold. She had yawned and folded the baby blanket she had been working on. Placing it in a wicker sewing basket, she announced that she was going to bed. Johnny had knocked out his pipe and remarked in injured tones:

"While you two are sleeping cozy and warm, I'll be shivering the skin off my bones. The wind comes underneath the door and climbs right into my buffalo robe."

While Nemia blushed prettily and put aside the small moccasin she was beading, Jonty exclaimed, "Why didn't you say something before, Johnny? I have plenty of quilts. You can use as many as you want."

When Nemia giggled, and the Indian's bronze face turned a dull red, she blushed too. She hadn't realized what Johnny had been hinting to Nemia.

But Nemia had known, and smiling shyly, she had said softly, "Perhaps during these cold winter nights we can double up."

Johnny's firm lips had lifted at the corners a bit and Jonty thought to herself, you sly dog, it hasn't taken you long to worm your way into Nemia's heart.

She had picked up the lamp and carried it to her room, and as she closed the door she could hear the rustle of clothes being removed. Before she got her gown on, a different kind of rustling had begun. A perplexed frown marred her forehead as she recalled all the love play she and Cord had indulged in before the actual coupling of their bodies. The long kisses, the caressing of each other's bodies. Was the red man unaware of this delightful practice, the added pleasure he'd derive from it?

Maybe someday she'd get up the nerve to ask Nemia.

Jonty grinned mischievously now. When Johnny cleared his throat, reminding her it was time she sought her bed, maybe she would tease him a bit. She would continue to sit before the fire, make him wait for his time with Nemia.

But when the hint had been given and ignored for several minutes, Jonty changed her mind at a glowering look sent her way. She wouldn't put it past Johnny to take her by the arm and escort her to her room.

She rose, picked up the lamp, said goodnight to Nemia, who was already under her buffalo robe, and started for her room. "No good-night for me?" Lightfoot called after her.

"I don't say good-night to randy old men," she retorted, laughter hovering over the words as she closed the door. She heard Johnny chuckle, then tell Nemia that he knew a little girl who needed her behind whacked.

A few minutes later she lay in bed, a shaft of pale moonlight coming through the window and bathing her stomach. She rested her hand on the bulge of her body, waiting for the gentle stirring she had experienced a few nights ago. Nemia had said that it was her baby coming alive.

I hope it's a little boy, she dreamed, one who will look like his father. "Or do I want it to look like his father?" she asked herself. Wouldn't it be too painful to have Cord's likeness always before her? Would her heart ever heal, seeing him in his son all the time?

Cord's face suddenly swam before her and she flung an arm across her eyes to shut it out. It didn't work. He hung there in front of her, just as he did in her heart.

It had been quiet in the other room for some time before Jonty fell asleep, thinking of Cord, knowing painfully how he was spending his time, snowbound in the mountains. The long evenings would pass swiftly for him as he and Tina made love.

The following day, back on Devil's Mountain, the tall spruce and pine bowed before the heavy blasts of wind as Cord urged the stallion on, a weariness behind his gray eyes.

As usual, he had been up since the first streak of dawn, checking that his stock was all right, that none were bogged down in snowdrifts, unable to free themselves. Since the snow's heavy arrival, he'd had to shoot five horses due to broken legs from slipping on ice, or falling into gulches half hidden by drifts. His men had killed an equal amount as they scoured the range.

Thankfully, he'd found that his biggest worry that first snow-covered morning had been unfounded. He had feared for the welfare of his vast herd in the hidden canyon. Before he had begun penning them in, they had most likely come down into the valley when winter set in. Were they finding shelter now, food to eat?

But after urging Rawhide through drifts up to his flanks, he had pushed open the big, heavy barrier and swept his eyes down the long floor of the valley. For a moment he went weak with relief. The wild ones crowded the lee side of the granite walls where high shelving overhangs kept them free of the wind and snow. And just as important, there were long stretches of wind-swept grasses. They were brown and dry, yet would provide enough nourishment to get the animals through until spring.

The ranch buildings came into view, and without enthusiasm, Cord headed home. He had hired a cook for his men and they now ate in the long kitchen Jones had added to the bunkhouse. He would have preferred eating with the men, but Maria always had a meal waiting for him. He didn't want to hurt the kind-hearted woman's feelings by not eating what she had taken pride in providing for him.

At least he wasn't pestered with Tina anymore. Cord's face lightened somewhat. Evidently she had taken his advice, for these days the young wranglers got all her attention. He hoped, for her parents' sake, that she didn't get herself in trouble. The young, very virile riders wouldn't turn away from the opportunities he'd had with the girl.

Cord dismissed Tina Perez from his mind and thought gloomily of the long evening ahead. Should he join his men for a few hands of poker after supper, or do what he usually did—sit before the fire, staring into the flames, hollowed out with longing for Jonty.

An inner voice warned him that he should have company, that tonight might be one of those times when his pain was unbearable. On such nights he always turned to the whiskey bottle, drinking until the alcohol softened the edges of his bleak reflections and made him sleepy. He would stagger off to bed then, impatient for spring to come so that he could take up his search for Jonty.

CHAPTER 22

JONTY CAME AWAKE AT HER USUAL HOUR, WHEN THE SUN was just rising and bringing the furniture out of the shadows. She stretched within the warm cocoon of her quilts and sniffed the air. The scent of the pine tree in the main room beyond was tangy-sharp.

Johnny had chopped down the small tree yesterday, no doubt muttering about the strange customs of the whites as he dragged it home.

"Didn't you ever see a Christmas tree before, Johnny?" she had asked, after she had asked him to cut one and he had scowled at her.

"Yes, I've seen them," he'd grumbled. "A healthy tree chopped down so that foolish women and children can tie ribbons on it."

She and Nemia had repressed their giggles as he picked up the axe beside the door and stamped outside.

Jonty suddenly hugged herself. A very happy event had occurred before Johnny returned with the tree.

She had been rolling out a dough mixture of flour,

salt, and a red juice Nemia had concocted from
berries and tree bark. She would cut them into
different shapes, bake them, then hang them on the
tree. And as she reminisced about Christmases when
she and Granny had decorated a tree, Nemia sat
beside the fire making small bows from material left
over from the very dress she now wore. Then, into the
companionable silence came several raps of a fist on
the door.

"Who could it be?" Nemia jumped to her feet and
hurried to stand beside Jonty, her black eyes full of
fear.

"I can't imagine." Jonty frowned, wondering why
Wolf wasn't raising a racket. The dog had gone
immediately to the door, his ruff standing straight up,
but the hair had quickly smoothed down, and now he
was sniffing eagerly and whining a greeting to whoever
stood outside.

She had started for the rifle hanging over the mantel
when a gravely voice called, "Jonty, let me in. I'm
near frozen."

Relief spread over the two women's faces. "Uncle
Jim!" Jonty squealed and, rushing across the room,
flung the door open.

With a deep rumbling laugh, Jim LaTour wrapped
her up in big bear hug. Jonty clung to him, laughing
and crying, breathing deep of the pleasant scent that
was all his—the soap he used, the small cigars he
smoked, and now the fresh smell of outdoors.

"How did you ever get through the snow?" She
tipped her head back, her eyes sparkling with happiness.

"It was no trouble at all." LaTour released her and
stepped aside so that she could see into the yard.

"Well, aren't you the smart one." Jonty gave a
tickled laugh as she gazed at a heavy plow horse whose
breath jetted like steam from his nostrils, and then at
the sled that was hitched behind him. Then she closed
the door and helped LaTour shrug out of his heavy
coat.

"I can't take credit for it." He removed his fur cap and leaned his rifle against the wall. "Some farmer's kid came into town with the sled to buy supplies and it hit me that the vehicle was a perfect way to get out here to the ranch. I made a deal to rent it from him and had the smoothest ride of my life. I have to get it back to him tomorrow."

"Oh, that means you're going to stay overnight!" Jonty hugged him again.

"I thought I might." Jim tweaked her nose. "That is, if you can find me a spot to sleep."

Jonty hit him playfully on the chin with her small fist. "You know there will always be a spot for you. You can have my bed."

LaTour threw back his head and laughed. "I can just see myself taking your soft bed while you sleep on the floor. I've got my bedroll on the sled."

He moved further into the room and smiled a greeting at Nemia, who stood shyly nearby. "You're lookin' well, Nemia," he said, then looked around the room. "Where's Johnny?"

Jonty gave a small laugh. "Would you believe he's out chopping us a Christmas tree?" She hurried to pull the coffee pot forward on the stove. You can imagine the grumbling Nemia and I had to listen to." She patted the back of a chair. "Sit down and have some coffee while we wait for him. He should return soon."

"I've got a few things on the sled I'll bring in first," LaTour said, and went back outside.

A smile glimmered in Jonty's eyes as she sat up and scooted off the bed. It had taken Uncle Jim two trips to bring in the "few" things. Packages, large and small, square and round, now lay under the Christmas tree.

And what fun it had been, decorating the tree after supper. Jonty slipped her arms through the sleeves of a heavy woolen robe and secured it with the attached belt. She hadn't been so happy in a long time. Even Johnny had "helped," although Nemia had quietly,

with an amused smile on her face, followed along
behind him rearranging most of the items he placed
on the scented branches.

Jonty slipped her feet into the fur-lined moccasins,
still thinking of the night before. When the tree was
finished, cheerfully filling up one corner of the room,
they had all sat before the fire, catching up on news,
events, and people back in Cottonwood.

Tillie was fine, LaTour assured Jonty. "She runs the
kitchen like a drill sergeant, barking out orders to the
two Mexican boys I hired to help her. They're scared
to death of her.

"Old Janie? She's fine too. Still sits in her door,
puffin' on that stinkin' pipe of hers, and asking me
every other day when that youngun' Jonty is comin'
back."

"Isn't Tillie giving her a plate of food every night?"
Jonty frowned.

"Yeah, she does." LaTour took a sip of whiskey
from the glass at his elbow, then grinned at Jonty. "I
guess, just like me, the old woman misses you."

Jonty reached for his hand and squeezed it. "I miss
you too."

LaTour studied the small face, the hint of sadness
far back in the blue eyes. "Are you happy here,
Jonty?" he asked. "Do you get lonesome, snowed in?"
He wanted to ask if she missed the no-good rancher,
but didn't. The less said about that one, the better.

Jonty remembered that conversation as she entered
the big main room. She had hurriedly answered that
she was totally happy, that she never got lonesome,
that Johnny and Nemia were excellent company.
Never would she admit that she missed Cord dreadfully.

She walked softly over to the large body rolled up in
blankets, and squatted down beside it. Her gaze went
over the beloved face, its harsh lines softened in sleep.
She loved this man dearly. He was the nearest thing to
a father she'd ever known.

Jonty started when suddenly the deep blue eyes

opened. She sat back on her heels, bemused, when the firm lips smiled, then whispered softly, longingly, "Cleo, my beautiful Cleo." Had Uncle Jim mistaken her for her mother? She wasn't aware that he had even known her.

She shook LaTour's shoulder gently. "It's Jonty, Uncle Jim."

LaTour's dream-filled eyes cleared, and rising on one elbow, he shook his head as though to clear it. "Mornin', honey," he said after a moment. "What are you doin' up so early?"

"I want to get the turkey in the oven." She spoke in low tones, not to awaken Johnny and Nemia. "Go back to sleep."

"No, I'll get up now." LaTour threw the top blanket aside. "I want to head back to town early this afternoon and I don't to waste any time with you by sleepin' it away."

And no time was wasted. Much talk and laughter went on through breakfast, and during the opening of the packages Jim had brought with him. He had remembered everyone. There was a new rifle for Johnny, with a large supply of ammunition, and a large skinning knife. Jim's eyes twinkled, and he slid his cousin a mischievous look as he handed Nemia her three packages. And though Lightfoot glowered when the bundles were opened, Nemia squealed her delight. There was a silk dress, a pair of dainty high-heeled boots, and a nightgown. All in bright red.

"I don't want her looking like a whore, Jim." Lightfoot growled, and looked as though he might grab up Nemia's gifts and toss them into the fire.

Nemia smiled and stroked Johnny's stiff arm. "Nemia will wear them only for you," she said softly, causing him to look uncomfortable at her display of affection. He said no more about the Christmas gifts.

For Jonty, there was a fashionable warm coat, a silk scarf, leather gloves, and a bottle of perfume. "I sent a couple of the girls to Abilene to pick out the finery," LaTour explained when Jonty made mention that she'd had no idea such fine quality merchandise could be found in Cottonwood.

The last package to be opened, a large bulky one, made Jonty exclaim in delight. She stretched forth a hand and set a beautiful, hand-crafted cradle in motion. "I love it, Uncle Jim." She smoothed a palm over the small soft quilt tucked around an equally small mattress.

"I wanted it to have a feather tick," LaTour grumbled, "but Tillie insisted that it would be too soft, that the baby's bones wouldn't grow straight.

"So, she made one. Probably stuffed it with rocks, the old harridan."

Jonty smiled to herself, imagining the argument that must have gone on. She looked up at LaTour apologetically. "I'm sorry we have nothing for you, Uncle Jim, but we had no idea you would be able to get out here."

"Don't worry about it, honey," LaTour dismissed her explanation. "Seein' and bein' with you is present enough."

The turkey and its accompaniments were eaten shortly after the unwrapping of the gifts, and then it was time for LaTour to leave.

Jonty and Lightfoot followed him outside, where the horse stood waiting, stamping his great hooves in the snow. "Well, Jonty, have a nice Christmas next week." LaTour hugged her tightly. "And take care of yourself. Don't go outside unless you have Johnny to hold on to." A bleakness slid into his eyes. "I don't want you fallin' and have somethin' happen to you."

He climbed onto the sled, then, and called to the horse to move out. Jonty watched through tear-blurred eyes until he faded from sight. Johnny took her arm then and led her back inside.

Christmas passed, January came, cold and more snow. February followed, still cold, but the spells of snow seemed to have come to an end.

Thank God, Jonty thought, staring out the window.

Her nerves were stretched as taut as a fiddle-string and she couldn't have taken many more days of that white, falling blanket.

The baby inside her gave a hefty kick, and she rubbed her swollen stomach. "Pretty soon, baby," she whispered, "I'll be holding you in my arms."

She was about to turn away from the window when she gave a start and leaned closer to the glass, peering through it intently. She was sure she had seen a horse and rider slip through the stand of tall spruce down by the barn. The rider had reminded her suspiciously of the fat man, Paunch. Her heart raced with dread. Had he somehow learned of Nemia's whereabouts?

Maybe I just imagined it, she thought after straining her eyes for several minutes and seeing no movement among the trees. Still, she had a niggling doubt. She would say nothing of her suspicions to Nemia, maybe scaring her unnecessarily, but she wouldn't rest until she went down there and checked for hoof prints.

Wrapping a heavy shawl around her shoulders, wishing that Johnny hadn't gone off hunting, she took down the rifle and said to Nemia, "I'm going to take a short walk to the barn, get some fresh air in my lungs."

"Walk carefully, Jonty." Nemia reminded her, "and take Wolf along. LaTour would have Johnny's skin if anything should happen to you."

"I'll be careful." Jonty assured the fretting woman, then grabbed the door frame as Wolf almost knocked her over in his rush to get outside. "Maybe I should leave this fellow behind." She laughed. "I don't know if he'll protect me, or break my neck."

"He seems to have caught some scent," Nemia said as the dog ran straight to the spruces, his ruff raised.

"Probably a deer." Jonty managed to keep her voice calm, although inside she felt anything but. "I'll check it out," she said over her shoulder as she hurried after Wolf.

The big dog was sniffing around one particular area

when Jonty came up to him. Her heartbeat raced. She hadn't been mistaken. She had seen someone. And judging from the deep, hoof-trampled snow, that someone had sat there a long time, watching the house. And she could tell by the low growling in Wolf's throat as his nose skimmed over the snow that it was a man Wolf knew and didn't like.

Apprehensively, Jonty remembered that the dog had hated the fat man, and when he darted off through the trees, tracking the prints that led off through them, she yelled sternly, "Wolf! Come back!" Paunch could still be lurking around and wouldn't hesitate a second to shoot her beloved pet, her protector.

Thankfully, Wolf obeyed her order and Jonty hurried him to the house, fearful that any minute she would hear the pounding of hooves behind her.

Jonty was thankful again that, when she entered the cabin, Nemia was occupied with mending a shirt of Johnny's and barely glanced up as she asked, "Was it a deer?"

"Yes," Jonty answered as she made sure she dropped the bar securely in its groove. She hung up her shawl and joined Nemia at the fire. And while the squaw rattled on about the days of her youth, Jonty kept her eyes on the clock, waiting for Lightfoot's return.

She hadn't long to wait before Wolf's joyful bark alerted her that the Indian was coming. Again she flung the shawl around her shoulders and hurried outside, pretending not to hear Nemia's "Where are you going, Jonty?" She wanted to talk privately to Johnny.

The Indian's face grew sober as Jonty related how someone had watched the cabin today, and of her suspicions who it was. He nodded, a dangerous look coming into his eyes. "It was him. And you know what this means, Jonty." He looked soberly at her. "You and Nemia must not leave this cabin unless I'm with you."

"And you must be careful also, Johnny." Jonty shivered with dread. "I'll never rest easy, now that Paunch knows where we are."

"Don't worry about him, Jonty." Lightfoot kept his own worry out of his voice and off his face. "You two women just stay inside until the thaw begins. I'll go after him then. I'll not have you and Nemia living in fear of that one."

Christmas came and went on the mountain also. Winter progressed and spring arrived.

The early chill of the March morning struck through Cord's coat, making his teeth chatter. Damn, it's still cold, he thought, pulling up his collar. But at least the long, freezing winter lay behind. Yesterday Jones had reported that the passes were open, news he had been waiting for. Tomorrow he would send a couple of men into Cottonwood, there to take turns watching Trail's End, night and day. The breed knew where Jonty was, and sooner or later he would lead them to her.

The sun, shining on Cord's lean features as he walked the stallion, hunting fresh game, revealed new lines around his mouth and eyes. His cheeks had thinned, were almost gaunt from the weight he'd lost. And the gray eyes that peered through the trees and brush were now like cold, dark steel. The long winter nights of worrying about Jonty, and longing for her, had taken their toll. He looked every one of his thirty-three years.

It was nearing noon and Cord was about to admit defeat. It appeared he wasn't going to scare up any game today, when there came the sound of an elk horn on a dead branch. He dismounted, rifle in hand, and started out on foot. It took him close to fifteen minutes of careful stalking before he had the animal in the sights of the rifle. He slowly squeezed the trigger and the elk dropped, the bullet taking him in the heart.

The animal was a yearling, which pleased Cord. It

wouldn't be difficult to sling it over the stallion's back. He put his fingers to his mouth to whistle the mount to him, then paused. Had he heard a twig snap, as if under a foot? He slowly pivoted around, his eyes missing none of the area. Nothing stirred. He came to the conclusion that probably an Indian was also out hunting. With the red man, it was an inborn instinct to move secretly.

Cord raised his fingers to his lips again, and this time completed the whistle. Rawhide advanced with his ears erect, snorting suspiciously at the scent of blood. But he stood quietly at Cord's command and let him tie the carcass behind the saddle.

"Good boy." Cord patted the broad rump and swung into the saddle. He had barely settled himself comfortably when he felt a searing heat along his left arm, then heard the report of a rifle. The stallion squealed and reared, and Cord, at the unexpected move, fell to the ground, landing on his right side, the Colt solidly beneath him. He tried to flip over on his back to jerk the gun from its holster, and felt a wrenching pain in his leg. His right foot was caught firmly between two rocks.

As he seethed in frustration, desperately trying to free himself, there came the crackling of brush directly in front of him. A moment later, he was not surprised to see his old enemy step from behind a stunted pine. With sickening clarity he knew he was going to die as the fat man moved toward him, the gun in his hand aimed at his hammering heart. Paunch was utterly unscrupulous and wouldn't hesitate to shoot an unarmed man.

Cord waited, every sense and thought concentrated on the man who came slowly nearer and nearer, purposely prolonging the agony in his quarry's mind. And adding to the suspense of waiting for that fat finger to squeeze the trigger, was the eerie mystery of why Paunch didn't speak.

He didn't speak until the sing of a bullet passing over his head brought a string of oaths spewing from between his thick lips. When he wheeled and lumbered off through the brush as fast as his weight would allow, Cord turned his head to look behind him, to see who had saved his life.

A tall young brave stood in the shadow of a large boulder, a smoking rifle in his hand. As Cord stared at him, the young man came and squatted beside him. Placing his rifle on the ground then, he eased Cord's foot free of the rocks. "I"—he tapped his breast—"a friend of Johnny Lightfoot. He say you a fair man. Treat red man and white man the same."

When Cord sat up, the Indian helped him ease the jacket off his injured arm, then slit open the blood-soaked shirt sleeve with a broad hunting knife. After a close scrunity of the wound, he grunted, "You lucky. Bullet only grazed arm."

Cord lifted his eyes from studying the long, red gash, meaning to thank his benefactor, but the brave had jumped into a shallow gulch, and before Cord could open his mouth, he had loped away out of sight.

"I'll be damned," he muttered, rising to his feet, "I'd of sure liked to thank that young man." He finally managed to single-handedly pull himself into the saddle. Raging inside, his arm throbbing, still bleeding, he debated going after Paunch. A few minutes of thought, however, told him that it would be a waste of time. The fat man knew the area almost as well as he did, and it would be a simple matter for the man to elude him, or worse, wait behind a tree or boulder and shoot him in the back.

As Cord turned the stallion homeward, he knew he hadn't seen the last of his ex-horse wrangler. Like most weak men, there was a stubborness about Paunch that would drive him on to kill the man who had humiliated him.

Cord's lips firmed into a thin line. He'd be ready for the bastard the next time.

CHAPTER 23

AT LAST THE VALLEY WAS RELEASED FROM THE FROZEN shackles of winter. The air was tangy with the sharp scent of pine and sage, and there was bird song among the trees.

Jonty also came alive with the arrival of spring. She was very large with her baby now, and was slowly putting to the back of her mind thoughts of its father. Only occasionally did Cord invade them. Also, adding to her peace of mind, there had been no more sign of Paunch hanging around the small ranch.

The gentle months of May and June passed, then July was upon them. A haze of heat lay over the valley, the leaves on the trees hanging lifeless and fixed.

On such a night, in the middle of the month, when even the wolves and coyotes were quiet, Johnny Lightfoot paced outside, while inside Jonty, soaked with perspiration, writhed in pain, crying out Cord's name as her body was wracked in labor. Surely Cord McBain's ears rang from the curses and threats the Indian called down on his head.

It was nearing dawn when Lightfoot finally heard the angry squall of a newborn and rushed inside the cabin. He found that Jonty had delivered a son—a son who, from his first wail, was the image of his father.

"You've done a real good job, Jonty." He smiled proudly at the worn-out mother. "I'd say he's at least nine pounds."

"He felt more like twenty." Jonty smiled tiredly as Nemia laid the snuggly wrapped infant in her arms.

She turned back the soft covering and gazed down at the small head, liberally covered with blond fuzz. Her heart leapt. It was the exact color of his father's. She examined the tiny, wrinkled features then, and seeing Cord's imprint in miniature, fear gripped her. Cord must never see his son. He'd know immediately that the child was his, and he was ruthless enough to steal him away from her.

According to Uncle Jim, Cord's ranch was flourishing and he was fast becoming a wealthy man. And not being the marrying kind, he would grab at the chance of having an heir without the bother of a wife.

As though he read her thoughts, Lightfoot said, "The man puts his stamp on everything he owns. McBain will want his son."

"Not if he's unaware of the child's existence!" Jonty cried.

"But, Jonty, how can you keep your child a secret?" Nemia asked. "It won't be long before everyone in Cottonwood will know of him. Your uncle Jim will boast of him."

"I know." Jonty smiled suddenly. Nemia's words had solved her problem. "He will brag to anyone who will listen to him, and that is good. If Cord should hear that I've had a baby, and that Jim LaTour is proudly talking about it, he will automatically think that Coty is Jim's."

"So, that is what you will call this young man?" Nemia stroked the soft little head.

"Yes, Coty. Coty Rand." Jonty hugged the whimpering baby to her chest. "Isn't he handsome, Nemia?"

"Very handsome," the squaw acknowledged. "And he is a very hungry fellow right now. Time you fed him."

Jonty shyly untied the ribbons of the fresh gown Nemia had helped her into and bared a firm, white breast. Nemia helped her to guide a nipple into the small, searching mouth. As it drew hungrily, Jonty knew a joy she had never experienced before. Her arms tightened around the small bundle. "He will never take you away from me," she whispered.

"You can depend on it," Lightfoot said quietly. "Jim and I would have something to say about that."

Nemia, the pessimist, shook her head doubtfully. "McBain is a very determined man. If he should learn he has a son, I don't think even the Devil could stop him from taking Coty."

"Maybe the Devil couldn't stop him," Lightfoot said grimly, "but Jim's knife in his heart would sure as hell stop him."

"Oh, I wouldn't want it to come to that!" Jonty's eyes grew wide.

Seeing the worry in Jonty's eyes, the Indian shot the squaw a warning look and said confidently, "Don't worry about it, Jonty. You're not going to lose your little brave, nor is anyone going to get killed. Things have a way of taking care of themselves."

Lightfoot breathed a long silent breath at the relief that shot into Jonty's eyes, and he turned to Nemia. "The cow is carrying on. I think she wants to be milked."

He and Jonty winked at each other. Nemia and Buttercup didn't get along well together, hadn't since the first time Jonty, too big in her pregnancy to squat beside the cow, had given the squaw her first lesson in coaxing milk from the little Jersey.

Jonty gave a thankful sigh when Lightfoot followed Nemia to the barn. The pair would linger in the barn this morning. Nemia bringing the tall Indian the release that the birthing of her Coty had interrupted. And she would have some time alone with her little son.

Inserting a finger in the little hand that rested on her breast, she talked softly to the nursing baby as her thumb stroked the feather-soft skin. "We will be the best of friends, little boy. When you grow tall and straight you will help Mama run the ranch. We will build it up to be the best cattle ranch around. People will point at you and say 'there goes Coty Rand, the biggest rancher in the territory.'"

Coty Rand. Jonty's face took on a frown, tinged with concern. Carrying her surname would tell the world that her son was a bastard. That might not be easy for Coty to live with. It hadn't been easy for her. Would he, in time, blame her, grow to hate her for the stigma she was placing on him?

She recoiled from the thought, her eyes filled with pain. Was she wrong, keeping her son from his father? Cord would give the boy his name, announce to the world that this was Coty McBain, son and heir to Cord McBain.

"But my little boy would never know me." A tear slid down Jonty's cheek and her arms tightened around the now sleeping Coty. "He would never know a mother's love, never know tenderness. He would grow up hard and unfeeling, a carbon copy of his father."

She couldn't give him up. Not only would it tear her apart to lose him, she owed him a mother's love and guidance. Besides, Uncle Jim could always adopt him. Her son could be Coty LaTour.

Soothed by that thought, when Nemia returned to the cabin she found both mother and son sleeping peacefully.

CHAPTER 24

JONTY STOOD ON THE CABIN'S PORCH WONDERING WHERE the summer had gone. September had slid around again, the nights clear and cold, with crackling frost. All day an autumn mist had enveloped the valley, but now, at sunset, the wind had come up, clearing the air.

She smiled at Lightfoot when he joined her on the porch. "I have to go hunting tomorrow," he said. "Our meat supply is spoiled. Nemia says it's fly-blown. I'll be taking Wolf with me, so be careful while I'm gone. Keep the shutters closed and the doors locked, and when you have to do the chores, keep your little derringer on you."

"Don't worry, Johnny, I'll be very careful." Jonty shivered, thinking of fat Paunch.

"I'll be leaving before daylight," Lightfoot said, stepping off the porch. "I'll sleep in the barn tonight so as not to awaken Coty in the morning."

Jonty remained on the porch until darkness, like a black mantle, settled over the valley and the air grew cold. She left off the unsettling thoughts of Cord that always came whenever she found a moment's relaxation, and returned to the warmth of the house.

Nemia was lighting the lamp when she stepped inside. "Is Coty asleep?" she asked, glancing at the cradle her son was fast outgrowing.

"Oh, yes. He fell asleep right after you nursed him," Nemia answered. "Coty is a good baby." She looked away and said shyly, "I'll be going to the barn now. Make sure you lock the door behind me."

Jonty hid her grin at Nemia's not very subtle hint that she wouldn't be coming back to the cabin tonight. Love was certainly in bloom with that pair, she thought, following the squaw to the door and sliding the heavy bar home behind the sturdy figure. She walked into her bedroom then and knelt beside her sleeping child. She gazed lovingly at the little face which daily grew to look more like his father's. She gently stroked the blond hair that was beginning to curl, feeling a twinge of guilt that his father didn't know about him.

She firmly dismissed that weakness and rose to her feet. Cord McBain never had any such feelings about her, why should she have any for him? He had Tina to love, and Jonty had Coty. Everything was equal.

Jonty returned to the kitchen and quietly filled a basin with the warm water Nemia had left on the stove. When she finished her sponge-bath, she crawled into bed and fell asleep before fully stretching her tired body.

Nemia's knock on the door awakened Jonty the next morning. The sun was well up, and when she opened the door to the squaw, she couldn't help teasing, "Johnny got a late start, it seems."

Nemia blushed, and when there came a painful low from the barn, she hurriedly changed the subject. "Poor Buttercup, her udders must be bursting with milk."

Coty fussed from the bedroom, and Jonty left off her teasing. "I'll go milk her as soon as I nurse Coty."

A short time later, she was dressed and ready to leave for the barn. "Be careful out there, Jonty," Nemia cautioned as Jonty picked up the milk pail and the basket she used for gathering the eggs. "You know what Johnny told you."

Jonty patted the pocket where the small gun rested. "If anyone or anything gets in my way, I know how to use this hardware." She left the cabin, cautioning Nemia to bolt the door behind her.

All was quiet outside. Jonty assured herself that there wasn't a soul within ten miles of the cabin as she robbed the chickens' nests, collecting eight eggs. When she left the small building and walked to the barn, her roving glance still detected nothing out of the ordinary.

She hummed softly to herself as she forked fresh hay for Buttercup, then knelt to milk her. It was while the two streams of milk splashed into the pail that a prickling of apprehension traveled up her spine and into her scalp. She left off squeezing the teats and listened. There was no sound except that of the cow munching hay.

She gave a derisive grunt, and chastizing herself for being so spooky, she finished the milk.

Jonty was closing the barn door when Nemia's shrill scream split the air. She spun around, and terror contorted her features. Her suddenly lifeless fingers dropped the pail of milk, splashing her dress and forming a white puddle around her feet.

The front door of the cabin stood open, and red, hungry flames were shooting out of it. In her moment of paralysis Jonty saw the fat figure of her old enemy hurry from the cabin, then disappear behind it.

The sight of Paunch released Jonty's limbs and screaming "Coty!" she sprinted toward the cabin, frantic with dread of what she'd find. She sprang through the door, unmindful of the flames that tried to lick her clothing as she groped her way through the smoke to where her son lay crying and choking.

Subconsciously, she noted that tables and chairs had been knocked over, silent evidence that Nemia had tried to fight Paunch off.

When Jonty gained the bedroom, she almost tripped over Nemia cowering beside the cradle, whimpering in despairing agony. "Nemia!" she cried as she swept Coty from the cradle, "get up, we must get out of here."

But the squaw only rocked herself and moaned. "She's in shock," Jonty said, and rushed her son outside to breathe fresh air. She carried him several yards away from the burning cabin and laid him on the ground. When his little chest rose and fell evenly, she rushed back into the cabin to rescue Nemia.

When Jonty bent over the squaw to help her to her feet, she flinched at the condition of the woman's face. Paunch had brutally struck her with his fists several times. Her bottom lip was split open, and both her eyes were blackened. Jonty swore silently at the finger marks beginning to darken around Nemia's throat.

Half-carrying, half-dragging, Jonty got the softly crying Nemia outside. With their arms around each other's waist, and helpless rage in Jonty's heart, they watched the cabin burn.

Nemia had gained control of herself now, and Jonty asked, "How did he get in, Nemia? Surely you didn't open the door to him."

"No, of course not, Jonty! I would rather let the Devil in." Nemia wiped her eyes. "I stepped out onto the porch to get some firewood and there he was. He moved so fast, and I was so startled that he had pushed me into the cabin and closed the door before I knew what was happening."

"Why didn't you scream then? Why wait until the house was on fire?"

"I didn't cry out because I was afraid I would waken Coty and that he would cry. I was afraid of what that awful man might do to him. Maybe kill him."

Jonty looked down at the battered face. "Did he . . . you know . . ."

Nemia's face crumbled. "Yes, hitting me in the face all the time. I lost consciousness for a while, and when I came to, the cabin was on fire and he was running out the door. That's when I screamed."

"You are a very brave woman, Nemia," Jonty hugged the shivering shoulders. "I shall never, ever forget what you have done today."

"Oh, I was very scared, Jonty, not brave at all." Nemia rubbed a fist across her wet eyes. After a slight pause, she sent Jonty a beseeching look. "Please don't tell Johnny what the fat man did to me. I'm so ashamed."

"Of course I won't, Nemia," Jonty said gently. "Not if you don't want me to. But surely you know you have nothing to be ashamed of? How could you help yourself? Anyway"—a feral light of satisfaction gleamed in Jonty's eye—"just believing that Paunch beat you is enough to make Johnny kill him someday."

The roof was caving in when Lightfoot and the dog returned. His staring eyes took in the blazing cabin, then swept to Nemia's half-naked state. It was the first time Jonty had ever seen the usually stoic face lose control. He gathered Nemia into his arms and, gently stroking her bruised face, asked, "Who?"

He made no response when both women answered simultaneously, "Paunch." But though he spoke no word, the fierce expression that came over his face said that the fat man wasn't long for this world.

Still silent, he wheeled and strode to the barn, returning shortly with a gray horse blanket. Draping it around Nemia's shoulders, he finally spoke.

"Nemia, see to Coty, and Jonty, gather up your chickens while I hitch up the wagon and catch the cow and the mare. I want to reach Cottonwood before dark."

"Poor Uncle Jim." Jonty shook her head. "Saddled with me again. How tired he must be of it."

Lightfoot gave her a stern look. "That, young lady, he would never be."

In hardly any time, it seemed to Jonty, they were pulling away from the smoldering ruins of her home. With an arm around Wolf's neck, she looked back until the glowing coals disappeared from sight. She faced around then, wondering what the future held for her and Coty. She had been almost happy on her little ranch.

Jonty sat in troubled silence beside Lightfoot. She also had something else to consider, to worry about. Cord. The chances of his seeing his son had increased, what with her and Coty living in town. She would have to be exceptionally careful until another cabin was built—if Uncle Jim would even consider having another one built. Her shoulders drooped dejectedly.

The sweating team pulled into Cottonwood just as the sun was about to slip over the distant mountain. Lightfoot steered them to the back of the saloon and brought them to a stop. They stood with heaving sides as he dropped the reins and jumped to the ground. As Jonty nimbly swung herself off the high seat, he assisted Nemia and Coty out of the wagon.

With the Indian leading the way, the three hurried toward the kitchen door, sniffing the air. "Tillie is starting supper," Jonty said, eager to see her friend again. "Smell that steak frying?"

As Lightfoot pushed the kitchen door open, Jonty gave a friendly nod to the old woman, Janie, sitting in her back door, as usual puffing on her long-stemmed clay pipe. A bemused look came into the pale eyes and Jonty knew she hadn't been recognized yet. There were a lot of people who wouldn't recognize her, she thought as she followed the Indian inside the kitchen.

A startled Tillie straightened up, a pan of biscuits she'd just taken out of the oven in her hands. "You scared me half to death, Johnny," she scolded, setting the hot pan down, then tossing the two pot holders down beside it. "What brings you to Cottonwood at this hour? Who's watchin' the wimmen and baby?"

Lightfoot grinned and stepped away from Jonty and Nemia. LaTour's new cook let out a yelp, and her eyes sparkling her delight, she opened her arms wide, exclaiming, "Jonty!"

Jonty flew into the motherly arms, crying, "Oh, Tillie, it's so good to see you again. I've missed you terribly."

After a tight squeeze, the smiling Tillie held Jonty away from her. "Let me get a good look at you."

Her eyes ranged over the delicate features, the cloud of black hair falling to slim shoulders, and on down to the full breasts and slender curve of the hips. She shook her head slowly, as though Jonty's arrival were going to bring a great disruption to the scanty peace of Trail's end.

"We're gonna have to keep you here in the kitchen durin' your visit, Jonty. If any of that bunch in the saloon sees you, LaTour will have to shoot half of them."

"I certainly hope not." Jonty laughed, then grew sober. "I'm afraid Uncle Jim is stuck with me again for awhile."

"What's happened, child—?" Tillie began, then was diverted by a wail coming from the blanketed bundle in Nemia's arms. She smiled a greeting at the squaw, then took the irate baby from her. "Let me take a look at this little scutter," she said. "Sounds like his daddy when he's on the rampage, don't he?"

"My God, and looks like him too," she exclaimed as she folded back the covers. "I never saw the like." She laughed as she held Coty up in the air. "Your daddy sure put his stamp on you, baby." Coty's face grew red, and his little legs and arms flayed the air. "What a temper." Tillie laughed again.

"He's hungry." Jonty defended her son's tantrum, taking him into her own arms and, sitting down, opened her bodice. "Otherwise he's a very good baby."

"I expect so," Tillie muttered, not persuaded that Jonty's claim was true. She'd bet good money the child also had his father's quick temper.

She turned to gaze at Nemia, and Lightfoot, seeing

the pitying look she gave his woman's face, frowned
darkly. The old hag was blaming him for the condition of the battered face. He took the squaw's arm and
said gruffly, "I'm going to take Nemia upstairs and
find her some clothes, Jonty." He turned a meaningful
look at Tillie. "Tell her what happened."

While Coty nursed, Jonty related what had happened, and of the burning of her home. When she
finished, Tillie stared down at her clasped hands
resting on the table. "That man," she said, shaking
her head. "I can't believe the black depths some men
sink to. It makes you wonder why God lets such
people live."

"Oh, his end is coming, and soon," Jonty said,
placing Coty over her shoulder and patting his back.
"He'll live only until Johnny can find him."

"That coward will be long gone from these parts by
now," Tillie snorted. "He'll know that LaTour will be
after him for burning down your home, endangering
two lives. He's got no desire to tangle with Jim."

"Unless he can slip up behind Uncle Jim someday
and shoot him in the back," Jonty said worriedly.

"Who's gonna shoot me in the back?" A deep, rich
voice spoke from the door separating the kitchen from
the saloon.

"Uncle Jim!" Jonty immediately started sobbing.
As LaTour hurried to her, Tillie took the baby and
Jonty was drawn into warm, comforting arms.

"What is it, Jonty? What has happened?" LaTour
smoothed her back with soothing motions of his
palms.

The handsome breed's anger was barely controlled
as Jonty sobbed out everything that had happened.
"Nothing ever goes right for me, Uncle Jim," she
ended with a wail.

LaTour continued to hold Jonty, his hand still
stroking her back. What could he answer her? Everything she said was true. Life had a habit of turning
sour on her, thanks to him. If he hadn't been on the
wrong side of the law when she was born, she'd have

not been raised in a whorehouse, would not have had to pose as a boy, would not have fallen into Cord McBain's clutches. Would not have a bastard baby.

He pressed her head to his chest. If only he could tell her who he was. But that he didn't dare do. She would hate him. Just like Maggie, she would blame him for her mother's death, for all the misery she had endured through the years.

No, he mentally shook his head. He could never tell her that he was her father.

When Jonty's crying ceased, with only an occasional sob raising her chest, LaTour fished a handkerchief from his hip pocket and pressed it into her hand. "It can't be done now, honey," he said, "what with winter comin' on, but come next spring I'll have another cabin built for you, and you can move back to your own little ranch."

Jonty pulled away from the comforting arms and wiped her eyes. "You've already done so much for me, Uncle Jim, and I hate having you lay out more money for me, but I'll be forever grateful if you do put up another cabin. Just a small one. Three rooms would be plenty for me and Coty."

LaTour tried to interrupt her, but Jonty continued talking. "I did a lot of thinking on our way here, figuring ways I could earn our keep while we're here. One thought kept coming back to me."

"And what was that?" LaTour finally managed to break in.

Jonty searched his face, knowing that he wasn't going to like her idea, that she would have an argument on her hands. She drew a deep breath. "I have a lot of poker knowledge, thanks to you, and I want to put it to practice. I want to be a poker dealer for you."

Tillie gasped and LaTour's eyes widened until Jonty wondered if they could get any bigger. Finally his tongue was released. "Are you crazy, Jonty?" The words tripped over themselves, so rapidly they were shot at her. "Do you have any idea what a ruckus your presence would cause in there?" He jerked a thumb

toward the saloon. "I have enough fights to contend
with every night as it is. I couldn't handle all the ones
you'd cause."

"Uncle Jim, that's nonsense and you know it,"
Jonty scoffed. "All you'd have to do is wave that knife
of yours around a couple of times and lay down the
law that I'm off bounds and no one would dare bother
me."

Before LaTour could answer, Jonty said thoughtfully, with a rueful grimace, "Unless, of course, you don't
think I play well enough, that I'd lose money for the
place."

"You play well enough." LaTour began to pace the
floor. "Next to me, you're the best. But dammit." He
wheeled around to scowl at her. "I don't want you
around the sort of men who come here. I want you to
have a nice, respectable life. To meet a decent man
and marry him."

Jonty glanced over at Coty sleeping peacefully in
Tillie's arms. "Uncle Jim, do you honestly think a
decent man would marry me now?"

"Of course I do. You're decent." LaTour smoothed
a hand over her black hair. "And so beautiful. Any
man would be proud to call you wife."

Pain flickered in Jonty's eyes. "You're mistaken,
Uncle Jim. There's one man who wouldn't. Cord
McBain."

The handsome breed began to pace the floor again.
"Damn the man," he grated. "I'll kill the bastard yet."

Jonty grabbed his clenched fist as he passed by.
"You promised you wouldn't," she reminded him
gently.

LaTour drew a ragged breath. "I know, but look
what he's done to you, reduced you to dealin' poker in
a saloon."

"Does that mean you'll let me work for you?"
Jonty's eyes sparked hope.

"It's against my better judgment, though." The
answer came sourly. "But there are some rules you'll
absolutely have to abide by." LaTour pinned her with

serious eyes. "Number one, I'll choose the gowns you'll wear. Number two, you don't make friends with the whores. And three, you don't hang around the saloon when you're not dealin'."

"Of course I won't hang around the saloon," Jonty snapped indignantly. "What do you think I am, a loose woman?"

"No, by God, I don't, and you know it," LaTour shot back. "But it would be just like you to pick up empty glasses and wipe off tables, makin' sure you're earnin' your keep."

Could he read her mind? Jonty wondered with a half smile. She had planned on doing exactly that. She smiled up at LaTour, knowing that was out of the question now. "I promise I won't do anything but sit at the table and deal cards," she said soberly.

"All right then," LaTour said reluctantly. "You can start tomorrow night. Now let me have a look at this young man." He hunkered down beside Tillie's chair and laughed in wonder as he gazed at the sleeping child.

"Cord McBain all over again." A frown creased his forehead. "I don't like to think what might happen if that wild man ever sees Coty."

"Neither do I, Uncle Jim." Jonty lifted Coty from Tillie's arms and hugged him protectively. "We've all got to be very careful that he doesn't until I get out of here again."

CHAPTER 25

CORD MCBAIN SAT IN FRONT OF THE CAMPFIRE, CAREFUL NOT to look into the flames. If a man had to look out into the darkness, he wouldn't be able to see, and that might mean an arrow or a bullet in his heart.

A pack of coyotes came nosing around, keeping in the shadows, howling and barking. Cord never felt so desolate in his life. He looked up at the moon. He felt in a strange mood tonight, like he could feel Jonty's presence . . . no, not that exactly, more like a sense of her. That she was unrestful, unhappy, calling out to him.

Where was she? All summer he'd had two of his men taking turns watching Trail's End and asking discreet questions. Each man had reported back that they'd seen no sign of Jonty, not even the dog or the Indian. And it appeared that LaTour never left town.

The two men would have been fired had Cord known that, at the breed's instructions, they had been lured upstairs by a whore every time he wanted to go visit Jonty.

Cord fought the idea that Jonty was crying out to him, and it died away. He was the last person she would ask help of.

Still, with a ragged sigh, he wondered where she was tonight, what was she doing. Was she with the breed? Were they, at this very moment, making love?

He supressed the groan that rose to his throat. "Don't think about it, man," he whispered fiercely. "You're gonna drive yourself crazy if you don't get her out of your mind."

He turned his head and grimaced wryly at the different tones of snorts and snores coming from his companions, asleep hours ago.

For three days, he and his riders had camped in the hidden valley, branding and taming the wild mustangs. One more day and they would head for Cottonwood with another hundred head for the Army. Cord rose and stretched sore muscles. It had been a strenuous few days and it was time he hit the blankets too.

He was in the act of kicking dirt over the fire when he heard a sharp, crackling sound coming from the edge of a sparse growth of nearby brush. He spun around, his hand coming up lightening quick, the Colt snug in his palm.

"Sing out your business here, mister," he ordered sharply.

There was a rustling movement, then a weedy and strained voice quavered, "I have a message for Cord McBain."

Was it a ruse to get him to sheathe his gun, Cord wondered, then have a half-dozen rustlers step out with drawn pistols? On the other hand, the voice was old and cracked, hardly the type to trail with outlaws.

Keeping his gun trained on the bushes, he said, "Come on in, hands in the air."

A small gray burro picked his careful way out of the brush, his ears laid back, reminding Cord of the one that had kicked their camp apart one night when he was bringing Jonty to the ranch.

But after one swift look at the little animal, he kept

his eyes on the rider. The man was old, as he had expected, white-haired and weather beaten. When he pulled the little animal in, only feet away, Cord growled, "State your business. What is your message?"

His manner defiant, the ragged stranger growled back, "Old Janie sent me."

Cord's heart thundered against his rib cage. He took a step closer to the mean-eyed little mount and closed his fingers around the bony leg dangling free from the worn saddle. "Does Janie know where Jonty is?"

The old man looked at the coffee pot set on the edge of the nearly dead fire. "You think there might be any coffee left in that pot?" He ignored Cord's question. "I've been ridin' a fur piece and it would taste mighty good."

Cord released the thin leg, saying tightly, "I think there's a cup or two left." He took a clean tin cup from the chuck wagon, and as he poured the still warm liquid into it, the old man hinted behind him:

"Ain't ate nothin' today. Feels like my stomach has stuck to my backbone."

Cord swore impatiently under his breath. This cagey old devil wasn't going to tell him anything until he had his gut filled. And from the looks of him, he'd been half-starved most of his life.

He went back to the wagon, took out a tin plate, and filled it with half-cold stew from the pot Cookie had left sitting on the tail gate. He added a spoon and a large piece of sourdough, then tried to contain himself while his visitor gulped the food down.

Finally, the last piece of meat had been shoveled into the toothless mouth, and the old man sighed his satisfaction. "All right now." Cord stood over him. "Give me the message."

"Don't reckon you got any baccy?" The old man brought out a short pipe. "It's been a long time since I've had me a good smoke."

"No, I don't have any baccy, you old reprobate,"

Cord thundered, at the end of his patience. "Now, dammit, give me the message. What did Janie tell you?"

"Well, first I want to tell you that my name is Thadus King, and that me and Janie have been close friends for fifty years or more. She and—"

Cord's control snapped. "Look, you old windbag." He grabbed the thin shoulders and shook them. "I don't care if you and Janie have been friends for a hundred years. Now, damn your wrinkled old hide, for the last time, what is Janie's message?"

Thadus gave him a reproachful look and, rubbing his shoulder, muttered, "Jonty is back in Cottonwood." When Cord would have interrupted him with a dozen questions, he held up a hand. "But he ain't no boy anymore. He's turned into a woman. And that ain't all. Jonty has—"

"I know all about that, old man," Cord broke in, "so don't yammer about it half the night." He hurried to Jones's hunched form and shook him awake.

"What? What?" Jones sat up, staring wildly at Cord.

Cord laid a finger to his lips and shook his head for silence. "Listen," he said quietly, "something's come up. You're gonna have to take the herd into Cottonwood. I just got word that Jonty has returned there."

Jones scratched his head. "Who told you, one of them coyotes that's been howlin' his head off?"

A slight grin twitched Cord's lips. He jerked a thumb over his shoulder. "We've got company. That old gent over there by the fire brought me the news."

Jones stared at the scowling old man. "Do you think he's tellin' you the truth?"

"Yeah, he is." Cord stood up. "I'm leavin' as soon as I can saddle up. If things go the way I want them to, I'll probably beat you back to the ranch."

Jones nodded and said softly, "Good luck, Cord."

Cord was cinching Rawhide's belly belt when Thadus ambled over to him. "You leavin' for Cottonwood now?" he asked, a hint of surprise in his voice, his breath vaporizing into a small frosty cloud as he spoke.

Cord nodded. "What about you? You gonna ride with me?"

The old man avoided his eyes, looking instead at the scuffed toes of his boots. "I kinda like this country," he mumbled, "thought maybe I'd hang around for a while." He looked up at Cord. "That is, if you don't mind."

Cord sighed heavily. The cantankerous old devil had to be in his mid-seventies. He'd probably be more of a hindrance than a help. But could he kill the hopeful look in the faded blue eyes?

He decided that Thadus could still push a broom, keep the bunkhouse swept out, maybe give Cookie a hand. "Stay as long as you like," he said over his shoulder as he bent and started rolling up his bedroll. "My foreman, Jones, will direct you to the bunkhouse in the mornin'".

A wide grin split the weathered face. "Thank you, McBain. And I know where the house is. I went there first. A sulky Mexican girl told me where I'd find you. Looked down her nose at me, she did." He followed Cord around as the rancher gathered his gear. "Janie said you wuz a square one, McBain."

"She probably meant I had a square head," Cord said, sarcasm directed at himself as he fastened the bedding on the saddle, then swung onto Rawhide's back. He lifted a hand to the old man, and with a signal to the stallion it wheeled and thundered away, sending clumps of sod and gravel flying as Thadus smiled happily.

Low-drifting clouds had been gathering all night, and by the time Cord arrived at Cottonwood, it had been raining for an hour. "It sure as hell rains a lot in this part of the country," Cord muttered, reining in the stallion and slipping tiredly to the ground. It had been pouring the last time he came to this miserable town.

He stood a moment beside the stallion, adjusting his gun belt, checking that the handle of the Colt was handy to his touch. He had no idea what awaited him inside the saloon, but he would be ready for it. Nothing was going to stop him from seeing Jonty, doing his damndest to talk her into leaving this hell-hole.

He squared his shoulders and stepped up on the wooden sidewalk, paused a second, then pushed open the swinging doors of the Trail's End. Inside, he stepped to one side and, leaning against the wall, let his gaze wander over the large room.

Nothing had changed, he thought. The same discordant mingling of the heavily beaten piano, laughter, shouting, and the tramp of dancing boots to the tinny music. He gave a start when his eyes fell on a table far back in the room. Four men and a woman sat around it, the suspended kerosine lamp casting a soft glow on the woman who studied a fan of cards in her slim fingers.

"Jonty," he whispered in wonder. "How beautiful you are." Where had the boy-girl gone? he wondered, half sad, as his eyes ranged over the fully developed body of a woman. And though the black silk dress was buttoned to her throat, it only made a man imagine what it concealed.

Cord's face suddenly became hard and tight as he discovered he wasn't the only man looking and wondering at her. He pulled his stetson down until it covered his upper face, then moved to the edge of the watching men crowded around the table.

She's good, he thought, watching Jonty's agile fingers manipulate the cards, then topping them together before slapping the cards down in front of each player, face up. "Five card stud," she said in that throaty voice that would always stay with her. "No draw. You play what you get."

Cord's eyes ranged hungrily over Jonty, surprised and pleased that her face wasn't painted. She looked very much the lady, he thought proudly, continuing to watch her swift, dexterous hands shuffling and dealing the cards.

Cord noted after awhile that a slight, angry frown now creased Jonty's forehead. It seemed to deepen every time one particular gambler raised her bet. He folded his arms across his chest and kept his eyes on the player. His eyes narrowed as a new hand began. The bastard was cheating, and it was clumsy and crude. Cord's eyes flickered to Jonty. Her angry expression told him that she knew it too. He was wondering how best to help her when LaTour's tall frame pushed its way through the throng. He gave the gambler a hard look, then leaned over Jonty and whispered something in her ear. She nodded, then excused herself and left the table.

Jealousy tied Cord's stomach in knots at the intimate act. He should have known that LaTour would be near, watching over Jonty. He had seen the man cheating and had stepped in, ready to take care of what she had been unable to do.

Damn the man! Cord ground his teeth in frustration. He was always in the background of Jonty's life, directing it, smoothing her path, shaming him for things he should have done and had not. Well, he was going to ask Jonty to marry him. That was more than the breed was willing to do.

Cord remained where he was a minute or so longer, gathering his courage to follow this new, self-confident Jonty. He would need every argument at his command to convince her that what she'd seen that morning back at the ranch wasn't what it had appeared to be. That he hadn't welcomed Tina's embrace.

Firming his lips, he began pushing and shoving his way to the door Jonty had disappeared through, ready to fight, and to win, the biggest battle of his life.

At first he thought the large kitchen was empty, it was so quiet. His gaze moved over a long table where several pies were lined up, then to the stove where three pots simmered, an aromatic steam escaping the lids. His eyes next skimmed over a window that looked out onto a frost-killed vegetable garden. Had Jonty gone outside?

He took a step toward the back door, then paused, arrested by the sound of a soft crooning. His eyes sought a shadowed corner, then froze, a look of incredulity coming into them.

Sitting in a rocking chair, unaware of his presence, Jonty held a nursing baby in her arms.

For what seemed an eternity to Cord, he couldn't move. The woman he loved had given birth to another man's child. As he stood there, the numbness slowly left him, and an anger began to build inside him. An anger that was so black, so hot, it seemed to sear his brain.

The bitch! While he had scoured the countryside for her, been sick with worry and love for her, she had been wallowing around in LaTour's arms with never a thought for him.

A sharp prickling along Jonty's spine alerted her that someone was in the room with her. She had a sudden ominous feeling that whoever it was wished to do her harm. Her arms tightened around Coty as she slowly lifted her head.

"Cord!" She gasped, staring at his hard, still face. "What are you doing here? What do you want?" she floundered, hurriedly flipping the corner of the blanket over the baby's face.

"It's for damned sure I don't want *you* now," Cord said harshly, moving across the floor to stand over her. His eyes raked her contemptuously. "You're tarnished. I'd never take the breed's leavin's."

Jonty drew in a sharp breath at his crude insult. In the charged silence that built, she thought how easy it would be to fling his churlish words back in his face. All she need do was lift the cover off Coty's face.

But that, of course, she didn't dare do. She stared back at Cord unflinchingly. "I didn't hear myself asking you to," she said quietly, thinking that it must be her imagination that he looked tormented, that he suffered.

She was sure of it when Cord sneered, "No, you didn't, nor are you likely to. You were raised in a whorehouse, and you're happy to be back in one. When LaTour tires of you, there will be plenty more men eager to take his place."

His lips twisted bitterly. "You're a hot little piece in bed and you'll make yourself a lot of money. Who knows, I might even visit LaTour's new whore once in awhile. That is, if I really get hard up."

Please, God, make him go away, Jonty prayed silently. *I can't hold back my tears much longer.*

Why isn't she spitting back at me? Cord wondered savagely. He wanted her to, to fuel his anger until he couldn't keep his hands off her. But damn her, she only sat there, her arms around her brat, refusing to even look at him. Before he opened the door and stepped back into the saloon, he tossed one last insult at her.

"It's only fittin' that you have a bastard, bein' one yourself." He closed the door behind him and Jonty's body slumped with a ragged sigh. Her pain was beyond relief-giving tears now.

She gave a tired sigh and rose, careful not to awaken Coty as she carried him into the bedroom. She laid him in the small bed across from hers, then adjusted the board that would keep him from rolling to the floor in his sleep. He was a very active baby, even in his sleep.

She leaned over her son, stroking the soft blond curls, the curls the only thing he had inherited from her. Tears glistened in her eyes. How sad that he would never know his father. She dropped a kiss on the sleep-flushed cheek and straightened up. It was time she got back to the poker table. Of course, Uncle Jim wouldn't care if she never went back into the saloon. He still objected strongly to her playing.

She lit the lamp on her bedside table, turning the wick low until only a small circle of light glowed in the room. Coty didn't like the dark. He became frightened of anything he couldn't see.

Jonty's fingers were swiftly doing up the buttons of her bodice when the bedroom door quietly opened.

"Tillie?" she whispered, peering in the near darkness as the door closed. There was no answer, just a tall, broad-shouldered figure moving toward her. Her hands flew to her throat. "What do you want now, Cord McBain?" she whispered. "Haven't you said enough?"

Cord gave a harsh laugh as he dropped his hat to the floor, then shrugged out of his jacket. Then, his fingers busy undoing his shirt, he sneered, "You know what I want. The only thing I'll ever want from you."

He pulled the shirt out of his pants, slid his arms out of the sleeves, and dropped it beside the hat. "That ripe body is constantly in front of me, making my blood boil, tearing me up inside with wanting it. So, my little whore, you're gonna soothe me, take away my hurt."

His hands were at his belt now, and Jonty had backed away as far as she could; the bed was nudging the back of her knees. "You get out of here, Cord McBain!" she whispered furiously. "I'll never let you touch me again. I hate and detest you, you cold, uncaring bastard."

"Good," he whispered back, stepping out of his trousers, then sliding his underwear over his narrow hips. "I sure as hell am not lookin' for any tender feelin's from you." Before she could move, his fingers were at her bodice, quickly undoing the rest of the buttons, then sliding the garment over her shoulders. When he ran knowing, insulting eyes down the length of her body, then stared pointedly at the vee of pubic hair clearly seen through the sheer muslin, she grew rigid with anger and humiliation.

She shook her head vehemently when he said harshly, "That is all I want of you. To put myself in there, keep it there until my mind is free of you."

And though she kept shaking her head, even put out a hand to stop him, he stripped off her remaining clothes. Then, stepping away from her, he coaxed hoarsely, "Look at me. See how I want you."

"No," Jonty whimpered, her blood already like warm syrup in her veins as she turned her head from him.

"Yes," he ordered, grasping her chin and forcing her face around.

In the lamp's small light, Jonty helplessly looked at the magnificent body. Her eyes passed over the flat stomach and went directly to the large manhood, full and throbbing with need. She recalled how it had once torn her, made her bleed before bringing her an incredible feeling of joy. A small moan escaped her constricted throat.

"You want it, don't you?" Cord pressed himself against her. "You want me inside you, you want to feel the slide of it, its largeness filling you, making you pant and clutch my shoulders."

"No! No! I don't," she whimpered weakly as he pumped his hardness between her thighs.

"Why do you lie?" Cord brushed a thumb across a pebble-hard nipple. "Your nipples give you away," he taunted. "Look at them, all hard and pouty, just waiting for me to take them into my mouth, strip them between my teeth."

"That's not true," Jonty denied weakly. "I don't want . . ."

The words died on her lips. Cord had dipped his head and fastened his mouth over one breast. "Oh, God," she moaned as he suckled her. Why couldn't she fight him? she asked herself. Why wouldn't her body respond to what her mind was telling it?

She unconsciously arched her body into his, and lifting his head, Cord drew her into his arms, smashing her breasts against the hairy mat of his chest. "What were you sayin' about me bein' cold?"

Jonty heard the mockery in his voice and words, and for a moment self-respect returned. He was playing with her, tormenting her senses. She put her hands on his chest, to push him away. But as though he sensed her recoiling, Cord cupped her buttocks and pulled her tightly up against his hard arousal. Bucking it against her in slow even jabs, he whispered huskily, "You're not cold either. Come on, be honest, you want me inside you. You remember how good it was between us."

The blood was pounding in Jonty's ears, and her lower body grew weak with longing. It had been so long. Still, when Cord nudged her to lay down, she protested and tried to pull away from him.

"Dammit," Cord grated impatiently, "you know you want me, so stop foolin' around."

"I don't! I don't!" She half sobbed.

"We'll see about that," Cord grated and gave her a slight push on the shoulder so that she fell back across the bed. "I'm gonna make you beg for it now," he whispered, and dropped to the floor, his hands on her knees.

He ran his palm up her legs and stroked the insides of her quivering thighs. Jonty shivered and gave a low moan when he parted the vee of black silky hair and buried his face in it. When his tongue flicked inside her, she leaned up and gripped his shoulders, begging, "Please, Cord, don't."

Cord lifted his head long enough to say, "I'll stop when you admit that you want me."

Jonty endured the thrusting tongue, the nibbling teeth, until she was sure she was going to faint from the need of having Cord inside her. "All right," she panted. "I want you."

The torture stopped. "You want me—what?" Cord asked huskily. "What do you want? Tell me."

When several seconds passed and Jonty made no response, Cord lowered his head again. "No!" she cried. "Not that. I want you inside me."

"That's my good girl," he mocked, sliding up her body. Jonty felt the trembling of his body and knew that he was in as bad a state as she was. He couldn't have held out much longer.

As he hung over her, he took her hand and guided it to his arousal. "You know what to do," he whispered softly.

Jonty closed her fingers around his large shaft, remembering how he had taught her how to guide him inside her. Cord caught his breath as she placed the first two inches of his manhood inside her, then wrapped her legs around his waist. She raised her small derriere then, and slowly her working muscles swallowed him.

Cord caught his breath, savoring each inch she drew him inside her, not letting it go until he filled her to overflowing. "Oh, God," he moaned when the black hair meshed with the blond. "Just like I remembered —silky, sweetly tight, sucking at me."

He started a slow, evenly paced thrusting, murmuring breathlessly, "Come on, honey, suck it, draw it deep inside you."

Ten, fifteen minutes passed as Cord, his body soaked with sweat, worked over Jonty. She had climaxed twice, and still his body rose and fell, rocking her back and forth. She raised a hand to his wet face. "Is something wrong?" she whispered.

"Nothing's wrong," he whispered back. "I want to make it last."

He continued the rocking thrust a few moments longer, then, as though her tender touch had broken his control, he slid his hands under her buttocks, and lifting them off the bed, he held her steady as he moved faster and faster inside her. A moment later he gave a hoarse cry and Jonty felt the flow of his seed pumping inside her.

How wonderful to feel his body against hers again, she thought, taking his weight as he fell limply on top of her, his passion-spent manhood still jerking inside her. She gently stroked his wet head. Surely, after this, he would have no more harsh words for her. Their love-making had been so beautiful; he had been so gentle. She waited for him to speak, to say the words she longed to hear.

When Cord finally did speak, she wished that he had been struck dumb.

Slowly withdrawing his depleted self, Cord rose and groped for his clothes. She heard the rustle of them as he dressed, heard him lightly stamp on his boots. She saw the dim outline of him standing at the foot of the bed, and a great pain stabbed her chest when he spoke:

"You're still damned good, lady," he mocked. "How much money should I leave on the dresser?"

Please, God, he didn't say that. Jonty closed her eyes in agony. But she knew she hadn't misunderstood him. He was holding true to form, lashing out at her in the most cruel way he could think of.

With sick, dull eyes, she managed to say calmly, "It's on the house . . . for old time's sake."

She saw the big body jerk, and smiled tightly. He hadn't expected that serene answer. He had expected her to lash out at him, give him the chance to say more bitter, hurtful things to her. A silence grew, which Cord didn't know how to break. Finally, he turned and made his way to the door, tripping over Jonty's slipper in the middle of the floor. He swore softly, jerked open the door, and almost walked into Tillie, reaching for the door knob.

"Hey! what are you doin' in here?" the sharp-tongued woman demanded sharply.

Cord brushed by the bristling body. "Ask her." He jerked a thumb toward the bed.

When the door had closed behind Cord, Tillie hurried into the room and turned up the lamp. "Wasn't that Cord McBain?" She turned to look at

Jonty. When the tear-stained girl hurriedly pulled the quilt up over her nakedness, Tillie cried, "Oh, honey," and sat down on the edge of the bed. Smoothing the damp hair off Jonty's forehead, she asked softly, "Did that hell-raiser rape you?"

"Not exactly, Tillie." Jonty swiped at the tears running down her cheeks. "He sort of . . . talked me into it." She sat up and threw herself into Tillie's arms. "Oh, Tillie," she sobbed. "He's so slick, so cruel."

Tillie rocked Jonty back and forth, her gnarled hands smoothing up and down her back. "Sometimes, Jonty, a man acts the way he does because he's torn up inside, hurtin' terrible himself."

"That's not the case with Cord McBain," Jonty said with sure conviction. "Nothing would hurt that one. Except maybe getting his pride stepped on. I guess I did that by leaving him, not giving him the chance to order me away."

"Did he see Coty?" Tillie held Jonty away, her eyes looking worried.

"No. Surprisingly, he was very quiet, as though not to disturb Coty." She frowned thoughtfully. "Do you think he did that out of kindness, or was he afraid that if he awakened Coty, his cries would bring someone to my room?"

"I don't know, honey." Tillie shook her head. "Some men take their pleasure silently, while others carry on like a ruttin' buffalo."

Cord hadn't been exactly silent. Jonty remembered his words of praise, his coaxing instructions, but all huskily whispered to her.

Tillie braced her hands on her knees and pushed herself to her feet. "Why don't you put on your gown now and try to sleep. You're in no condition to deal cards anymore tonight."

"Yes, you're right," Jonty agreed, then asked, "Tillie, you know that tea you . . . you brew for the girls so that they don't . . ."

"I'll bring you a cup of it right away, honey," Tillie

interrupted her. "We don't need any more hell-raisers runnin' round, do we."

When Cord walked out of the saloon, old Janie was waiting for him. Guilt and dejection muddling his brain, he almost tripped over her scrawny body hunched down beside the door.

"I did good, huh, young feller?" she started right in. "I got you word that Jonty was back."

"You did good, Janie." Cord blindly reached into his pocket and withdrew some greenbacks. "Thanks." He shoved the money into her waiting, grubby hand.

The arthritic fingers closed greedily over her reward. Then, giving her cackling laugh, she said slyly, "Surprised us all, Jonty did. Come back a woman with a baby." Her eyes scanned Cord's face carefully. "Who do you think the father is to her little bastard? I ain't never seen her around any man ceptin' LaTour."

When Cord would have walked past the old woman, afraid that he might hit the wrinkled face if he didn't get away from the words spewing out of the toothless mouth, words that sliced at him like a knife, Janie stood up, blocking his path.

"The breed is awfully fond of her. Treats her like a queen. He's crazy about the baby too. It's a little boy, you know."

"I gotta go," Cord said almost desperately, taking the old woman by the arms and firmly lifting her out of his way.

Rawhide whinnied a greeting as Cord undid the reins looped over the hitching post. He swung into the saddle and the stallion moved out.

"Get her out of your mind," Cord told himself. "If you don't, you'll be pullin' stunts like that the rest of your life."

It was a bitter, grim-faced Cord who nudged the stallion into a mile-eating lope.

CHAPTER 26

SOFT FEMININE LAUGHTER, DEEP MALE CHUCKLES, AND high childish squeals mingled in the large kitchen. Eight people watched one-year-old Coty Rand's small fingers rip the colorful wrappings from his birthday packages. His gray eyes sparkled at each treasure revealed.

"Unca Jim." He thrust a long narrow box at LaTour, his face flushed with irritation, and when "Unca Jim" pretended not to hear, Coty threw the box on the floor and made a noise that sounded a lot like swearing.

"Coty!" Jonty chided while everyone else laughed. "Don't laugh." She bent stern eyes on LaTour and Lightfoot, the two who had laughed loudest. "I can just imagine what's going to come out of him when he really starts talking. He'll pick up on everything he hears."

Tongues were bitten, repressing more laughter as young Coty beat his spoon on the table, his wide smile revealing small pearly teeth.

Jonty glared at LaTour and snapped, "Open the blasted package."

LaTour, struggling to keep the smile off his face, cut the string with his knife.

"Here you are, young fellow." He handed the package over to the eagerly waiting child. "This is from your Uncle Johnny."

Colorful paper joined the pile on the floor, and Coty gave a delighted squeal. Lightfoot's lips spread in a pleased smile as the youngster pulled a small wooden gun from a box, yelling, "Bang, bang!"

Jonty frowned, but did not voice her disapproval. Not only would Johnny's feelings be hurt, but Coty was a male, and in this sparsely settled wilderness he would probably one day carry the real thing. She could only pray that it would never be turned on another human being.

She rose and cut the cake waiting in the center of the table, and a semblance of quiet settled in as everyone sang "Happy Birthday" to Coty.

As Jonty consumed her own slice, she let her gaze drift around the table, lingering a moment on each guest. Uncle Jim was becoming quite respectable these days. He had cut all his ties to his old gang, and was now being spoken to by ladies of Cottonwood when he passed them on the street.

Jonty's eyes moved to Tillie, sitting next to LaTour. What a dear friend she was. If Jonty Rand had ever done one wise thing in her life, it had been befriending this woman.

Her gaze moved on to Johnny and Nemia, and a softness grew in her eyes as she watched the squaw slide a second piece of cake onto her lover's plate. Such a tight bond had grown between those two. One day they would leave the little room they shared upstairs, for both longed to be with their people again. How sad she would be when that day came.

Jonty turned her gaze to the stranger among them. John Stewart. Doctor John Stewart. Thirty years old, a little under six foot tall, almost bone thin, brown eyes and hair, and a gentle nature. Originally from St. Louis, Missouri, he had arrived in Cottonwood six months ago and set up his office next door to the saloon. Later, after they had got to know each other, he had grinned and explained that he figured that would be the best place to hang up his shingle. "What with the fist fights and gun battles that erupt in Trail's End so often, I figured I'd be kept busy sewing up wounds and busted heads." He'd laughed.

She had first met John when she took Coty to him with a bad cold. She had paid scant attention to his staring at her, for she had grown use to men ogling her. But his gentleness with her son, his quick wit and smiling warm eyes, had made her take a closer look at the man. She saw him often after that, on the street, in the saloon, patching up knife stabs or gunshot wounds, always cleanly shaven and impeccably dressed in his poplin suits.

She caught John's eyes on her now and smiled at him. It had taken him a month to get up the courage to ask her to go on a picnic with him down by the river, then another month of courting before he kissed her.

Jonty dropped her eyes from the doctor's. She knew that John was in love with her, and that he would ask her to marry him before long. What would her answer be? she wondered. She felt a warm affection for him, but would that be enough? There would be no rocky spots in an union with John. His was an even nature and there would be no fits of temper, no demanding dominance of her.

But would that be good enough? If she was to be truthful, wouldn't her own fiery nature soon become bored with John's tenderness? It would be too late if that were the case. To her, marriage was a lifetime commitment.

A rueful smile touched her lips when her eyes fell on old Janie. She was forever comparing John to Cord, pointing out John's weakness and Cord's strength. Nor did she ever miss a chance to remark on how much Coty looked like his father, and wouldn't McBain be proud if he knew he had a son.

One day, hot and tired, and having listened to Janie ramble on and on in the same vein, Jonty had reached the end of her tether with the old woman. She had glared into the peaked, wrinkled face and ground out, "You know, Janie, I think the older you get, the more ornery you become, and I'm fed up with it." Then, slapping her hand on the table, emphasizing each word, she let the old woman know what she feared from her and what the consequences would be if her suspicions proved true.

"I know, old woman, that it's on your mind to let Cord McBain know about Coty. But you'd better think twice about it. For if you do, there will never again be a plate for you at supper time, nor a nip of whiskey."

Janie had blustered a bit, denying that she had any such intention of speaking to McBain. Then, giving a sniff, she had turned and entered her run-down shack. That evening, however, she had been at the kitchen door, waiting. And a week later she was back to her old song. But Jonty knew the fear of losing her one good meal a day would keep her from sending any messages to Devil's Mountain.

Jonty returned to the present with the realization that Coty's party was breaking up. Tillie was bustling around the stove and Nemia was helping her little charge from his high chair, while LaTour and Lightfoot were pushing away from the table and rising to their feet.

She also rose, giving Janie a boost up. "Coty, thank everyone for your presents," she reminded the child whose head now nodded sleepily on Nemia's shoulder as he was carried toward the bedroom for his daily nap.

Everyone laughed when Coty's only response was an irritated frown.

Jonty sighed and shook her head, then gave Janie a

threatening look, stopping the old woman in mid-sentence as she cackled, "That youngin' gets more like his—"

I wish people would see more than Coty's naughty side, she thought as everyone except the doctor filed out of the room. Everyone got a big kick out of that which was so much like his father—quick temper, short patience. They never saw, as she did, that there was much of his great-grandmother in him also—the seriousness that could grow in his gray eyes, the way he sometimes cocked his head and listened intently when she was explaining something to him.

On her way to the sink with a stack of cake plates, Jonty was struck with a sudden thought. Sometimes, when Coty smiled, he looked like Uncle Jim. She shook her head at the foolish thought. That was impossible. There was no blood tie there. She set the heavy china down and turned to smile at John Stewart.

"Would you like another cup of coffee, John? There's plenty left in the pot."

The doctor fished a gold watch from his vest pocket, looked at the time, and shook his head. "I'd better not, Jonty." He returned her smile. "It's time I got back to my office. There's probably a dozen patients waiting for me already."

"You are kept busy, aren't you?" Jonty walked the slim man to the door. "I've never seen so many ailing women since you hit town." Her blue eyes teased him.

"There are a few." He lifted a hand and lightly flicked her nose with a long finger. "But the only one I'm interested in never seems to become ill."

Jonty shrugged and smiled up at him. "Some women just never seem to ail."

The levity left Stewart as a seriousness grew in his eyes. "Can I see you tonight?" When Jonty shook her head, he coaxed, "There's a full moon tonight. We could take a buggy ride along the river. It would be cool there."

"It sounds wonderful, John, to feel a cool breeze for a while, but you know I have to work tonight."

The doctor's disappointment was clear. He stroked her cheek with his soft palm. "It seems an awfully long time until Sunday."

Jonty laughed softly. "Silly, it's only a day after tomorrow."

"I know, but every hour away from you seems like a day."

"My, you are full of pretty speeches, aren't you?" Jonty opened the kitchen door with a smile and stood holding it open for him to pass through.

"You're a hard woman, Jonty Rand." He grinned down at her, then kissing her cheek, he called good-bye to Tillie and left.

"I'd say the young doc has it pretty bad," Tillie said when Jonty joined her at the sink and picked up a towel and began drying the dishes draining on the rack. "What are you gonna say to him when he asks you to marry him?"

"I don't know, Tillie." Jonty hung the towel up to dry, then dropped into a chair. "My brain is worn out from thinking about it. I like John an awful lot, have tremendous respect for him. I enjoy his company, and I know he'd be kind to Coty. He's not the kind of man who would hold a child's illegitimacy against him. I'm pretty sure he'd even adopt Coty, give him his name."

"Yes, I think he would," Tillie said, joining Jonty at the table and sitting quietly while she waited for her to continue speaking her thoughts.

"Coty is a very intelligent child, and sooner or later he's going to start asking questions. Questions that will be hard for me to answer." She looked up at Tillie. "Don't you think it's important that Coty have a father?"

"Yes, honey, it is," Tillie answered after a thoughtful pause. "But it wouldn't be fair, nor wise, to marry a man just to give your child a name. Marriage to a man you love can sometimes be very hard. Married to one you don't love can mean a lifetime of hell."

"Love!" Jonty dismissed the word with a scornful wave of her hand. "It can be hell to love a man also, Tillie. It can humiliate you, rip your insides to shreds, make you bleed, tear up your mind."

"I don't know, honey," Tillie said sadly. "It's been a long time since I've had a tender feelin' for a man. But it seems, as best as I can remember, that it was a wonderful feelin'."

"Your love must have been returned then." Jonty stood up. "I'm going to lie down a little while before I have to go to work."

Tillie watched the young woman she loved like a daughter leave the room. "I'd like to take a whip to Cord McBain," she whispered.

CHAPTER 27

DAMIT TO HELL, TINA, ONCE AND FOR ALL, STAY AWAY FROM me." Cord marched the Mexican girl from his bedroom, his grip firm on her arm. "I thought I made it clear I don't have any romantic notions about you. And," he added, pointing her down the hall, "I have too much respect for your parents to simply use you."

Clad only in her nightgown, Tina jerked her arm free of his grip and Cord took a step backward as the hatred of a woman scorned seemed to reach out and scorch his skin.

"You'll regret this night someday, *hombre*," Tina muttered over her shoulder as she wheeled and ran out of the house.

Hah! Cord thought, turning back to his room. He regreted the day he'd ever brought her here. He crawled back in bed and lay quietly, trying to coax back the dream he'd been having of Jonty when Tina slipped into his bed.

"Black-eyed bitch," he muttered when sleep wouldn't come and Jonty stayed firmly away.

Cord tossed and turned for a long time before he slid into a restless sleep. The sun was an hour high before he awakened the next morning. The clock in the front room struck seven and he jumped out of bed, swearing under his breath.

"Of all the times for me to oversleep," he muttered, walking across the floor to where he'd hung his clothes before retiring.

Today Jones and half the wranglers would start the trek to Cottonwood, driving before them his largest herd yet to be sold. The Army, liking his sturdy, well-broken mustangs, had ordered five hundred head.

As he slid on his trousers and shrugged into his shirt, Cord's mind was on the last-minute details to see to before the men headed out—check the chuck wagon, making sure Cookie had a plentiful supply of provisions; inspect the men's canteens, making sure they were filled with water and not whiskey. Some damn fools did that, taking a chance of dying from thirst.

Stamping on his boots, then buckling on his gun, Cord left his room. In the kitchen he ignored Tina, but nodded to her mother, busy at the stove, as he made his way outside to wash up.

As he filled a basin with water from a pail, he recalled with a sharp pang how Jonty had talked Jones into building the bench so that the men could wash up outside. He had thought her a young lad then, and had sneered at her feminine wish not to have the kitchen floor tracked up.

"Don't think about it, man," he muttered, and dipped his hands into the water.

The morning mountain air was cold as Cord dried his face on a towel that had already been used many times. He smiled ruefully. Always before, Tina had brought him a clean one. He'd be getting no more special treatment from her, he was sure. He could still feel the stab of her eyes when he passed through the kitchen. But that was good. That was how he wanted it.

Maria, however, was her usual cheerful self when he sat down at the table. "You slept late this morning, Cord." She placed a plate of bacon and eggs in front of him. "Was your sleep not restful?"

"I was sleepin' real good at first, then somethin' woke me up. After that I had a hard time gettin' back to sleep." He slid a look at Tina, surprising a look of hatred on her pretty face.

"You know," Maria said as she watched Cord dig into his breakfast, "something woke me up last night. Sounded like footsteps." She turned to Tina standing stiffly beside the sink. "Did you have reason to get up last night, Tina?"

Cord hoped the mother would see the guilty flush that spread across her daughter's face and question her further. But when Tina turned her back to them and muttered, "No, Mama, it was not me you heard, maybe it was some mice skittering around," Maria agreed and turned back to the large pot of chili simmering on the stove.

A few minutes later, Cord finished his second cup of coffee and stood up. "That sure smells good, Maria." He smiled at his housekeeper, slapping his stetson on his head. "I look forward to a bowl of it for lunch." He felt the shooting sparks of Tina's dark eyes boring into his back as he left the kitchen.

Cord rode up the mountain, his shoulders hunched in his jacket. Indian summer had come and gone on the mountain weeks ago, and a cold wind from the north had taken over. Of course, it was still reasonably warm farther down in the valley; it was always several degrees warmer in the lowlands. Until winter set in. Once it arrived, the whole world seemed frozen.

The stallion made one last lunge, and the holding pens lay before Cord. He held the big horse in for a moment, stirred by the sight of whinnying, snorting mustangs racing around in the enclosures, looking for an escape hole in the stout pole corrals. The sight never failed to thrill him.

He peered through the clouds of dust kicked up and frowned. Where were the men? He nudged Rawhide and moved on, a bit riled that his riders were nowhere in sight. He rode around a clump of brush and boulders and spotted them. The men stood in a circle, looking down at a man stretched out on the ground. With a start, he recognized the long, angular body immediately. Jones, his foreman.

In seconds he was kneeling beside his friend. "What happened, Jones?" He noted how the rider was clutching his shoulder.

"My dad-ratted horse threw me, Cord," Jones answered through white, pinched lips. "I'm afraid my shoulder is busted."

"Let me take a look at it." Cord took Jones's right arm and gently started to raise it. Midway to his head Jones let out a screech.

"It's not your shoulder." Cord laid the arm back down. "It's your collar bone. If it was a broken shoulder, you'd have let out a yell as soon as I lifted your arm." He stood up. "I'll take you back to the ranch and bind it up. That's about all you can do with that kind of break. It'll mend by itself if you don't move it."

One of the men brought Jones a more reliable horse and Cord helped him to mount. "Bend your elbow and support it with your other hand," he advised the man, who was obviously in pain.

It took longer than usual to reach the ranch house, due to holding the mounts to a walk so as not to jar Jones too badly. As they rode past the house, Maria stepped out onto the porch. "What is wrong with Jones?" she called anxiously.

"His horse threw him," Cord called back. "Bring me some strips of cloth to the bunkhouse, will you please, Maria?"

In less than fifteen minutes, Jones was divested of

his shirt, his shoulder bound, and his arm resting in a sling. His face still pale, and disgust for himself in his voice, he said to Cord, "You're gonna have to take the herd in now. That Army man will only deal with me or you."

That thought had already entered Cord's mind, and it was an unwelcome one. He had planned never to go into Cottonwood again, never take a chance of running into Jonty. He couldn't trust himself around her. The only thing he could do was get in and out of town as quickly as possible, not stopping anywhere.

He pressed the foreman's uninjured shoulder, and forcing a cheerfulness in his voice, said, "I need to get off the mountain for a while, raise a little hell." He lifted an eyebrow at his friend. "Wouldn't you agree?"

"I sure would, and make sure you do," Jones agreed wholeheartedly. "Spend a night or two with a good whore, get some of that meanness out of you."

Cord grinned down at the disabled man, then heading for the door, said, "I'll see you in two or three days."

Two pair of eyes watched Cord as he loped away to join his men. "I hope he comes back happy," Maria said, while her daughter silently muttered that she hoped he'd catch a disease from the whores he was going to lie with.

As Cord had surmised, Indian summer still lingered in Cottonwood as he and his men drove the herd to the holding pens a couple of miles beyond the town. The government man was waiting for him, and after a thorough checking and counting of the horses, passed Cord a check, the amount agreed upon by mail.

Cord folded the white slip of paper and stuck it in his shirt pocket. He had just enough time to get to the bank and cash it. He had a few words with his riders, explaining that he would be hitting the trail for home, but that they could stay on overnight. After cautioning them to stay out of trouble, he pulled his hat low on his brow and reluctantly steered the stallion down the main part of town. Maybe, if he were lucky, no one would recognize him.

The bank building was in the middle of the street, and when Cord entered through the heavy door he was greeted with much respect from the president himself. By now he had an impressive bank account in the establishment. He was fast becoming a wealthy man. When his business was transacted, he shook the banker's hand and left.

As Cord rode down the street, anxious to get well away before sunset, to make camp before dark, he vaguely noticed the Indian woman coming toward him, a papoose strapped to her back. He gave the woman an idle look as he drew opposite her, then slid the same to the child. He liked little tots.

Suddenly the stallion was whistling a protest as he was pulled in so sharply that the bit tore into his mouth. Cord sat the mount as though paralyzed, his face blanched white as he stared at the child in disbelief. It was no Indian boy on the squaw's back. The child was white. And moreover, he was the spitting image of himself.

The woman passed him before he found his tongue. "Hey, you squaw," he called after her, "where did you get that youngun?"

Nemia gave him one fleeting, frightened look, then sprinted away. By the time Cord swung to the ground and looped Rawhide's reins over a hitching post, there was no sign of her. "No matter." His lips tightened in a grim line. "I know where the mother is."

As Cord burst through the back door of the kitchen, Nemia entered from the saloon. The little tune Jonty was humming died in her throat, and the rolling pin in her hand came to an abrupt stop on the dough.

There was a slumbering threat of destructive violence in the man who stood in the door, glaring at her.

"What do you want, Cord?" she finally gasped out.

A cynical smile drew down Cord's lips as he said, "It's always the same question with you, huh, Jonty? What do you want, Cord?"

He stepped into the kitchen and closed the door. "Well," he said, "this time I'm after something entirely different from what I usually want from you." He looked past Jonty to the Indian woman standing behind her and added, "And I think you know what I'm talkin' about."

Jonty swung around and saw for the first time that it had been Nemia who had rushed through the door, and that Coty was peering over her shoulder.

Suddenly drained, she lowered herself into a chair. "So now you know." Her words sounded dead.

When Cord advanced on her, his eyes like pieces of gray steel, she thought that he had turned into the hardest-looking man she'd ever seen. She flinched when he spoke.

"Why didn't you tell me about him that night?" His voice was dangerously quiet.

Jonty lowered her lids to hide her fear, and surprisingly, also guilt. Neither emotion lasted long. He didn't dare strike her, and she'd had good reason not to tell him about his son.

She lifted her eyes to Cord, and affecting a careless shrug, said coolly, "I didn't think it would matter to you." Her eyes became challenging. "After all, he's only a little bastard—I believe those were the exact words out of your mouth the first time you saw him."

"Damn you, Jonty." Cord winced. "You know I didn't know he was mine then."

"Oh, I see." She shot back at him. "Now that you know who sired him, he's no longer a bastard. Is that what you're saying?"

While Cord struggled for an answer to her charge, Jonty stood up and walked to stand beside Nemia and Coty. "In case it hasn't entered your mind, Coty still doesn't have a father. He's known as Coty Rand, bastard child of Jonty Rand."

Cord's long fingers clenched into fists. "Will you stop callin' him that!" he yelled. As they glared at each other, as though preparing to do battle, Coty sensed the turbulence in his mother and began to cry. Jonty took him from Nemia and spoke soothingly to him until he quieted and laid his head on her shoulder.

"You can settle down, Cord," she said quietly. "After tomorrow that stigma will be taken away from Coty. He'll have a father."

"What in the hell are you talkin' about?" Cord closed the distance between them, grabbing her, his fingers biting into her arms.

"Will you keep your voice down." Jonty glared at him, trying not to feel the painful grip of his hold on her. "And to answer your question, I'm getting married then, and my new husband is going to adopt Coty."

"The hell he is!" Cord shouted, his face dark with rage. "I'll straighten that out with LaTour right now."

"I'm not marrying Uncle Jim!" Jonty had to shout over Coty's renewed crying.

Cord pulled up in his hurried stride toward the saloon door. His eyes narrowed on her suspiciously, he asked, "Are you tellin' me that LaTour has tired of you already, that he's willin' to let you marry some other man?"

"I'm not telling you anything, Cord McBain," Jonty hissed, handing the squalling child back to Nemia. "Just be advised that I'm getting married day after tomorrow and that my son will have a name."

For a moment Jonty thought she saw a flicker of pain in the gray eyes, but when Cord spoke, his voice was as hateful and arrogant as ever. "Oh, you're gettin' married all right. But it's gonna happen tomorrow, and I'm the man you're gonna marry."

Jonty's breath left her body in a gasp. "Marry you!" She scoffed, bitingly sarcastic. "Are you out of your mind? I'd never marry you, you big bully—you *womanizer*."

Cord flinched at her sneering description of him, then quickly shrugged it off. Walking over to the stove and pouring himself a cup of coffee from the pot that was always kept full and hot, he drawled coolly, "That's up to you, but either way I'm takin' the boy back to the ranch with me." He pinned Jonty with resolute eyes. "No other man is gonna raise my son. He will call no other man father."

"Uncle Jim will stop you!" Jonty cried, her eyes wide with apprehension.

"I'll stop him first—with a bullet in his heart."

Jonty saw the determination in the gray eyes and knew that he would indeed, if necessary, shoot Jim LaTour, That nothing or nobody was going to stand in his way.

She hid her shaking hands under her apron. It was happening, just as she had feared it would. She had dreamed of his offer of marriage—but what kind of marriage would it be? He didn't love her, and she could never bring herself to sleep with a man just to satisfy his lust. She glanced up at Cord, then quickly away. He was watching her, a mocking smile on his face. Damn him, he was enjoying himself. He knew he had her cornered.

"Is Tina still at the ranch?" she shot at him.

Cord hesitated, guilt flushing over his face. Then, not looking at Jonty, he mumbled, "She is, but like I told you before, she—"

"Then I wouldn't have to share your bed." Jonty cut him off.

Cord took a careful breath. It sounded as though his threat of taking Coty away was working. He hated blackmailing her with the boy, but he was desperate. As for sharing his bed, well, time would take care of that. Given the chance, he knew how to change her mind.

He looked at Jonty coolly and gave a scornful grunt. "I don't need you, Jonty, to warm my bed," he lied.

"Good." Jonty hoped the single word didn't betray the emptiness she felt inside. She should have known that Tina was still taking care of that department.

"Does that mean you agree to the marriage then?" Cord tried to hide the breathlessness in his question.

Jonty's fingers played nervously with the buttons on her bodice. Then, with a sigh of resignation, she looked at him challengingly. "On one condition. You don't carry on your affair with Tina in the house. I won't be shamed by your openly taking her into your bedroom every night. Besides, Coty is very bright and would eventually ask questions."

Cord stiffened and opened his mouth to refute her assumption that Tina spent her nights with him, started to protest that the girl never had, and that if Jonty hadn't been so mule-headed that morning over a year ago, all the misery and pain they both had suffered would have been unnecessary. But Jonty had disdainfully turned her back on him, and his own stubborness rose up.

"Fine," he said stiffly. "After I've spoken to my son, I'll go look up a preacher."

He started toward Jonty's quarters when the roar of a gun in the saloon halted them both in their tracks. While he and Jonty stared at each other, there came loud outcries from both men and women, and the kitchen door banged open.

Jake, the bartender, stood there wild-eyed, his face white with alarm. "LaTour's been shot, Jonty! Someone fired through the window from outside. I think it's bad."

"Oh, my God!" Jonty rushed to the door, shoving Cord out of her way. "Send someone for Doctor Stewart," she called, darting into the barroom, leaving Cord staring after her.

"She should ever be that upset over me," he muttered bitterly, then followed her.

Jonty was down on her knees beside the fallen man, his head in her lap, when Cord walked over to stand beside her. The fear and anguish on her face sent a hot tide of jealousy through him. Maybe LaTour had tired of her, and maybe she had planned on marrying another man, but by hell, it was plain she was still crazy about the breed.

"Stand aside, let me through." A brisk, commanding voice made a path through the crowd for the well-dressed, slender man with a small black bag in his hand. When he knelt on the other side of LaTour, Jonty looked up at him with beseeching eyes.

"Oh, John, help him. I think he's badly wounded." She motioned to the pool of blood forming on the floor.

"Jake." The doctor looked up at the bartender as he unbuttoned the wounded man's shirt, "Clear the room, would you please?"

The big man began shooing everyone out, and when Cord would have followed the others, LaTour opened his eyes and panted, "Stay here, McBain. I want a word with you later."

Puzzled, Cord nodded, then took a seat in a nearby chair, noting that Jonty also looked a little shocked.

He was toying with an empty glass on the table, wondering what the breed wanted from him, when the doctor, without taking his eyes from his patient, ordered shortly, "Bring me a basin of warm water." Cord stood up and glimpsed the ragged hole in LaTour's side as he hurried to the kitchen. If the man survived this, he was a tough one.

When Cord entered the kitchen, Nemia straightened up from placing Coty in his high chair. Alarm washed over her face and she hovered protectively over the child.

"It's all right," Cord said quietly. "I'm not going to take your little charge away. Would you get me a basin of warm water for the doctor?"

The squaw stood uncertain a moment, then, as though accepting the fact that if the rancher did pick up his son and walk out the door, she couldn't stop him, did as she was asked. Her body stiff with silent protest, she moved away from Coty and picked up the tea kettle from the stove.

While she filled a pan with water, Cord knelt down in front of his son. His eyes full of love and pride, he smiled widely. "Damn, boy, but you look like me."

Coty grinned back at him, then chortled, "Damn, damn, damn."

"Hey, fellow, you shouldn't swear like that." Cord

laughed, then looked guilty when Nemia chided behind him:

"You shouldn't swear in front of your son. Jonty doesn't like it."

Cord stood up and smiled sheepishly as he took the basin held out to him. "Looks like I'll have to start watchin' my language."

Back in the saloon again, Cord placed the water within the doctor's reach. John Stewart dropped a piece of guaze into the basin and glanced up at Cord. A slight change in his eyes said that he had recognized Coty's father. He nodded curtly, then turned his attention back to LaTour.

And Cord knew by the instant flash of jealousy in the man's eyes that here was the man Jonty had planned to marry. His own jealousy rose, the bitterness of it almost choking him. Had the doctor known the joy of holding Jonty in his arms, made love to her? He wanted to fly at the man, beat the thin face to a pulp.

Don't go loco, he commanded himself, get hold of yourself and try an keep calm. Anyway, for the man to lose Jonty to another would be punishment enough. He sat back down in the chair and watched the clear water in the basin quickly run red with LaTour's blood as the doctor sponged the gaping wound.

Three times during the next half hour Cord returned to the kitchen for fresh water. In that time his temper was tried again and again as Jonty continued to hold LaTour's head in her lap, tears slipping down her cheeks as the man moaned at the doctor's probing fingers and sharp scalpel.

Jonty's small face showed her weariness when at last LaTour was swathed in bandages from mid-chest to slim waist. The doctor snapped his bag shut, then stood up. "Let's get him upstairs to bed."

Cord and the bartender carefully lifted LaTour, who still clung to Jonty's hand, and slowly mounted the stairs. In his room, Jonty gently withdrew her hand and hurried to turn back the covers of the big bed. "Careful," she cautioned as they placed LaTour on the bed, making Cord tempted to bounce the man up and down on the mattress. When her fingers tugged at LaTour's belt buckle, to divest him of his trousers, Cord struck her hands away.

"I'll get him undressed," he grated.

Jonty blinked, and LaTour grinned faintly, then gave a sharp grunt when his pants were yanked, none too gently, down over his hips.

"Cord!" Jonty's slim hand slapped the back of his head. "Don't be so rough."

Cord straightened up, gaping at her in surprise and anger. "Watch it, Jonty," he snarled, smoothing down the hair her action had stood on end. "You may be the mother of my child, but I'll still turn you across my knee if necessary."

"Hah!" Jonty snorted, turning her attention to the doctor's strained face as Stewart carefully measured out laudanum into a glass of brandy.

"This should deaden his pain and allow him to sleep," he explained to Jonty, ignoring Cord as he took her arm and led her away from the bed.

"How bad is the wound?" Jonty looked at Stewart anxiously, her hands clutched in her apron.

"The bullet entered his left side, two inches below his ribs, passed through his body and came out on the right side. We'll have to wait and see if there have been any vital parts wounded. We'll know in a few hours."

"How will we know?" Jonty looked at LaTour's pale face. "Will his pain increase?"

"Not necessarily. We'll know by a high fever and delirium." The doctor's brown eyes searched Jonty's face. "Will I see you later, just for a minute?"

Jonty knew that Cord was watching them, probably heard every word. She tossed her head defiantly. Whether it riled him or not, she owed it to this gentle man to explain privately the change that was taking place in her life.

She nodded and said gravely, "Yes, John. I'll have a cup of tea with you at the cafe. I have to talk to you."

Stewart's eyes moved from Jonty's pale face to Cord's glowering one, then back to Jonty again. As if he divined the seriousness of her talk, his eyes took on a bleakness. Jonty took a step toward him as he headed blindly for the door. Cord's hard grip on her arm halted her.

"LaTour wants to talk to us." He gave her an unnecessarily hard jerk toward the bed.

Jonty sent him an irate look before sitting down next to LaTour and picking up his hand. "What is it, Uncle Jim?"

The laudanum was taking effect and LaTour's words came slow and thick. "I want you to take Coty and go away with McBain until I'm on my feet. I won't be in any condition to protect you for a while."

The long spaces between the words said plainly to the couple hanging over him that the wounded man would soon be asleep. In fact, as Jonty pulled the sheet up under his chin, LaTour was already beginning to snore softly.

"Dammit!" Cord swore. "We didn't get to tell him that we're gettin' married, and that I'd be takin' you away in any case."

Jonty didn't even acknowledge that Cord had spoken as she rolled down her sleeves and stepped out into the hall. Cord strode along behind her, and as they descended the stairs, he spoke words that brought her up short, almost tripping as she spun around to stare at him.

"What did you say?"

"You heard me. I said that I've decided we'll get married today. Right after you've spoken to Stewart. I can see no reason to wait. This way we can get an early start to the ranch."

"You're crazy!" Jonty sat down on the step as her legs gave out beneath her. "That's only hours away."

"So? How long does it take a preacher to make us man and wife? Fifteen minutes, ten?" Cord sat down beside her. "You go see Stewart at his office, and I'll go round up a preacher. An hour from now, you'll be Mrs. McBain and Coty will have a legal father."

"I won't do it!" Jonty jumped to her feet. "I don't know what your big hurry is. Coty is over a year old, and I can't see what a day's difference is going to make."

It could make a lot, Cord thought darkly. What was to say that when she met the doctor tonight they wouldn't do the same thing he wanted to do—sneak off and marry on the sly.

He mentioned none of this as he stood up beside her. He said instead, "I can see that as usual you're gonna buck me at every turn." He continued down the stairs and headed for the kitchen. "I'll just get Coty and head for home."

Jonty's feet barely touched the floor as she sped after Cord. "All right," she panted. "We'll do as you say, you devil."

Jonty would never let herself remember those few minutes in John's office when she told him that she would be marrying Cord, and why. "If I don't marry him, John, he'll take Coty away from me. Uncle Jim can't help me now. And I couldn't bear losing my son. He is my whole life."

She had run from the room then, not looking back as John called after her.

She did remember occasionally her wedding, and the short time leading up to it. On her return from talking with John, she found a bewildered Reverend Parker waiting for her when she entered the kitchen by the back door, as well as Johnny Lightfoot, Tillie, and Nemia. Before turning her attention back to the preacher, she noted that Tillie wore a smile almost as bright as her silk dress.

"Jonty." Parker returned her greeting. "Have you given this sudden marriage a lot of thought? It was my understanding that you and the doctor were going to wed."

"She changed her mind, Reverend." Cord was

suddenly there, pushing in between them, his hand gripping Jonty's possessively. "It happens sometimes —love at first sight, you know." He smiled down at Jonty. "Go get yourself dressed, honey. Everyone else is ready."

Jonty noticed for the first time that Cord and Johnny wore suits and Nemia had donned a beautiful fringed shift. They all look so happy, she thought, and giggled hysterically inside, wondering why Janie wasn't here. She was Cord's biggest admirer.

Her shoulders slumped. They didn't know the hellish years that stretched ahead for Jonty Rand. The awful days of being tied to a man who had no regard for her.

"Hurry up, honey." Cord touched her arm. "We gotta get over to the church."

"Church?" Jonty blinked up at Cord. He wanted this sham ceremony performed in a house of God? No! Not in church. That would be sinful and she'd have no part of it. If this devil insisted on marriage it would be done here, in the kitchen, and in the clothes she stood up in.

She turned cold eyes on Cord and caused several gasps when she said firmly, "Let's make no pretense here, Cord. For you and me, the kitchen is fine—as are the clothes I'm wearing." She looked at the preacher and added, "Let's get on with it."

Disapproval was on everyone's face as the preacher sighed and motioned the couple forward, then directed Tillie and Lightfoot to stand beside them.

Suddenly, as he opened his much-used bible to the passage that would make the glowering man and stony-faced woman husband and wife, the last rays of the setting sun struck through the window and shone on the pair as if in benediction. Everyone's face lightened, as though they had decided that there was hope for these two people after all.

It was over then, and Cord was being told to kiss the bride. Jonty obediently raised her face and Cord's lips brushed gently across hers. At the touch of the firm softness of his mouth, a tingling started in her lower body and she quickly stepped away from her new husband and turned to smile weakly at the small audience.

Nemia shyly kissed her cheek, as did Lightfoot. Then Tillie was folding her in warm arms. "It's gonna be all right, honey," she whispered. "You'll see." She held Jonty away from her, and with her ribald sense of humor, winked and said, "I hope you're feelin' strong. He looks lean and hungry."

Jonty felt her face flushing. "He'll look that way for a long time if he's planning on me to feed his hunger."

"Jonty!" Tillie gave her a little shake. "I know you had a taste of him at least twice, and a man like that"—she sighed, rolling her eyes—"a woman could never get enough of."

Irritated with herself because Tillie had come too close to the truth, Jonty became a little coarse herself. "In case you haven't noticed, Tillie, there's more to a man than that—that appendage that hangs between his legs."

Tillie's rowdy laugh bubbled through her lips. "But, honey, that's the best part of a man."

Jonty jerked away from the teasing woman. "Not to me, it isn't."

The sense of elation Cord had been experiencing ever since the preacher's words made Jonty his seeped away as he overheard the exchange between her and Tillie. The old familiar feeling of helplessness came over him. He was a fool for thinking that Jonty could so readily put the past behind her and fall into his arms. She had Maggie's pride and would not let him come near her until she believed in him. And he would make her do that if it took him the rest of his life.

Coty toddled over to Cord and tugged at his pants leg. At least I've given my son his rightful name today, Cord thought, reaching down and picking the boy up.

I'll be able to see him grow, direct him in his young years.

Challenge grew in his gray eyes. He wasn't forgetting, either, how Jonty responded to his love-making. If he had to win her through the dictates of her body, he'd do it. And he could think of no more satisfying task.

Heat flushed through his body. Would it be possible to begin his wooing of her tonight? No, not here, he couldn't. Jonty would be concerned with LaTour, probably wouldn't even go to bed.

He set Coty on his feet and poured himself a drink from the bottle on the mantel. He stared thoughtfully into the flames of the fireplace a moment, then tossed the whiskey down his throat. What he was going to say to Jonty now would send her temper soaring.

Tillie and Jonty looked up when Cord approached them, Jonty looking wary as usual. "If you two are through gabbing," he said, "I'd like to get started for the ranch."

Jonty stared at him as though he had pulled a gun on her. "Are you out of your mind?" she finally exclaimed. "I can't leave here now. We don't know yet how serious Uncle Jim's wound is. Then there's the packing of my and Coty's clothes." She finally ran out of breath.

His voice cool and uncompromising, Cord said, "I checked on LaTour just before we got married. He's restin' easy and there's no sign of fever. I have a wagon waitin' at the livery that has a thick pile of hay to sleep on. It can't take you long to pack your clothes." Cord also ran out of breath.

"This is ridiculous!" Jonty stamped her foot. "There's no reason we can't wait until tomorrow morning to leave."

Although he didn't want to do it, Cord fell back on his old way of handling Jonty. His voice cold and belittling, he said, "You forget, Jonty, how early we get snow on the mountain. It might very well be snowing there now. You may not care, but I don't want my son caught out in a winter storm."

Jonty felt the sting of his voice and was made to feel foolish as she had in the past. Of course there was no argument against such reasoning. She swung on her heels and stamped into her room to prepare for the trip.

CHAPTER 28

APART FROM THE CREAK OF WAGON WHEELS, A STILLNESS hung over the plains; the air was clear and invigorating. An hour later everything was bathed in moonlight.

Jonty sat in front of the campfire Cord had built, Coty snuggled between her crossed knees. She looked up at the full moon and thought how relaxing it was out here after the noise and stench of Cottonwood.

A thoughtful sigh fluttered through her lips. She was thankful to get her son away from the saloon and the men who came there. Uncle Jim had given up on rebuilding a house on her ranch. Twice he had tried, but each time it had been burned down before completion. By whom, they weren't sure, but in their hearts both blamed the fat man, Paunch. Uncle Jim had men out looking for the man.

But what awaited her at Cord's ranch? she wondered. Tina was still there, and no doubt he would still carry on with her. She dropped her chin on Coty's curly head. She hoped that Cord would be discreet

with his affair with the Mexican girl. He had more or
less promised, but she didn't put much faith in his
words. She tried to assure herself that, if for no other
reason, respect for his son would lead him to use
prudence in his relationship with the girl.

Jonty gazed unseeing into the fire. What would be
her position at the ranch house now? Would Cord
expect her to take over the running of it, be the
mistress? Or would she be looked upon as a guest—an
unwelcome one, tolerated only because of Coty.

Or what if Cord expected her to take up her old
duties as a wrangler, leaving her son to the care of
Tina or Maria?

At the thought of Tina being in charge of Coty,
Jonty's arms tightened around the youngster so hard,
he gave a protesting cry. Never, ever, she thought
grimly. I will fight Cord all over that ranch before I'll
let that happen.

She jerked back to the present when Cord came out
of the darkness and dropped a grub sack beside the
fire. "You hungry, son?" He smiled at the chortling tot
who held out his arms, coaxing to be picked up. Cord
reached down and tossled the blond hair, whether or
not intentionally, letting the back of his hand brush
against Jonty's breast.

"I can't hold you now, sprout," he said. "Your dad
has to make supper."

Coty fussed a minute, then relaxed against Jonty.
And she, watching his father bustle around camp, was
in shock. Cord hadn't ordered her to prepare the food.
She caught her breath when he looked up and smiled
at her.

"The grub will be ready soon," he announced, his
wicked-looking Bowie knife slicing through a slab of
salt pork. "Are you hungry?" He laid the thin slices of
meat in a frying pan that was obviously new.

"A little," Jonty answered, not knowing quite how
to react to this smiling, charming man.

She remembered then a warning Granny had given
her once. "Jonty, men are always at their best when

they are trying to impress a woman. The only way you can protect yourself is to learn how to judge them. Is he honorable, or is he a scamp, out for only one thing?"

Well, Jonty thought, I don't have to wonder what this one has in mind. Twice he had seduced her into making love with him, but his soft words and inviting smiles wouldn't work on her again.

When Cord announced that the meat and beans were ready, Jonty busied herself with feeding Coty, answering in monosyllables as Cord sought a conversation between them. He finally gave up and they finished the meal in silence.

But as they sat drinking the rich, fragrant coffee, Cord's banked anger overflowed when Jonty innocently wondered out loud how Uncle Jim was faring. "I hope he's still free of fever."

"Dammit to hell!" he burst out, slamming down his cup, coffee splashing into the fire, "is that man all you ever think of? He's like a disease with you!" He rose to his feet and stood over her. "I don't want to hear you call him Uncle ever again! It's an insult to intelligent people. Women don't usually sleep with their uncles."

Jonty didn't yell back as she wanted to, to scream at him that he was insulting, that she had never slept with Jim LaTour, but Cord's loud tirade had frightened Coty and the little one was beginning to cry hysterically.

"You listen to me, you loud-mouthed jackass," she ground out through her teeth. "My son is not used to screaming and yelling, so you'd better learn to control that hellish temper around him. If you want to rant and rave, get out of hearing distance and yell your damned head off."

It was a silent, abashed father who watched the mother try to calm their son. When only hiccups escaped the small mouth, Jonty changed him, then without a backward look at the man who stood helplessly beside the fire, she climbed into the wagon and settled Coty between the blankets. He kept a close look on her she took off her shoes, then pulled her dress over her head.

She was just drifting off to sleep when the wagon shook with Cord's joining them. She started to rise, to order him out, when Coty's even breathing told her he had fallen asleep. She let her body relax. She would not have him upset again. Anyway, what could Cord do with the child lying between them? She closed her eyes and slept deeply all night.

The sun was well up when Cord gently shook Jonty awake the next morning. As she sat up and looked around in bewilderment, knowing that Cord always liked to get an early start at whatever he was about, he explained. "I figured Coty wasn't used to gettin' up while it was still dark outside."

Jonty could only stare at him, having never seen this softer side of her new husband before. She forgot for a moment how angry she'd been with him last night, and gave him a sleepy smile.

"He's not," she said, "and it was thoughtful of you to think of that and let him sleep."

"I'm not all rock-hard." Cord looked at her soberly. "I have my moments . . . especially for those I love."

Jonty lowered her lids, hiding the pain that jolted through her. He meant Tina, of course, and he wanted her to know it. Coty stirred and yawned, then smiled sweetly. "Hand him down to me," Cord said. "I've made him some oatmeal."

My goodness, you are full of surprises, Jonty thought before saying, "I'll have to change him first. I'm sure he's soaked. I've been trying to train him, but I haven't had much luck yet."

"When we get back to the ranch I'll give you a hand with it," Cord said, then grinned. "I'll take him in hand and show him how it's done."

Jonty felt her face beginning to burn and hurriedly started putting Coty into fresh clothing. That probably was how little boys learned not to wet their pants—watch how Daddy did it.

To her amazement, when she lifted Coty down to Cord, he carried the youngster over to the fire, then, holding him on his lap, began spooning the warm cereal into the hungry little mouth himself. She shook her head in wonder. This hard-faced man was going to make a fine father—far different from the kind of husband he'd make, that was for sure.

Jonty visited a clump of tall, thick brush, then walked back to camp and washed her face and hands in a basin of water Cord had warmed for her. As she used the new towel he had hung on the tail gate, a rueful smile touched her lips. There was a time, not too long ago, when this same man had made her wash up in cold water, usually in a river.

She reminded herself that Cord hadn't known her sex in those days, and hunkering down beside father and son, she filled a plate with salt pork and fried potatoes from a skillet that was fast losing its new look.

The morning meal was finished, but some twenty minutes later they were still sitting in front of a fire that was burning itself out. When are we going to break camp? Jonty wondered, as the sun rose higher and higher. She slid a glance at Cord, who continued to lean back against his saddle, sipping coffee and smoking a cigarette. At this rate, they'd have to spend another night out in the open.

But that would be all right with her, Jonty told herself, pouring another cup of coffee and sipping at it. She had missed the occasional sleeping under the stars. And it was quite nice, sitting here with Cord, no bitter words between them. It was almost as it had been a long time ago. Before she had found him in bed with Lucy that day.

They broke camp at last, although reluctantly on Cord's part, Jonty felt. He moved about it so slowly, not at all in his usual swift, sure movements.

Excitement began to build in Jonty as the wagon bumped along and she began seeing familiar landscapes. She had missed this beautiful country. After a while she turned to Cord and asked him about Jones and Red, and how the new wranglers were working out.

Cord answered that Red was as wild as ever, then told her of Jones's accident and that he'd be laid up for a while. As for the new riders, they were all good, dependable men when it was necessary for them to be so.

Jonty shivered suddenly, realizing that the closer they came to the mountain, the colder it was becoming. If Cord didn't whip up the team they would be camping out again, and this time it wouldn't be so enjoyable.

But Cord kept at a leisurely pace, and although Jonty felt they could still make it to the ranch by nightfall, he pulled the team into a stand of spruce and set the brakes while the sun was still a couple of hours high. She opened her mouth to protest, then remained silent. She had never won an argument with this stubborn man and she wasn't likely to now.

Again Cord made camp and prepared supper. Jonty had to admit that it was very cozy, the leaping flames of the fire warming the area where they sat eating their pork and beans. How nice it would be if this sense of well-being lasted after they reached the ranch.

A gray fog had descended when Cord announced they'd probably better retire to the wagon. "I think I'll add another blanket tonight. It's gettin' quite chilly." He pulled forth the extra one he'd folded beneath the wagon seat, along with the towels and Coty's small clothes. "This dampness can go right through a person."

Jonty climbed into the wagon and waited for Cord to hand Coty to her. "Get settled in first," he said, keeping the boy in his arms.

Jonty's eyes flashed. Did he think she was going to get undressed while he stood looking at her? "Then turn your head," she said stiffly.

Cord's gray eyes mocked her. "I've seen you in your petticoat before, Jonty. If you think back, you'll remember that I've seen you without it too."

"Enjoy the memory," Jonty flashed back, feeling her face flush, "because it won't happen again."

Cord's eyes said different as he turned his back to Jonty. Time would tell.

Jonty hurriedly slipped off her shoes and whipped her dress over her head. She did not trust him not to wheel around and watch her. But his back was still turned as she slipped between the blankets and called to him that she was ready for Coty.

Cord laid his sleeping son in Jonty's arms, his hands gentle as he tucked the extra blanket around them. He gazed at his wife's beautiful face a moment, then, fighting back the desire that leapt inside him, he walked around the wagon to his side. He removed his boots, shucked down to his underwear, then settled himself beside his son.

It was around midnight, Jonty thought by the position of the moon, when Cord shook her awake. "What is it?" she whispered, alarmed.

"Coty has wet the bed, and me along with it," he whispered back, his tone insulted.

Jonty knew she shouldn't laugh. It was unpleasant waking up and feeling a warm wetness seeping into your clothes. She, too, had experienced that a few times. But the thought of her small son having the audacity to pee on this big, proud, arrogant man was too much. Her giggles turned into soft peals of laughter.

"It's not funny, Jonty," Cord hissed. "What are you gonna do about it? I haven't got any other underwear either."

"Why should I do anything about it?" Amusement still lingered in Jonty's voice. "I'm not wet."

"Aw, come on, Jonty." Cord sat up as he pleaded. "You've got to think of something."

"Cord," Jonty spoke on a serious note. "I don't

know what to do about it. Do you have another blanket we could put over the wet spot?"

"No, dammit." Cord growled as Jonty watched him, biting her lips not to grin at his dilemma. Then Cord's face lightened. "I think I have a solution." He fumbled beneath the wagon seat again and in a moment he was smoothing out the thickness of two towels over the damp spot in the blanket.

As Jonty watched in the semi-darkness, Cord carefully lifted his sleeping son and laid him on the towels. "Now." He grinned, jerking his wet underwear off. "You scoot over beside him and I'll slide over to your side."

"What?" Jonty gasped, and before she could add to the single word, he was crowding in beside her.

"There now." He wiggled around, making himself comfortable. "Everybody's nice and dry."

Every nerve in Jonty's body was aware of Cord. His clean, masculine smell, the heat of his bare leg lying across her own. She tried to put some distance between them. She didn't want the sensations that were beginning to creep through her body.

Calling back the anger that was fast deserting her, she snapped crossly, "Do you have to lie so close? I feel like a sardine squashed between you two."

"I can't help it," Cord complained in a little-boy tone. "I'm smack up against the wagon now." There was a pause before he whispered, "Maybe if I lie on my side."

And before Jonty could protest, inform him that *she* would turn over on her side, he had put action to his words. Now, not only did she have the touch of his leg against her, she felt the pressure of his arousal against her hip. And though an answering hunger racked through her in waves, she said through clenched teeth, "Forget it, Cord."

"Forget what?" he asked innocently, raising up on an elbow and leaning over her, his fingers toying with the narrow strap of her petticoat.

"You know what," Jonty snapped, then gasped

when suddenly he had one breast bared and his lean brown fingers were closing over it. "Stop it, Cord." She tried to pull his hand away, knowing what would happen if she allowed those cunning hands to continue their mind-shattering movements.

"I can't, Jonty." Cord's lean, stormy face leaned over her.

She braced her hands against his chest, but their puny strength was as nothing as he lowered his head and settled his mouth on hers.

Jonty forced herself to lie quietly, passively, as Cord's lips moved coaxingly, hungrily over hers. Pride demanded that she at least make a token gesture of rejection. But all was lost when his lips trailed down her throat and settled over a puckered nipple. As his tongue laved it, stripped it through his teeth, all her defenses were shattered. She felt the violent beat of his heart against her arm and gave a little moan, her hands going to his head, pressing it closer to her breast.

He was taking her lips then, kissing her with ever-deepening passion. Long-repressed desire scorched through Jonty and her lips were as demanding as his.

"Ah, Jonty," he groaned. "It's been so long." His fingers stripped her single garment down to her waist, down past her hips, where she raised them high enough for him to slide the slip over her feet. He sat back on his heels and adored her body with his eyes. Since Coty's birth she was more beautiful than ever, more desirable.

Gently parting her legs, he stretched himself out on her. "I'm sorry, honey," he whispered, "but I've got to be inside you right now. It's been too, too long."

He groaned as she took him in her hand and eased him inside her. "Oh, God, you feel so good," he whispered. "So tight, so smooth."

Jonty raised her arms and wound them around his shoulders, her nails biting into his shoulders as his largeness filled her, stretched her. She whispered his name and he began a rhythmic thrust, his hard, long length sliding in and out, driving a little deeper with each thrust.

His pace was slow at first, then mounting passion made him lose control. Jonty felt the quickening of his body and a rush of desire sent her own body reaching for his and they moved feverishly together.

"Oh, Cord!" Jonty cried softly, and, his heart hammering, his body arching in spasm after spasm, Cord groaned her name as he plunged them both into physical fulfillment.

As their breathing returned to normal Jonty stroked Cord's sweaty head lying on her breasts. There had been such a feeling of rightness in the love-making they had just shared. Still, she thought as her hand paused in its caressing movement, the word love still hadn't passed between them.

When Cord began to suckle her breasts again, and his great size began to grow hard inside her, she could only pray that it was love that made him desire her so wildly. "For I am helpless against this," she whispered inwardly as once again he was moving against her, holding her hips steady so that she would feel the full force of his stroking manhood.

There was no sleep for Jonty as the night wore on, and only short intervals of rest as time and again Cord claimed her. He apologized once, saying, "I'm sorry, Jonty, but I just can't get enough of you."

When daylight broke and Coty stirred, Cord reluctantly released her. He gazed down at her face, then gently stroked the purple shadows under her eyes. "I've worn you out, haven't I?"

She nodded and smiled gently. "It's a nice tiredness, though." But later, as she tended Coty, she thought she had never felt so tired and battered in her life. She had love bruises all over her body, some in very embarrassing places. And her legs didn't seem to want to come together anymore.

But her husband, she noticed, moved around, full of energy, whistling, playing with Coty. Jonty's lips twisted ruefully. He could probably make love again at a moment's notice.

It was time to break camp then and begin the last leg of their journey. Cord placed his hands around Jonty's waist and settled her in the back of the wagon. "You're to sleep," He pulled the blankets up around her. "I'll keep Coty up front with me."

Jonty didn't argue, and was asleep almost before Cord finished tucking a blanket around her.

Jonty awakened to a cold wind blowing across her face. She lay a moment, wondering at the gray darkness looming overhead. Of course, she thought, sitting up. I'm in a wagon on my way to the ranch. And it looked as if the storm Cord had predicted was coming to pass. She rummaged in the bag that held her and Coty's clothes and pulled out a woolen shawl. She placed it over her head, tied it under her chin, buttoned up her jacket, and climbed over the seat to sit beside Cord.

He turned his head and smiled at her. "Looks like we're in for some rough weather. I'm thankful we're only a couple of miles from home."

"Here, let me have Coty." Jonty reached for the youngster clasped to his father's broad chest, a blanket shielding his face from the change in the weather.

Coty fussed a second, then snuggled up against her, falling back to sleep. Cord glanced down at his son, then grinned at Jonty. "He wet me again. Do you tell the little dickens to do that?"

Jonty grinned back. "No, I haven't, but it's not a bad idea. It would tell anyone who got within smelling distance of you that you're a father."

"Hah!" Cord snorted. "I've got a better way than smellin' like a pee-pot. I'll tell anyone who'll listen that this young man is Coty McBain, my son." He glanced again at his sleeping son. "Actually, that won't be necessary. One look at him and even a stranger would know he's mine," he said proudly. He put an arm around Jonty's shoulders and hugged her. "Thanks, Jonty, for a wonderful gift."

"Happy to oblige you, sir." She twinkled up at him. "Maybe later you'd be grateful for another such gift. Maybe one of the female gender."

"The sooner the better." Cord leaned forward and gave her a hard kiss on the lips. "If this storm wasn't practically upon us, I'd stop the team and get the little girl started."

Jonty smiled and leaned her head on his shoulder. "I wouldn't be surprised if she started last night."

The velocity of the wind rose as the wagon bumped and jolted along, Cord now cracking his whip, urging the team at a faster pace. His aim was to outride the storm, but the wind was steadily increasing in volume, and in no time the storm-blast was upon them. The air became a fleecy white curtain, swirling around them, stinging their faces like pellets of ice.

Jonty arranged the shawl around her face until only her eyes showed, then wrapped the blanket tight around Coty, covering his face completely. She couldn't see a foot ahead of her now, and she wondered how Cord was managing the reluctant team that fought to turn their tails to the wind. How tired his arms must be, and how could he see where he was going?

A burst of love and faith swept over her. He would get them through.

"We're almost there, honey." He patted Jonty's knee as he whipped up the horses.

"You look like a snowman." Jonty ran her eyes over Cord's face, his eyebrows and lashes heavy with snow.

"I feel like one too. I can't wait to get to Maria's warm kitchen and drink about a gallon of coffee."

Maria's kitchen? Jonty frowned. Why not her kitchen? The Perez family was no longer needed at the ranch. She was Cord's wife and quite capable of running a household. She would mention the fact to him tonight. After they had gone to bed.

She blinked when a picture of flashing black eyes and red lips swam before her. She had forgotten about Tina. What if Cord insisted the Mexican family stay on? Her arms tightened about Coty. That would mean only one thing. He had no plans to give up the daughter.

Jonty stared ahead. Cord would be put to the test tonight. Good or bad, she would have an answer. If it were negative, she would be left a shell of a woman.

"We're here!" Cord's voice was exuberant as he broke into Jonty's troubled musings.

Light spilled out of the kitchen window as Cord halted the tired team next to the back porch. Jonty stared at the dim outline of the house, remembering how unhappy she had been within its walls. Would it be different this time? God, she hoped so.

Unnoticed by Jonty or Cord, a female figure about to step upon the porch paused a second, then stepped back into the shadows. Hate glimmered in Tina's eyes as Cord hopped to the ground, then lifted his arms to a woman who held a baby clutched to her breast.

"So." The word hissed through her lips with the sibilance of a snake. "Mister Cord McBain has brought his own private woman back with him—with a child yet."

Tina's eyes narrowed and glittered at the tender way Cord lifted the gringa to the ground, the action showing the high esteem he felt for the woman. When he took her arm and guided her onto the porch, Tina put the first step of her revenge in motion.

As Cord took hold of the door knob, saying "Smell that chili, Jonty, I can't—" his sentence was cut short by a pair of arms thrown around his neck.

"Oh, Cord," Tina cried happily, "I'm so glad you're home. I've missed you so!"

"What the hell!" Cord staggered back at the impact of her weight. "Cut it out, Tina," he said brusquely, tearing her arms away when she attempted to pull his head down for a kiss.

Tina laughed, stepped away from him and teased, "Don't be so shy, Cord." She smiled up at him provocatively and murmured, "You'll lose your shyness later on tonight."

Cord gave her a puzzled, threatening look then turned his back on her. The bitch was up to mischief. He shot his wife a worried look. He could only see her profile, and it looked very stiff. With an inward sigh, he took her rigid arm and led her into the kitchen. If there weren't a blizzard raging outside, he'd send the Mexican bitch packing right now.

Maria turned from the stove, a long-handled spoon in her hand, a welcoming smile on her pleasant face. "Cord! I didn't hear you ride up, with all this wind howling." She turned to gaze at Jonty. "And you've brought company with you."

Jonty pushed the shawl off her head and Cord placed an arm around her waist. "Not company exactly, Maria," he said, then added proudly, "I want you to meet my wife." And while Maria and Tina gasped their surprise, he uncovered Coty's face. "I also want you to meet my son, Coty."

"Your wife, Cord?" The stunned housekeeper hadn't taken her eyes off Jonty. She studied the beautiful, smiling face, the curly hair the color of a raven's wing, tumbling about slender shoulders. Finally, she said, in some wonder, "My, my, doesn't she look like Jonty. Are you related to him, dear?"

Cord's deep laugh rumbled. "Don't you recognize her Maria? That *is* Jonty."

"No!" Maria fumbled for a chair and sat down.

"So much is clear now," she said at last, as though to herself. "It wasn't a weak little lad I felt sorry for, doin' all that hard work I knew he wasn't up to."

She turned angry eyes on Cord. "Why did you do that to her?"

"It's a long, long story, Maria," Cord said, his face a shamed red. He took the rousing Coty from Jonty.

"I'll explain it all to you another day. Right now, take a look at my son. Who do you think this fine-looking fellow takes after?"

Maria scanned the tiny features, which at the moment were squeezed into a scowl, the forerunner of a tantrum. She laughed. "He looks exactly like you when you're gettin' ready to cuss out one of the hands." She turned to her daughter. "Isn't he a handsome little fellow, Tina?"

Tina's gaze flicked briefly to Coty, a grimace of distaste twitching her lips. Then, ignoring her mother's question, she looked at Cord with feigned sympathy as she laid a hand on his arm. "Why didn't you wait until you could talk it over with me?" she asked softly. "Together we'd have come up with a solution better than marrying LaTour's cast-off."

Black rage smoldered in Cord's eyes. He pushed Coty into Jonty's arms. Female or not, he was going to rock Tina Perez's head.

Maria beat him to it. Following an angry burst of Spanish, she delivered her daughter a smack across the face that sent her stumbling against the table. "Why do you say such things?"

Tina shrank back as Maria lifted her hand again. But she didn't strike the girl. She took her arm instead and jerked her toward the door. "Get home. Your father will deal with you later." She slammed the door on the crying Tina, then looked embarrassed at Jonty. "I'm so sorry, Jonty. I don't know what came over her."

Jonty could have told the woman that jealousy had come over her daughter, black, raging jealousy. She waited for Cord to speak, to denounce Tina, to say he wanted her off the ranch immediately. When he said nothing, what little faith in him that remained died inside her.

Still numb, she allowed Cord to take her arm and lead her to her old bedroom. "We'll turn my room into a nursery for him," Cord said as she laid Coty down on his great-grandmother's bed. When she made no response, he looked at her pale face and thought how tired she must be.

"Look, honey, It's a couple of hours until supper. Why don't you and Coty take a nap in the meantime? I'm gonna walk over to the bunkhouse to see what's been goin' on while I was away, and to see how Jones is comin' along."

He lingered a moment, watching Jonty's still face, then dropping a kiss on top her head as she bent over Coty, he turned and quietly left the room.

Her mind a turmoil of emotions, Jonty put dry clothes on her son, set him on the floor, then walked over to the window that looked out onto the barn and stables. How could he be so unfeeling? she asked herself, gazing at the snow that still fell heavily. She knew he wasn't going to the bunkhouse. He was going to find Tina, to console her, to kiss away her tears.

She closed her eyes and shook her head. Why had Cord insisted on marrying her? It was clear he loved Tina. He hadn't tried to shut her up when she slashed his wife's face with her hateful words.

His wife. What a laugh. He no more thought of her as a wife than he did old Janie. But he would tolerate her presence, because she was necessary to him now, to tend Coty. He at least had sense enough where Tina was concerned to realize that she would neglect his son. When Coty was older, however, and able to take care of himself, his mother would be sent away.

Jonty's breath had steamed up the window and she listlessly began to clear it with a finger. Cord, on his way to the stables, glanced up at her window and thought that she was waving at him. He smiled widely and waved back, thinking that Jonty wasn't angry after all as he continued on.

He had gone but a few steps when he heard hurrying footsteps behind him. Before he could turn around, Tina was at his side, catching his hand and jerking it up until his arm lay across her shoulders. "Damn you, you bitch." He grated between his teeth, trying to pull free. "It won't work." He panted from his effort. "I've put Jonty wise to you. She didn't believe the little act you put on back there."

"Didn't she?" Tina smiled slyly, still clinging to his hand, keeping his arm around her shoulder. "We shall see." She followed him into the barn.

And to Jonty watching them, it looked very lover-like as they passed into the darkness of the stables. Oh, God, she thought, what more proof do I need? Cord can't even wait until nightfall to make love to Tina.

Coty tugged at her dress, his little face puckered, ready to cry. She picked him up and sat down on the edge of the bed. The little fellow was hungry, but could she bear to sit at the supper table with the lovers, knowing that just recently they had been in each other's arms? Could she pretend ignorance of the fact?

"I can, and I will," she whispered, staring grimly ahead. Not by look or action would either know of the empty feeling inside her. Cord had deceived her for the last time, torn her apart for the last time. And he was far off the mark if he thought he would ever share her bed. Tina would have to be sufficient for the randy tomcat.

She stood up, adjusted Coty to her hip, and with head held high, left her room, walked down the short hall, and entered the cozy, warm kitchen.

CHAPTER 29

THE DELICIOUS AROMA OF STEAMING FOOD ON THE LONG table hit mother and child. Jonty's mouth watered, and Coty began bouncing and kicking his short little legs. It had been short rations on the trip from Cottonwood, and they were both hungry.

Maria, her face flushed and slightly perspiring from the heat of the cookstove, smiled at Jonty's entrance and held out her hands to Coty. "Come on, little one," she coaxed, "your high chair is waitin' for you, right between your mama and papa."

Coty hung back a moment, not a child to readily make friends. Then, deciding that he liked this pleasant, smiling woman, he leaned toward her. As Maria placed him in the chair that had ridden all the way from Cottonwood, Jonty smiled a greeting at Carlo Perez, then glanced around the table. Only one other person sat there.

Her smile widened and she hurried over to sit down next to Jones. "How are you, Jones?" she asked, supressing a giggle. Her old friend's face was a study of profound bemusement. His eyes bulged and his prominent Adam's apple bobbled so fiercely, she thought it was ready to jump out of his throat.

Finally, he blurted out, "Cord said you had turned into a woman."

Jonty's laughter pealed out at the wrangler's choice of words. "And a wife and mother also," she managed to get out. "Meet my son, Coty."

It took Jones several moments to pull his gaze away from the most beautiful woman he'd ever seen. His mind raced with disturbing questions. Had he ever bathed naked in the river in front of her? Worse, had he ever relieved himself in front of her?

God, he bet he had. He mentally slapped his forehead. That was why no one had ever seen her take a leak. The men had joked about the *boy* bein' shy.

The bothersome thoughts of what this young woman must have seen during her time spent on the ranch made Jones look quickly away from her and begin to talk about Coty.

"He's sure a fine lookin' boy, Jonty. Cord could never deny that he's his son. He's a McBain through and through."

"With his father's temper too." Maria laughed as the child began pounding his spoon on the empty bowl before him, his small face pulled into an angry scowl that looked exactly like his father's when he was displeased about something. Jonty removed the spoon from the small waving fist and Maria took the bowl to the stove and filled it with soup from a steaming pot.

As Jonty spooned the vegetable mixture into the waiting eager little mouth, Maria gave a nervous look around the table. "I don't know what's keepin' Cord and Tina. Should we start without them, Jonty?"

Jonty delivered more soup to the small mouth that gaped open like that of a baby bird. Did Maria know what was going on between her boss and her daughter? Certainly Jones looked ill at ease.

"We might as well." She directed another filled spoon toward Coty. "They're probably so involved in something they've forgotten all about supper." Jonty hoped that she had kept the sarcasm out of her voice.

"Yes, I expect so," Maria said, taking a seat next to her husband. "Cord is probably checking the brood mares that are in foal, and Tina is most likely in the house pouting."

No one spoke as a platter of steaks was handed around, then a bowl of potatoes, followed by another of string beans. The silence continued as everyone ate, only Coty jabbering away now that his stomach was being filled.

Jonty couldn't have spoken to save her life. The anger she had known in her room couldn't compare with what burned inside her now. How dare Cord insult her like this in front of the hired help. Couldn't he at least make a pretense of a normal marriage? Was he so besotted with the Mexican girl that he didn't care about keeping up appearances?

The meal was halfway finished when Cord came hurrying into the kitchen, Tina close behind him. He gave the girl a startled look, then began apologizing for his lateness.

"Old Thadus cornered me, and he was so full of questions about Cottonwood and old Janie, I couldn't get away from him."

As he passed in back of Jonty's chair, he leaned over and kissed her cheek. It was all she could do not to slap him across his handsome, deceitful face. And when Tina slid into a chair across from her, a triumphant look on her face, it was almost impossible not to lunge across the table and grab a handful of black hair.

"What do you think of my boy, Jones?" Cord asked, filling his plate and digging in.

"He's a fine lookin' youngin', Cord," Jones said soberly, and to Jonty's ears there was a hint of warning in the foreman's next words. "I don't expect you'd ever want to lose him." She knew for a fact that Jones's eyes slid to Tina as he spoke.

If Cord caught any caution in the solemn words, he didn't show it as he answered, "I surely wouldn't. The little fellow is almost as precious to me as his mother is."

Jonty almost strangled on a mouthful of coffee. Who in the hell did he think he was fooling? Why, she could smell Tina's scent on him even as he spoke his lies.

A quick glance from the corner of her eye showed Cord smiling at her, waiting for her to make a loving response. She continued to sip her coffee as though she hadn't heard him. She sensed that he continued to watch her and could almost read his mind, guess the questions that were running through it. Had she seen him with Tina? Had she seen them enter the barn, and if so, how could he best convince her that nothing had happened between them, consequently enabling him to make love to her tonight?

She gave a startled jerk when Cord asked for a cup of coffee. Should she, as his wife, wait on him? Would it look strange to everyone if she didn't? If she wanted Cord to make a pretense of a normal marriage, shouldn't she also do the same?

It was an unnecessary question. Tina had already jumped to her feet and grabbed the coffee pot. Jonty watched the girl lean over Cord, her breasts brushing against his shoulders as her free hand gave one stroke to the back of his head. As the hot stream of coffee filled the cup, she wished she had the nerve to dash it into her husband's lap. That would cure his lust for a while.

Her lips curled scornfully when Cord frowned and sat forward, pretending an irritation she knew he didn't feel at Tina's action.

It was a lengthy meal, what with the three men discussing what had gone on at the ranch in Cord's absence. Jonty developed a throbbing headache, and Coty was tired and sleepy and was working up to one of his tantrums. The solitude of her room was a soothing thought.

She pushed back her chair and stood up. The others could talk all night if they wished, but she and Coty were going to bed. As she bent over to lift Coty from his chair, her eyes accidentally met Tina's. The mocking look on the pretty face sent red-hot anger rushing through Jonty's veins. You bitch, she thought, I'll wipe that look off your face.

She shifted her gaze to Maria, who had risen and was gathering up the dirty dishes. "Maria," she said, "having cooked this big meal all by yourself, you must be dead tired. Take your apron off and go home. Tina can do the washing and tidying up."

Maria straightened up, her surprised gaze moving to her spoiled daughter as the young woman cried, "But Mama, I have—"

"I'm sure an hour or two won't interfere with— with whatever it is you think more important than helping your mother," Jonty cut in tersely, expecting Cord to countermand her order any moment.

Maria nervously twisted her hands together, caught between the determination of her young mistress, and that of her sullen-faced daughter. She opened her mouth to say that she didn't mind cleaning the kitchen, but Jonty didn't let her get started.

"Go on, Maria. Go with your husband, sit before your fire, and relax together." Although she didn't say it, her tone conveyed the suggestion that the daughter too often came first with her housekeeper.

Evidently, Maria got the message, for her eyes widened a bit; then, smiling at Carlos, she removed her apron and handed it to a highly irate Tina. As her parents left, she sent a baleful look at Jonty. Sparks seemed to fly from her eyes when her new mistress smiled at her complacently.

As she lifted the fussing Coty from his chair, she glanced at Cord. How was he taking her ordering his beloved Tina around? His face was expressionless as he rolled a cigarette. Her eyes narrowed thoughtfully and she came to the conclusion that he had a good reason for keeping his mouth shut. One word in the girl's defense would play the dickens with his getting into bed with his wife tonight.

Coty's fussing turned into aggravated crying, so Jonty said a general good-night and left the kitchen. Inside her bedroom, she firmly bolted the door behind her. She smiled down at her son with caustic mirth as she prepared him for bed. "Isn't it a shame, Coty, that your daddy played it safe for nothing. He wasn't going to sleep with us anyway, huh?"

Coty was sleeping soundly and Jonty had just slipped her gown over her head when the door knob was turned. She held her breath, waiting for the soft knock that soon sounded on the door. Her mouth twisted with grim humor. "Knock ahead, Mister McBain," she whispered. "Knock until your knuckles bleed."

And that was precisely what Jonty thought was happening as the rapping became louder, a regular tattooing on the sturdy panel. And adding to the racket was Cord's thundering voice.

"Jonty! Are you deaf? Open this door!"

Jonty sighed. Coty was stirring, and his blasted father was going to awaken him. She would have to say something to the stubborn jackass, otherwise he'd knock all night. She moved to the door and whispered loudly, "What do you want?"

"What in the hell do you think I want? I want to go to bed." His voice grew soft and thick. "And I want to make love to my wife."

Jonty gritted her teeth, pushing back the wave of desire his honeyed words caused her to remember. But she couldn't have this happening all the time. She closed her eyes tightly. Some day, or night, he would find her resistance low and she would be lost to his powerful attraction. For even now, knowing that he had made love to Tina only hours ago, there was an ache fomenting inside her, screaming for satisfaction.

There was only one thing she could do. She must make him so angry with her that he wouldn't want to come near her. She closed her eyes, digging deep inside her for the courage to tell her lie.

"About our love-making on the trail, Cord," she began. "That was a mistake that won't happen again."

It grew deadly silent outside the door, only Cord's heavy breathing giving evidence that he was still there. Jonty swallowed and continued, "I'm not putting all the blame on you for breaking your promise that we were marrying only to give Coty his rightful name. You see, it had been a long time since I was with a man, and I got carried away."

Jonty had to bite her lips not to cry out at this last lie. She waited a moment, blinking back her tears, then put finish to there ever being a romantic interlude between them ever again.

"To me, Cord, it is wrong to sleep with a man you don't love. I'm sorry, but you won't be sharing my bed."

When Cord finally spoke, his voice was tight with fury. "Keep your love!" he thundered. "I never asked for it. But I'll tell you this, that hankerin' you've got for LaTour will shrivel up and die before you share his bed again. I'll kill the bastard before I'll let you shame me by goin' back to him."

Jonty leaned weakly against the door, tears streaming down her face as she listened to Cord stamp down the hall, then slam the kitchen door behind him. Her tears ran faster. He was going to Tina.

Jonty crawled into bed and, gathering her son in her arms, stared into the darkness as she faced some bleak facts. She was caught in a loveless marriage, and would most likely be trapped on this mountain for quite a few years. Cord would keep her here, not only to tend Coty, but to save face. It would not matter to him what Jonty Rand might want or need.

The next morning, as Jonty sat at the kitchen table teaching Coty how to handle his spoon, to bring the warm cereal to his mouth and not on his cheeks or ears, she heard Cord's bedroom door open.

Her heart started fluttering like that of a bird. He

hadn't spent the night with Tina—unless he had dared to bring the girl into the house. Her lips narrowed to a thin line. He had better not have. That she would not endure, and she had told him so.

When Cord walked into the kitchen she darted him a fast look from beneath lowered lids. From the looks of him, he hadn't spent the night in wild love-making. He looked as though he hadn't slept well. His rough-hewn features looked almost haggard, and there were dark circles under his eyes. He'd probably look more refreshed once he shaved off the blond stubble on his cheeks and chin, she decided.

In the strained silence that immediately filled the room, Cord, his face a cool, impassive mask, nodded a greeting to Maria, then sat down next to his son and ruffled the boy's curls.

"So." He smiled. "My son is a big fellow now. He can feed himself. What are you eatin' there, Coty?"

"Good!" Coty held a filled spoon toward his father's face.

Jonty ducked her head to hide her amusement at Cord's dubious look at the unappetizing lump of dripping mush. Would he take his son's unsavory-looking offer?

Cord did, but with his eyes shut. He even managed to smack his lips as though it was the finest food he'd ever tasted.

He loves his son at least, Jonty thought.

Cord looked away from Coty and smiled up at Maria as the housekeeper poured him a cup of coffee. "How many eggs do you want for breakfast, Cord?" she asked, then sent Jonty a beaming smile. "Your chickens have multiplied while you were gone. We now have fresh eggs every morning for breakfast, and fried chicken for supper every once in a while."

Jonty opened her mouth to say she was pleased to hear that, but Cord spoke ahead of her. "I'll only have coffee this morning, Maria. I'm not very hungry."

Maria gave him a surprised look. He usually had three eggs, steak, and potatoes. She smiled. Love did make one lose one's appetite. Jonty was only having coffee too.

"What about supper, then?" she asked Cord. "What should I cook?"

Cord drank the last of his coffee and stood up. "That's up to Mrs. McBain. She's in charge of the house now." And while Jonty gaped her amazement, Cord kissed the top of Coty's head, then left the room without a look or a word to his wife.

"So, Mrs. McBain." Maria's eyes sparkled teasingly. "What will we have for supper?"

It took Jonty a minute to pull her mind away from Cord's surprising remark and to concentrate on the housekeeper's amused question.

"I think a pork roast," she answered in the same bantering vein. "And stop calling me that Mrs. McBain nonsense."

Maria laughed. "A pork roast sounds real good, Jonty, but as you very well know, there's not a pig within a hundred miles of here."

"I know." Jonty stood up and carried Coty's empty bowl to the sink. "I just thought it sounded good, too. What about fried chicken? I can't remember when I had chicken last." She returned to the table, the coffee pot in her hand. She refilled her cup, then Maria's.

"What about stewed chicken?" Maria suggested as Jonty took the pot back to the stove and returned with a wet cloth to wipe Coty's face. "There's a rooster out there that I've been threatening to put in a pot for a long time. He's a mean one, always fightin' with the other roosters. He even took after me one day when I was feedin' them."

"Sounds good." Jonty sat down and gave Coty a spoon to play with. "Do you know how to make dumplings?"

"No." Maria shook her head. "I'm afraid I never learned how. Our people aren't much for them."

"That's all right, I'll make them," Jonty said, eager to work in a kitchen again. "Maybe I'll bake some pies too. Do we have any fruit?"

"Out in the barn are some apples, buried in the hay so they won't freeze. Red got hold of a whole bagful from somewhere."

"Good. I'll—"

Tina's jarring laugh cut Jonty off in mid-sentence, and she looked up at the Mexican girl. She hadn't heard her enter the room and didn't know from what direction she'd come. From Cord's room? she was wondering suspiciously as Tina gave her a smirking look and sat down at the table.

"I see you're giving Mama orders now," Tina remarked, her eyes following her mother as Maria rose to pick up the coffee pot, then poured a cup for her.

Jonty frowned at the older woman waiting on the younger one. Tina Perez was spoiled rotten. She gave the girl a level look and said coolly, "That's right. And you'll take orders from me too."

While Tina looked at her rebelliously, she added, "There's dust balls all over my room, and probably throughout the house. After you've finished breakfast, give the place a thorough cleaning. I like things neat and clean."

Tina's anger-sparking eyes flew to her mother for support. But Maria stood at the sink, keeping her back to the two women. Tina turned her enraged gaze back to Jonty. "Cord has never complained about the house. It satisfies him, so I don't see what business it is of yours."

Jonty's voice was acid as she answered in measured tones, "Cord is no longer in charge of the house, Miss Perez. It's me you're going to have to satisfy, and I'm far from being happy with the way things look around here."

Tina glared at her new boss a minute, then dropped her eyes, a sullen pout to her full lips. Jonty sipped her coffee, wishing the Perez family was a thousand miles away. Besides, they were no longer necessary here. She had done the cooking and housecleaning before and she could do it again.

But, she thought with an unhappy sigh, the snow by now had blocked the way out of the valley, so she would be stuck with them until the spring thaw. There was also Cord to consider. Would he allow her to get rid of them?

Jonty stood up and lifted Coty out of his chair and stood him on the floor. She gave Tina a threatening look. "Don't take your spleen out on my son by *accidentally* stepping on him."

Before the girl could make a response, Jonty left the kitchen and walked into the big front room. She hadn't been in this part of the house since her return.

She was met with a pleasant shock. In her absence, several pieces of furniture had been added, reminiscent of the pieces that had burned along with her cabin. Cord must have purchased them from the same man Uncle Jim had. The long couch was upholstered in the same long-wearing hop-sacking, only in a warm blue where hers had been a darker color. There was a small maplewood table with a pretty lamp placed on it. It hadn't been used, she noted, looking at the wick that bore no burned edges.

In fact, Jonty got the impression that the room hadn't been used since she was last there. That was strange. She'd have thought Cord and Tina would have spent all their evenings in here. It was such a pleasant room.

"I guess they spent their time in the bedroom," she muttered under her breath. As she knelt to strike a match under the carefully stacked kindling someone had laid out, she added making a fire here every morning to the list of Tina's duties. From now on, she would keep that one off her lazy ass. The bitch would be glad to leave here when spring arrived.

Jonty went back to the kitchen, picked Coty up, and retrieved a piece of dried mud from his mouth. Muttering that she would soon put a stop to mud being tracked into the house, she started for her room. Coty was soaking wet and needed to be changed.

She was wondering when Cord would start training

his son not to wet his pants when, just as she reached her bedroom, Tina came from Cord's. "I was just checking to see if I'd left any of my things in Cord's room," she said slyly.

Although Jonty inwardly flinched at the girl's words, she looked at her empty hands and managed to say calmly, "Evidently you didn't find anything."

"No." Tina smirked. "I guess Cord looked his room over carefully before leaving it." She edged past Jonty and swished her way toward the kitchen.

"Bitch!" Jonty hissed under her breath, and just before Tina disappeared at the end of the hall, she called after her, "Set a big pan of water on the stove to heat. I want you to scrub the kitchen floor before you do anything else. It's a disgrace. And I mean for you to do it, not your mother. She has enough to do. I'll inspect it after you've finished."

Jonty smiled gleefully as the kitchen erupted in a torrent of angry Spanish. "Lucky your mama doesn't understand the language, huh, Coty?" She smiled at her son.

The morning was cold and still as Cord led Rawhide out of the barn and swung into the saddle. It had stopped snowing last night around midnight, but the drifting clouds that obscured the mountain top promised it would snow again.

The stallion's great hooves made a muted crunching sound in the snow as Cord sent him up the mountain in search of game. To hunt deer was only an excuse for him to get off by himself, to think. For there was more than half a steer back at the ranch, hung high in a tree, out of reach of predators.

And now, alone, Cord let his face show his bitterness, his despondency, his total weariness. He gave a ragged sigh of resignation. He had been a fool to think that Jonty would ever forget or forgive his previous cruel and shabby treatment of her. She might have forgiven that, he thought, for he had thought her a male, but later, after he knew better, he had blundered on with his insults, accusing her of sleeping with the customers of Trail's End. He hadn't for a moment believed that when he threw it in her face. Pain and anger had made him say it.

A pinched look came to his mouth. He still had his doubts about the breed, though. There was a strong attraction between them. It was love on Jonty's part— but LaTour? He hadn't made his mind up yet just what kind of feelings the man had for her. They were strong, whatever they were.

Cord shook his head in self-contempt. His hopes had been so high after making love to Jonty on the way to the ranch. There had been no pretense in her response to him. She had held nothing back, had given herself completely. Never had he felt so thoroughly sated, so contented.

And her sweetness had lasted until that bitch, Tina, out of revenge, had thrown herself into his arms. But that shouldn't have affected Jonty. He had explained to her about Tina the morning after their first night of love-making. Hadn't she believed him when he swore that the Mexican girl meant nothing to him, that he had no desire to sleep with her?

No, he thought gloomily, it wasn't jealousy that had brought the coolness to Jonty's attitude, her refusal to sleep with him. It was the damn breed. She'd had time to think and remember the man, and that was when her resentment had grown for the one who had taken her away from him in forced marriage.

Cord swore savagely, silently. The warning he had given her last night still stood. He would kill LaTour before he'd see her return to the man.

A grimace of distaste for himself curved Cord's lips downward. He was still taking advantage of Jonty, treating her in a shabby way. He knew she would never leave her son. His broad shoulders sagged. He couldn't help it. Both Jonty and his son had too strong a hold on his heart. He could only hope that time would soften Jonty's feelings toward him, and that eventually she would forget the breed.

It was going to be a long, hard winter, he thought with a ragged sigh. It would be hell being forced into Jonty's company daily by the weather. Would he be able to keep his hands off her? Even now his loins ached with the need of her. How many times, he wondered, would he needlessly go hunting?

CHAPTER 30

THE FROZEN DAYS OF WINTER DRAGGED ON, KEEPING EVERY-
one housebound. Necessary chores were quickly tak-
en care of, then the warmth indoors just as quickly
sought.

It had snowed off and on all through January, and
now in mid-February it still stormed, only not so
often or so hard. Nor had there been any change in
Jonty's and Cord's relationship.

Jonty maintained a cool and aloof attitude around
Cord, hiding the hurt that was like a wound inside
her, one she was sure would never heal. And Cord's
face grew stonier with each passing day, as though the
long months of winter had hardened his heart and
soul.

When the coldness of her room forced Jonty into his
company, to share the warmth of the fireplace, his
demeanor was distant, coolly remote. They never
spoke to each other when alone, their only utterances
to the boy who chattered to both of them.

Their behavior with each other differed little when in the company of others, when they used only the barest minimum of words when forced into talking. Maria sent the couple many wondering looks, while Tina never missed a chance to send Jonty a mocking one. Jonty would grit her teeth, knowing that the girl was aware that Cord didn't sleep with her. Even if he hadn't told her, Tina made up his bed every morning. She'd know.

Jonty squirmed inwardly this early morning. How pleased that must make the little bitch feel. She didn't think that Tina came to Cord's bed anymore, for she had taken to leaving her door open in order to receive some heat from the fire that burned all night in the living room. Since Coty's birth, she was in the habit of sleeping lightly, should he cry in the night, and she would have heard the girl walk down the hall.

Her eyes took on a bleakness. That wasn't to say that the two didn't come together anymore. Every night, around the same time, Cord would rise from his chair, and without saying a word, leave the house. She wasn't positive about how long he was gone, for she made it her business to be in bed before he returned.

And that was what kept the taunting smile on Tina's lips, and the ache in her own heart. Her husband preferred another woman to his wife.

And yet, Jonty thought as she moved about the big room, dusting the furniture, she'd swear that sometimes she saw hate in Tina's eyes when she looked at Cord.

But that didn't make sense. She paused thoughtfully, the dust rag in her hand. It hadn't been hate on the girl's face that summer she hung all over Cord. Still, she was puzzled about Cord's attitude toward Tina. There seemed to be open dislike in his eyes when he looked at her.

Jonty resumed dusting, mocking herself silently. It was all a sham, a cover-up for their real feelings. "Oh, Tillie, I miss you," she whispered, dropping the cloth and going to stare out the window. "I'm so hungry for female talk, the comfort of crying on your shoulder."

It was difficult to have a friendly little chat with Maria over a cup of coffee. Tina was always there, her lips in their perpetual sneer whenever she was around. Jonty smiled wryly. She had to depend on Jones and old wind-bag Thadus for any adult conversation.

And strangely, she found them interesting to talk to. Both were full of stories to tell. But it wasn't female talk. She couldn't ask them how long was it going to take her to get over Cord. What she should do about Tina. Should she deny the girl entrance to the house?

Her hatred for the girl was growing daily. She was afraid that one day Tina would say something that would break her control, make her fly at the smirking face and scratch it to ribbons. She turned impatiently from the window, putting a stop to her uneasy reflections. She needed to get outside for a while, get some fresh air, get rid of this restless discontent.

She stamped on her boots, tied a scarf around her head, then shrugged into the fur-lined jacket that Lightfoot had given her on her eighteenth birthday, eons ago it seemed.

"Maria," she said as she entered the kitchen, pulling on her gloves, "I'm going for a short walk. Will you listen for Coty? He's taking his nap. I should be back before he wakes up, but you never know with that one."

"Of course, Jonty, you go right along." Maria smiled at her. "You need some fresh air. You've been looking peaky lately."

Jonty stepped outside, stood and breathed deep of the thin, pine-scented air. After a moment she stepped out onto the shoveled path to the stables. She slid open one side of the big double door and Beauty whinnied a welcome as she stepped inside.

"Hello, pretty girl," she crooned, scratching the sharply pointed ears. "You're missing our rides, too, aren't you?" She ran a hand over Beauty's rounded belly. "Are you getting fat, or did Rawhide get at you? You'd better be careful, little one, he's just like his master." She visited with the mare a few more minutes, then went back outside.

As Jonty bolted the door behind her, her eyes caught a movement on top of the small hill in back of the barn. She wondered what Cord and Red were doing up there until she saw that they were trying to pull a young colt out of a snowdrift.

The young horse was frightened and fought the two men with all his strength. Finally, he pulled Red off his feet, and as he tossed the wrangler around like the arms of a windmill, Jonty burst out laughing, and called loudly, "Ride 'em, cowboy!"

Startled, and caught off balance at her call, Cord spun around, slipped, tried to catch himself, failed, and tumbled awkwardly down the hill, scrambling and cursing and landing finally within a foot of Jonty.

She stared down at him, trying to restrain her mirth. His body was completely covered with snow, and he resembled a huge snowman, sprawled out on its back.

"Jonty," Cord growled warningly, a curious huskiness in his voice, "don't you dare laugh."

Jonty bit her lips, her tongue, but to no avail. "I can't help it," she choked out, and throwing her head back, her throaty laughter pealed out, making the mountain ring with its sound.

Her hilarity was short-lived. Lean fingers grabbed her ankle and jerked. Before she knew it, she was on her back and Cord was leaning over her. The wind knocked out of her, she stared up at him helplessly.

"Cord," she began, then his face was coming toward her, fierce with desire and longing. His mouth took possession of hers, and it was as if it fed an already raging hunger, a physical starvation. Against her will, her senses leapt wildly in response. Her arms had started to go around his broad shoulders when he broke off the kiss.

His eyes full of tenderness as he gazed down at her, he groaned, "God, Jonty, let's not fight anymore. It's drivin' me crazy the way you ignore me."

When indecision filmed Jonty's eyes, he hurried to add, "I'm not askin' you to sleep with me, Jonty, if you don't want to. Just talk to me. I'm god-awful lonesome for you."

"I don't know, Cord." Jonty absently brushed the snow out of his hair. "Tina is always—"

"Jonty, don't start that again," Cord interrupted impatiently. "I told you the girl means nothing to me, never has, never will."

There flashed before Jonty all the things the Mexican girl had said to her, the flagrant admittance that she and Cord were lovers, the embraces she had seen them share, his disappearance from the house each evening.

Cord had to be lying. She shut her eyes, the thought a sad one. More than anything in the world, she wished that he wasn't. Still, her nerves were being stretched tight with the coldness between them. If they were at least on speaking terms, it would make the long evenings seem shorter. It would also be better for Coty to see his mother and father talking to each other.

She would give Cord a chance, she decided. But if she caught him in one more lie, her trust and faith in him would be utterly ruined for all time.

She opened her eyes to Cord's anxiously waiting face. "All right." she said, "I'm willing to try—being civil to each other, I mean."

Cord laughed softly with a sigh of relief. "You'll never regret it, Jonty, I swear it to you," he said sincerely. He gave her another short, hard kiss, then jumped to his feet, reaching down a hand to help her up.

As Jonty stood beside Cord, she saw Tina leaning against the corral. The malignant look she received from the flashing black eyes made her shiver.

"I'll bet you're freezing." Cord put an arm around her shoulders, pressing her close to his side. "Let's get you inside and warm you up."

Surprisingly, he didn't even glance at Tina, who stood staring daggers at him.

The rest of February moved smoothly in the ranch house following Jonty and Cord's agreement that there would be no more cold silences between them. They shared breakfast now with their son, whose vocabulary was growing daily. Maria was teaching him Spanish, and maybe because of this new language, he swore less.

Cord had laughingly said that the little dickens probably thought he was saying naughty words in the new language.

The only thing that marred Jonty's content was the threatening presence of Tina always hovering in the background. She used the word threatening because that described the looks the girl shot Cord everytime he ordered her to fill their coffee cups, especially if it was for his wife.

The evenings were also pleasant now—first, because Tina wasn't there, but mainly because the heat of the fire was shared in harmony. Their stockinged feet stretched out to the fire, Jonty and Cord would talk—mostly Cord, telling of his youth, the death of his father in the war, the different jobs he'd had before finding the fascination of chasing wild mustangs.

There were other times when few words passed between them, but it was a comforting time, a warm, companionable time. Nervousness only gripped Jonty when she stood up and said good-night. A wistfulness, a pleading, would gaze at her from smoky gray eyes.

But she was still leery of this new Cord. It would take more than just a few weeks for her to have faith in him again. He had hurt her too cruelly, too many times. Her wounds were nearly healed, but not quite.

Once while they were talking, Cord, in his fashion

by tone as much as by words, let her know how sorry he was for his earlier treatment of her.

"You're old for your age, Jonty," he said in his normal voice after she had expressed an opinion of why some people were the way they were.

She had shrugged and smiled. "Uncle Jim reckons that a woman matures early because of the harsh events in her life."

Cord was silent a long time before he said in a remorseful and strained voice, "God knows you've suffered a lot in your short life."

Jonty continued to stare into the fire, not daring to look at Cord. She knew she would see the guilt in his eyes, the asking for forgiveness, the hunger. And she would weaken. It was getting harder and harder not to respond to him. Every time she walked into a room his eyes traveled over her with open desire. He was slowly chiseling away at her heart and mind.

A cold March spring finally arrived. Cord no longer spent his days in the house, but was out with his men breaking and branding horses, preparing for another drive to Cottonwood. Jonty wished that she could go with him. She missed Uncle Jim and Tillie dreadfully, and she was anxious to know how Uncle Jim was mending.

She also missed Cord's presence in the house, as did Coty. A dozen times a day she listened to the same refrain. "Where daddy? When daddy comin' home?" Then, tearfully, "I want mine daddy."

And aggravatingly, Tina had started dropping her innuendos again. "Look, Tina," she said one morning when the girl hinted that she had been with Cord the night before, "I don't know why you make up those lies, but you're wasting your time telling them. We both know that you were not with Cord last night."

A craftiness shone in Tina's eyes. "Are you trying to tell me that he was with you—slept with you?"

Jonty sucked in an angry breath, knowing that Tina

had just made up Cord's bed. Well, she could tell lies too. She stuck her chin in the air and said coolly, "If it's any of your business, yes, I did sleep with my husband . . . most of the night." Before Tina could respond, she added, "The kitchen floor needs scrubbing. Get to it." She slammed the door in the spluttering girl's face.

"Why do I let that bitch bother me?" Jonty asked herself later that night as she prepared a fussing Coty for bed. "I'm almost positive that Cord no longer has anything to do with her, and I'm beginning to wonder if there ever was anything serious between them. On his part, at any rate."

Coty's fussing turned into yowls as she pulled a little nightshirt over his head. He no longer needed a diaper. His father had finally showed him how it was done.

"I no go bed til daddy come home!" he yelled at the top of his voice, his angry little face beet red.

"Coty," Jonty tried to reason calmly, "Daddy may not be home for hours. He's out with the wranglers tending to the horses. You'll see him in the morning."

"No, no, no!" Coty threw himself on the bed and beat the mattress with his tiny fists.

"What's wrong with my boy?" Cord stood in the doorway, exhausted looking but with a wide smile on his face.

"He's having a McBain temper tantrum, that's what's wrong with him," Jonty snapped. "I'm tempted to whack his little bottom."

Coty's crying stopped immediately when he heard Cord's voice, and a watery smile wreathed his baby lips as he held out his hands. Cord picked him up, and as the curly head nestled itself on his shoulder, Cord said softly, "I promise this won't happen again, son. We'll have our time together every night."

Coty put his arms around the thick, muscular throat, gave the whisker-rough cheek a kiss, then yawned widely. Five minutes after Cord laid him on his little bed, he was sound asleep.

"I expect you're hungry," Jonty whispered.

"Starved," Cord whispered back and followed her to the kitchen.

Jonty drank coffee while Cord wolfed down thick slices of beef roast and potatoes. When his plate was polished clean, she rose and brought him a large piece of apple pie and refilled his coffee cup.

"I missed your pies while you were gone, Jonty." Cord picked up his fork and cut into the flaky pastry. "Actually, I missed all those dishes you used to cook up."

"You know, Cord." Jonty put down her cup and sat forward, "I've been thinking that there's no reason to keep the Perez family on. You know that I'm quite capable of taking care of the house and cooking. I did it before."

An uncomfortable red washed over Cord's face. "I know you did, Jonty, that and much more. That's why I want you to take it easy now, just take care of my son."

Jonty sat back, the suspicions that always lingered just back of her mind coming to the front. Was he speaking honestly? Or had the growing conviction inside her that nothing existed between him and Tina been wrong?

"Look, Cord," she said sharply, "if that's the real reason you're keeping the Perezes here, put it out of your mind. I don't like taking it easy. I have always worked, and that is how I like it." She paused, then, "And I don't want them here any longer."

The slashed grooves alongside Cord's mouth deepened in a grin. "I didn't know you felt that strongly about it, honey," he said. "I'll send them back to Cottonwood as soon as the pass thaws out."

Cord finished his coffee and stood up, then stretched his sore muscles. "I'm dead beat." He yawned. "Would you mind if I went straight to bed?"

"Of course not." Jonty rose too. "It's late anyhow. I'll just clear the table, then go to bed myself."

She started to walk around the table as Cord headed

for the door. Their head-on clash couldn't be avoided.
Cord's hands went out automatically to steady Jonty.

"Oops, sorry," Jonty smiled up at him. "I should
have watched where I was going."

She waited for him to release her arms, but his
fingers only tightened. She tilted her head to look at
him and the eyes that gazed back at her were slumberous with desire.

"Cord," she warned, pressing her hands against his
chest, feeling the beat of his racing heart. As though he
hadn't heard her, couldn't help himself, he pulled her
into his arms, melding the length of her body against
his. With one strong arm firmly across her back, he
moved a hand down to her small rear and pulled her
into the warmth of his spread legs.

A tingling shot up her spine when his hard arousal
throbbed against her stomach. "No, Cord." She began
to struggle, to get out of the embrace that was turning
her blood to molten fire.

"Just a kiss, Jonty," he begged huskily. "Just one
kiss."

His lips came down on hers then, possessively,
gently sweet, teasing them open, impelling her to
respond. She moved her head back and forth to escape
the raw hunger, but Cord moved with her, drawing
hungrily on her mouth. Before she was aware of it, she
was weak and shaky with her own desire, and she was
clinging to his hard body, her lips as fiery as his.

Then his hand found her breast, and the shattering
effect it had on her feelings brought her back to the
real world. *I'm not ready for this yet*, she wailed
inwardly, *I'm still not sure of him.*

With a hard twist of her head, Jonty tore her lips
away from the insistent ones and, taking Cord by
surprise, managed to wrench her body out of his arms.
Panting slightly, she put the table between them as she
said, "I'm sorry, Cord, but I need more time. I won't
be rushed off my feet this time by your love-making. I
will never again listen to the dictates of my heart
instead of my head."

"Dammit, Jonty!" Cord glared at her. "What more do you expect? The past few weeks have proved that we enjoy each other's company. We're fine in bed together, and we have the common bond of a son between us." He reached across the table and stroked her flushed cheek. "I expect makin' love to you is the nearest I'll ever come to heaven."

Oh, Cord, Jonty thought sadly, looking into the gray eyes, where desire still lingered. You've said everything but what I most want to hear. Can't you say that you love me, even though you'd be lying?

She was saved a response to Cord's arguments by a knock on the door. Startled, they both swung around, Cord swearing under his breath. "Who in the hell is that at this time of night?" He strode to the door and whipped it open.

"I'm sorry to bother you, Cord." Jones stood on the porch looking anxious. "But one of the mares is deliverin' her foal, and she's in trouble."

Jonty didn't linger to hear what Cord would answer, but took the opportunity to flee to her room. Cord could be very persuasive when he wanted to, and her body still ached for the relief his promised. There would be no contest between them if he should get her in his arms again.

Bolting the door behind her, the first time for quite awhile, Jonty disrobed, pulled on a gown, and crawled into bed. She heard the kitchen door close, then all was quiet. Cord had gone to the barn with Jones.

And he's so tired, she thought compassionately.

As she lay staring at the ceiling, her compassion grew for the man whose aloofness, hardness, said that he needed no man's help, that he was all powerful in all ways.

Gradually, as Jonty thought back, honestly and unemotionally, pulling forth in her mind every run-in they'd ever had, emotional or physical, she realized that Cord McBain wasn't all rock-hard. There was a great tenderness beneath that hard, rough exterior. The gentleness in the way he handled his son, the

softness in his voice when he talked to him were
obvious signs. And although when he made love to
her, he was possessive and sometimes ruthless, always
he was caring and gentle.

Jonty lay a long time in the darkness, thrashing out
the pros and cons of a life with Cord McBain. She
finally came to a decision. It would be a cold, empty
life without him in it. If there had ever been anything
between him and Tina, she firmly believed it was over.
He had made no fuss about the Perezes leaving when
the weather permitted.

She tried to stay awake, waiting for Cord to return.
She had made up her mind to go to him tonight, to
start their real marriage.

The next thing Jonty knew, the morning sun was
shining in her face. She smiled wryly. She had fallen
asleep as she waited for Cord.

She glanced at Coty, who was sleeping soundly, and
should do for at least another hour. She slid quietly
out of bed. Wouldn't Cord be surprised when he
awakened to find her lying beside him. It would be
better this morning than it would have been last night.
After a night's rest, her husband would have more
stamina.

She giggled softly. He would need all the strength he
could dredge up, for she had a need for that magnificent body that would be a long time in sating.

She slipped down the hall, her bare feet making no
noise. She stood in front of Cord's bedroom door,
surprised that it was closed. He never closed it. What
if he was no longer interested in her? Maybe he was
tired of chasing her, had decided he didn't need her
after all.

Her suddenly sweaty hands closed over the door
knob. No, I don't believe that, she thought, and
pushed open the door.

What Jonty saw brought a pain to her chest so sharp
it stilled the breath in her lungs. Cord lay on the bed,
sleeping soundly, Tina snuggled up beside him.

She never knew what propelled her into the room, pushed her to stand beside the bed. It was as though she had left her body, no longer had any power over it—not even over her tongue when Cord mumbled something, then turned on his side and gathered Tina in his arms.

She watched, paralyzed, as his mouth covered the Mexican girl's.

She was swaying on her feet when suddenly Cord jerked up his head, bleary confusion in his eyes. What happened next, happened all at once. Tina sought to pull his head back to her, and he saw Jonty, standing white-faced, loathing staring out of her eyes, in the doorway.

"You Mexican bitch!" he yelled, giving Tina a shove and tumbling her onto the floor. He scrambled out of the tumbled bedclothes and hurried after Jonty, who had wheeled and run sobbing down the hall. She slammed and locked the door on Cord's anxious voice and Tina's shrill, triumphant laughter.

Jonty paid no attention to the hammering on her door, nor to Cord's alternate pleading and threatening. Especially, she closed her ears to his explanations. She had heard them all before. Her mind was open only to her present plans. To get away from Cord McBain. To never be hurt by him again.

She glanced at her son, whose father's racket had awakened. It would break her heart to leave him, if only for a short time. But he was too young, and the early spring weather too cold, to take him on the long ride to Cottonwood. But he would remain here only until the weather warmed and Uncle Jim was well enough to come back here with her to make sure Cord allowed her to take him away.

Jonty took clean clothes from Coty's drawer, had him use the little chamber pot, then dressed him, only vaguely listening to his childish chatter. She sat him on the floor, and breaking a strict rule of no playing with his wooden blocks before breakfast, placed the

box beside him. The two of them would eat after she
was sure Cord was well away from the house.

She started choosing what few clothes she would
need to take with her, carefully opening and closing
the drawers. Cord must get no inkling that she was
leaving him. She wouldn't even tell Maria, she decided. That good woman would try to talk her out of
it, and certainly she would get word to Cord as soon as
possible. His big stallion would soon overtake her
little mare.

"No," she muttered, "I'll just leave, let everyone
think I'm going for a ride. I can be almost to Cottonwood before Cord comes home for supper."

She smiled mirthlessly. Even then, it wouldn't
occur to him that she had gone off and left Coty. He
was sure that her son was the key that would keep her
here.

Cord made one last attempt to talk to Jonty. There
was a moment when she softened toward him a little,
toward the soft pleading in his voice, the sincerity.
Then the next minute he was swearing, "To hell with
you. I don't give a damn whether you believe me or
not."

Jonty felt relief at Cord's anger. That she could
fight. It was his softer side that was usually her
undoing. It tore her up, though, when Coty, hearing
his father's voice, wanted to go to him. Big fat tears
rolled down his baby cheeks as he cried, "I want
daddy. Eat mine breakress with daddy."

Finally, she distracted the child by letting him play
with her box of shiny, many-colored beads, saved
from her days of playing poker.

A soft sigh escaped her as Coty's little fingers dived
into the velvet-lined box. She wasn't looking forward
to dealing cards again.

An hour passed before Jonty saw Cord ride away
with Jones, headed up the mountain to the horse
canyon. She took her bundle of rolled-up clothes,
shoved them into a pillow case, eased open the

window, and tossed them outside. She'd pick them up on her way out.

She managed to stay calm, show her everyday face as she shared breakfast with Coty, wondering where Tina had taken herself off to. It was just as well the girl hadn't put in an appearance, for she doubted she could keep her hands off the bitch.

When finally Coty's large appetite was sated, Jonty wiped his face and stood him on the floor, then casually said, "I think I'll go for a ride, Maria, if you don't mind keeping an eye on Coty for a while."

"Not at all, Jonty." Maria readily agreed. "Me and Coty get along fine, don't we, little man?" She ruffled the blonde curls.

Ten minutes later, Jonty returned to the kitchen, booted, her fur-lined jacket on, a black stetson pulled low on her forehead. She swept her son up in her arms, choking back her tears as she hugged the little body. Through blurred eyes, then, she left the kitchen and made her way to the barn.

She was cinching Beauty's belly strap when old Thadus spoke at her elbow. "You ain't goin' ridin', be you, Jonty?"

"I thought I would." Jonty kept her face from him. The old man's eyes were still keen and he wouldn't miss the evidence of her tears.

"It's not a good idy, Jonty. See them dark clouds hangin' over the mountain? There's a snow squall brewin'. Looks like a bad one."

"Don't worry about it, Thadus. I won't be caught in it," Jonty said, pulling on her gloves and vaulting into the saddle. If a squall should hit, she'd be well out of its reach.

"Where you be ridin' to?" Thadus looked at her worriedly.

"Oh, up the mountain somewhere," Jonty lied. She pretended to fuss with her stirrups, getting her feet into them, until the old man turned and went back into the barn, shaking his white head. As soon as he closed the door she headed Beauty toward the back of the house. She leaned down and swept up her bundle of clothes as she passed by the window.

Jonty reached the valley, keeping the mare at a walk. The snow had melted considerably, but there was still several inches on the ground, and sometimes it was quite slippery. It would be this way for miles until she rode farther south.

She had been riding a couple of hours when Beauty slipped on a piece of ice and went lame. Jonty slid from the saddle and examined the projection just above the back of the right rear hoof. It was swelling rapidly.

"Damn!" She looked back over her shoulder with troubled eyes. What should she do now? It would be cruel to make the mare carry her weight. Besides, she doubted the little mount could make it to Cottonwood unburdened. And certainly she couldn't walk that distance.

And on top of everything else, the clouds old Thadus had pointed out to her were becoming blacker and blacker. If the rising wind meant anything, the squall would arrive at any minute, could already have arrived on the mountain.

Wanting to cry, and swearing at the fates that always seemed against her, Jonty turned the little mare around and headed back toward the mountain and the ranch.

It was imperative she get home before Cord. She would never be able to slip away again if he found out about her attempt today.

The thought was but a moment old when the snow came with a howl, hard, whirling flakes that stung her face and eyes.

Half an hour later, the squall died as quickly as it had sprung up, leaving everything threateningly quiet. Something drew her gaze north. A black dot moved across the snow, rapidly becoming larger at its approach. Her heart gave a lurching beat. Wolf pack! As it drew nearer and nearer, she could hear its steady drumming.

Beauty caught the animals' scent and began rearing, whistling her terror. Convulsed with her own terror, Jonty opened her mouth and loudly called Cord's name before folding mindlessly to the ground.

CHAPTER 31

THE MORNING MIST HAD MELTED WITH THE RISING SUN AS Jim LaTour and Johnny Lightfoot rode along. The Indian sent the breed a sidewise look. "She might not want to come back with you, Jim. Maybe she and McBain have patched up their differences and are gettin' along fine."

"You're loco, cousin. I'd bet my last dollar that long-legged McBain forced Jonty into marryin' him, just so he could get hold of Coty. If I hadn't been flat on my back and half out of my mind, she'd have never married him."

"Maybe." Lightfoot's stoic expression didn't change. "He's got a deep feelin' for Jonty, regardless of how he acts. And she returns it. But it's so stormy between them, so many misunderstandings—like McBain carrin' on with that Mexican girl, which I think he does just to rile Jonty."

A smile twitched Lightfoot's lips. "Your daughter is just like you, Jim. Proud as an old timber wolf. If McBain hasn't been behavin', you can bet she'll come back with you. But if he's walkin' straight, she'll stay with him."

"If I find Jonty happy and content, I won't even mention her comin' back with me. But by God, if I see that same pain in her eyes I'll take her off that mountain so fast, McBain will miss it if he blinks."

"Well, I just hope he's not around if you do," Lightfoot said as the mounts were lifted into a lope, Wolf at their heels.

The two men stopped beside a stream around noon, letting the horses drink while they chewed on pieces of beef jerky. "Looks like it's snowin' up on the mountain." Lightfoot gazed at the distant peaks over which lay a white mist.

"Probably a squall," LaTour answered. "Won't last long."

A quarter mile away, a lone rider pulled his mount in also, a rider who had followed LaTour and Lightfoot from the time they left Cottonwood. He swung his obese body from the saddle and, hunkering down beside the horse, took a piece of jerky from his coat pocket. Biting off a piece from the strip of dried meat, he chewed, his hate-filled eyes on the distant two men.

"I'll get you this time, breed," he muttered, "and that bastard McBain at the same time."

When Lightfoot and LaTour climbed back in the saddle and led off, Paunch did the same.

A couple of hours later LaTour's and Lightfoot's mounts were treading through snow. "You were right, Jim, a squall did sweep through here," Lightfoot said. "And look, there's hoof and boot prints."

"Yeah." Jim slowed his mount to more closely scrutinize the tracks. "The horse is limpin'. See how the right rear hoof hasn't cut the snow as deeply as the others."

Lightfoot grinned at the idea of his cousin telling him about reading sign. "From the size of the boot tracks it's a youngster who's leadin' him."

Both men stared against the setting sun when, from a distance the yowling of running wolves carried on the air. "Them yowlin' bastards give me the shivers," LaTour said. "Always have."

"The wolf is lord out here, Jim." Lightfoot grinned. "You should know that by now. Look over there to your right. You can see them. They're runnin' prey."

LaTour spotted the bunched group and frowned. "You don't suppose they're after that kid and his horse, do you?"

"Could be." Lightfoot kicked his mount into a hard gallop. "We'd better find out."

In only minutes they saw the horse struggling to get away from the slight figure who fought to hold it still. The wolves were only yards away, bearing swiftly down on the pair.

A cold chill went down LaTour's spine when he recognized the terrified voice that called out to Cord McBain. Johnny Lightfoot also recognized the voice, and with guns shooting into the air, they sent their mounts thundering toward the figure now crumpled in the snow.

LaTour was off his stallion before it came to a full stop. As he ran to Jonty, the Indian began to shoot into the pack, yelling to Wolf to stay back. The air was filled with yips and painful yelps. In seconds, the pack was disappearing down the valley, leaving behind four dead companions.

"She's fainted." LaTour shoved at Wolf, who sniffed eagerly at Jonty's face. "I'm gonna rush her to the ranch. You bring Beauty in."

He swung into the saddle and Lightfoot handed Jonty up to him. "I'll damn well find out what she was doin' out here alone, and why there's gear tied to her saddle. Somethin' tells me she was on her way to Cottonwood and that it had to be somethin' bad to make her go off and leave Coty."

The advancing twilight was still and cold, black in the shadows, as Cord sat in the saddle, his head cocked, listening. Then, although he was hoarse from calling Jonty's name, he loudly called it again, desperation in his voice.

The only sound that came back to him was a coyote's bark, answered by another.

His shoulders drooped a little lower. Evidently his men, who were scouring the mountain also, were having no better luck. There had been no gunshots, a prearranged plan should anyone find Jonty.

He looked up at the glimmer of sunshine that was fast growing dim. His hopes of finding his wife, already very low, slipped farther in the thickening darkness.

He wearily and reluctantly turned the stallion's head homeward. If he waited much longer, he wouldn't be able to find his way down the mountain. He could only hope and pray that she was all right, that she had heard him calling but, to punish him, had refused to answer.

"Damn Jonty's stubborn pride," Cord muttered. "Couldn't she have given me a chance to explain everything? That I was dreamin' I was kissin' her?"

Tina's action that morning had finally made him realize just how dangerous a woman scorned could be. He knew now the girl hated him, and was out for revenge. God knew how many lies she had told Jonty.

Well, Miss Tina Perez wouldn't cause any more trouble between him and Jonty. Cord's lips firmed grimly. He had told her flatly to stay in her parents' house until he could return them to Cottonwood. And God help her if she didn't heed his order.

Full darkness had fallen, and there was a glimmer of light shining from the kitchen when Cord rode out of the fringe of spruce back of the house. He could hear his men riding in from all directions.

He was about to ride on to the stables when he spotted the mount tied to the hitching post alongside the porch. His heart lurched hopefully, for reasons he didn't know, and he was off Rawhide's back and onto the porch in one leap.

Maria met him at the door, her face beaming. "Jonty's back, Cord!" she exclaimed. "Mr. LaTour found her."

"LaTour found her?" Cord looked stunned. "Where?"

Maria dropped her eyes and nervously twisted the material of her apron. "I guess Jonty was runnin' away, goin' back to Cottonwood. But Beauty went lame on her."

She peeped up at Cord's stony face, then away at the bitterness in his eyes. "Mr. LaTour and Johnny arrived just in time to save her from a pack of wolves."

"Where is she?" Cord looked like a wild man as jealousy and concern chased across his face.

"In the front room. Mr. LaTour is tryin' to warm her up." As Cord made for the big room, Maria hurried behind him. "She's near frozen—got caught in a snow squall."

LaTour was rubbing the circulation back into Jonty's feet when Cord burst into the room, bringing with him all the hurt and humiliation that had sent Jonty fleeing. White-lipped and tense, he stood over her, willing her to look at him. But after one wide-eyed stare, she looked straight ahead into the fire.

Cord let out a long, slow breath, and ignoring LaTour, who had risen to his feet, he said, "I can't believe that this man means more to you than your son does. That you would just go off and leave Coty."

Jonty looked at him then, blue fire in her eyes. She opened her mouth to say defensively that she hadn't left her son for all time, only until she could return in warmer weather and reclaim him. But as she glared at the angry man, she became aware of the anguish far back in his eyes. Was he really hurting that she had left him?

She gave a startled jerk when LaTour fairly shouted, "Shut your mouth, McBain! Don't play the hypocrite with her. She left here only because she couldn't stand any more of your lyin' ways—bringin' your woman into her home, sleepin' with the bitch in a room right next to hers."

Cord tried to interrupt, to deny all the charges fired at him, but the enraged man glaring at him raved on, not giving him an opening. Finally, in the middle of it he wheeled and walked from the room, barking at the housekeeper, "Stay here, Maria. I want you also to hear somethin' in a minute."

LaTour lifted a questioning eyebrow at Jonty, and when she shrugged her ignorance at Cord's abrupt leaving, he knelt beside Jonty and took up rubbing her feet. "I guess I shut that four-flusher up," he grunted.

"I don't think so, Jim." Lightfoot had quietly entered the room. "He'll be back, then we're gonna listen to some explanations. That was one angry man who left here."

"It will be interestin' to hear whatever lies he cooks up," LaTour said. He had started on Jonty's other foot when Cord returned, shoving a white-faced Tina before him.

While everyone looked at the sullen, though constrained girl, Cord snapped, "Go ahead, tell them— and your mother." He nodded toward Maria, who had moved to stand anxiously beside her daughter. "Tell them all the mischief you've been causin'."

And with some prodding and leading questions from Cord, Tina began to speak. Sometimes shrilly defiant, sometimes so low-toned the listeners had to strain to hear her as she disclosed all. She ended with how she had, just minutes before Jonty discovered her, slipped into Cord's bed and snuggled up against his sleeping body.

Tina was crying when she finished speaking, the sound of her sobs mingling with those of her embarrassed mother. Jonty gave the girl a glacial look, jumped to her feet, and ran to her room, too ashamed to face Cord.

While LaTour and Lightfoot looked at each other uncomfortably, Cord looked pityingly at his housekeeper. "I'm sorry I had to do this, Maria," he said kindly, "but I'm fightin' to keep my wife, to keep my marriage goin'."

The woman nodded her understanding as the tears continued to roll down her cheeks. Cord laid his hand on her shoulder and said gently, "You realize, don't you, that you and Carlos can't stay on here? I'll be takin' you back to town in a couple of days. Evidently the pass is open." He shot LaTour a dark look.

Maria wiped her tears with the corner of her apron and squared her shoulders. "I know, Cord, and I am so ashamed that I raised such a daughter. Carlos will give her a beatin' she won't quickly forget." She grasped her daughter's arm, jerked her into the hall, and marched her outside.

The door no sooner closed on the Perez women than Cord wheeled to face LaTour. His fists on his lean hips, his eyes like ice, he snarled, "And now, breed, it's time you get a few—"

His words froze in his mouth, for suddenly LaTour clutched his chest as almost simultaneously shattered glass showered the floor and a rifle cracked outside.

"Good Lord!" Cord cried and jumped to catch the falling man just as a bullet whined over his head, striking the mantel. Lightfoot hesitated a split second, then ran out into the darkness.

Blood was flowing from between LaTour's fingers, and his face was paper-white as Cord lowered him to the floor. He looked up at Cord through pain-blurred eyes.

"I think I'm done for, McBain," he said weakly. "But first there's some home truths you must know." He paused a moment, gathering strength, then half whispered, "You damn fool, Jonty is my daughter."

Cord stared at the man in stunned, incredulous surprise. He could see it now, who Jonty had always reminded him of. The eyes were a dead giveaway if a man only took the time to look.

"Does Jonty know?" he asked quietly.

"No she does not." The words came faint, but firm. "And damn your soul to hell if you ever tell her."

"But she has the right to know. The girl loves you."

"She would hate me if she learned that I deserted her mother in her time of need."

"You're crazy, man. You must tell her."

"No!" This time the voice was definitely strong, as was the hand that grabbed Cord's arm. "Promise you won't tell her."

"All right, I won't," Cord calmed him. When Jonty burst into the room, there was a glaze of delirium in LaTour's eyes.

"Uncle Jim!" she cried out, rushing across the floor to kneel at his head. Her face convulsed in dread and fear when she saw the blood that still trickled from between the slim brown fingers.

Wild-eyed, she looked up at Cord. "Cord, please tell me that you didn't do this."

"Jonty, of course not!" Cord soothed, a reproachful note in his voice. "Didn't I promise you that I would never shoot him?"

"Then who?"

"The fat man, Paunch," Lightfoot said quietly from behind them. "I saw him slinkin' off through the trees back of the house."

"We'll get him later," Cord said. "Right now let's get Jim into my bedroom and let Jonty see what she can do for him."

"Yes," Johnny said, and helped Cord to carefully lift the semi-conscious man from the floor. As they carried him down the hall, he added, "But I will be the one who will get Paunch."

Jim was placed on the bed, his limbs straightened out, and an extra pillow placed under his head. While his cousin hurried to the kitchen for hot water, Jonty rushed to her room to gather up medical supplies. Meanwhile, Cord cut away the blood-soaked shirt and breathed a sigh of relief. When Jonty returned, the little black bag in her hand, he stood up.

"I don't think it's as bad as we first thought, honey. The bullet hit low on his shoulder instead of the chest."

Jonty's face blanched as she looked down at the ugly-looking hole in the fleshy part of Jim's shoulder. "Cord," she said, "get me a sheet from my bottom chest of drawers and tear it into wide strips. When I get the wound cleaned out I must pack it, stop the bleeding."

Cord rushed away, and she smoothed the black hair off the broad forehead. "Don't you dare die on me, Uncle Jim," she whispered. "Don't you dare. I couldn't bear it if you did."

Cord returned and Jonty worked feverishly over Jim for several minutes. Half an hour later, his shoulder was tightly bound, and Cord and Johnny finished undressing him and tucked him beneath the sheet and blanket.

"Why don't you go lie down and rest awhile, Jonty," Cord said, frowning at her tired-looking face. "I'll sit with him."

Jonty shook her head as she pulled a chair up to the bed. "I'll be fine, Cord. The next few hours will be the crucial ones."

She picked up LaTour's lax hand and held it in her own. "He hadn't fully recovered from his last wound, and losing all this blood again, I've got to watch him carefully."

"Would you like a cup of coffee, somethin' to eat?"

"I'm not hungry, but a cup of strong coffee sounds good."

Cord gave her shoulder a gentle squeeze. "I'll be right back with it."

An hour passed, in which Cord had brought the coffee, then left, sensing that Jonty wanted to be alone with LaTour. She sat sipping the strong brew, the only sound in the room the wounded man's labored breathing.

As she prayed silently, over and over, for God to let

this wonderful man live, LaTour started moving restlessly, mumbling incoherently. She left her chair and sat on the edge of the bed. When she laid her hand on his hot forehead, LaTour brought his fever-bright eyes to focus on her face.

"Ah, Cleo," he whispered, "I have missed you so." He fumbled for Jonty's hand, and as she quickly gave it to him, he brought it to his cheek. "Do you forgive me for not bein' with you when our little girl was born?"

Jonty stared down at him in complete bewilderment. What in the world was he talking about? Her puzzled mind raced. What baby? As far as she knew, her mother had only one child.

LaTour was rambling again, off into the world of yesterday, and Jonty was swimming in a world of confusion. Then, his words quite lucid, LaTour said, "Jonty, my sweet little daughter."

Shaken to her depths, Jonty stood up and fumbled for her chair. She sat for a long time, her mind going back to that day when a handsome, blue-eyed man showed up in the kitchen of Nellie's place. She remembered vaguely that Granny had not been pleased to see him, but Jonty had loved the big man on sight.

She traced the years—the way he always showed up for her birthdays, was always there when she needed him most, love and assurance in the eyes that she now realized were so like her own.

But why had this been kept from her? she asked herself. Granny had to have known that Uncle Jim was her father. Why hadn't she told her?

Because she always blamed him for my mother's death, Jonty answered her own question. She never forgave him. Even on her death bed she called him a breed and tried to make her promise never to go to him.

Jonty bowed her face in her hands. "Oh, Granny, I pray God has forgiven you your deception. It would have meant so much to me, knowing that this man is my father."

Toward morning, LaTour's fever broke and he slipped into that deep sleep which is near to death. An hour or so later, when Cord stuck his head in the door, both father and daughter were sleeping peacefully, side by side.

The jingling of his spurs brought both pairs of eyes open. Jim looked at Cord, then at Jonty, whose smile was like a piece of sunshine.

"Well good morning, Jonty." LaTour returned her smile.

"Good morning . . . Father," she answered.

LaTour stared at her a moment, then swung angry eyes on Cord. "Damn you! You told her."

"It wasn't me." Cord held up a protesting hand, his own smile wide. "I've got a feelin' you told her yourself . . . in your delirium."

LaTour turned a questioning gaze on Jonty. "That's right," she answered the silent question. "You came right out and called me your beautiful little daughter."

Her father looked deep into her eyes as he asked, "You don't hate me?"

Jonty sat up, real anger on her face. "If you weren't already flat on your back, I'd have Cord put you there. What a foolish question to ask me." She gave his black hair a hard yank. "What I do mind is your keeping the fact to yourself all these years."

"I thought it for the best, honey," LaTour said sadly.

"You all right, Jim?" Lightfoot spoke from the door.

"Yeah, I'm fine, Johnny. Weak and sore, but thanks to my daughter, I'll make it."

A hint of a smile stirred the Indian's lips. "Finally, she knows." LaTour nodded, clasping Jonty's hand. "I'll be off then," Lightfoot said. "Red just saw Paunch skulking around back of the barn." He paused, then said stoically, "I'll be goin' after him now."

He looked at Jonty, a softness in his eyes. "Little cousin, will you step outside with me for a minute?"

Jonty smiled, pleased that the Indian had acknowledged their relationship, and scooted off the bed.

Her smile disappeared when as they stood on the porch and Johnny said solemnly, "I won't be comin' back, Jonty. Me and Nemia are leavin' for our people's village as soon as I return to Cottonwood. We'd have gone a long time ago, except I've been waitin' to kill that fat bastard first."

"Oh, Johnny." Jonty gazed up at him, tears shimmering in her eyes. "I wish you wouldn't go. I'll miss you and Nemia so. It will be like losing a part of my family."

The Indian looked away from Jonty's tears and patted his dog's head. Trying to bring some levity into their conversation, he said, "I'm leaving Wolf with you. My people might get hungry and make stew out of him."

"Oh, Johnny." Jonty's eyes squeezed tight with tears. When she opened them, Lightfoot was gone. She sighed raggedly and returned to the bedroom.

She was smoothing LaTour's covers when there came a blast of a gun, followed by an agonized squeal. As everyone stared at each other, the gun spoke again. For several minutes, then, at spaced intervals, each bringing forth a scream of pain, the gun barked. Cord and Jim looked at each other knowingly. The Indian was putting his shots carefully, in places that would hurt unbearably but not bring the relief of death.

Evil Paunch would be a long time dying.

Jonty leaned against the porch post, her face soft with contentment. The Perez family had been gone two weeks now, and she was sole mistress of her home. Daddy Jim was up and around, and best of all, she was secure in the knowledge that her husband loved her dearly.

There came the sound of loping hoof beats, then

Cord came riding up to the house. He dismounted and threw the reins. He came toward Jonty, and as usual his hard, handsome looks made the breath catch in her throat. He climbed the two steps and silently took her into his arms.

Jonty silently whispered, "Thank you, Granny, for being so wise about this man."